APR 1 5 2010

W9-BWZ-499

THE LAST FIX

Also by K. O. Dahl

The Fourth Man
The Man in the Window

THE LAST FIX

K. O. Dahl

Translated by Don Bartlett

MINOTAUR BOOKS

A Thomas Dunne Book
New York

A THOMAS DUNNE BOOK FOR MINOTAUR BOOKS.
An imprint of St. Martin's Publishing Group.

THE LAST FIX. Copyright © 2009 by K. O. Dahl. Translation copyright © 2009 by Don Bartlett. All rights reserved. Printed in the United States of America. For information, address St. Martin's Press, 175 Fifth Avenue, New York, N.Y. 10010.

www.thomasdunnebooks.com
www.minotaurbooks.com

ISBN 978-0-312-37571-3

First published in Great Britain by Faber and Faber Ltd

First U.S. Edition: April 2010

10 9 8 7 6 5 4 3 2 1

THE LAST FIX

PART 1

THE GIRL ON THE BRIDGE

1

The Customer

There was something special about this customer, she was aware of that at once, even though he wasn't doing very much – that is to say she noticed the door open, but as the person in question went to the holiday brochure shelf instead of walking straight to the counter, Elise continued to do what she was doing without an upward glance. She sat absorbed in the image on the screen, trying to organize a trip to Copenhagen for a family of three while the mother on the telephone dithered between flying there and back or squeezing their car on to Stena Saga and taking the ferry crossing so that they were mobile when they arrived.

Elise looked at Katrine and established that she, too, was busy. The headphones with the mike held Katrine's unruly hair in place, although a blonde lock had fallen over the slender bridge of her nose, and she was concentrating on the computer screen. Katrine had that characteristic furrow in her forehead, which she always had when she concentrated. Her eyes shifted from keyboard to screen, her long dark eyelashes moving slowly up and down. Like an elegant fan, Elise thought, studying Katrine's face as she bent over her work, her profile with the somewhat pronounced nose above reddened lips, and that top lip of hers which had such an effect on men because, on one side, it was a little swollen.

Now and then Elise felt she could have been Katrine's mother. Katrine reminded her of her eldest girl, except that Katrine was much more spontaneous. She was quicker to laugh than her daughter.

Nevertheless every so often Elise felt it was her daughter sitting there, and Katrine was probably aware of this, she thought. The unnecessary attention might even have annoyed her.

As the customer approached the counter a few moments later Elise put down the telephone, looked up and prepared to greet him. But when the man ignored her, preferring to stand in front of Katrine, Elise returned to what she had been doing, noticing that Katrine had sent the customer a friendly peek and uttered an automatic 'Hello' long before finishing her on-screen work. Elise also had time to think that she would have a word with her about that bad habit. She formulated the admonition in her head: *Don't say 'Hello' until you have eye contact with the customer. The customer always feels important. The customer perceives himself as the centre of the universe. If one divides one's attentions, the customer will become annoyed. This is quite a normal reaction.*

From the corner of her eye Elise could see Katrine taking off her headphones and saying something she didn't quite catch. What happened afterwards is what stayed in her mind. The customer was a relatively tall man, equipped with what Elise liked to call vulgar 'totem signals'. He was wearing a black leather waistcoat over a sunburned bare upper torso. His jeans were worn and had holes in the knees. Even though he must have been over forty his long, grizzled hair was tied up in a tasteless ponytail; he wore a large gold earring in one ear and when he went to grab Katrine Elise saw an enormous scar on the man's lower arm. In short, this man was a thug.

The thug launched himself over the counter and made a grab at Katrine, who, panic-stricken, kicked her chair away from the counter, rolled backwards and slammed into the wall. 'Call the police,' Katrine screamed as the chair tipped up and she crashed down on to the floor with her legs in the air. Elise also had time to think how ridiculous she seemed – lying on her back in the chair with all her hair in front of her face and her legs thrashing wildly, like a dumb blonde in a 1960s romantic comedy. While she was thinking the words *ridiculous* and *comedy*, Elise jumped off her chair and stared at the thug, an authoritative expression on her face which, afterwards, she could hardly credit herself with having had the where-withal to muster in such a situation. She had never been robbed before, and that was the thought that went through her mind now: *My God, we're being robbed. How will we survive the psychological repercussions?*

At that moment the brutal man seemed to sense Elise's presence in the room. He flashed her a quick glance and then re-focused his attention on the blonde on the floor. He seemed to take a decision, seized the counter as if intending to jump over it. Then Elise broke the silence. In a loud, piercing voice she said: 'I beg your pardon, young man!' She was to smile at that line many times later. But however incongruous it sounded at that moment, it worked. The thug stared at her again and hesitated. In the end – it must have been after a few seconds, though it seemed like several minutes – he changed his mind and headed for the door with a wild look in his eyes as he shouted to the blonde girl struggling to her knees and holding her head. 'You do as I say, right? Have you got that?'

The door slammed behind him.

Elise stood gaping at the door. It looked no different from how it had been a few seconds ago, it was the same door in the same room, yet it was being seen through different eyes, judged by a different consciousness. 'What was that?' she managed to exclaim, bewildered, numb and not entirely sure what had in fact happened.

Katrine had risen from the bizarre position she had been in, swept back her hair, put her hands on her hips, brushed down her skirt and limped around the counter. She had lost a sandal, and staggered over to the door with one sandal and one bare foot. She locked the door and turned to Elise. For a few seconds she leaned against the door, breathing heavily. She was wide-eyed and her hair dishevelled. A button on her blouse had come loose and she held the two sides together with one hand. Standing like that, leaning against the door with a short skirt and untidy hair, Katrine looked more like a bimbo from a TV soap opera than the daughter about whom Elise liked to daydream. Elise was standing stock still, motionless, petrified. Not a sound could be heard in the room, apart from Katrine's heavy breathing and the telephone that had started to ring behind the counter.

'Aren't you going to answer the phone?' Katrine asked at last.

'Of course not. Are you crazy?'

At once Elise saw the comical side of the remark. They exchanged looks and Katrine began to laugh. Elise smiled at herself and asked again: 'Who on earth was that man?'

Katrine, too, lowered her shoulders in the changed atmosphere. 'Oh, crap, I've gone and hurt myself.' She grinned. 'My bum hurts.' She turned and looked out on to the busy street, pressed down the door handle, opened the door and peered out. 'He's gone anyway,' she said, closing the door and limping back behind the counter. She slipped on the other sandal and picked up the chair. 'It's stopped ringing,' she confirmed and pulled a face.

Elise, curious: 'Is he someone you knew from before?'

Katrine avoided her gaze. She breathed in, arranged her blouse, sat down and adjusted the back of the chair. It was obvious she was thinking feverishly, and it was also obvious she was struggling to decide what to say.

Elise waited patiently with a stern look on her face.

In the end, Katrine said: 'I think it frightened him when I shouted to you to call the police – and I don't think he'll be back.' Her face became more impassioned and desperate the clearer it became that the other woman did not buy her story. 'Elise,' she drawled. 'It's true. I thought he was just a normal customer.'

Elise did not answer; she observed Katrine with suspicion, feeling like a sceptical school teacher.

'I don't know what else to say.'

'What do you mean by that?'

Katrine turned to her, and it seemed to Elise she could read a kind of genuine despair in her expression. But it was never easy to say with Katrine. At this moment she reminded her of one of her own children on Sunday mornings when lies were told about how long they had been out. Slowly Elise rose to her feet and took plodding steps to the front door. It was her turn to lock up now. Broad and plump, she stood with her back to the door and leaned back hard, her arms crossed in an authoritarian manner. 'Katrine.'

'Hm?' Her blue eyes were innocent blue and glazed, a child's eyes, ready for a fight.

'Is it safe to work here?'

Katrine gave a slow nod.

'Because I'm over fifty and would like to imagine I will be here until I'm sixty-seven. I like travel agency work. I like the fringe benefits. I like flying to Sydney for next to nothing. And I'm not interested in taking early retirement because you're incapable of distinguishing between old friends and old lovers.'

'Elise . . .'

'I hate to have to say what I'm going to say now,' Elise continued. 'I don't know if I can express myself in a befitting manner, either. I thought we were going to be robbed. I'm all shaky and my stomach hurts.'

Katrine tilted her head. 'I'm sorry,' she said. 'But I had no idea . . .'

'The man who was here,' Elise interrupted with force. 'He's the nearest I have come to what I would describe as a thug.' She didn't give Katrine, who had raised both palms in defence, a chance. 'You and I have never talked about the past,' Elise persisted, but she was full of regret when she saw the effect her words were having. 'We don't need to talk about the past, not even now, but I would like to know whether I can feel safe working here. If not, I'll have to take further steps. Has this roughneck got anything to do with your past?'

Katrine smiled with the same glazed, light blue, childlike eyes. And Elise could have bitten off her tongue. She should never have asked in that way. Katrine laughed a nervous, artificial laugh and reassured her: 'No, Elise, he has nothing to do with my so-called past.' And Elise knew Katrine had lied. That was why she blamed herself. Katrine had lied and now they were moving into terrain where she had no wish to be with this young woman. She felt she lacked words and could see Katrine was aware of this shortcoming; from Katrine's face it was clear she realized Elise had seen through the lie. Silence hung in the room. Katrine made no attempt to retract the lie, and Elise did not want to wait for the sound of cars and trams to penetrate the window, making the situation workaday and wearisome – for that reason she interposed: 'So next time he could just as easily come in and attack me?'

'Of course not.'

Elise breathed in. 'So he's only interested in you?'

Katrine looked away. Elise waited.

'Yes. He is someone from my past,' she conceded at last.

Elise breathed out and closed her eyes. In a way this admission was the most important thing that had happened so far today; the admission was more important than the incident with the man. The admission made it possible for the balance between them to be re-established. More than that, the relationship between them was no longer threatened by lies. 'Thank God,' she mumbled, unlocking the door and strolling back to her chair. 'Thank God.'

The door jangled. The two women were startled. They looked at each other and Elise felt her mouth go dry.

But it was not the man returning. The customer who opened the door turned out to be a young woman wanting Mediterranean travel brochures.

The next few hours were hectic, and even though it was a quite normal Saturday with quite normal Saturday tasks, sluggish computers and indecisive customers, Elise felt a little shudder go down her back every time the door opened. Every time the familiar jangle sounded, she peered up at the customer and glanced over at Katrine who, irrespective of whether she was busy or not, was sitting ready to meet her gaze with neutral, light blue eyes.

It was almost two o' clock before the room was quiet again. Elise swung her chair round to face Katrine, took a deep breath, but then paused.

- 'I know what you're going to say,' Katrine said, massaging her temples. 'You want me to ring the police.'

'Don't you think you should?' Elise said in a low voice. 'He threatened you.'

Katrine nodded. 'I need to think a bit,' she said.

'Katrine . . .' Elise started.

'Please,' Katrine retorted. 'Let me have a think!'

'What did he want?'

Katrine went quiet.

'Is he an ex-boyfriend?'

'He might have considered himself one once, a long time ago.'

'So he's jealous?'

'Believe me, this has nothing to do with love.' Katrine sighed. 'He and a load of other people are just shadows for me now. It's funny, but until he walked through that door I had forgotten what he looked like.'

'What's his name?'

Katrine had to puzzle for a few seconds. 'Raymond,' she said at length. 'Just imagine, I had even forgotten that.'

'But what did he want?'

Katrine stood up. 'I promise I'll tell you,' she said. 'But not this minute. I need to think; I'll have to ask for some help to know how to tackle this. Then I promise I'll tell you.'

Elise nodded slowly. 'Fine,' she said. 'What are you going to do this evening?'

'I'm going to do something I have next to no interest in doing.'

Elise smiled and at once pictured Katrine's skinhead boyfriend. 'Are you going to finish with him?'

Katrine smiled and shook her head. 'With Ole? It'll be him who does that with me, I suppose. But he's accompanying me at any rate.'

'Where to?'

'To a party.'

'It must be quite a party if you're that keen to go.'

'That's the point,' Katrine said with a heavy sigh. 'I have absolutely no interest in going, but I have to.'

2

The Afternoon Atmosphere

Ole had eased his body from a recumbent into a sedentary position on the sofa. It was a terrible sofa to sit on, one Katrine had bought at a flea market, a 70s sofa bed, with a solid, uncomfortable pine frame and a seat that was so deep it was impossible to sit with your back supported; you either had to lie or you had to sit with your legs beneath you. It irritated him that she had this sofa. It irritated him to think that all her visitors had to confront the same problem: Shall I lie down or what? When Katrine sat on the sofa she always drew her legs up beneath her – she invited a physical intimacy in everything she did. He could feel his irritation growing as he thought about this too, that Katrine was a woman who invited a physicality in all situations. A pling sounded on the TV. Someone had put Stavanger Viking ahead. But he was watching Molde playing against Stabæk. Crap match. Frode Olsen, the goalkeeper, might just as well have started doing gymnastics on the crossbar, and the cameramen seemed to be more interested in the trainers on the Molde bench than the ball. Katrine sauntered by, not wearing clothes of course, her hair wet from the shower. She turned down the volume without a word to him.

'What is it now?' he asked.

'Nothing.'

'But why can't I watch TV?'

'My God, you can watch TV. But you can manage with the volume down can't you? I have to make a call.'

With that she was gone, slamming the hall door behind her. The contours of her body became a blurred, pale shadow behind the door's frosted glass. He could see her sitting beside the telephone. This was Katrine in a nutshell: sitting naked, phoning and making sure he couldn't hear. A form of behaviour and secrecy he could not stand. But now he didn't know what provoked him more, her nonchalant nakedness or her slamming the door, as though he had no right to know what she was doing. He felt a sudden fury surge up inside him; he got up and tore open the door. 'You're the one who's loud!'

She peered up at him with the telephone receiver tucked under her chin. He stood following the line of the cable coiled around one of her breasts. It looked like a pose for a men's magazine.

'And why aren't you dressed?' he barked.

'My dear Ole, I've just had a shower.'

'But you could get dressed, couldn't you?'

'Ole, I live here. I do as I like.'

'But I'm here now.'

She put down the telephone and leered. 'You're not usually that bothered whether I'm dressed or not.' She rose to her feet, took the towel hanging from a hook on the wall, made a big show of wrapping it around herself, so that it half-covered her breasts and reached mid-thigh.

She sat back down beside the telephone, held it and looked up. 'Happy?' 'No,' he said, irritated, still provoked and aggressive because she had put on her cool tone – she seemed to be sitting there and making a fool of him.

Then her eyes flashed. 'I have to make a call. Would you please go away and let me talk in peace.'

'Who are you ringing?'

'It's got nothing to do with you.'

Ole Eidesen felt the blood drain from his face. 'It's nothing to do with me?'

Katrine sighed and crossed her legs before adjusting the towel. 'Ole,' she said, 'drop it.'

'I want to know who you're ringing.'

'Why?'

'Because.'

'Ole, I never ask you who you ring.'

'But I want to know who you're ringing.'

She took a deep breath and closed her eyes. 'Why?'

'I have a right.'

Her eyes narrowed. He hated it when her eyes narrowed, hated the determination that lay behind her cold, hard blue eyes.

'Ole. Don't start. You have to respect my wishes.'

He closed his eyes for a second. He didn't want to feel this. But it came. He was unable to stop: 'Closing the door on me is not right.'

'What did you say?'

'Don't close the door on me.'

'I decide if I want to be alone,' Katrine said in a low snarl. 'And everyone has to respect that. You, too.'

'You're not alone if you're talking to other people.'

Katrine dug deep. She stared at the wall as though counting to herself. Then she groaned and said in a low, imploring voice: 'Ole, don't. I've had enough of jealous men!'

'I want to know who you're ringing. You have no right to be so secretive.'

Katrine, cool, almost in a whisper, 'Don't I?'

Ole took a sudden step forward. Before he knew what he was doing, he had grabbed her plait and pulled her into a standing position.

'Ow,' she screamed, tottering forwards. She lost her towel; a soft breast fell against his arm. 'Let me go!' she gasped.

Just as suddenly as he had grabbed her, he let go, his innards cold as ice. 'Sorry,' he stammered and moved to embrace her. But she was juggling with the towel and shoved him away with tears in her eyes. 'Out,' she said.

'I'm so sorry.'

She put a hand to her hair. 'You're completely insane.'

'I said sorry, didn't I!'

'And I'm asking you to go,' she screamed. 'Out. I have to make a call.'

Stupefied, Ole backed into the sitting room. 'You have no right to keep secrets from me,' he mumbled. 'You have no fucking right!'

'Out!' Katrine hissed. And slammed the door again.

Ole sat staring at the outline of her body through the wavy glass. Watching her pull herself together, get up and stand in front of the mirror with her back to him. She paced to and fro. He followed the silhouette of her body as she sat down beside the telephone and took the receiver. He saw how her body language changed, how she flicked her hair and brushed it with long, casual strokes. Her voice was low and tender, a voice talking to another person, a voice articulating words he could not distinguish. He could hear her laughter, though. In the pit of his stomach, the embers of jealousy smouldered. He wanted to know who she was calling. She couldn't bloody do this. She would soon fucking see what happened if she went on like this.

The crowd cheered. Ole Eidesen watched the slow-motion replay. Frode Olsen, horizontal in the air, got three finger tips to the ball and pushed it over the bar. A blue Molde player clenched both fists in a demonstration to the spectators of how disappointed he was. Ole wasn't interested. He couldn't get his mind off Katrine, who had now cradled the receiver and was about to call another number. In his heart he was cold. She was cheating on him. She was sitting three metres away from him and cheating on him. Before his very eyes.

3

The Party

Annabeth and Bjørn had set the table in the large L-shaped room. The table was L-shaped, too. The longest part of the table had been placed in the longest part of the room. There was a neatly written place card on every plate. Katrine had been given a seat at the rectangle forming the short end of the letter L. Most of the guests were unknown to her. The only ones Katrine knew were those from the rehab centre; from where she sat, she could see just Sigrid and Annabeth. Annabeth's husband, Bjørn Gerhardsen, was opposite her. This could become tricky, she had thought as for a few brief minutes they stood facing each other. This could become very tricky. But Ole was there too, in the chair next to him as it happened. Ole and a plump guy she knew from sight at the centre; she had no idea what his name was – he may have had some function on the administrative board. In addition, she had an inkling that he was gay. He had all the buffoonery and the feminine movements. Between Ole and the gay man sat a woman in her late twenties. She didn't know her, either, although Ole seemed quite taken by her; he was indulging in furtive sidelong glances. The woman for her part was encouraging him by playing coy. That didn't bode well, thought Katrine, who had been able to study the woman's figure for the brief moments they had stood before taking a seat – she was not that tall, yet she had endlessly long, nylon-clad legs. The legs took the focus off other details, such as lifeless hair with split ends and stubby fingers with nails chewed down to the stumps. However, the face, despite a few irregular features, bore a deep sensuality with two sensitive eyes and wonderful, golden skin. The fact that the chemistry between Ole and the unknown woman seemed to be working so well led Katrine to examine her own feelings. She wondered whether Ole's undisguised interest in the other woman ought to have made her feel jealous. The strange thing was that it did not. All she felt was irritation; she was irritated by his clumsiness, irritated that he wasn't better at chatting her up. And this lack of jealousy frightened her. It made her think of her therapy sessions, what she had gone through with respect to her emotional life and the danger signals. She speculated on how she should interpret this. In a way the fact that Ole only irritated her by showing interest in another woman made Bjørn Gerhardsen loom larger, seem more powerful and dangerous. It became harder to avoid his gaze. For this reason conversation around the table seemed to be desperately sluggish. And, worst of all, she felt she was responsible for this sluggishness. Her irritability was putting a damper on others. The idea was silly. She knew that, but was still unable to stop herself thinking it. She was sweating and wished she were anywhere but here. The hushed lethargy was broken at various junctures by Annabeth standing up at the corner of the L-shaped table and shouting '*Skål*'. They were doing a lot of toasting over where the table joined the second room. Katrine toasted with mineral water and held her hand over her glass when Bjørn Gerhardsen tried to fill it with red wine.

After the main course the long-legged woman took out a cigarette. Gerhardsen fumbled in his jacket pockets. Ole didn't notice anything. But the plump gay man was first out of the blocks and lit her cigarette with a gallant bow.

'I won,' he grinned at Bjørn Gerhardsen.

Everyone laughed. The childish outburst relaxed the atmosphere. Even Katrine laughed. The laughter was liberating.

Annabeth squealed from the corner with a raised glass. '*Skål*, Georg!'

'Goggen,' shouted the gay man. 'Everyone calls me Goggen...' To the young woman with the long legs he said: 'Did you see the new guy on TV on Saturday night? Do you remember the joke he told about the psychologist?'

The long-legged woman was already laughing. Cigarette smoke got caught in her throat and she started coughing. Ole was staring down the gap between her pitching breasts.

I don't belong here, thought Katrine.

'So the patient said: *I'm not the one...*' Goggen sat up in his chair, puffed out his cheeks and put on a stupid face. Katrine realized this was meant to be an imitation. Goggen, in a lumberjack voice: '... he said to the psychologist. *You're the one who's obsessed about sex. After all, you're the one doing the asking.*'

The woman with the long legs screamed with laughter. Ole did, too. But Katrine felt icy tremors run up her spine because a foot was stroking hers under the table. It couldn't be Ole's. She didn't dare to look up. Don't let it be Bjørn's, she thought. Bjørn could not be so revolting. There was no one else it could be, though. It had to be Bjørn Gerhardsen. She shivered and flushed; she was sweating. The foot caressed her leg higher up. Up and down, up and down, slowly.

Katrine closed her eyes and kicked the foot away. And then there he was. The moment she opened her eyes he was there, Bjørn Gerhardsen, with a gentle, provocative smile.

She felt someone's gaze burning on her cheek and twisted her head. It was Annabeth. There was no mistaking where Annabeth was looking. For some reason Annabeth must have guessed something. The knot Katrine felt in her stomach went ice cold. Annabeth knows, she thought. The bloody bitch. She knows. And Bjørn knows she knows. So he must have told her. She turned her head and focused on Annabeth's husband again. He smiled; he had been following her eyes and now he winked at her without the slightest attempt at concealment. Who noticed anything? Annabeth, of course, and Goggen. The fat homosexual scented the magnetism in the air like a deer scents watchful eyes in the gloaming. Georg studied her with renewed interest. And Gerhardsen kept smiling. She lowered her eyes and, at the same time, despised herself for having lost the battle. She stared down at the table cloth and felt the perspiration trickling down her neck.

'It's so smoky in here,' she exclaimed. 'I could do with a bit of air.' So saying, she got up and stumbled towards the veranda. A woman's hand opened the door for her. As she staggered on to the terrace she heard the company at the table breaking up. Annabeth's voice boomed: 'Coffee with liqueurs in the lounge! Please help yourselves! I have just put it out, and I don't have the energy to serve you . . . self-service!' The voice cracked on the last word.

Katrine breathed in the fresh air. It was a grey June evening and she leaned against the terrace railing. She looked down at an illuminated swimming pool. *You could dive in from here*, she thought. The blue, luminous water formed the centrepiece of what looked like a tiled courtyard. And beyond the tiles grew a few fruit trees.

She could make out a lit street lamp between the trees; it cast an orange light on the pavement outside the fence. She let her eyes wander further afield and noticed that the view of Oslo was blocked by a large canopy of trees in the distance.

She knew he was there before he spoke. Knowing he was standing behind her caused perspiration to break out again.

'Is this where you are?' the smooth voice whispered.

The sound of his heels on the slate tiles was repugnant. She didn't turn. She didn't answer.

His reflection appeared in the pool below. 'Cognac?' he asked, putting a glass down on the broad balustrade. A square reflection of the light yellow veranda door formed on the glass containing the brown liquid. His fingers were rough, the skin around his wedding ring seemed swollen. His wristwatch was a bluish watch face inside a thick metal chain; it was naff, something that would not look out of place in a James Bond film.

'No, thank you,' she said. 'Have you seen Ole?'

'Do you like our garden?' Gerhardsen asked as though he had not heard the question. She observed her own reflection in the blue water beneath her. And she observed Gerhardsen's. Naff man in naff clothes beside a blonde wearing make-up. Shit, it was just like a James Bond film. 'Big garden,' she said politely. 'Must need a lot of work.'

He was leaning back against the balustrade sipping from his glass. 'Couldn't you come and help us from time to time?' he said with a smile. 'You're so good with your hands, aren't you?'

She stiffened. His smile was macho, self-assured. But that didn't matter. These looks, these blatant advances were familiar territory to her. I can overcome this, she thought; she concentrated, looked him in the eye without any emotion and felt her nerves relax.

'You have a good memory,' she said, regretting the words at once, they could have been easily misunderstood. It was like giving him rope which, of course, he grabbed greedily.

'You, too,' he said.

The silence was transfixing. The sound of laughter and the usual drunken revelry carried from inside the house.

'If you want, I can show you round the garden now,' he said with a crooked smile.

Her face was numb. She could feel her mouth distorting into an artificial, transparent smile as she tried to stare him down. 'You are one big arsehole,' she said slowly and clearly so that he caught every single syllable. But it didn't help. She saw that. This was his arena. His home. She was here at their invitation. She was a part of the decoration for the evening, something exotic Annabeth and Bjørn could show off: *Would you like to see the house – the African vase, the carved masks on the wall, the Italian table and the poor drug addict Annabeth managed to get back on an even keel. Which one is she, do you think? Yes, her over there, the blonde, and she's so good-looking, isn't she?*

19

At that moment she felt his hand stroking her backside. 'Don't touch me,' she hissed as tears welled up, forming a humiliating, misty film across her vision.

He cleared his throat. His hand slid between her thighs.

'I'll scream,' she said, despising herself even more for these stupid words. Had it been anywhere else, in the street, on the staircase in a block of flats, any other place except for here, she would have kicked him in the balls and spat at him into the bargain. But she was a stranger here, and paralyzed.

He removed his hand. 'Just wait before you scream,' he said in a cool voice.

She turned and saw Annabeth through the glass door searching for her husband.

'Your wife's looking for you,' she said.

'No,' he said with a sardonic smile. 'She's looking for us.' He raised his glass and sought her eyes. Katrine stared into space and heard herself say from a long way off:

'You are nothing, nothing to me.' And sick of this game, sick of playing the role of an idiot, she stormed towards the door and into the smoke-filled room.

As she made her way between the people she could feel their gazes burning into her body. From the corner of her eye she saw heads huddled together. She lumbered across the floor feeling like an orangutan on a stage set for a ballet. She was completely numb. At the other end of the room she saw Ole bending over the woman with the long legs. He was whispering something in her ear. She was giggling and tossing back her hair. Apart from them, she recognized only the faces of Sigrid from the rehab centre and Bjørn Gerhardsen.

She appeared at Ole's side and he immediately lost his composure. He coughed and mumbled a forced 'Hi'. The stork woman fumbled for a cigarette. Katrine stood her ground. The stork woman was professional, turned away and moved on.

Ole took her arm. 'Shall we mingle?' They entered the room with a piano where Georg, alias Goggen, was sitting. Ole held her back. 'Not that man,' he whispered into her ear. 'He's a poof.' She sent Ole a weary smile and felt alienated, even by him. She said: 'Shout for me if he tries anything on you.'

They took their place in the circle around Goggen, who was talking about himself and an ex-lover – a waiter – and some fun they had had with a female TV celebrity. According to Goggen, the woman had thought it exciting to have been left alone with two gay men. They had been drinking hard all night, all three of them. In the daylight hours they had become very intimate, and during a guided tour through her flat all three of them fell on to her large four-poster bed and 'did it'. 'We had her, both of us,' Goggen wheezed. 'And I mean at the same time.' He winked at Katrine and said to Ole: 'You know, he parked himself where pricks prefer . . . (pause for effect, audience cheering) while I found a spot a little further back.' (More cheering.)

Goggen continued with a raised voice, at one level below shouting: 'I was very aroused because we could feel our pricks rubbing against each other all the time. After all, there was just a thin membrane between them!'

Katrine peered up at Ole. Either he was embarrassed or he was furious. At any rate, his face was red. As red as Goggen's. You're all the same, she thought, and her eyes wandered back to Goggen, who was now employing body language. He was miming, leaning backwards, overweight, flushed. With his face distorted into a sick grimace, he puffed out both cheeks as though blowing a trumpet. Then he sat with his mouth open and revealed the white spots on his tongue. His eyes, dead and vacant, staring into empty space, Goggen said: 'She was screaming all the time.' Saliva dripped from his full bottom lip as he imitated her. 'Aah . . . aaahhh.'

Ole wanted to leave and grabbed her arm. She felt her alienation tip over into aggression. A sudden fury that had been building up. But now it was being released by Ole's smug self-righteousness. She stayed where she was. From the corner of her eye she could see that he, too, had chosen to stay.

The laughter among the listeners died away, and the long-legged woman, who in some mysterious way had also appeared among them, whispered to the man next to her so that everyone could hear: 'Now that was a bit vulgar, don't you think?'

'Oh dear!' he said, miming a stifled yawn and patting his mouth with his hand. 'Just so long as he doesn't tell the story about the piano stool. Whoops.' He recoiled and added, 'Too late!'

'I was in Hotel Bristol,' Goggen said. '. . . I went in and saw a quite magnificent piano stool in the bar, and I simply could not resist. I sat down and played a light sonata and I hardly noticed that I was playing until I sensed the silence around me. But, by God, it was too late to stop then – so I kept going, and when I finished I could feel there was a man standing next to me . . .'

'A man!' Stork woman shouted in an affected voice. 'So exciting!'

Her neighbour: 'Yes, talking about piano stools and women, have you heard about the fat woman who's so good at playing she breaks two stools every concert!'

Ole grinned. He didn't mind joining in when Goggen was thve victim. Ole's eyes shone.

The stork woman winked at Ole. 'Breaks the piano stool?'

'Yes, of course, they're very fragile affairs!'

'I felt . . .' Goggen screamed with annoyance. 'I felt a hand . . .'

A voice from the crowd: 'It's not mine!'

Laughter.

Goggen was offended. 'Very droll, very droll. Well,' he continued with everyone's attention back on him again. 'I was sitting there playing and I felt a hand on my shoulder,' his voice entranced, his eyes half-closed, the pale whites gleaming. 'I turned,' he said with dramatic emphasis, 'and I looked up . . . and was startled to hear a voice say: *Nice.*'

Goggen, who had the audience with him now, paused. 'A beautiful, rounded, warm voice,' Goggen placed a hand on his own shoulder as though trying to feel the same pressure as he had long ago; he twisted in the chair pretending to hold the hand and turn to see who owned it. '. . . *That was very nice*, the voice said and then this man let go and gave me . . .'

'Come on,' one of the women at the table shouted. She turned round to make sure the others were with her. 'What did he give you?'

A voice from the table: 'Goodness me! With a hand, too!'

'The man,' Goggen, undeterred, continued. 'The man was a venerable man of the theatre. Per Aabel!'

The words had an impact. A wave of deep rapturous sighs passed around the table. Goggen surveyed those around him with a nod of triumph and repeated, 'Per Aabel!'

Katrine noticed Annabeth standing in the doorway. She was drunk as was everyone else. All those self-righteous people who dealt with others' drug abuse problems were pissed. Pissed and horny and old. She felt nauseous.

A man who had not quite got the point of Goggen's story looked at the others with a little grin. 'Christ, Goggen, isn't he the same age as you?'

Everyone burst into laughter.

'Who said that?' Goggen stood up, raising an arm in the air, his bloated cheeks quivering with rage. 'Who said that? I challenge whoever it was to a duel.'

'Sit down, you old goat,' a woman shouted. 'Sit down and tighten the truss!'

More laughter and raised glasses. Katrine turned because she sensed a movement by the door. Annabeth was staggering towards her, and Katrine squeezed Ole's hand and let him take her in tow.

Annabeth blocked their way. She was swaying and struggling to keep her balance. 'Katrine,' she called with warmth in her voice. 'I hope you're having a good time,' cutting off the ends of her words, because she was drunk. Katrine smiled but felt sick. 'The food was lovely, Annabeth. Very nice.'

Annabeth took her hand. Katrine looked down at Annabeth's

hand. It was the hand of an ageing woman, pale brown skin, wrinkled fingers covered in rings. She looked up. There was a lot of blusher on her cheeks. And dark shadows under the powder.

'We love you *so much*, Katrine,' Annabeth said and began to cry.

'Are you crying, Annabeth?'

Even though Katrine wished she were many miles away, she managed to find the right note of sympathy. In front of her stood Annabeth, the director of the rehab centre, completely pissed. The stab of discomfort she had felt in her stomach from the first moment she had set foot in the house, the little stab she had been fighting to keep down freed itself now from the claws in her stomach. Katrine could feel the discomfort and disgust spreading through her body like wildfire, a numbing hot pain that started in her stomach and spread outwards. As her body gradually surrendered to the pain and repulsion, her mind was clear enough to remember the many times she had seen more wretched gatherings than this. She closed her eyes, opened them again and saw Ole. He was standing behind Annabeth and staring at her, rapt. For a few seconds Katrine experienced deep, violent contempt for him and all the people around her: Annabeth and her smug acquaintances knocking back wine, beer and spirits to find the courage to tell each other secrets, to slag each other off, to smooth the path for infidelities and other hypocrisies. And there was Annabeth whispering secrets to her she didn't have the energy to hear. But the painful stabbing in her stomach also numbed her thinking. There was a rushing noise in her ears and she discovered she could not hear what was going on in the room. Annabeth was swaying and her lips were moving. Her teeth were long with black joins. They were the teeth of an old person. A person who has smoked too many cigarettes and uttered too many empty words. Annabeth's eyes were red, wet with tears, swimming with water. In her hand she was holding what looked like an open bottle of red wine. She waved the bottle and teetered again, took an unsteady step to the side and the bottle exploded as it hit the door frame. In slow motion a shower of red wine enveloped Annabeth; it was as though someone had torn off her skin, as though blood were spraying out, wetting her hair, streaming down her face and neck, a naked red wound that had once been a face. At that moment Katrine's hearing returned; it returned as the old woman let out a hoarse scream. The sound was just an undefined rush in Katrine's ears. For one second she gazed into Annabeth's eyes; she stared into two dark, empty tunnels in a brain which was no brain, just a pulsating mass of white worms. Katrine's stomach heaved. She knew she was going to throw up, there was no doubt in her mind; the contents of her stomach were on their way up right now. Her vision became even hazier. The white worms came closer, and the red liquid streamed down Annabeth's neck, like blood, as though from a fountain of blood.

* * *

Someone was supporting her. Katrine felt the cool tiles against her knees and knew she was throwing up. She vomited into a toilet bowl. Sounds from the party penetrated the lavatory door. She peered up. Ole was standing over her. His expression was anxious. 'I want you out,' she groaned.

'You fainted,' he said. 'The bitch smashed the bottle of wine and you passed out. Great party. You shouldn't drink so much.'

She looked up at him. 'I don't drink. I haven't touched a drop all evening.'

'Why were you sick then?'

She was unable to answer before the cramps in her stomach started again. This time it wasn't food; it felt like she was disgorging burning hot tea. She groped for toilet paper. Her fingers grabbed some cloth. Ole had passed her a towel.

'Don't know,' she groaned. 'May have been the food.'

He flushed the toilet. The noise drowned out the sounds of the party. She dried the mucus, the snot and the tears from her face.

'Why are you still here?' she asked. 'I want to be alone. I don't want you to see me like this.'

He mumbled: 'Do you think I want to be on my own with that lot outside?'

She nodded and had another violent retch. She brought nothing up. Yes, she did, a drop of caustic bile rolled off her tongue. She felt the draught of the door as he opened and left. That was a relief. She felt better.

Ole was full of lies, too. This place suited him. He slotted in among these people. Ole could make conversation, he could drop small compliments to the ladies and engage in small talk with other men. Ole was at home. Only she was at sea. She had no business being here. And she wanted to go home. She should be with people who made her feel good. That was the solution. Go home. If home existed.

She recovered a little and dragged herself up by the toilet seat. She sat on the bowl staring at herself in a large mirror. In this house you could sit on the toilet and admire yourself. Annabeth's husband, Bjørn Gerhardsen, too. Perhaps he stood here in front of the mirror, jacking himself off before he went to bed. She shook her head to remove the sight from her consciousness. Her stomach was empty. She was not nauseous any longer. But her stomach muscles ached after the attack. She sat like a teenage prostitute after her first OD, before the darkness came. Knees together, mucus running down her chin, watery eyes, sickly pale skin and vomit-stained hair hanging down in two big tangles over her forehead. The tears that had been forced out as she spewed had made her mascara run. She thought about the insane sight of Annabeth spattered with wine. And instantly felt sick again. She swallowed. Sat there with closed eyes, swallowing until the nausea subsided. Now she knew what she should not think about. Slowly she opened her eyes and regarded herself in the mirror. The sounds of music, laughter and screaming carried through the door.

If she had not been a conversation topic for that lot outside before, she was now. *Have you ever heard anything like it? The poor welfare case feels unwell and throws up at Annabeth's party – have you ever heard anything like it?*

There was a knock at the door.

She wanted to be alone, quite alone. There was another knock. Banging, social-worker-type-banging. I-will-never-give-up-banging. Shall-we-talk-about-it-banging. Old-woman-banging. 'Katrine?' It was Sigrid. 'Katrine? Are you OK?'

Katrine wanted to be alone. No, she wanted to be with Henning, to sit and drink tea with Henning and not to feel the quiver of expectation in the air, or the looks.

'Katrine!' Sigrid kept on banging.

Katrine stood up and opened the door a fraction.

'My God, what do you look like, my little girl!' Sigrid was caring, as always. She pushed her way into the room and began to wash Katrine's face. 'There we are, yes, are you better now?'

'I think I'm going home,' Katrine said, pulling a face at herself in the mirror. 'Could you ask Ole to ring for a taxi?'

'I'll do it for you. Ole's gone into the garden.'

'In the garden?'

'Yes, Annabeth wanted people to swim in the pool. And she has a new fish pond she wants to show off. Just wait and I'll find you a car or see if anyone can take you.'

'There isn't a soul here left sober.'

Sigrid, her brow furrowed: 'It might seem like that, but there are quite a few people who don't touch a drop.'

'Just forget it,' Katrine sighed.

They observed each other in the mirror. Sigrid, middle-aged, slim and grey-haired, attractive and educated, with soft, caring hands. Katrine, young with a somewhat weary expression in her eyes. 'You should have been a nurse,' Katrine said and put Sigrid's arm around her shoulder. Portrait of girlfriends in the reflection. 'I can see it now as large as life.'

'What?'

'You walking round in a white uniform on the night shift with several male clients waiting for you in the dark, waiting for a glimpse of their dream woman tiptoeing through the door.'

Sigrid smiled at Katrine in the mirror, flattered but still with a caring, concerned furrow on her forehead. 'I'm old,' she said.

'Mature,' corrected Katrine, freeing herself, 'but I'm young and don't have the energy for any more tonight. I'll ring someone to pick me up. You go back to the party.'

Katrine felt a sudden desire to have Ole with her, to have him holding her. She wanted Ole to say: *Stay here, with me.* She stood in the doorway looking. First of all for Sigrid, who had disappeared into the crowd. She stood and watched Ole come in from the terrace. Ole and the long-legged lady from the dinner table. Their intimacy had become more open. Katrine closed her eyes and could see them before her, naked in bed. She could imagine it quite clearly, but felt no jealousy, just a leaden despondency.

What did she want Ole to say? *I'm sick of this place.* He could say that. He could come here, hold her and say he would take her home and stay with her. She could feel herself becoming angry. Why didn't he do that? Why wasn't he the person she wanted him to be?

At that moment her eyes met his. He was walking towards her. She closed her eyes. She saw it vividly. The row that was coming. All the nasty things she would say; all the nasty things he would say. She opened her eyes again. For every step that Ole took, she wished it were Henning. Henning and no one else.

'How's it going?' he asked.

'Better,' she mumbled. 'You're enjoying yourself too, I can see.'

He followed her gaze, to the woman with the legs watching them. As soon as Ole turned, the long-legged woman left and was lost from view.

'Some people are going to hit town,' Ole said after a pause. 'Smuget. The queer and a few others. Do you feel like joining them?'

'No,' she said. 'Do you?'

'Not sure. Maybe.'

'I'm going home,' she said.

'Home?'

She gave a tired smile. 'You don't need to join me. Relax, stay here. Or go with the others to town.'

He brightened up. 'Quite sure?'

She nodded.

A crowd of noisy guests forced their way between them. Goggen patted Ole on the bottom. 'You going to join us, sweetie?'

Ole grinned.

Goggen grabbed his waist and swung him round in a slow waltz. Katrine retreated to the toilet, locked the door and waited until she was sure the hall was empty. Voices and strident yells penetrated the walls. Someone was mistreating the piano. When she was sure that all those in the corridor had gone, she crept out, lifted the receiver of the telephone hanging on the wall and called Henning's number. She checked her watch. It was not midnight yet. At last she heard a sleepy hello at the other end. 'Katrine here,' she said quickly. 'Are you in bed?' She couldn't restrain herself from asking, and then grimaced, as though frightened he would say yes and be grumpy.

'Me? No.' Henning yawned aloud. So he had been asleep.

'Have you got a car?' she asked.

'My brother's, the big old crate.'

'Can you pick me up? I'm at Annabeth's. Now?'

Thank God for Henning, who never asked any questions. 'Start walking now,' he said. 'And I'll meet you.'

4

Night Drive

Twenty minutes later the house was a hundred metres away and she was alone in the darkness. She strolled down the quiet road. It was grey rather than dark outside, the murky gloom of a summer night. She felt a lot better, but her stomach and diaphragm were still taut. The fresh air caressed her face. She passed under a lamp post. The electric lamp buzzed and projected a pallid gleam, unable to illuminate better than the night itself. She continued on down the road. Her heels echoed on the tarmac. The electric buzz was gone, soon to be replaced by a mosquito next to her ear. Shortly afterwards she heard the drone of a car. Next she saw the beam of headlamps behind the massive trees alongside the road. Oslo opened up far beneath her. The whole town smouldered with lights, like the embers of an enormous dying bonfire. The black sea of the inner Oslo fjord reflected and amplified the glow. The drone of the engine increased in volume and soon she saw the reflection of car headlamps on the trees and a line of cars rounded the bend. The first car was low with an open top. Henning's long hair blew in the gusting side wind, and he had to brush it away from his face. He pulled up and she jumped in.

They sat looking at each other, smiling. 'What's up?' he asked.

Her smile became broader. 'What do you think?'

'Have you won loads of money?'

She grinned. 'No.'

'Tell me what it is!'

She collected herself and closed her eyes.

'Something wonderful has happened to you,' he said.

She nodded, unable to restrain her smile.

'Are you going to tell me what?'

'Later,' she said, squeezing his hand. 'Later,' she repeated, stroking the dashboard with her hand, and asked, 'Where did you find this?'

'It's my brother's,' he said. 'I look after his car while he's abroad.'

'Do you mean that? You've got a brother who just lends you this kind of car?'

He gave a lop-sided smile and cocked his head. 'He is my brother after all.'

'Tired?' she asked.

'Not any more.'

'What do you feel like doing?'

He shrugged. 'How much time have you got?'

'All night.'

He leaned his head back so that the little goatee stuck up like a tuft of moss on the end of his pointed chin. 'Then it's as clear as the stars in the sky,' he mumbled. 'I know what we can do.'

'But I want to eat first,' Katrine said. 'I feel like some really greasy, unhealthy food.'

Her hair fluttered in the wind in the open-top car. Henning accelerated past Holmenkollen hill which loomed up in the night like a huge mysterious shadow. They bumped into each other in the hairpin bends going down the ridge, and her hair became tangled and lashed at her eyes. Without hesitating for a second she removed her blouse and tied it around her head like a scarf. Henning glanced across. 'This is like Fellini,' he shouted through the rushing of the air. 'I drive my convertible through the night with a babe in a black bra!'

She leaned forward and turned on the car stereo. The music boomed out as though they were sitting in a concert hall. Leonard Cohen first took Manhattan by storm and then Berlin. They exchanged glances. She turned the volume up louder. Henning changed down and accelerated. The speedometer showed 130 km as the road levelled out. As the yellow street lamps flashed by like disco lights on Henning's face Katrine felt like they were in a tunnel. The wind against her body, rock 'n' roll and the urge to cleanse yourself of educated manners, of social graces, of double entendres and hidden agendas, of clammy hands and middle-class arrogance. If this party had taken place more than three years ago, she thought to herself, she would already have been sitting on the floor with a needle in her arm. She felt a faint yen for that kind of kick even now. But it was faint, like the longing for a particular kind of sweet you ate when you were young. And so it will ever be, she thought, but three years ago I had no control over things, three years ago I wasn't even able to enjoy the pleasures of rejecting a man I didn't like, of not caring whether people saw me leaving a party alone, of not caring what others thought or of not caring what clothes I wore, especially when sitting in an open car.

Three years ago the great secret was just a black, impenetrable void. If she thought enough about the great secret she might be re-born.

She smiled to herself. Re-born. Henning would call that kitsch. But then Henning had never wished he had not been born.

Henning parked at the bottom of Cort Adelers gate. Aker Brygge, a shopping precinct, lay like a fortress in front of Honnør wharf, the City Hall square and Akershus Castle on the other side. Although it was around midnight, it didn't seem like night. They strolled down the tramlines, passed a taxi rank, and two younger taxi drivers whistled after Katrine who was walking by the broad display windows in Aker Brygge. She glanced at her reflection. It felt good to see herself. It felt good to make faces at her reflection: to be saucy but not tarty. Confident, but not cheap. This is me, she thought. This is how I am. Not naked, not dressed; not hungry, not satiated.

They made friends with a drunk in the queue at McDonald's. He grabbed Katrine's hand and winked at Henning. 'Christ,' he said. 'I wish I was young like you.' Katrine bummed cigarettes off him. A street musician sitting on one of the benches in front of the ferries to Nesodden began to play Neil Young's 'Heart of Gold'. The drunk asked Katrine to dance. She did. The guests at the café tables along the promenade sat like dark shadows in the summer night, shadows who might be friends, who might be enemies. She didn't care about the shadows scowling at her, not understanding what was going on. Tourists in shorts and white trainers with purses on strings around their necks strutted past them in the dark.

Afterwards she feasted on a double cheeseburger, chips with a dollop of ketchup and a large Coke. Henning had a milkshake as always, a vanilla milkshake. That was Henning.

'Didn't you get any food up on Holmenkollen?' he asked once they were back in the car.

'I spewed it up. Guess why.'

'Mr Nice Guy?'

She nodded.

'He tried it on?'

'As always.'

Henning produced a small joint from his shirt pocket, lit it and took a noisy suck. 'It's what I've always said,' he gasped, holding his breath for a few seconds before continuing, 'The guy is enough to make anyone spew.' He was breathing normally again. The smell of marijuana spread around them. Henning said: 'But I wouldn't have thought you would chuck up. I thought you were normal.'

'Shit, I hate being normal.' Katrine grinned through a mouthful of chips and ketchup.

Henning took another noisy suck on the joint. 'Would you like to be normal?' he asked with tears in his eyes.

She tossed back her head and screamed: 'No! And it's wonderful!'

They drove along Mosseveien to the sounds of a gentle night-time voice speaking through the car's speakers. Henning turned off on the old Mossevei by Mastemyr, passed Hvervenbukta beach and drove at a leisurely speed along the night-still road. Katrine switched off the radio and stretched her arms in the air. The wind tried to flatten her arms; the verdant tops of the trees formed shadows against the sky; there was a smell of grass, of camomile. The smell of summer came streaming towards them. Henning turned right, down the road to Ingierstrand.

He stopped and parked in a kind of gravel parking area, under some large pine trees, with the bonnet facing the calm Bunnefjord and a narrow beach further down.

Both of them turned at the sound of another car. They were not alone. A light came round the bend, a car braked and came to a halt further back.

Henning smiled and started the engine again. 'Never any peace. I want us to be alone.'

She said nothing. She was considering what he said and wondered whether to say anything.

Henning reversed and drove back the way he had come. But at the crossing with the old Mossevei he took a right. They drove carefully round the bends and parked by Lake Gjer. It was a wonderful undisturbed area. A table and bench and a few bushes. Henning drove in between the trees. They could see across the lake; a few hundred metres away they could make out the silhouette of the gigantic car tyre marking Hjulet caravan site.

Henning switched off the engine. For a few moments they heard the chirping of a cricket. Soon it too was quiet. The quietness around them made them feel as if they had entered a void.

She wanted to tell him how she felt, to communicate to him the trembling sensation she had which was making her skin nubble, here and now. But she could not find the words. They gazed at each other. In the end the silence was broken by the click of the electric lighter. Henning's face glowed red as he lit his cigarette.

The leather seat creaked as she leaned back and peered up at the blue-black sky where the stars sparkled, like the gleam from a lamp covered with a black sieve. She said aloud: 'Like the gleam from a lamp covered with a damn great black sieve.'

They looked into each other's eyes again, so long that she almost felt part of her was drowning in his dark eyes. She wondered whether it would always be like this for her, whether the boundary between friendship and love would always be confused.

He said: 'If we can move away, step back far enough, here on earth, we see a kind of system in what is only fiery chaos. We can see two stars, one may have died years ago, and been extinguished, and the other may be in the process of exploding right now. We consider it a system, but everything is in constant flux. The earth falls, the sun falls, stars explode in the beyond and create time!'

The cigarette bobbed up and down in the corner of his mouth and his eyes shone with enthusiasm. He is a little boy, she thought, taking the cigarette from his dry lips. She held it between her long fingers and kissed him tentatively. He tasted of smoke and lozenges. The stubble of his beard rasped against her chin. He said something she didn't catch; the words caressed her face like silent breaths of wind between fine beach grass. She opened her mouth as he went on, parted her lips to blow at the whispering voice.

'Imagine a woman,' he whispered. 'A beautiful woman a long time ago, one who is a bit wild . . .'

'Wild?'

'It's a long time ago anyway, and one day she is walking along a path and comes to a river. There's a bridge over the river, one of those old-fashioned ones made with tree trunks, with no railing . . .'

'Is it spring or autumn?' she asked.

'It's spring, and the river is running high and she stops to look down, into the foaming torrent. She stands there playing with her ring, but drops it in the water . . .'

'What sort of ring is it?'

'I'm coming to that. The ring has been passed down through generations. And the ring falls in the water and is lost. Many years later she meets a man. He's from Canada . . .'

'Where is she from?'

'Hm?'

She smiled at the bewildered expression on his face. 'You said he was from Canada. Where is she from?'

He thrust out his hands. 'She's from . . . from . . . Namsos.'

'You see. It takes so little for you to lose your composure.'

'But you ask so many questions. You're ruining my story.'

She smiled. 'That's because you get so excited. Don't be annoyed. Go on.'

'The two of them marry. But all his life he walks around with an amulet around his neck. It's a small Indian box carved out of wood; inside he has a secret, something he found in the stomach of a salmon he gutted as a young man . . .'

'The ring!' she exulted.

Despairing intake of breath from Henning.

She grinned. 'Are you denying that the ring is in the amulet?'

He, also with a grin: 'The ring is indeed in the amulet. But that's not the point.'

'OK, get to the point.'

'The point is that he dies.'

'Dies? Hey, you're evil.'

'. . . And when he's dead, the widow opens the amulet he wore around his neck all his life . . . what are you grinning at?'

'You're such a hopeless romantic.'

With another grin: 'I'm never going to the cinema with you.'

'Yes, you will. Let's go to the cinema. Let's go tomorrow.'

'But you don't let anyone finish what they're saying.'

'I don't go to the cinema to talk!'

'No, but I'm sure you'll sit there commenting on the film. I hate it when people talk in the cinema.'

'I promise to be quiet if you come with me to the cinema tomorrow.'

'What will Ole say if you and I go to the cinema?'

'Don't bring Ole into this. I'm talking about you and me.'

'And I'm talking about the system,' he insisted, remaining objective. 'My whole point is that it is not chance that made this man

36

live his life with her ring round his neck. No two rings are identical; it's the same ring she lost before they met. He caught a fish with the ring in its stomach. However, the ring and the man, plus her and the salmon, along with the ring, are all part of the system, a pattern which becomes logical if it is put in the right perspective. If you step back far enough.'

'And you're floating on a pink cloud,' she said, taking a last drag of his cigarette. She held it out to him with a quizzical expression, then crushed it in the ashtray in the car door when, with a wave of his hand, he refused. She said: 'The strange thing about this story is that she didn't know about the ring the man had around his neck all his life. After all, they were married.'

He sighed again. 'You're the one who's hopeless,' he whispered, and after a little reflection went on: 'OK, but I think this guy had the ring in the amulet around his neck because he dreamed about the woman who owned it, and I think he didn't want to reveal the dream to his wife because he loved her so much. He didn't want her to know about this dream he had about another woman.'

'And in fact it was his wife who owned the ring. It was her he was dreaming about all the time.' She nodded deep in thought. 'In a way, that's beautiful.'

Henning leaned forwards, groped around the dashboard and pressed a button. A buzz came from the roof of the car as it closed above them.

'Wouldn't you like to see the stars?' she asked with sham surprise.

'I'm a bit cold,' he answered – as though quoting a line from a book.

With the roof over their heads and the windows closed it was like sitting in front of a warm hearth. The car bonnet reflected the glow of the starry sky. An insect brushed against her forehead, leaving her with a mild itch which she rubbed with her index finger.

'What I am trying to point out is the pattern,' he continued. 'Imagine the hand that gathers strength to cast the bait, a second in an ocean of seconds, but still this second is part of a system. It is at this second that the salmon takes the bait – so that the man can land the fish and find the ring in its stomach. For one moment, imagine that moment – the sun reflecting on the drops of water and the metal hook – a hundredth of a second that fulfils the fish's feeling of hunger and its drive to swim up the river. This hundredth is one link in a system. Everything is connected: fate, man, woman, salmon, time and the ring she fidgets with on the bridge. Together they are points in a greater unity. Take us two. Or imagine two people, any two young people, two people who love each other without being aware that they do.'

'But is that possible?'

He shrank back, stole a glance and said: 'Of course it's possible. These two people see each other every day, they may meet every day at work – or not even that – for that matter they might see each other every day at a bus stop – or on a bus in the morning rush hour. She may run past a window where he is standing and waiting every morning. Think about it: every morning she runs past a particular office window to see him, and he rushes to the window to see her; this is a moment of contact neither of them can analyze or understand to any meaningful extent until a lot of time has passed. Later, with more experience, with the passage of more time, they think back and know in their hearts that what they had felt at that moment was a kind of love. They know that they already loved each other then.'

'But, Henning,' she said, stroking his beard with her lips. She placed a light kiss on Henning's mouth and whispered: 'You can let them meet again because you're in charge, you're telling the story.'

He whispered back: 'You have to remember that these two met in the way they did without knowing they were meeting. It was just something that happened. Past meetings of this kind are a source of the loss or the warmth they carry inside – for the rest of their lives.'

'But you can let them meet once more,' she insisted.

'OK,' he said.

'Tell me now they did,' she begged. 'Tell me they met again.'

'OK,' he repeated. 'The two of them met again. This is how it happened: he was sitting on a train going south. The train stopped at a station and he got up to look out of the window. Then he saw her. Because another train was standing in the station too. She stood looking out of the train window – the train going north, in the opposite direction. A metre of air separated them. Can you imagine that? Her standing with the wind playing in her hair. She was wearing a white summer dress which was semi-transparent; through two train windows he could see the dress clinging to her body – he could see the outline of her stomach muscles under the dress. They saw each other for five seconds, looked into each other's eyes until the trains moved off. One train went north, the other south. And they were separated again.'

She caressed Henning's chin with her lips. 'What's her name?' she whispered.

He grinned and shook his head. 'This isn't about me. This is a story. This is something that happens every day. To someone. The one thing you can say is that there is something beautiful about the moment the two of them experience.'

'And you're in a world of your own,' she whispered. 'Do you fantasize about her?'

'Of course.'

His smile was sad: 'The only comprehensible thing you can take from the system that affects those two is the poetry. The language, the words we say to each other form a box in which we can collect the beautiful things in life and reveal them to each other at moments like now – here, you and I in this car, tonight. Language and poetry are our way of sensing the incomprehensible because we cannot step far back enough, outside ourselves, to a place where you can enjoy the logic and the inevitability of reality.'

He was breathless from all the speaking. Henning is actually very charming, she thought, Henning is naïve, child-like and charming. She said:

'I don't agree.'

'Eh?'

'You're good at storytelling, but you don't know anything about reality.'

He sent her a gentle, sarcastic smile. 'That's how easy it was to get off with you.'

'Now you listen to me,' she said. 'Outside Kragerø there is a little place called Portør. It's not the name of the place which is important; the point is that you can see the whole horizon from there. It sticks out into the sea – all that is between you and Denmark is the Skagerrak. Once upon a time there was a dead calm. Do you know what that is? Dead calm. That's when the water is like a mirror, not a ripple. I was swimming, early in the morning, the sun was shining, the water was warm, not a breath of wind and the sea was completely still. I began to swim, towards the horizon. You know how I love swimming. And I swam and I swam until I felt so tired I needed to rest. I lay floating on my back looking up at the burning sun. I could see my white body under the surface of the water and I glanced around. And do you know what? I had swum so far out that it was not possible to see land anywhere. Whichever way I looked there was just calm, black sea. I couldn't see anything, not a boat, not a sail, not a strip of land. And I lay there thinking about the black deep beneath me, thinking that I had no idea which way led back to where I had come from, and I closed my eyes. Lying there like that was the biggest kick I have ever known, before or since. I knew in my heart that this was what it is all about. This is life; this is what actually happens every day. Every second of the day is like lying there, alone in the sea.'

'But you found the way back?'

She smiled. 'Of course I did. I'm here, aren't I?'

'Yes, I know, but how? Was it just luck that you swam in the right direction?'

'Maybe. It might have been luck, but that's not the point. The fact is that it was the most important experience I have had in my life.'

'Why do you think that?'

'It was what made me decide to come off drugs. But perhaps even more important than that was the revelation.'

She smiled and whispered softly. 'My single thought while I was out there was that nothing is predetermined. There is no system. You tell great stories, Henning, but this business about predetermined systems is just bullshit. My life begins somewhere between me and the sea. I believe in myself and in reality. That's it.'

The final word hung quivering in the air. Neither of them said anything. They sat close together and Katrine could feel the heat from Henning's thighs against her own. 'What kind of amulet did he have?' she asked.

'Who?'

'The guy from Canada.'

'Oh, him . . .' Henning tried to force a hand down into his trouser pocket, but had to raise his bottom first. 'Here,' he said, passing her a beautiful, small, white box. She took it. There were neat drawings in gold on the lid. 'The kind we used to keep our amphetamines in,' she said, weighing the small box in her hand.

'Not like this one,' he said, taking off the lid.

'Marble,' she burst out. 'Is it made of marble?'

Henning nodded. 'It's the same technique they use in the Taj Mahal. The mother-of-pearl and the blue stone have been worked into the material. Feel,' he whispered, stroking the smooth surface of the lid with his finger. At that instant their eyes met. She slowly lowered the white box and put it in her lap. Then she loosened the thick band of massive gold with two inlaid jewels she was wearing on the ring finger of her left hand. She dropped the ring in the box where it fell with a dry thud. She closed the lid and passed him the box. Henning took it with a gulp.

They huddled close together and the intimacy between them grew. She stared at Henning's glowing skin, at his black eyes shining in the dark. Sinews and veins formed dark shadows in his skin. That's how I want him, she thought. And that was how she took him. She forced Henning under her and fucked him, there in the car; she rode him until the constellations in the sky made small reflections in the beads of sweat on his forehead. She could read in his dark pupils how his orgasm was building up, and when he came inside her, she covered his mouth with hers and let him scream as much he was able, deep down into her stomach.

* * *

Afterwards she dozed off. Her body ached when she woke up; her right leg felt bloodless and numb. That's the first time I've slept in a car since I was little, she thought. It was colder now. Henning was emitting low snoring sounds. She loosened her arms from around his neck and sat up straight. In the mirror she saw that her hair had become tangled. She looked like a woman waking up in the arms of a man in a car in the middle of the night. My leg has gone to sleep, she thought, and began to massage her calf and thigh. And I am cold. Outside there were still stars in the sky. The tiny crescent moon that had hung over the water had moved further south, and the sky, above the treetops on the other side, was lighter, had a bluer tinge. 'Fancy that,' she said in a husky voice. Henning was mumbling in his sleep. She glanced at the clock on the dashboard. It was past two o'clock.

She shivered, put on her thin blouse and straightened her skirt. She examined her face in the car mirror and wished she had a comb. The inside of the car windows had steamed up. She was hungry. And she needed a wash. She searched the glove compartment for cigarettes, but it was empty apart from the log book and a few paper napkins. She dried the condensation on one of the side windows. Outside it was dark behind the spruces. She rolled down the window. The air was wonderful, fresh, but light and cool to the face. Her upper arms began to get gooseflesh. She grabbed the gear lever, eased her leg across to find the clutch pedal. At last she got the car into neutral and manoeuvred her hand around the steering wheel without waking Henning. Then she turned on the ignition. The car started, and she put on the fan heater. The white cone of the headlamps picked out a tree trunk and a mass of green vegetation. Henning was still fast asleep. She thought about going for a wash in the water. It would be wonderful to rinse away the taste of smoke from her mouth. But there didn't seem to be an obvious path. The area between the road and the lake was a murky jumble of trees, bilberry bushes and sharp ends of bare branches. She shuddered. She thought of snakes, horrible coiled snakes slithering between the dead leaves on the ground; she thought of spiders and huge anthills, crawling with millions of ants, and she shuddered again.

In the end she opened the car door and staggered out on stiff legs. She hopped around until the blood slowly returned to her sleeping leg. Ants in the blood. It hurt and she bit her lower lip. She brought her heel down on a sharp stone. It hurt so much she screamed 'Ow', then began to walk. She stumbled around the car like an electric doll with stiff legs and limbs. Barefoot, she walked over the cold, sharp stones and soon felt her circulation returning.

All of a sudden she heard a sound and stopped to listen. She stood quite motionless and a chill crept up her spine. She stood like this for a long time, listening, but didn't hear the sound again. At the same time she scanned her surroundings to see what could have caused it. The night was grey, not pitch black, and in the light from the moon and the stars she saw her shadow on the ground. The only sound to be heard was the low rumble of the idling car engine. What was truly black were the trees and the surface of the water struggling in vain to reflect the stars.

When, at last, she was sure that she had imagined the sound, she decided to go down to the lakeside. She walked down the road with care, looking for a path. And caught sight of a wonderful flat stone she could stand on at the water's edge. A cool gust of air blew against her ankles and legs as she approached. She stopped, bent down, put her hand in the water and felt the temperature. Lukewarm. In the dark she found the stone and went down on her knees. She scooped up water and threw it into her face; it was not cold at all. She stood up, peeled off her panties, kicked off her shoes and stepped into the lake bare-legged. Her feet sank down to her ankles in the mud which felt like cool, lumpy cream. It was unpleasant, but it didn't matter. It was only for two seconds. She raised her skirt to her waist, faced land, squatted down and washed herself.

What was that?

She sprang to her feet and listened.

A sound. But what kind of sound?

She stood quite still listening. But now the silence was total, not even the sound of Henning's car was audible. Just the sound of insects fluttering their wings against the water broke the frozen silence. She suddenly became aware that her skirt was bunched up around her waist, and she let go.

Something had changed. There was something strange about the silence. She tried to work out what was different. She could not, but she didn't like standing there, alone and exposed in the water. The deep gloom and the unbearable silence caused her to feel a clammy sense of fear spreading outwards from the small of her back, a fear which numbed her fingers, which drained her arms of strength, which dried out her mouth and which stopped her breathing. As the darkness was a summer darkness, she could make out the contours of rocks and branches protruding into the air. A clump of black, impenetrable spruce trees blocked her view of the road. It was not possible to see through the wall of spruce foliage.

Walk, she told herself, *wade to the shore and go back to the car.* But for some reason she did not want to make any noise. Because, she thought, because . . . it would drown the other sounds. Which sounds? She stood quite still concentrating, but she couldn't hear a single thing.

Shout, she thought. *Shout for Henning*! But she couldn't make herself do that, either. Instead she waded to the shore. She tripped and almost fell, but managed to regain balance and scrambled on to the shore. She tried to force her wet feet into the shoes. It was difficult; her feet refused to go into her shoes of their own accord.

Once she was ready, she stood with her body tensed, listening. Not a sound to be heard, not even insects. Her eyes seemed to be drawn to the thick wall of spruce on the right. There were spruce needles and tiny pebbles in her shoes. It was unpleasant, but she repressed the feeling. She was focused on the air and the dark wall of spruce. There. There was that sound again. And it came from somewhere behind the spruce trees. She was breathing through her open mouth. Panicky breathing which she had to keep in check. She closed her mouth and held her breath. She stared intently at the clump of trees. There it was again. The rustling noise. She closed her eyes.

'Henning?' she whispered. Her voice didn't carry.

The rustling stopped. She cleared her throat to regain her speech.

'Henning?' she shouted and listened. A twig cracked. Other twigs stirred. 'Is that you, Henning?'

A silhouette detached itself from the clump of trees, a white silhouette. A silhouette that had been there all the time, but she had not seen it until now, when it started moving. It was in human form. White human form. With no clothes on.

PART 2

THE LITTLE GOLD RING

5

Kalfatrus

Police Inspector Gunnarstranda observed the shape of his face in the glass bowl. The reflection distorted his appearance and made it pear shaped. The mouth with the white, artificial, porcelain teeth resembled a strange, long pod full of white beans. His nostrils flared into two huge tunnels and around his face there was the suggestion of a grey shadow, no Sunday shave as yet. He searched for words to say to the goldfish. He was standing in front of the book shelf on which the goldfish bowl was placed, looking at the fish and himself in the glass. Behind his pear-face, the reflection caught everything in the flat: the book shelves and the table with the pile of newspapers. 'Are you lonely?' he asked. The question was ridiculous. He re-phrased it: 'Do you feel lonely?' And, as usual, he put words into the mouth of the red and orange fringetail swimming around in the bowl with an air of leisure. 'Of course you feel lonely; I'm lonely, too.' Saying the words gave the policeman a pang of conscience. He ought to have bought more fish to give the fat red and orange goldfish some friends, to create a fish community in the bowl. However, at the same time he feared that buying more fish would mean he would lose contact with this one. It looked at him with its strange eyes, its beautiful tail flapping in slow motion. 'Yes indeed, we're both lonely,' he concluded, straightening up and ambling into the kitchen to brew up some coffee in the machine. Four spoonfuls of Evergood, five if it was a different brand. That's how it is; with some brands of coffee you need to put more spoonfuls in the filter. Not something you can discuss. It's a question of taste. He hooked his braces over the shoulders of his vest. 'Do you know what the worst thing about it is?' he said to the fish. 'It's that you can't be alone with your loneliness any more. Now it's fashionable to be lonely, now they have programmes about loneliness and everyone talks about it, and they broadcast programmes for the lonely.'

He switched on the coffee machine and leaned against the door frame. There was a portrait of Edel hanging over the fishbowl. What expression would she have on her face and in her eyes now? But why? Was it because he spent his time conversing with a fish? Perhaps she's jealous, he thought, jealous because I don't talk to her? But he did talk to her, in his head. The fish was different; the fish was like a dog. 'Yes,' he heard Edel chide him. 'But dogs have names,' she said.

Exactly, thought Gunnarstranda, trudging back to the bowl. He took the yellow packet of fish food, opened it and tapped a bit out with his forefinger. Tiny flakes floated on the surface of the water. Giddy with happiness the fish about-turned, swam to the top and nibbled at the food. 'Would you like a name?' he asked the fish and considered the three wise men in the Bible. The name of one of the wise men might suit the fish. If the Hindus' theories were right, if the fish had high negative karma, it might indeed have been one of them. But Gunnarstranda could not remember the names of the wise men. Yes, he did, one of them: Melchior. Rotten name for a fish. One was called Balthasar. That was better, but not very original. He kept thinking. 'You could be called . . . you could be called . . .' This was not his strong suit. He had a sudden inspiration. 'Kalfatrus,' he said aloud and straightened up with satisfaction. 'Good name. Kalfatrus.'

The moment the word was spoken the telephone rang.

Gunnarstranda checked his watch and met Kalfatrus's eyes. 'I don't think we'll be seeing each other so often in the future,' he said to the goldfish and turned towards the telephone. He padded across. 'It's Sunday morning,' he continued. 'I haven't shaved, and, in fact, I had a few plans for today. If the phone rings at moments like these it can mean only one thing.'

He placed a hand on the telephone, which continued to ring furiously. The two of them looked at each other across the room for two brief seconds. A policeman and a goldfish exchanging glances. Inspector Gunnarstranda cleared his voice, snatched at the receiver and barked: 'Please be brief.'

6

Vinterhagen

Neither of them had much appetite after the autopsy. They stood outside in the car park, gazing pensively into the air. It had stopped raining, Frank Frølich confirmed. The wind was making the trees sway and dispersing the clouds; the hot sun was beginning to dry the tarmac. He considered what they had found out and wondered how to tackle the case, or to be more precise: how Gunnarstranda thought the case should be tackled. In the end, the latter broke the silence: 'Did you see the news last night?'

'Missed it,' answered Frank Frølich.

'Quite a big deal. Pictures of a helicopter and the whole shebang. But they had a pretty good portrait, a facial composite. I suppose that gave them the lead.'

'Sure,' Frølich said, uninterested. The problem was matching them, matching the lifeless flesh on the table with a name, with a living woman. 'Katrine,' he said with a cough. 'Wasn't that the name?'

Gunnarstranda repeated the name as though tasting it on his tongue. 'Lots of women called Katrine Bratterud. Unusual tattoo on the stomach, so it looks as if we've got something to go on. But having something to go on is not enough.' Gunnarstranda studied his notes and pointed to the car. 'To Sørkedalen.'

They drove in silence with Frølich behind the wheel. Gunnarstranda sat crouched in the front seat with his light summer coat pulled tight around him, mute. Frølich was still searching for music he liked on the radio. Every time the voices in the speakers turned out to be commercials he changed channel. He kept clicking until he found music he liked. Gunnarstranda looked down with annoyance at the finger pressing the search button. He said: 'I've heard that voice three times now. If you click on that station again, I'm going to demand to know what she's talking about.'

Frølich didn't answer. There was no point. He continued to search until the husky voice of Tom Waits emerged through the speakers.

They passed Vestre cemetery and drove from Smestad up Sørkedalsveien past camouflaged houses and protected conservation areas. For a while they were driving side by side with a train on the Østerås Metro line. Two small children in the front carriage were banging their hands on the window and waving to them. The radio was playing quiet blues music as they passed Røa; they went on to Sørkedalen through a June-green cornfield caressed by the gentle breeze and glistening like velvet in the sun. Frølich switched off the radio when the commercials returned. 'This is Oslo,' he said, opening his palms with passion. 'Five minutes by car and you're in the country.' The road had a few tight bends, and on reaching the top of the hill, they could see blue water between two green mountain tops, large-crowned deciduous trees growing along a winding, invisible stream and in the background the fringe of the massive Oslomarka forest. Frølich slowed down. 'Should be somewhere round here,' he mumbled, hunched over the steering wheel.

'The white arrow over there,' Gunnarstranda said.

The arrow was a sign pointing to Vinterhagen. Frølich turned into a gravel car park. There were big holes in the gravel after the heavy torrents of rain. The car bumped along and pulled up in front of a green thicket. They got out. The air was fresh and a little chilly. The holes in the gravel were still full of rainwater. Frølich peered up. The sky seemed unsettled. Right now the sun was shining and was very hot, but all around clouds were gathering for what might be a sudden downpour, perhaps accompanied by thunder. Frølich stood next to the car for a moment before taking off his jacket and hanging it casually over his shoulder. They walked down a narrow pathway with a greyish-black covering of compressed quarry aggregate and past a greenhouse with a door open at one end. Someone had painted *Vinterhagen* on the glass in big, fuzzy, yellow letters. A woman in her mid-twenties, wearing shorts and a T-shirt, watched them through bored eyes.

'I suppose this must have been a folk high school at one time,' said Frølich as they strolled between a large, yellow building and a piece of ground that had been cleared for an allotment. There were attractive vegetable patches with tidy rows of new shoots. 'Idyllic,' intoned Gunnarstranda, looking around. 'Idyllic.'

'And this looks like an accommodation building,' Frølich said with what seemed to be genuine interest, causing his partner to frown with suspicion. Climbing roses attached to a trellis ran along the wall. Frank pointed to an official-looking redbrick house. 'I suppose the offices must be over there.' They walked on towards a group of young people standing around an old, red tractor. 'A red devil,' Frølich exclaimed with enthusiasm. 'An old Massey-Ferguson.' At that moment something soft smacked on to the ground. They stopped. Then another tomato spattered against one of the windows in the yellow building, right behind them. The tomato disintegrated, leaving behind a wet, reddish stain on the dark glass. Frølich ducked, but not quite fast enough to avoid being hit in the face.

* * *

Inspector Gunnarstranda turned and regarded the woman who had been following them from the greenhouse. She had another tomato at the ready. When Frølich started running towards her, she dropped the tomatoes she was holding and sprinted like a gazelle across the vegetable plot and jumped with consummate ease over a fence. Frølich lumbered like a wounded ox. His massive upper torso rocked from side to side and the flab bounced up and down. His white shirt detached itself from his trousers and his tie fluttered over his shoulder. After a few metres he came to a halt, gasping for breath.

A hint of a smile could just be discerned around Gunnarstranda's thin lips. The crew around the tractor were roaring with laughter. Frølich waved his fist after the receding tomato-thrower, turned and plodded back, rummaging through his pockets for a handkerchief. 'Now and again I ask myself whether we're in a real profession,' he sighed, wiping tomato juice off his hair and beard.

'What would you have done if you had caught her?'

Frølich glanced at his boss, but didn't reply.

Gunnarstranda patted the corner of his mouth. 'Here,' he said. 'Tomato seeds.' Frølich wiped his mouth and glared at the youths by the tractor who were still amused by the incident. 'I don't understand them,' he said. 'Why does anyone who has been on drugs hate the police so much?'

'Perhaps because the police have a tendency to run after them,' suggested Gunnarstranda succinctly.

'Reflex action,' Frølich said.

'You run, they flee. The game is that stupid. Look at them.' Gunnarstranda pointed at the group around the tractor. They were making pig-like snorting noises. He took a roll-up out of his pouch, lit it and headed for the office building with Frølich trailing after him. Frølich shook his jacket which had fallen on the ground. They stopped when Gunnarstranda had a coughing fit.

Frølich looked back at the kids around the tractor. 'They remind me of the time when Eva-Britt had two kittens. She had been given them by a farmer who brought them in a wicker basket. But they had had very little contact with people and had gone feral. They hid under the sofa in her living room, came out some time during the night, ate the food she had put out and shat and pissed all over the furniture. I was staying there and went to pick one up. Christ, that cat was wild. It clawed my hand and tore my shirt.'

Gunnarstranda had his breath back. 'Kittens?' he mumbled without much interest and stopped in front of the entrance to the office building. He had two more drags before pinching the glow of the roll-up and putting it into his coat pocket. The floor inside was laid with large flagstones and the ceiling fans whirred. A young man with a goatee and long hair held in a ponytail was sitting behind a table, talking on the telephone. A dog, a boxer, lay on the floor beside the desk. It had placed its head on the floor as though it were holding the stones in place while scowling up at the two men approaching.

The young man on the telephone apologized and put down the receiver.

'Annabeth Ås,' Gunnarstranda said with an irritated glance at Frølich, who was still drying his beard with a handkerchief.

A tall woman wearing a wide tartan skirt appeared from behind a partition. She proffered her hand to Frølich. 'Gunnarstranda?'

'Frank Frølich,' he said, lightly squeezing her hand.

The boxer stood up too, stretched and gave a cavernous yawn before padding over to the three of them, looking up with anticipation.

'Then you must be Gunnarstranda,' said Annabeth Ås, proffering her hand. The policeman shook hands. 'Process of elimination,' she said with a nervous smile. She had rather short, spiky, brown hair and a lined face, but her smile was friendly, though rehearsed, and her teeth were long and discoloured by nicotine. The yellow fingertips also revealed a heavy smoker.

The two policemen were silent.

'Well,' she said with a questioning look at Gunnarstranda. 'Should we go into the office perhaps?'

'We would like you to come with us,' Frølich said, clearing his throat. 'We would like you to help us.'

'What with?' asked Annabeth, alarmed.

'We need you to identify who it is we're dealing with,' Frølich said, and added: 'The deceased . . .'

'Hm . . .' Annabeth hesitated. 'You mean to look . . . at . . . her?'

Frølich nodded.

'I had been hoping I wouldn't have to.' Annabeth Ås sent a quick glance at the man with the goatee. The latter returned a stiff glare, then lowered his eyes and concentrated on the papers on the desk in front of him.

'But I suppose it is best if I do it,' Annabeth concluded, stroking her chin thoughtfully. 'Give me a couple of minutes,' she said, disappearing behind the partition again.

The two men left. The sun was strong and Gunnarstranda produced a pair of supplementary sunshades from a case he kept in his inside pocket. They clipped on to his glasses. 'Trouble in paradise,' he muttered. Through the glass doors they could see Annabeth Ås and the man with the goatee in lively discussion. The latter was gesticulating. Both stopped the moment they discovered they were being observed. The policemen exchanged looks and ambled back the way they had come.

'What did you do in the end?' Gunnarstranda asked standing by the parked car.

'Eh?'

'What did you do with the kittens?'

'Oh, them . . .' Frølich said, lost in thought. He was searching through his jacket pockets for a pair of designer reflector sunglasses. He put them on, checked the reflection in the side window of the car and pulled a face. 'The kittens? They're dead. Eva-Britt got fed up with them, so I shot them.'

Gunnarstranda had time to light the old roll-up and take five long drags before Annabeth came walking between the trees. There was something rustic about the way she walked, the long dress and the flat shoes, plus the way she stepped out, with such energy. Even her short hair bounced in rhythm. On her back she was carrying a small, green rucksack. She shouted to the youths by the tractor and waved her arms. She was wearing a shawl over her shoulders, tartan too; she gave the impression of being the arts and crafts type. Gunnarstranda held the rear door of the car open for her.

'My God,' she said. 'The back seat. Like a criminal.' But she got in, a little more reserved, and waved to the tomato-thrower who was back by the greenhouse door now.

'She just hit me in the face with a tomato,' Frølich conversed cheerfully as he turned out of the car park.

'I beg your pardon?' Annabeth said with deliberate hauteur. 'My dear man, I hope you weren't hurt.'

Frølich observed her in the rear-view mirror and looked across at Gunnarstranda, who had half-turned in his seat to say: 'There was something else I was wondering about. This young man in the office, is he a patient or an employee?'

'He's doing social work for his military service, so in a way he's an employee.'

'What's his name?'

'Henning Kramer.'

'And the missing girl. Why do you think her parents have not reported her missing?'

'Our patients very often do not have much contact with their parents. Or they come from other parts of the country.'

'And?'

Annabeth wound her arms round her rucksack. 'Isn't that answer good enough?'

'I mean in this case. What happened in this case?'

'Gunnarstranda,' said Annabeth, leaning forward. 'We in social welfare are very well versed in matters concerning professional oaths of client confidentiality.'

Frølich searched the rear-view mirror for her face. His sunglasses straddled his nose like a hair slide. You could see he disapproved of the woman's answer by the way he examined the mirror. 'This is a murder investigation,' he emphasized.

Annabeth Ås cleared her throat. 'And I am entitled to exercise my discretion,' she said coldly. She cleared her throat again. 'What's going to happen now?'

'We would like you to come with us to the Institute of Forensic

Medicine,' Gunnarstranda said. 'There we would like you to answer yes or no to one question.'

'And what is the question?'

'Is the body you see in front of you that of the girl you reported missing, Katrine Bratterud?'

* * *

'Yes,' said Annabeth Ås. She looked away as Gunnarstranda pulled the cloth up over the face of the dead girl. 'That's her. The air in here's making me feel sick. Can we go out?'

Outside on the grass they found a bench, one of the solid kind, a combination of a seat and a table that you find in lay-bys in Norway. Annabeth slumped down without removing her rucksack. She breathed in and stared into space, her eyes glistening. 'That was that,' she said. 'Almost three years fighting for her life, all for nothing.'

They sat in silence listening to the cars rushing past some distance away from them. An acquaintance strolled by and waved to the two policemen.

'Do you know what it costs to rehabilitate a drug addict?'

The woman's question was a reaction; the two men both understood that she was not interested in an answer.

'My God,' Annabeth repeated. 'What a waste, what a dreadful waste!'

The following silence lasted until Gunnarstranda prompted her: 'What is a waste, fru Ås?'

Annabeth straightened up. She was on the point of speaking, then paused and instead dried her eyes with the back of her hand.

'Tell us about the three years,' Frølich interjected. 'When did you first meet Katrine?'

Annabeth sat thinking for a while.

'Why do you think . . . ?' she began at length. 'Was it assault? Rape?'

'When did you first meet Katrine?' Frølich repeated patiently.

Annabeth sighed. 'It was a few years back. It was in . . . 1996. She came to us *of her own unfree will,* as we are wont to say, referred to us by Social Services. She wavered for a bit, by which I mean she absconded several times. They often do. But then up we went into the mountains to see how invigorating life can be without any artificial stimulants. She became more motivated, agreed to treatment and followed a three-year course. We divided it up into stages – she was in phase four – and would have been discharged in the summer. She took advanced school-leaving examinations while she was with us and finished last year. Brilliant exam results. God, she was so intelligent, so smart, lightning-quick at picking things up. She got three damned As. She rang me up. *Annabeth, Annabeth*, she screamed down the phone. *I got As.* She was ecstatic, so happy . . .'

Annabeth was becoming emotional and stood up. 'Excuse me . . . I'm just so upset.'

Gunnarstranda looked up at her. 'I suppose that patients do sometimes die,' he commented.

'What?'

'Don't drug addicts sometimes die?'

Annabeth stared at him, speechless. Her mouth opened and shut in slow motion.

'And after school,' Frølich interrupted in a composed voice. 'What did she do then?'

Annabeth glowered at Gunnarstranda, closed her eyes and sat down again. 'She got a job in no time at all,' she said. 'Well, I think she should have aimed higher, started at university, taken an honours course. She could have done political science. She could have become a journalist. With her looks she could have walked into any job she wanted. My God, she had so many options!'

'But where did she get a job?'

'In a travel agency. I can give you the phone number. Such a ridiculous young girl's dream. That's such a bitter thought, too. Here

we have this delicate soul who I assume – I say assume because it
was impossible to get anything out of her, as is so often the case –
and this poor soul goes and gets abused by some man or other
while still a child. Please don't misunderstand me. There are some
drug addicts who just want their kicks in everyday life. I mean,
some patients can't seem to live intensely enough in the world we
call normal. But . . .'

'. . . but Katrine wasn't the type?' Frølich suggested.

'Katrine was so full of . . . what should I say? . . . she was so vulnerable. And girls like her often start taking drugs at the age of
twelve, with hash anyway. Start smoking reefers, as they call them,
then it's glue-sniffing and alcohol and the first fix when they're
fifteen. Then they drop out of school. It's the usual story: leave
school, leave home, then start picking up punters on the streets.
These poor young people have no childhood. They don't have the
ballast that you and I . . .'

She paused for a few seconds while Gunnarstranda, still thinking, sprang up and placed one foot on the seat to roll himself a
cigarette.

'Go on,' Frølich said in a friendly voice.

'Where was I?' she asked, disorientated.

'You were talking about drug addicts who lose their childhood.'

'Ah, yes. And what do you do when you haven't had a childhood? You catch up of course. That was what was so bad about
Katrine. Good-looking girl, attractive figure, intelligent, quick. But
just a child, just a child . . . what was your name again?'

'Frølich.'

'A child, Frølich. This child in a woman's body could sit down
and stuff herself with sweets – watch cartoons, read rubbishy romantic magazines like a twelve-year-old girl – with stories about
princes who ride away with Cinderella into the sunset – blow out
candles on her birthday, wear a crown on her head – she always
wore a crown on her birthday. She loved it. Writing her boyfriend's
name on her hand. Spur of the moment wheezes like having a

61

bread-eating competition or making paper boats. She revelled in these things.

'It's often like that. Young girls in women's bodies, experienced in life and so driven that they can wriggle their way like eels around men and authorities. This dual nature is perhaps the biggest problem of all. Women like this can seem like wounded animals grabbing whatever they need at any particular moment, without any scruples, while still being children with dreams of the bold brave prince who will ride away with them, take them on trips around the world. Katrine was no exception. Imagine, with all the talent she had, she preferred to sit at a computer in a travel agency! What about that? A travel agency!'

Frølich nodded his head gravely and watched Gunnarstranda flick a strand of tobacco off his lower lip while staring into space. A magpie stalked across the grass behind him with purposeful intent. The bird was like a priest, thought Frølich, a stooped priest, dressed in black with a white collar, his hands behind his back. In fact, the two of them, the magpie and the vain policeman, were very similar.

'You said she wrote her boyfriend's name on her hand. Did she have a boyfriend before she died?' Frølich asked.

'Yes, she did. A bit of a strange choice. I'm sure you know the type. Looks like a car salesman or a football player. Goes to a tanning salon and watches karate films.'

'What's his name?'

'Ole. His surname's Eidesen.'

'What sort of person is he?'

'Run of the mill . . . a young . . . man.' She shrugged.

'But what's the link between them? Why did they become a couple?'

'I think he must have been a tennis coach or something like that,' she said with a resigned grin. 'No, I was joking. He was a driving instructor or a language teacher. I haven't a clue really, but it was something as banal.'

'What impression did you have of Ole?'

'He was an ordinary sort of chap, superficial . . . in my opinion, and hence boring . . . and very jealous.'

The two detectives looked at her.

'Although he wasn't brutal. Just jealous. I don't think he ever did anything . . .'

'Just a boring, jealous man?'

'Yes.'

'How did the jealousy manifest itself?'

'Dear me, this is just what I've heard. I don't actually have any impression of him.'

'What do you think Katrine saw in a man like Ole?'

'Status.'

'What do you mean by that?'

'I mean what I say. This chap looks like one of those models in a deodorant commercial – you know, shaved head and trendy clothes. For Katrine he was a status symbol she could show off to other women. Meat.'

'Meat?'

'Yes, that's what our young people are good at, pairing up, and I assume this chap was well-suited for that.'

'She had a large tattoo around her navel. Anything symbolic in that?' Frølich asked.

'No idea,' Annabeth answered, adding, 'I would guess not. It's part of the tawdry art that characterizes our patients. Something erotic, I would guess, a sex thing.'

'Do you know if she had a past in prostitution?'

'They all do.'

Frølich raised both eyebrows.

'Most anyway.'

'But Katrine? Did she?'

'She had also experienced that segment of reality, yes.'

Gunnarstranda coughed. 'When did you last see Katrine?'

Annabeth looked perplexed. 'On Saturday.' She cleared her

throat and took the plunge. 'At a party at our place. She became ill and then just left.'

'In other words, you were one of the last people to see her alive.'

Annabeth stared into the policeman's eyes for a few seconds and lowered her gaze. 'Yes . . . I was, with several other people.'

'You said she became ill.'

'She had a bit of a turn and was sick. I was very shaken because I thought she was drunk and it would not have looked good if our patients were seen to be drinking and spewing up at my house.'

'But she wasn't drunk?'

'No, she hadn't touched a drop of alcohol all evening. And it can't have been the food either because no one else was ill.'

'So it was a turn,' Gunnarstranda said. 'And she left the party with her boyfriend?'

'No, she must have taken a taxi on her own.'

'Must have taken? You don't know if she did?'

'No, to be honest, I don't know how she got home.'

'She never did arrive home.'

Annabeth closed her eyes. 'Don't make this worse for me than it already is, Gunnarstranda. I don't know how she went off. All I know is that someone was taking care of her. I know she left the party and I assume they put her safely into a taxi.'

'But do you know when?'

'I would guess at around midnight.'

Gunnarstranda nodded. 'Fru Ås,' he said, 'we have now reached a point in the conversation where I have to explain that the parameters have changed somewhat.'

'Oh?'

Gunnarstranda did not reply at once.

'Changed? Surely you don't think . . . ? Oh, my goodness, what . . . ?'

'We don't think anything,' the policeman said gently. 'The change is that you are no longer required to protect client confidentiality. If you are not already aware, I can release you from any

professional oaths with immediate effect, if necessary, with authority from the highest . . .'

'That won't be necessary,' Annabeth assured him. 'Should there
be any problems we can discuss them as they occur.'

'Very well,' said Gunnarstranda. 'Earlier today a post-mortem
was carried out on Katrine Bratterud.' He tossed his head to indi-
cate where it had taken place.

'Yes,' said Annabeth.

'Frølich and I were present.'

'Yes.'

'It is very important for us to have this vomiting business clear,'
the detective said. 'Are you positive she was sick?'

'I didn't stand watching, if that's what you mean.'

'What food did you serve at the party?'

'Why is that?'

'I would like to compare it with what we found in her stomach.'

A shudder went through Annabeth. She said: 'Filled mussel
shells as a starter. After that it was a buffet: salads, cured meats and
tapas – you know, marinated olives, artichokes, that sort of thing,
because it's easy, then a bit of cheese at the end . . . red wine . . .
beer . . . and mineral water for those who wanted it . . . coffee with
cognac.'

Gunnarstranda nodded. 'We found fragments of skin under her
nails,' he continued. 'This and a number of other details suggest
she defended herself.'

'You mean she scratched?'

The policeman nodded.

'Poor Katrine,' Annabeth muttered to herself, and as neither of
the policemen said anything, she added: 'Well, I haven't run into
anyone with a scratched face, if that's what you're wondering.'

'Why do you think Katrine's parents didn't report her missing?'

'They're not in a state to miss her.'

'And what do you mean by that?'

'It means that fru Bratterud, who lives like a gypsy, either at home in her hovel – excuse the expression; some might call it a house – or sharing a bed with any one of a variety of men, is an alcoholic and hardly knows how old Katrine is. I don't think her mother remembered a single birthday while she was with us.'

'And the father?'

'He died when she was ten or eleven. Originally she came from a foster home and was adopted.'

'A foster home,' Frølich said. 'So Katrine was adopted by a drunk?'

'I presume the mother was not a drunk when she adopted Katrine.'

'Nevertheless.'

'Mistakes are made by all public authorities, Frølich. For all I know, there may be people doing twenty years in prison because of your mistakes.'

The younger detective was about to contradict her, but she swept him aside: 'At the centre we have a girl of fourteen who lost four teeth as a result of police brutality.'

'Fourteen? Rubbish.'

'The people who beat her up were more concerned with the fact that she was taking part in an anti-racist demonstration than her age. The point is that mistakes are made everywhere, Frølich. And I have dedicated half of my life to trying to correct such mistakes. Care for drug addicts is a continual process of repair. One shot of heroin for a thousand kroner in the street can be the start of a slow suicide or several years of fighting against addiction, costing society ten million kroner. Even if Katrine does end up as a statistic at some point, you don't need to rush to put her on the list. It would be better to find out who killed her.'

'Where did she grow up?' Gunnarstranda intervened.

'In fact, I'm not sure, but I think it was Krokstadelva or Mjøndalen, Stenberg, somewhere around there, in one or other of the innumerable clumps of houses between Drammen and Kongsberg.'

'And Katrine's biological parents?'

66

'Katrine knew that her real mother died when she was very young and that was all. I didn't talk with her about that much.'

'What did you talk about?'

'A lot about her father. She really loved him. The father who died when she was ten or eleven. That may be a possible explanation for her syndrome, feeling drawn to a father figure, but all that is just speculation.'

Gunnarstranda nodded slowly. He said: 'There's one thing we need to know. You said something about sexual abuse in childhood years. Does that apply to Katrine, too?'

'I don't know.'

'What do you mean by that?'

'Katrine was inscrutable in this respect. I have my suspicions, but I don't know for sure.'

'What do you base your suspicions on?'

'I have my own ideas. There are often such stories behind a great many cases like hers, as I said. These symptoms of hers – prostitution, withdrawal, drug addiction – they can be explained by a variety of factors. But picture a girl with a strong attachment to a father, then the father dies, the mother turns to drink and strange men wander in and out of the house . . . I don't know. As I said, she was inscrutable.'

'Is there anyone who could help us clear up this point? Someone who was particularly close to her?'

'There's Ole, of course. They were together for quite a while, even though it was sporadic.'

'Sporadic?'

'Yes, he wanted a closer relationship than she did. You have to understand . . . Katrine didn't like people getting too close . . . then there's Henning, the conscientious objector you met at our place. He spent a lot of time with Katrine. There's Sigrid, a social worker with us. Sigrid Haugom. Katrine often confided in her, but I doubt Sigrid knows any more than we do. It is not our practice to keep secrets about our patients – amongst ourselves, I mean.'

Gunnarstranda reacted. 'But isn't that what all confidentiality is based on? Do you mean that the patients at Vinterhagen cannot rely on the employees' ability to keep secrets?'

Annabeth stared at him in bewilderment.

'You were very quick to hide behind client confidentiality,' the inspector continued.

'Successful treatment depends on openness, Gunnarstranda.'

The policeman glared at her.

'In fact, that is part of our ideological platform. Complete openness,' she explained in a gentle voice.

Gunnarstranda dropped the subject. He said: 'As far as her male circle of acquaintances was concerned . . . was there any competition? Did Katrine's boyfriend have rivals?'

'To be honest, I have no idea,' Annabeth said. 'Don't take too much notice of me. I may have imagined this jealousy of Ole's. I know very little about these things.'

Gunnarstranda was making motions to return to the car.

'You don't need to drive me back,' Annabeth said. 'I need some fresh air and it's late. I'll stretch my legs.'

'Before that I need the names of everyone at the party on Saturday.'

Annabeth Ås reflected. 'Is that really necessary?'

'I'm afraid so, fru Ås.'

She took a deep breath and met Frank Frølich's eyes. 'Come on then,' she said. 'Take notes.'

* * *

They sat watching her. She could have graced an illustration in a Norwegian fairy tale. The long skirt, flat shoes and a small square rucksack on her back. *Kjerringa med staven.* The Woman with the Walking Stick. Except that this woman had no walking stick. 'Do you know why all women teachers walk around with a rucksack like that on their backs?' Frølich asked with a thoughtful air.

'For books,' Gunnarstranda suggested.

The other man shook his head. 'It fits exactly into the kitchen sink,' Frølich said.

'The rucksack?' Gunnarstranda asked.

'Yes, so they're firmly in position when their old man wants to give them one.' Frølich laughed at his own joke.

Gunnarstranda peered up at him with disgust.

'The rucksack on the woman's back,' Frølich explained, 'is stuck in the sink . . .'

'I understood,' Gunnarstranda cut in. 'I don't think being single is doing you any good.' He stood up. 'You'd better check out the travel agency. And now we have a few names to be getting on with.'

'And you?'

Gunnarstranda looked at his watch. 'I have to go home. Change clothes. Go to the theatre.'

'You?' Frølich burst out in dismay. 'To the theatre?'

Gunnarstranda ignored the comment. Instead he perused Frølich's notes. 'I'll take in this Sigrid Haugom on the way there,' he said. 'See you.'

7

Domestic Chores

She must have been a nice sort of girl, thought Frank, pondering what the tattoo around her navel could have meant. It didn't have to mean anything. Even teenage girls had tattoos these days, around the tops of their arms, on their shoulders, buttocks, breasts. People had tattoos everywhere. But, he went on to think, that special tattoo still suggested that he might never have been particularly close to her. He had male friends with tattoos; Ragnar Travås had tattoos all over his upper torso. However, since he did not know any women with tattoos he automatically assumed it was probable that he would not have got to know this woman.

Frank Frølich found a gap between two cars and parked the police vehicle a few metres away from the drive to the block of flats in Havreveien. Standing alone in the slow lift up to the third floor, he was still wondering about the tattoos. Ragnar Travås considered tattoos attractive. But as for me, Frank thought, I could never look at a tattoo and see only that. After all, a tattoo is part of the body on which it is tattooed. Thus, Frank had to conclude, he regarded the body as part of the very decoration. Any body art that cannot be removed becomes part of the person. Or the person becomes part of the tattoo. *And in that case the motif is pretty important*, he thought. *Thank God she hadn't chosen something banal like a cat or . . .* Katrine Bratterud had had a kind of flower pattern with lots of flourishes tattooed around her navel. Irrespective of whatever stories Annabeth Ås and any of the others served up to him Katrine would stand out as the woman with the embellished abdomen – a dead body with a painting on her stomach; this painting would stand out and be an inseparable dimension of Katrine B whenever he thought about her as a living person. But that's my problem, he thought. I see Katrine's decision to adorn her stomach as one of her dominant traits, and that's where my assessment of her breaks down, he thought, opening the lift door to his floor. Because this was not just any flower. It was a lush, ornate flower – with two narrow but equally luxuriant petals licking their way down to her groin. Odd, he continued to think, that my mind is on the tattoo rather than all of the other stuff: the drug addiction, her childhood . . .

Frank's shoulders sank as he stopped in front of his own door. It was open. He knew what that meant. From inside he could hear the sound of the vacuum cleaner. This was the last thing he had wanted today. The day had been too long, there had been too much hassle and there had been too little food for that. He stood in front of the door for a few seconds thinking. He could cut matters short, flee into town, have a beer first and then work on the theory that she would have left after a couple of hours. No. Not now, not when Gunnarstranda could ring up any moment to discuss details. He pushed the door open and stepped over the yellow vacuum cleaner blocking the way.

She stood in her usual energetic pose, shouted a brief greeting over the noise but made no move to switch off the machine. 'There's food on the kitchen table,' she yelled.

Frank's mother had two children she looked after very well. For Frank's sister this sacrifice was a welcome relief. Two small children and a husband doing shift work meant that you appreciate a helping hand. It was different for Frank. He was annoyed by her reproaches regarding the mess in the flat and the beer bottles in the fridge, and her fussing.

So he flipped off his shoes and walked into the sitting room without paying any attention to her remark about the untidy shoelaces.

The TV was switched on, but there was no sound. Floyd, the English celebrity cook, was cutting ginger into long strips and throwing them into a casserole before focusing his attention on a bottle of wine.

Frølich slumped listlessly on to the sofa, put his legs up and rested them on the table that was not in fact a table – it was an old sea chest made of unplaned wood – but a multi-purpose piece of furniture: footstool, table and a perch for handy objects like a remote control and a mobile telephone.

He looked at the TV screen. Floyd, with his red-wine nose and red-wine smile, smelled the casserole and then straightened up, poured red wine into a glass and knocked it back in one almighty swig. Frank raised the remote control and switched off the television.

I may have seen Katrine in town, he mused. I might have turned my head for a second look . . . thought that she . . . or stolen a glance on the tram, noticed her profile when she was sitting with her nose in a magazine or a newspaper . . .

His line of thought was broken when the hall door was opened with a bang. Vacuum cleaner first, Mum next. That was how she was. Unstoppable, like the dentist's drill in *Karius and Baktus*.

'Take it easy!' he growled in a fit of irritation. But she ignored him as always and persevered with clenched teeth. The mouthpiece of the vacuum cleaner was already under the TV.

'Careful,' he shouted.

'Eh?'

Mum pushed the mouthpiece between the cables, the DVD player and the TV.

'Don't touch anything!' he roared, jumping up and over to the yellow vacuum cleaner and pressing the off button. The motor died with a slow whine. His mother straightened up and put her hands on her hips. She said nothing; she stood there with her stomach jutting forward, a pose which expunged all opposition.

'I can manage this myself!' he ventured – in a meek voice.

'Christ, I've got my loose hackle flies here.' He pointed to the feathered trout flies on one corner of the table. 'The bloody vacuum cleaner might have sucked up my flies.'

She sent him a stern look.

'I'm trying to think,' he ventured, in an even meeker voice.

'So think somewhere else!' Stomach first – out you go. 'Now I'm here, I'm going to help. Go into the kitchen and get some food down you.'

He was beaten; he padded out of the room, closed the kitchen door and sat by the window looking out on to Europaveien – E6 – and stared down at the queue of cars crawling its way past.

A corpse. A woman's dead body, with no clothes on, no jewellery, nothing. Just the eye-catching tattoo around her navel. Until the pathologist had cut open her stomach and folded the skin neatly to the sides.

But it wasn't her lying on the table. It was something else. It wasn't her thoughts, her terror as she felt the cord around her neck tighten – until she blacked out. It's the other her we have to deal with, he thought, and visualized the dead body someone had tossed away – tossed away like a used item, like so much rubbish, like an empty shell. The lack of respect appalled him. Of all the acts the unknown perpetrator had committed against this poor woman, none was as grotesque as tossing her away, leaving her to lie there without dignity.

I'm becoming soft, he said to himself. Tonight I'm going to sleep badly; I'm going to think about her.

Frank chewed at a piece of bread covered with salami and a thick layer of prawn salad. Then he got to his feet and opened the fridge. He took out a litre of milk, checked the date, ripped open the top and quenched his thirst from the carton.

At last there was silence in the sitting room. He could hear her reassembling the vacuum cleaner in the cupboard in the hall. 'No wonder you're not married,' she shouted to him. 'The way this place looks!'

He found some cups and poured coffee that she had brewed in the machine. He observed the polished sheen of the kitchen window. At once he regretted his recent aggressive tone. 'Thank you,' he whispered, somewhat ashamed, as she sat down at the kitchen table. 'I'll drive you home afterwards.'

'You won't ever get me on your motorbike again,' she swore and stood up to find some sugar cubes. Frank smiled at the memory of the time she had sat in the sidecar going down Ringveien. Mum holding on to her hat while being thrown around like a nut in a shell.

'I've got a car,' he assured her.

She shook her head. 'Then I'd rather take the Metro.' She smacked her lips as she chewed the sugar cube and took a mouthful of coffee. 'No one in the street is going to be able to say I was driven home in a police car!'

Frank cut himself another slice of bread. 'It's a civilian car,' he said. 'No police sign or anything.'

'Oh yes,' she said, indifferent. 'How's Little Napoleon?'

'As always.'

'I hope someone puts that little bugger in his place one of these days.'

'He's a good policeman.'

'He's what your father would have called a right basket.'

'You're only saying that because you don't know him.'

'Yes, thank God.'

Frank sighed. 'He's a widower. He hasn't got enough to do. That's the whole problem. In a way he's married to the job.'

'You are, too,' she said.

'You get hooked. You can't avoid it.'

'How's that?'

'It's like this murder. It's a crazy thing to happen but it's impossible not to be caught up. Nor to want to sort it out.'

'That's all, is it? Or is it because you daren't come to grips with other things in your life?'

74

There she went again. Frank shook his head in despair. Before he managed to say anything the telephone rang.

'Talk of the devil . . .' Frank's mother muttered. 'There he is, Little Napoleon ringing for his foot-soldier.'

'Are you alone?' Gunnarstranda asked.

'Like a mackerel in Drøbak Sound,' Frank said, taking the cordless telephone into the other room.

'Tell me when you're alone.'

'Now,' Frank said, sinking into the sofa again. 'I thought you were going to the theatre,' he continued.

'I am going to the theatre. Soon. I want you to go out to the rehab centre tomorrow. Talk to the lad with the goatee and ask him if he had anything going with the girl. If you can find anyone else who knows her, talk to them, too. Will you shut up!'

'I didn't say a word,' Frank said.

'I wasn't talking to you. I was talking to a woman grumbling away outside. That's done it. Now she's as mad as hell. Good, that's made my day. Well, see you.'

'See you,' Frank said, staring at the telephone.

8

A House in Town

The woman who opened the door was closer to fifty than forty and had at one time been very attractive. She was slim, of medium height, dressed in a nice grey suit with a skirt reaching above her knees. She regarded Gunnarstranda with expectation and mild interest, like a nurse.

'May I come in?' he asked straight out.

'Of course, my dear. Please excuse me,' she said, beaming a broad smile which made her even more attractive. Her hair was completely grey, like silver, and Gunnarstranda guessed it was dyed. He assumed she had been blonde once.

'Annabeth has told us everything. It has hit us hard. But I didn't expect a visit from the police so quickly.'

She was bare-legged and moved with grace, without a sound. She showed him into a living room and invited him to take a seat. 'Back in a moment.'

The sound of classical music could be heard through concealed speakers. It was *The Magic Flute*, Mozart, one of the few pieces the policeman knew well. The singing made him sentimental. It made him think of Edel. And as he pursued the memory, the man and the woman in the opera were singing in unison: '*Auf Wiedersehen, auf Wiedersehen.*'

Gunnarstranda looked around. The CD cover lay with today's newspaper on a coffee table in front of the suite. Otherwise the room was dominated by tables: small antique tables in elegant

76

mahogany, one table in each corner, one alongside each wall, several bearing antique lamps, American-looking Tiffany lamps with shades of coloured mosaics.

Gunnarstranda stood on an oval rug with an oriental pattern. The rug lay in the middle of the floor and softened the sound of his shoes which had made such a hard, formal click on the oak parquet flooring. He stood on the rug, rocking on the balls of his feet. He listened to Pamina warbling her way through an aria as Sigrid Haugom was rattling cups in the kitchen. On the edge of his awareness he could hear water running from a tap. He ran his eyes along the walls. A room of good taste, he thought, more taste than function: no books, no TV, but a suite of comfortable furniture, tables, lamps and pictures on the walls. His interest was caught by a potted plant on the window sill and he strode over. It was a bonsai tree and it was not thriving. He lifted up the pot and studied the plant with interest. His conclusion was that the poor tree was dying. He stood looking outside, lost in thought. The window was south-facing and the garden stretched gently down to a green hedge concealing a pair of tramlines behind. But over the hedge you could see the classic outline of the inner part of Oslo fjord, the islands, Bunnefjord and Nesodden. One of the blue Color Lines ships was rounding the headland towards Drøbak and into the Skagerrak.

'Sugar or milk?' came a voice from behind.

He turned and saw that the reason he had not heard her coming in was that she was barefoot. 'I take it black, thank you.' He put the plant pot back in its place, crossed the floor and sat down in one of the stylish chairs around the low oval coffee table whose wood gleamed wine-red.

She sat down on the sofa diagonally opposite him. After a moment or two she grabbed the remote control from the table and cut off the man's song. Tamino he supposed. They exchanged looks as the silence enveloped them.

'Gunnarstranda,' Sigrid said as though tasting the word. 'Unusual name.' She squinted at him with a cheeky smile playing on her lips: 'Do you like the name?'

The policeman examined the elegant porcelain cups for a few seconds, considered the question, scented the atmosphere in the room and noted his surprise that she had asked such a personal question without any unease. He stroked the gilt-edged plate, then looked her straight in the eye and smiled. 'What sort of question is that? No one likes their name, do they?'

She cocked her head, satisfied with the answer: 'I suppose you're right.'

'Yes,' Gunnarstranda said, sampling the coffee and informing her with a tiny nod of the head and an appreciative pursing of the lips that it was good. 'In our culture it's the women who have been obliged to change their names; man's lot has been to accept his identity and to perpetuate the name.'

She stared into space for a second before gathering herself. 'But if you didn't like your name you could have changed it, I suppose. It's possible.'

Gunnarstranda leaned back in the chair. 'I didn't come here to talk about me,' he mumbled, crossing his legs. 'But now that we're on the subject, I disliked my name as a child. And for a long time I thought everyone did – dislike their name. But that's not the case. And as I grew older I realized that I disliked people taking pseudonyms and aliases even more.' Taking in the room with a sweep of his arm, a gesture that was intended to include the splendid view, the lavish interior and her general social affiliation, he continued: 'Well, what is a lady like yourself doing in a place like . . .'

'. . . a rehab clinic for drug abusers? Nothing could be more normal,' Sigrid said. 'I belong to the mediocre majority of women in West Oslo. I am one of those who have tired of shopping and housewives' holidays on the south coast and have decided to go back to work now that their children rate friends higher than home.'

'When is that?'

'When children enter their teens, or the child, in our case. We went to school at the same time: Joakim to senior high school, me to Diakonhjemmet University to study social work. I've been working with Annabeth for three years now.'

'Joakim – is that your son?'

She nodded.

'What does he do now?'

'He's in the US, studying economics at Yale.'

'Not bad.'

'Very right and proper, you mean, for herr and fru Haugom of Grefsen.'

'So you're a little critical of the boy's choice of education?'

'Let's just say working with drug addicts puts Western capitalism and financial politics in perspective.'

'Interesting.'

'Why's that?' She curled her legs up under her on the sofa.

'Because you appear to be middle-class, but you choose to work with drug addicts and are critical of . . .' He searched for words.

'Of our official drugs policy,' she completed, pensive and focusing in front of her.

'How do you get on with the patients?'

'Pretty well actually. I would say I'm doing a good job.'

'You're thriving?'

'Yes, and the patients with me.'

'And Katrine?'

She nodded. 'Katrine was the young, silly type. Excuse my language. I liked her very much; she had looks, style, a future and all that, but at the same time she was envious of me.'

Gunnarstranda smiled in acknowledgement.

'She was envious of my life, house, money and the car I drive. Please don't misunderstand me. Such envy is healthy. That type of girl, however, needs clear, specific models; their personality is too fragile and their self-image too vulnerable to come to terms with the fact that life can be hard. Their whole problem is that when they come face to face with reality, when they are confronted by adversity and the going gets tough, they resort to drugs. That is a world they can control; the drugs milieu is full of clichés, as you know. Not even the worst soap opera on TV can be as superficial or hollow or as full of vacuous phrases as a conversation between two addicts.'

Gunnarstranda sipped his coffee and was on the point of saying something.

'I'm sorry,' Sigrid said, suddenly seeming depressed. 'It's just that I can't take it in that I'm talking about Katrine. Of course I know she's dead, but it's strange anyway . . .'

'If she had died in a different way,' the policeman said, 'let's suppose, of the classic overdose, for example, I daresay we would not have been sitting here discussing her.'

Sigrid Haugom closed her eyes and let out a deep sigh. Silence fell over the room. Gunnarstranda leaned back and watched her from beneath half-closed eyelids. She shifted position, cleared her throat and said: 'Death is not so unusual in this job, of course. We've had several patients who have died. Death and overdoses are daily topics of conversation – in fact. But addicts are never killed by someone else; they tend to kill themselves.' She looked down.

Gunnarstranda nodded. 'What did you think about fru Ås inviting her to a party at her home on Saturday?'

'I was against it, and I definitely thought it was premature.'

'What do you mean by *premature*?'

'The difficulty for our patients is that they often have to be fundamentalists to survive. They have to be off all drugs, off alcohol and off former friends. Do you understand? But the world isn't like that. The world is full of overlapping networks. Reality consists of people who build alliances. The world is full of double standards and territorial battles. At the Centre we do have occasional parties. Everyone does. But I didn't like Katrine being there. For our patients it's tough to face the fact that the very people who work every day at ridding them of their addictions turn to alcohol when they want to enjoy themselves. Everyone drinks with moderation. Well, maybe not everyone. Some drink themselves legless. The difference between an addict and a so-called normal person is that the latter can adapt their lives to the demands of everyday living. They go to work sober, drink a beer in the sun – but they stop there. In my opinion, the kind of party Annabeth has is a revolting ritual. *Revolting* is my word and I am against that kind of ritual. When a patient like Katrine takes part, the party changes character; it becomes a sort of confirmation ceremony, with the patient showing us that she can deal with the life to which she has to return.'

'A sort of initiation test into the normal world?'

'Not my words, but you've got my point.'

'But weren't you worried when she fell ill?'

Sigrid Haugom sighed and stared out of the window, sunk in her own thoughts while absentmindedly running a hand up and down her leg and scratching herself. The room was silent except for a wall clock and its hollow, raindrop-like, tick-ing sounds. Gunnarstranda peered up at it: old-fashioned craftsmanship with a dial made of matt porcelain, covered in stains. The Roman numerals were neatly painted and the same neatness was visible on the clock hands. A carved eagle adorned the wooden clock, and the pendulum that hung next to the wall swung from side to side between two weights, much like fir cones in appearance.

'Now she's dead of course, but as a rule we would have been worried, yes,' the silver-haired woman said.

'But at the time, during the party?'

'I tried to talk to her, but then she seemed to recover. She must have eaten something she couldn't stomach and then it passed . . .'

'So her behaviour didn't give cause for alarm?'

'Now that you ask, I think perhaps we should have taken the whole affair more seriously.'

'Has this sort of thing happened before? I mean that a patient is sick in this way?'

An eloquent smile played on Sigrid's lips. 'It was the first time I'd been to that sort of party. For the Centre, that is. Such parties are not that usual.'

'What was the occasion?'

'It was a party for the staff – an end-of-summer celebration. I suppose Katrine had been invited because she was leaving us for the big, wide world. Her treatment at the Centre would have been finished in the summer.'

'Are there many patients you can declare drugs-free?'

'Our statistics are not very good, no.'

Gunnarstranda sat looking at the floor. 'Are anyone's statistics good?' he asked at length.

'Yes, some are. Nothing exceptional, but there are better statistics than ours. However, even if Katrine was the patient who had achieved most, that doesn't mean that we don't have a lot to do. Some of the blame for the bad figures has to lie with the legislators. Patients come to us as a result of compulsion orders, but they only last for a little time, and if we don't have the authorization to hold them, they often go. It's the same as with many so-called normal people: they take the path of least resistance.'

'Why do you think she was ill that night? Do you think it had anything to do with the food?'

'I have no idea.'

Gunnarstranda waited while Sigrid reflected. She was sitting with her legs folded beneath her on the sofa, holding an ankle with one hand and supporting herself with the other. 'I remember Katrine and Annabeth were in conversation, and that I walked towards them. Her boyfriend, who was there, did the same. He caught her when she fell.'

'She fainted?'

'I don't know.'

Gunnarstranda waited.

'She might have fainted.'

'What did you do?'

'I followed the two of them, her and her boyfriend, to the bathroom and, after a while he came out, leaving her inside. He said she felt better and would be out in a while. I waited for a bit, and after a few more minutes I knocked on the door. But she wouldn't open up. A little later she shouted to me that everything was fine and opened the door. Then I went in; she was sitting on the toilet lid. I remember I washed her face. She seemed fine, but was a little shaky. I remember she asked me to call a taxi, but then didn't bother, that is to say she told me not to bother. She said she would come out of the toilet, but that she might leave the party early. So I went.'

'Did you say anything else to her?'

'No. Some time later I asked Annabeth, but she thought she had gone home early because she was ill.'

'What did you think then?'

'I was nervous. She was upset because of an incident that took place earlier in the day and –'

'What sort of incident?' Gunnarstranda interrupted.

'I think someone from her former life had appeared in the travel agency where she was working.'

'Who?'

'I don't know the name. But she rang me a couple of hours before we left for Annabeth's. It must have been about five o'clock, I think, so it was after she had finished work. She said something had happened.' Sigrid frowned. 'The whole thing was a bit incoherent, but I think she said someone from the drugs milieu she had been part of turned up at her workplace. That was why she had to talk to me. She insisted on it.'

'Why you?'

'Because . . .' Sigrid searched for words.

Gunnarstranda leaned back in the chair, silent.

'Because we talked a lot. We got on well.'

'But what did she want to talk about?'

Sigrid Haugom deliberated. 'I asked if we couldn't talk on the phone, but she said no. I remember I looked up at that clock.' Sigrid pointed to the wall where the clock in the brown box was ticking loudly. 'It was past five and we had to be at Annabeth's for half-seven. And I was working out how much time I would need for a shower and the other things I needed to do. I . . . well . . . I tried to make it all fit, let me put it like that, and asked if I should pop by before we went to the party, but she said no.'

'And how did she go on?'

Sigrid shrugged. 'Words to the effect of . . . then we can chat later, or something like that. I wasn't so happy with that because I knew she was very touchy in that area, about being rejected, so I asked: *Are you sure?* And once again I offered to drive down to hers. But then she asked me if I had time tomorrow, that is, the day after, on Sunday. And I said yes, but, well, that didn't materialize.'

'Can you remember what she said had happened, the precise words she used?'

The woman on the sofa turned this over in her mind. Gunnar-stranda sipped his coffee and sent her another complimentary glance.

Sigrid closed her eyes. 'She said: *I've had a visit . . .* or: *Something happened at work . . . I've had a visit from the past. I have to talk to you or I'm going to snap.* Something like that – I can't remember the exact words.'

'. . . or I'm going to snap?'

Sigrid nodded.

'How did you interpret that expression?'

'Not in any special way. As a way of speaking, like: *I think I'm going to faint* or: *I think I'm going to die*, as some people say.'

'And what did you answer?'

'I said: *Who was it then, my love*? Or: *My dear, who was it then*?'

'You were so intimate? My dear? My love?'

'Yes, in fact we were.'

'Do you address other patients in the same way?'

'I generally get on well with patients.'

'But you address them all in the same way?'

'You could say that Katrine was . . . I suppose it is true to say there was something special about our relationship.'

'Why was that?'

Sigrid took her time. In the end, she said: 'Because it was her, and it was me.' She thought a bit more. 'Maybe Katrine was different, yes, I think she was. Katrine was special.' Sigrid seemed to be clarifying her thinking to herself. She sat staring into space, lost in thought. 'There was something about Katrine,' she said at length, and added, 'Oh, I don't know. When it comes to the crunch it might just have been the chemistry, but on top of that she had confided in me over a long period.'

'Confided?'

'Yes, it wasn't perhaps very therapeutic, but she preferred me to many others.'

'But she didn't say who it was that had visited her or what had happened?'

'No. The conversation turned into a discussion of when to meet.'

'Did you try to contact her on Sunday?'

'I rang her in the afternoon, but got no answer.'

'How did you interpret that?'

'I thought she had forgotten or she would get back to me later. After all, we hadn't made any specific arrangement.'

Gunnarstranda coughed. He considered his next question. 'What sort of person is her boyfriend?'

'An empty shell.'

'Shell?'

'I think so. There's a lot of façade, but not much in here.' She tapped her temple with her middle finger. 'He was also jealous, not very mature . . . yes, in fact that covers it . . . not very mature.'

'Is he violent?'

'I don't think so.'

'Do you think he hit her?'

'No.' She shook her head. 'No, I would have known.'

'How did the jealousy manifest itself?'

'I guess he was afraid she was intimate with other men.'

'Was she?'

'I have no idea.'

'She didn't take you into her confidence about everything?'

85

'It would be more correct to say I wasn't interested in that type of confidence.'

'Did anyone at the party make advances to her?'

'Advances?'

Gunnarstranda looked her straight in the eye. 'I think you understand what I mean. Did anyone at the party follow her, have sexual intentions, that is?'

'I doubt it.'

'Why?'

Sigrid stared into space. She was thinking. 'Then the individual concerned must have left the party,' she said at last. 'And . . .' She continued to think. 'And so as not to be found out this individual must have returned . . .'

'Yes, that's a possibility.'

'No . . .' she took her time, staring upwards. 'That seems quite unlikely.'

'But does it seem impossible?'

'What do you mean?'

'Well,' said the policeman. 'You knew her, she confided in you some of the time and there is a good chance someone followed her. Whether it was feasible is another matter. Can you say, with your hand on your heart, that everyone at the party stayed in the house all that evening and night?'

'No.'

'Why not?'

'Some went into town. After all, the meal was over. Some were upstairs, some were downstairs, some were at the bottom of the garden or behind the bushes. Who knows.'

'Do you remember who went into the city centre?'

'A gang of them went to dance at Smuget . . . there was a man we called Goggen who was the leader and desperate to go – he's an ergonomist – his real name is Georg Beck. I know Bjørn Gerhardsen left . . .'

'The host, Annabeth's husband?'

'Yes, he's just an overgrown schoolboy. He wanted others to join them. Quite a few of the younger ones went along. I don't know how many there were. At any rate, Goggen and Bjørn Gerhardsen. Plus a few others. Katrine's boyfriend, Ole Eidesen, may have been with them.'

'Why do you think that?'

'I couldn't see him or Katrine anywhere. Either he went with Katrine or he went with Goggen and the others to town.'

'And you?'

'Me? I went hither and thither.' She put on a tentative smile. 'Do you think I . . . ?'

'We don't think anything, but we may need to hear some of the confidences.'

'How so?'

'She may have said something that has a connection with the case. So I would like you to contact us if you remember anything.' He rose to his feet. Sigrid followed suit. 'Of course,' she assured him.

Gunnarstranda: 'How did you hear about her death?'

'Well, at today's morning meeting I brought the issue up as I hadn't heard from Katrine, and someone had seen the news last night, an item about a dead woman being found in Mastemyr. I don't know why but suddenly everyone was frightened it could be Katrine. Henning, a social worker with us, was given the task of ringing her at work to check.' Sigrid's smile was weary. 'And I don't know if that was before or after you were contacted,' she added.

'And you have no idea why she fell ill at the party or where she went after leaving you?'

'Not a clue.'

'When did you leave the party?'

'I was picked up by my husband.'

'When?'

'Late, very late, it was beginning to get light.'

'You have a nice husband.'

'He's always there for me. When we were younger I thought this self-sacrifice was a bit wearing. Now it's just great.'

'But why did you stay so long?'

'We kept going. I talked to Annabeth for a long time. It was a cross between a sewing circle and a business meeting. The last guests left at around half past four, I think. Afterwards I helped Annabeth to tidy up. Before I left, Bjørn came back from town.'

'What time was that?'

'As I said, it was beginning to get light, so I would guess it must have been around four in the morning.'

'Was the party a success?'

'Yes, I think so.'

'Was there anyone in particular Katrine spoke a lot to during the evening?'

'Well, that's hard for me to say. She left the party early and I sat quite a distance from her during the meal. I saw her with her boy-friend having coffee. That was all I noticed about her – until she was ill.'

Gunnarstranda got to his feet and walked to the door.

'Very nice to meet you,' Sigrid Haugom said to his back. The detective inspector turned in the doorway. He stood thinking.

'Yes?' Sigrid said.

'Do you know anything about her background, her childhood?' Sigrid shook her head. 'I went home with her once.'

Gunnarstranda waited.

'It was very sad.'

'Why's that?'

'Her mother lives in a pretty derelict house. She was living with a man, but she was alone when we arrived. It was Katrine's birth-day and she hadn't remembered. The woman hadn't seen Katrine for two years, and she served up tinned spaghetti on paper plates.'

Gunnarstranda pulled a face.

Sigrid said. 'Katrine couldn't cope. She ran out and I think that was the last time the two of them saw each other.'

9

The Soirée

Police Inspector Gunnarstranda was sitting in his office. He had taken his place behind his cramped desk on which there was a black computer, an electric typewriter, a mug jammed with biros, a pile of periodicals, a hole punch, an empty, faded red ash tray inscribed with CINZANO in peeling white letters on the side and a great many loose sheets of paper.

He undid the buttons of his blue blazer and loosened the tight knot of the tramline-blue tie over his shirt. The chair creaked as he leaned back and crossed his legs, forcing the trouser material up and exposing one unusually white leg over the edge of the sock. One angry black shoe bounced up and down in the air.

The telephone rang. He lifted the receiver. 'And thank you, too,' he said. 'I've just arrived. Yes, it was great. I seldom go to the theatre. But that's what it's like being a policeman. I have to sort out a few things here even though it's late.'

One hand rested on the typewriter. The other pulled out the report he had just pounded into shape. He read through it as the voice continued to speak into his ear.

'The less we say about that the better,' he said, listening for a while, then he grunted a goodbye and cradled the telephone. He sat gazing out of the window. It was beginning to get dark outside. So it was very late. Nevertheless it was too early to see stars in June; all he could see was the flashing green light of a plane flying so high no sound could be heard.

There was a knock at the door. Frank Frølich stuck his head in. Gunnarstranda nodded.

'Like it?' Frølich asked, closing the door behind him. He lumbered over and slumped down in his chair, which groaned under the weight. He was wearing blue jeans, trainers and a T-shirt with a Friends of Beer logo beneath a blue denim jacket. His wavy, grey hair was in a mess and so long that it was growing over his ears. He needs a haircut, thought Gunnarstranda, a haircut and to go on a diet. Frølich's stomach bulged out beneath his ribs, and, sitting upright in a chair, as he was now, it was only a question of time before he would be able to use it as a coffee table.

'Like what?' asked Gunnarstranda.

'The play.'

Gunnarstranda took his time and looked down at himself. He straightened his tie and cuff links. 'No,' came the conclusion. 'I didn't.'

'What was wrong with it?'

'The crowd who took me there.'

'But they have nothing to do with the play. What did you see?'

'*Faust.*'

'I've heard it's supposed to be shit-hot.'

Gunnarstranda considered this. 'Well, I liked the play. The text is good apart from these temptations to which he's exposed. I mean, they were so banal: young women in suspender belts and all that. I had expected a bit more from Goethe, not to mention Mephistopheles!'

'Who did you go with?'

'Falk-Andersen, his wife and his sister.'

'Proper bit of match-making, eh?'

'Proper pains in the arse more like. Of course, they enjoyed the play.'

'And who is Falk-Andersen?'

Gunnarstranda sighed. 'A botanist. Retired academic. Even if I'd tried I'm not sure I could have offended any of them.'

'Very good,' Frølich said. He sat back in his chair with a glazed look, then said, 'I've been talking to the people at the travel agency where Katrine Bratterud worked.'

Gunnarstranda raised his arm and checked his watch. He realized he should have eaten a long time ago and tried to work out if he was hungry.

'Fristad rang,' mumbled the detective inspector. 'Director of Public Prosecutions.'

Then came the cough. He put his feet on the floor and succumbed to it heart and soul. Pains shot through his chest, his breathing was like a rotten elastic band and he knew he looked dreadful.

After the attack had finally abated, he swung round his chair, opened the window wide and took out a short, fat stump of a roll-up from his pocket.

'Don't think that's very healthy,' Frølich ventured.

The police inspector waited until his breathing was normal before answering. 'Nothing's healthy. Working's not healthy, sleeping's not healthy, even the food we eat makes us ill.' He stuck out his lower lip like a monkey as he lit the roll-up, so as not to burn his lips.

'Why don't you roll a new one?' Frølich exclaimed in disgust.

'If I light them several times, I can reduce my smoking to eight a day,' Gunnarstranda retorted. 'Eight a day.'

'So you think it's healthier to smoke that tarry goo than to have a few puffs at a fresh one?'

'You sound like Falk-Andersen's sister!' Not to burn himself Gunnarstranda was holding the tiny dog-end with the nails of his thumb and first finger. The fingers formed a circle and he pursed his lips as he blew the smoke out.

'I don't give a damn if you smoke yourself to death,' Frølich said in desperation. 'It's the aesthetics of it that I find distasteful.'

'OK, OK,' mumbled the inspector, swinging round and dropping the extinguished, brown tobacco-corpse in a long-necked ashtray behind him. He wore a lop-sided smile and fetched a new roll-up from his pocket. 'Nine a day,' he grinned, and lit up.

Frank Frølich shook his head.

'You're right,' Gunnarstranda said, inhaling. 'This one's better; this one won't make me ill. By the way, Fristad was wondering why we didn't trot out the standard phrases to the press – mutilated body, vicious rape, the worst I've seen in my police career and so on.'

'And what did you answer?'

'Nothing.'

'But was it rape?'

'Looks like it,' Gunnarstranda said.

'We have to find out what she was doing after midnight,' Frølich said.

'She went to a fast food place.'

'Is that right?'

Gunnarstranda nodded. 'They have identified the food we saw in her stomach as minced meat, bread and potatoes, most probably fast food. So it seems as if it was right that she brought up Anna-beth Ås's fine supper. Our problem is to find out when and where she ate the meal.'

'I was talking to her colleague,' Frølich said. 'A lady of about fifty, the aunty-type, you know, with grown-up kids, liked to keep an eye on the girl . . . she says she was good at the job and attractive and cheerful and happy and all that.'

'And?'

'Well, she knew the girl was undergoing treatment, off drugs and off bad influences. The lady at the travel agency says something odd happened . . .'

The telephone rang. Gunnarstranda sent it an angry glare. It continued to ring. Frølich asked, 'Aren't you going to answer it?'

His tooth enamel glistened and the lenses of his glasses flashed as Gunnarstranda snatched the receiver and slammed it down straight-away.

Frølich stared at the dead telephone.

'Go on,' said Gunnarstranda.

'On the day she disappeared a guy entered the shop and went for her.'

'That's the second person who's told us about the incident,' Gunnarstranda said. 'The girl rang Sigrid Haugom on the Saturday and said the same. What does she mean by . . . *went for her?*'

Frølich read his notes. 'A roughneck, about forty years old with salt and pepper hair, pony tail, earring and an ugly scar on his arm. The man threatened Katrine and tried to attack her but gave up when Katrine asked . . . Katrine asked me . . . asked me to call the police.' Frølich peered up.

'This lady,' Frølich said, 'was left in shock. She asked Katrine who he was and why he had flown at her. She says Katrine admitted she had known the man once, but she had not seen him for many years.'

'What is salt and pepper hair?'

Frølich reflected. 'Salt-and-pepper colour.'

'Black and white?'

'No, more grizzled, a bit like me.'

'You're grey, not grizzled.'

'Some say I'm grizzled.'

'How did he threaten her?'

Frølich read from his notebook. '*You do as I say*, or: *You bloody do what I tell you.*'

'So she had refused to do something for this man?'

Frølich nodded. 'Sounds possible.'

'It's not much of a lead, of course.' Gunnarstranda pulled a face. 'So we're looking for someone from the drugs scene who recently threatened our girl. The woman from the travel agency had better have a look at the rogues' gallery. And you can check with the boys in Narcotics if this salt-and-pepper roughneck rings any bells with them.'

10

Freedom Is Another Word

It was Frank Frølich's second visit to the Vinterhagen centre; this time he was not pelted with rotten tomatoes. He was sitting with Henning Kramer in what appeared to be a classroom. Beside the board hung a poster with the legend *Say No to Drugs* – and a picture of an athlete, presumably a sports star. Frank was not sure who it was. Her face meant nothing whatsoever to him. To fill the time, he let his eyes wander through the window where there was little to attract his attention except for the yellow accommodation building. The place seemed quite dead. There was no visible activity to be discerned at all. Not so strange perhaps, he thought. They must be affected by what had happened. Almost three minutes had passed since he asked a simple opening question to the man sitting on the dais. From that moment Henning Kramer had been studying a corner of the ceiling with his first finger resting against the tip of his chin as he ruminated. 'Feel free to answer,' Frølich said to Kramer.

'I'm thinking,' he said.

'From what I've heard you spent a lot of time together. You must have known what she was like.'

'Who she was or what she was like?'

Frølich sighed and faced the intense man who was still staring at the ceiling with the same concentration. 'Is there any difference?' he asked with a yawn.

'Perhaps not,' Kramer mused.

Frølich realized he had before him a man who weighed words and therefore he essayed a linguistic compromise: 'What sort of person was she?'

Kramer closed his eyes. 'Katrine was carrying a dream,' he said, opening his palms, 'the dream of being crazy, the dream of standing on the motorway and hitch-hiking and feeling free, jumping into a car and saying or doing something which would amaze the driver. *Bobby thumbed a diesel down just before it rained and took us all the way to New Orleans.* That's it, isn't it? The point, and Katrine didn't realize this, is that drivers are no longer amazed. You can't say anything that hasn't been heard before. There is nothing that has not been said before, or done for that matter, and the poor kids with flared pants and headbands hitch-hiking by the roadside or those rolling naked in the mud at the Roskilde festival, they might think they're demonstrating a counter-culture but they're just a tourists' sideshow, which for some people might be a nice reunion with another time. It's a bit like seeing those keyrings with the image of Jerry Garcia, the ones you can buy at Fisherman's Wharf in San Francisco. You don't believe it until you see them, but when you do, it's proof that the so-called youth revolution has finally been absorbed into history and canonized by the middle classes. So it's sad for those who still believe they're living in the sixties or the seventies because what they believe they're part of is nothing!'

Kramer jumped down on to the floor and strolled over to the window where he stood with his back to Frølich.

'Katrine never understood that it is pointless to escape into freedom,' Kramer said, and, roused, turned around: 'Freedom is not a state of mind or somewhere you can escape to. Freedom has to be grasped; it's here, inside yourself, and you find it in the things you do and think. It's about being your own master and master of the situation you find yourself in. You can't escape to freedom, only from it. It's only when you stand up and accept the world as it is, place yourself in it and grasp your own reality that you are free.'

Frølich stifled a yawn. Then he glanced up from his notepad. Kramer was out of breath, excited. Frølich looked down at the blank page in his pad and jotted in his neat handwriting: *Remember to ring Eva-Britt before four.* Julie, Eva-Britt's daughter, had a place in an after-school care centre in Majorstuen. Eva-Britt had a special meeting on Tuesdays and they had a tacit agreement that Frank would collect Julie on these days. But the timing was bad. He would have to send her a message.

As Frank couldn't think of any other things he needed to remember, he cleared his throat and asked in a toneless voice, 'But that's what Katrine was doing, wasn't she? From what I've understood she was ridding herself of illusions, she was officially clean and had a job with a travel agency.'

'She couldn't cut the mustard though because she couldn't be with normal people.'

'What do you mean?' Frank asked, elated to have steered the conversation away from abstractions.

'She couldn't be normal. She wasn't capable of it. It made her feel sick at that bloody party of theirs; she couldn't take the reality they had to offer.'

'So you don't think she was really ill at the party?'

'She was no more ill than I am now!'

'You mean she threw up because she could not take their reality?'

'Yes.'

'But what was it that she couldn't take? In concrete terms.'

'What?' Henning's smile was sardonic, caustic. 'She didn't want to be like *them*!'

'Them?'

Kramer's eyes flashed. 'She hated the thought of signing up to a culture where you change your personality as you change your clothes. These so-called *models* that Vinterhagen serves up, *they* waltz off from a job where *they* preach for a natural release of endorphins in the brain, where *they* repeat time after time how dangerous drugs are, how empowering it is to tell the truth, to admit to your own mistakes and to recognize that life in itself is one long intoxication, then *they* waltz off and don another dress, or suit, or hat, and instead of evangelizing that same claptrap *they* get plastered over supper before daring to say a few words of truth to each other and drink even more so that *they* can shag each other behind the bushes and blame the booze afterwards. Don't you see?'

'Aren't you one of these models yourself?'

'I hope not.'

Frølich watched him, unsure about how to continue. 'I understand what you're saying about seeing through double standards,' he said. 'But this person was an adult, academically bright by all accounts and she had a past on the streets. She must have known what the world was like, how it worked. She can't have thrown up because her hypotheses proved to be correct.'

'You're mistaken there,' Kramer said in a gentle tone. 'That is the precise reason why she spewed up. She spewed up the two of them: Bjørn and Annabeth.'

'Why?'

'Because . . .' Henning Kramer hesitated and fell silent.

'Tell me.'

'Once upon a time she screwed Bjørn Gerhardsen while she was whoring to get money for dope.'

Frank's brow furrowed with scepticism. That particular piece of information stank. He underlined his own perception by pulling a face and shaking his head.

'It's true,' the other man retorted – before continuing in a calmer key: 'Well, I don't give a shit whether you believe me or not. The point is that she recognized the guy from the past, and that's fine. Annabeth Ås is not that sexy, I suppose, so her old man rents himself a tart now and then. He's not alone in doing that. But the problem was that the guy didn't appreciate that he had to keep a low profile. My God, it traumatized her. She did have sex on the odd occasion, but it was a difficult thing for her. And then the guy turns it on and wants her again, right, for nothing, behind one of the bushes in the garden.'

'That night? At the party?'

'Precisely.'

'Are you sure about that?' the policeman snapped.

'She told me.'

'What did she say? Her exact words.'

'*He tried it on. Mr Nice Guy.* Those were the words she used. And that was all we said about the matter.'

'That was all she said. *Mr Nice Guy?*'

'We had talked about this business before, that she had, well . . . recognized Gerhardsen and so on. Both Annabeth and Bjørn are pretty pathetic, right, in their way, and when we talked about them . . . well, from then on we called him Mr Nice Guy. It was a bit like an internal code between two people. We joked about it because during the day he's the Vinterhagen chairman and during the night he buys himself a chunk of potential patients. We dubbed him Mr Nice Guy. Ironic, of course.'

Frølich studied his notes. 'And when did she tell you this?'

'After the party.'

Frølich straightened up in his chair.

'There was something special about that night, you see. I drove up to collect her. She called me.'

'She called you? When?'

'Saturday night. Around twelve. I was sleeping in front of the TV. She woke me, called me on my mobile.'

Frølich, excited: 'And you drove there to collect her?'

'Yes . . .'

'What make is your car?'

'I don't have a car. It was my brother's. He's abroad at some seminar. In the Philippines. I'm allowed to borrow his car when he's off on a trip. An Audi. She came to meet me in the road, wearing the same gear, right, provocative – her skirt was transparent with the street light behind her – her dream clothes. At that moment she saw herself as some chick in a promo video and she jumped over the car door. She didn't open the door – it's a convertible, you see, and then she tied her blouse around her hair, no, that was afterwards, but what I'm trying to say is that she got off on the car trip, on the night, on being in an open car with me. Her hair was blowing into her face, right, round the bends down Holmenkollen, and she cast around for something to tie her hair with, but she had nothing, so she took off her top, with just a black bra underneath, and that gave her a kick, sitting there in her bra. That was the dream. Like *feelin' free*. We drove down to Aker Brygge, to the McDonald's. It was her idea, and we ate there. She wanted a cheeseburger and stood there dressed as she was. It was like the fulfilment of this dream. Like . . . like . . . Christ, someone should have strung up that word *like*. I am so sick and tired of saying it. Anyway, I'm pretty sure she was a millimetre away from shooting up that night. She was high, really high, and when I asked, before we took off from Aker Brygge, what had happened like, or why she was so high, she ignored me, just for a second. I could see she didn't want to talk about it because she didn't want to come down from the clouds she was on, if I can say that. She like saw me for a second and said: *Mr Nice Guy. He tried it on* . . . And I just stood looking at her.'

'And then?'

'Then we took the E6 – the old Mossevei – almost as far as Ingierstrand.'

'And?'

'I parked there.'

'In Ingierstrand?'

'No, I stopped there at first, but we weren't on our own. After a while another car parked in the large car park there, so we drove on to the Mosseveien crossing and turned right, out towards Lake Gjer, past Tyrigrava. We stopped in a car park not far from the E18, facing the lake, very nice spot.'

'And?'

'Then we talked.'

'What about?'

'Life in general.'

'Not the party?'

'Not a word.'

'Nothing about her, about what had happened that day?'

'No, just about dreams.'

'And then?'

'Then we had sex.'

'I thought she was with a guy called Ole Eidesen.'

Henning Kramer shrugged.

'Were you jealous of Eidesen?'

'Not in the slightest, more the other way around – he was jealous of me . . . perhaps.'

'Why should he have been?'

'Katrine was more open with me, I suppose, and he suspected us of sleeping together now and then.'

'Did you?'

'Now and then.'

Frølich chewed his biro and waited.

'Not that often, only when she wanted it. The last time was a long time ago now, many weeks ago.'

'Did you think of the relationship as love?'

'Of course.'

'Let me be precise,' Frank said, sitting up erect. 'I'm asking you if you wanted a so-called official relationship with her, just the two of you.'

'It was just the two of us. She always came back to me. But I was the one who didn't want her so close. In that way we were closer on a soul level.'

'On a soul level?'

'Yes.'

'With a bit of body now and then?'

'Yes.'

'But that night who took the initiative? Who suggested inter-course?'

'She did.'

Frank was silent.

'It's incorrect to say *suggested*. It was in the air. You could say that we like had sex from the moment she sat in the car. Making love was just a kind of conclusion – the final bit that was missing.'

'Did you use contraceptives?'

'No.'

'Where did you make love?'

'In the car.'

'That night you say she was wearing a black bra and a top?'

'A blouse, black, and a skirt.'

'Was she wearing anything else?'

'Not as far as I know.'

'No panties?'

'I didn't see her taking them off.'

'So she was walking around naked under her skirt?'

'No, she was wearing them. She pushed them to the side . . . if we have to be technical.'

'So she was dressed when you were having sex?'

'Yes, that is, she was wearing a skirt and I folded down her bra.'

'And the blouse?'

'She put that back on later.'

'When?'

Kramer frowned as he deliberated. 'When I drove her home,' came the eventual answer.

'Was that long afterwards?'

'Maybe an hour or two. We slept for a while, at least I did.'

'How long did you sleep?'

'I woke up at just after half past two. She had left the car. She woke me up as she got back in.'

'And you're sure it was half past two?'

'02:37. I looked at the clock in the car.'

'And she'd been out?'

'Yes, I heard the car door slam and she was inside and I looked at the clock and she teased me because I was asleep. She asked if I had a cigarette. I did and so we both smoked a cigarette, and then she asked me to drive her to Ole's place.'

'What clothes was she wearing?'

'The same.'

'Jewellery?'

'Assume so.'

'What do you mean by that? Did she have any jewellery or not?'

Kramer didn't speak for a few seconds, as though thinking. 'Katrine always wore jewellery: gold rings . . . bracelets . . . rings with twisted snake patterns and big stones, and chains round her neck.'

'And what was she wearing that night?'

'Most of it, I assume. Rings. Yes, she always wore rings. That night, too.' Kramer shifted, ill at ease. The policeman watched him in silence.

'Yes?' Kramer coughed, changing position.

Frølich studied the man for a few more seconds. 'And you're sure she was wearing jewellery that night? Would you swear to it?' he asked.

'Of course.' Kramer's eyelids moved slowly up and back down . . . up . . .

'When she came back to the car, was she wearing jewellery?'

'I reckon so. But I didn't check her over.'

'So you're not sure if she was wearing jewellery when she came back?'

'I can't swear to it that she was.'

'But did you ask her what she had been doing outside?'

'No.'

'Why not?'

'It didn't occur to me.'

'It didn't occur to you?'

'No.' Henning Kramer shrugged. 'She might have been for a pee or perhaps she had just been stretching her legs.'

'Did she have anything else with her? A handbag?'

'Yes, she did. Not a handbag, but a small shoulder bag with a long strap that she wore across her back. I remember that well.'

Frølich nodded. 'When did you set off back home?'

'It must have been just before three or just after. I can't remember. I was shattered so I wanted to get home as fast as possible.'

'Where did you take her?'

'Not so far. She wanted to get out at the roundabout over the E6 – the one by Hvervenbukta where you turn off for Holmlia.'

'That's less than a kilometre from where she was found murdered,' the policeman said.

Kramer nodded.

Frølich cleared his throat. 'I have to ask you once again,' he said slowly. 'Are you positive you dropped her at this place?'

Kramer cleared his throat. 'Yes,' he answered.

Frølich scrutinized him again. 'Why did you drop her there of all places?'

'She wanted to walk to Ole's place. Ole lives in Holmlia. Not sure what the address is. But she wanted to go to Ole's and walk the last bit on her own. She said she didn't want him to see me, if he was waiting for her.'

'Why not?'

'He would have made a scene, I suppose.'

'And then?'

'I drove off.' Kramer paused. All of a sudden he seemed overcome by emotion. Frølich tried to imagine how he would have behaved in a situation like this. Regardless of whether the young man was telling the truth or not, it was clear that this conversation was a strain. It had started off quite light, with philosophical babble about the dead girl's attitude to life. Even the conversation about their love-making had gone smoothly. One thing was certain, though. It wasn't smooth any more. Kramer seemed very moved; his lips were quivering. 'She waved.' He fell silent again; his lips were still quivering. Frølich studied his face and said: 'Did you notice any other cars when you dropped her? Was there anyone following you?'

Kramer considered the questions, then shook his head slowly. 'I may have met the odd taxi down on the motorway. No, I don't know. It all seemed very quiet, but when I set out I'm sure I met a number of cars.'

'But you can't remember anything else about them?'

'No, I just drove, listened to music and drove.'

'And you didn't see her again?'

'No.'

'Did she stand waving to you as you drove off?'

'She wasn't standing. She was walking and she waved.' Kramer's lips quivered again. 'And I didn't see her again,' he concluded.

'Tell me the exact spot where you dropped her.'

Kramer cleared his throat and closed his eyes. 'We passed the car park by Hvervenbukta, the one on the left hand side as you're driving into town.'

'Along Ljansbrukveien?'

'Yes, I suppose that's what it's called . . . We went on, towards the roundabout and the bridge over the E6, and then she said: I'll jump out here. And then . . .' Kramer cleared his throat again. '. . . then I drove around the roundabout and across the bridge over the E6 . . .'

'Yes . . .' Frølich said patiently.

'I stopped at the end of the bridge where I would turn left to get down on to the motorway. She got out there.' Kramer went quiet.

'Go on,' Frølich said.

'Well, I joined the motorway and didn't see her again.'

'You said she started walking up . . .'

'Yes.'

'When you last saw her she was walking up the Ljabru road towards Holmlia?'

'Yes.'

'But then she would have had to go through a long tunnel, wouldn't she?'

Kramer looked up. He weighed the possibility and gave a slow nod.

'Yes, she must have done.'

Frank shifted his sitting position. 'It's quite a long way to Holmlia from there. She must have gone through the long tunnel and then up Holmliaveien. Now I don't remember whether there's a pavement in the tunnel, but it sounds very impractical to be dropped off before the tunnel . . .'

'I don't know the area,' Henning Kramer interrupted.

'But nevertheless,' Frølich said. 'It's two to three kilometres from the roundabout up to Holmlia. Why didn't you drive her all the way?'

'She asked to be dropped at the roundabout.'

Frølich sat observing him for a while.

Kramer stared back and coughed. 'Perhaps she went through the woods,' he suggested. 'Perhaps she took a short cut.'

'But I thought you said she started walking up the Ljabru road?'

'Yes, I did, but there must be a short cut through the woods.'

'It's possible, but did you see her walking through the woods?'

'No, all I know is she insisted on being dropped at the roundabout.'

Frølich desisted with that line of enquiry and checked his notes. 'A car followed you to Ingierstrand, is that right?'

'No.'

'I thought you said you couldn't be on your own in the car park.'

'That was just a car parked there. A couple out for a drive, like us, I would guess.'

'So there were two people in the car?'

'No. No idea. I didn't see if there were two or five people in the car. I didn't look.'

'Did you see what kind of car it was?'

'Don't remember. Ordinary car, saloon, Japanese or Ford or Opel, just a bog-standard car.'

'Colour?'

Kramer shrugged. 'No idea, dark, it was night – not much light.'

'The car didn't follow you from Ingierstrand?'

'Don't think so. We were alone in the car park anyway.'

Frølich ran this through his mind again. 'When you drove back from the place where you had intercourse, what did you talk about?'

'Nothing.'

'Nothing at all?'

'No.'

'You didn't even discuss where she was going to go or what she would say to her boyfriend if he asked?'

'No.'

Frølich gave a slow nod, regretful that he had done this interview on his own. He let out a deep sigh.

'What's the matter?' Kramer asked innocently.

'I'm afraid your status has changed. You were a witness, but now you're a suspect.'

Henning Kramer said nothing.

'Did you hear what I said?' Frølich asked.

'Katrine was the only person I have loved . . .'

'That's not how it works,' Frølich said, wearied. 'Katrine was found murdered and in a condition that suggests the murder was sexually motivated. In nine out of ten such cases the murder is committed with the intention of concealing another crime, in other words, rape. And now you claim that you had consensual sex a few hours before she was found murdered.'

'We did.'

'Well, that's possible, but the public prosecutor, the judge or the jury may not see that in the same way.'

'But what should I do?'

'At any event you will have to sign a statement and give a DNA sample. And then you'll have to think about all the exact timings.

They have to be as precise as possible because we will have to cross-check your statement with those of other witnesses. So if you can remember anybody or cars with passengers or anything that would corroborate what you have said to me, then things would look a bit brighter.'

Kramer stared darkly into the distance.

'Where did you go after dropping her off?'

'Home.'

'Where's that?'

'In Holmen, Stasjonsveien.'

'Is that your brother's place?'

'No, I live there with my mother.'

'Is it your mother's or your place?'

'My mother's.'

Frølich nodded and made a note. 'Was there anything Katrine said that night, anything at all, that made you uneasy or that you wondered about or you didn't understand . . .'

Kramer sat with his eyes closed. He was sweating. Once again Frølich rued not having a partner with him.

'There was one thing . . .' Kramer began.

'Yes?'

'She had a secret.'

'Uh-uh.'

'I'm trying to think. There was something about the electricity in the air when we met that night . . .'

'When you picked her up?'

'I asked her if she had won at bingo because she seemed so high and, like, happy, but she hadn't. She said something wonderful had happened.'

'Something wonderful?'

'Yes, and so I asked what it was, but she just shook her head and said she would tell me later.'

'Later?'

Kramer nodded.

'Was it your impression it was connected with the party?'

Kramer shook his head.

'Have you any theories as to what she might have meant?'

'Not an inkling.'

Frølich held out his hand peremptorily.

'Eh?'

'The car keys,' Frølich said in a gentle tone. 'You may not remember a lot of witnesses, but you do have one – the most important one for us in such cases. And that's the car.'

11

Naming the Thug

Elise Hermansen was obviously flustered when she came in. She stood in the doorway peering around. 'I've never been inside a police station before,' she apologized in an anxious voice, stroking her newly coiffured hair.

'You'll be fine,' Gunnarstranda said. He took her elbow and guided her towards the table in the middle of the floor. 'Please take a seat. Is there anything you would like? Coffee, for example?'

'No, thanks,' she said, sitting down. 'Do I really have to go through this?'

Gunnarstranda considered the question. 'You don't have to, but it would be nice if you would take the trouble.' He walked over to his desk, opened a drawer and took out a pile of photographs. He stood by the desk in silence for a few seconds, but when she showed no intention of answering, he continued: 'From your description the man who entered your agency was about forty years old, five-foot-eleven, wore an earring and was well-built, not fat.'

Elise Hermansen nodded.

'Well-built, but not fat,' Gunnarstranda repeated, looking her in the eye. 'Like the policeman you spoke to first – Frank Frølich?' Gunnarstranda gestured towards Frølich, who had just entered and was closing the door behind him.

Elise Hermansen blushed, gave a nervous smile and fluttered her eyelids.

Frølich grinned. 'Do you think I'm fat . . . rather than well-built? Was he slimmer than me?'

Elise Hermansen was reassured by Frølich's smile. 'I like men to be more than skin and bone,' she said with more relaxed intonation. 'Let's say he was narrower round the waist than you.'

'Great,' Frølich said, winking at her. He turned to the other policeman: 'I'd like to discuss a witness. I'll be outside.' He pointed to the other door and made a move to leave.

'Compared with you, he was slim in fact,' Elise Hermansen said to Frølich as he was leaving.

Frølich closed the door. The lady turned to Gunnarstranda. 'I didn't mean it like that,' she said.

'The man was good-looking in a brutish sort of way,' Gunnarstranda read aloud.

Elise nodded again.

'When you were asked what you meant by the expression "good-looking in a brutish sort of way" you answered that his face was a bit like an Italian actor's, such as Marcello Mastroianni or Sylvester Stallone.' She looked up again.

Elise nodded.

'Could you expand on that?'

'There was something about the mouth and the chin. But to be specific . . .'

Gunnarstranda nodded.

'A bit ravaged . . . masculine.'

'I see. And when you were asked what colour his eyes were you answered that you couldn't remember. Can you remember now?'

Elise shook her head in regret.

'You said he had salt and pepper hair, a pony tail and an ugly scar on his right forearm.'

Elise nodded.

'But you can't remember his name? Did Katrine Bretterud mention the man's name?'

'That's what I'm not sure about.'

'Mhm?'

'I think she may have mentioned a name.'

'When the two of you were talking?'

'No, when I was asking her questions afterwards she told me his Christian name, I think, but I'm sorry, I can't bring it to mind.'

'Never mind,' Gunnarstranda said in a friendly voice. 'I've passed on your information about this man to the archive ladies at Kripos, the Serious Crime Squad, and I asked for photos of people born in 1955 through to 1964. That's an age range of 35 to 45. Some people look older than they are, and some look younger, don't they. It depends on hair, clothes and so on . . .'

'It was a sort of thug's name,' Elise interrupted.

Gunnarstranda straightened his glasses. 'Thug's name?'

'Yes, the sort of name those brutes often have: Stig, Ronny . . .'

Gunnarstranda sat nodding. He mumbled. 'Bård maybe? Roger? Jim?'

Elise shook her head in despair. 'I might remember . . .'

'In the meantime,' the policeman said, 'I'd like you to take your time and have a good look at the pictures. You don't have to be a hundred per cent certain. You can tell me if you see a trait that rings a bell and Frank Frølich or I will discuss it with you afterwards. And you don't have to be afraid you're going to hurt anyone. If you recognize someone, what happens is that we talk to the respective person to try to clear up whether he could have had any connection with Katrine – or just eliminate him from our enquiries. All right?'

Elise nodded.

Gunnarstranda had to fight to suppress a coughing fit. He smiled in apology and went on: 'I should point out that even if a person has a photo in the police archives it does not necessarily mean he is a criminal. I say this so that you don't jump to any conclusions if you see someone you know in this pile. Still all right?'

Elise Hermansen nodded.

'Let's roll,' Gunnarstranda said, placing the pile of photographs in front of her on the desk.

* * *

'Wonder whether we'll be lucky,' Gunnarstranda said, closing the door behind him. 'There doesn't seem to be much wrong with the lady's memory. What did you want to talk about?'

'The young man with the goatee. We may have to consider Henning Kramer a suspect,' Frølich said, swinging round in his chair.

'I see,' said Gunnarstranda. He took Frølich's report and began to read it with interest.

'He says he picked up Katrine from Annabeth Ås's party, drove round with her and ended up on the old Mossevei – in Oppegård, almost right over by Tusenfryd amusement park – where he claims they made love. She was willing.'

'I see,' Gunnarstranda said, reading on. Frølich swung gently to and fro on his chair while his partner read.

At length Gunnarstranda raised his head and said, 'What do you think about this?'

'I think I . . .' the younger policeman began, but paused because Gunnarstranda was having one of his terrible coughing fits.

'I think . . .' Frølich held his breath as a series of new jerks ran through Gunnarstranda's lean body. The man was trying to suppress a cough that would not yield. That's no twitchy nose or the start of a cold, thought Frølich. The boss's cough was hollow, asthmatic and bronchitic, a cough that rumbled and hacked from a foothold deep and entrenched in the man's lungs. Like a rockslide, thought Frølich, trying not to show that he had noticed the stubborn muscular convulsions in Gunnarstranda's face. But it was not easy to pretend when the man's eyes were bulging and his lips pressed together so tight that his head went a deep burgundy colour as the air from his lungs pushed at his cheeks and mouth from inside. The detective inspector was beginning to resemble a frog. The rocks in his lungs were waiting to pile down the side of the mountain; it was just waiting for the first one to come loose. 'You should see a doctor,' Frølich said when he could stand it no longer.

'Wh . . . wh . . . hm . . . hm . . . why's that?'

'It could be emphysema. Heavy smokers get emphysema.'

The fit began to subside. The boss sent him a stiff glare until his breathing became more regular and the rocks inside had settled. 'It's not emphysema,' he answered with suppressed anger. He cleared his throat as if to confirm that the fit was over. The detective inspector mopped his brow. 'It's a smoker's cough,' he mumbled. 'A bog-standard smoker's cough.'

'Is that what the doctor says?'

'Yes.'

'You've got to give up smoking!'

'Of course. But I've got the cough under control now. I don't inhale so deep.' Gunnarstranda was already fidgeting with another cigarette. 'Besides, smoking is one of my pleasures.'

'But . . .'

'Shut up about my smoking! Talk to me about Henning Kramer. Is he a rotten apple?'

Frølich flinched at the other man's outburst. Then he hurriedly continued: 'Maybe. There's a flaw in his story. He seemed quite credible until the bonk in the car, but then he began all this weird stuff about driving her to the roundabout just by the crime scene.'

'Is he lying?'

'I don't know. It might have been nerves. Just suppose he was telling the truth in the first part; in other words, he drove her out there to have a love-in, but then . . .'

'. . . then she didn't want to, you mean?' Gunnarstranda nodded and went on, 'Suppose he tried it on, was rejected – after all she had a boyfriend. He raped her, left loads of sperm on her clothes. She resisted, tore his hair, scratched him. That would be a logical train of thought.' He nodded.

Frølich sat in silence for a few seconds.

Gunnarstranda crushed the cigarette between his fingers.

'I wasn't happy about doing the interview on my own,' Frølich said.

Gunnarstranda grimaced. 'What's done is done.'

'But he could be the killer.'

Gunnarstranda took a deep breath. 'Now I'm intrigued,' he grinned, pointing the glow of the cigarette in the air and watching it. 'Let's say Kramer raped and killed her. Tell me what he did afterwards.'

Frølich leaned forward in his chair. 'You said it yourself,' he acknowledged. 'That's the most logical conclusion. He removed her clothes; they were covered in his hair and sperm and bits off his clothing. He knew that one stain, one single hair was enough for DNA profiling to identify who had committed the rape. That explains why his powers of persuasion failed when he was talking to me. After all, he had to cobble together a plausible explanation for what he was doing. He may well have dropped her off in Mastemyr. The difference is that she was not alive. The truth may be that she was dead and that he pushed her over the safety barrier and into the ditch.'

Gunnarstranda waited.

'That must have been how it happened,' Frølich concluded.

'And now?' Gunnarstranda asked.

'What do you mean?'

'Should he be arrested?'

'That's what I don't know,' Frølich sighed. 'That's why I would have liked to have you along. Anyway, we're checking his car over now. So we'll have to wait and see.'

'You don't think there's a chance the evidence may have been destroyed?'

'Of course there is. He could have hidden her clothes and . . .'

'But there is reasonable cause for suspicion?'

Frølich hesitated.

'Well, let me ask again. Should he be arrested?'

Frølich stood up, annoyed: 'If you want to bring him in, for Christ's sake go and do it!'

'But would *you*?'

'What do you mean *Would I?*'

'Well, should he be arrested or not?'

'That's your decision!'

'But I have only your report to go on,' Gunnarstranda fumed, waving the papers he had just read.

'Don't you think it's good enough?'

'I didn't say that. But there are two factors which would hold me back from arresting Kramer!' Gunnarstranda stood up as well. He barked: 'First of all, we have to check out Kramer's story. Right now. We have to keep several options open, particularly because of one thing Kramer said and which I am surprised you didn't pick up on yourself!'

'And what's that?' Frølich asked.

'The fact that the man has already admitted sexual congress with the murder victim.'

On appreciating the full force of this piece of information, Frølich slumped into the chair and realized what Gunnarstranda meant. 'OK,' he said. 'I was too keen.'

'Kramer must be dealing from a straight deck,' Gunnarstranda continued, without showing any mercy. 'Because he admitted having had intercourse with her. Admitting intercourse with a rape victim is a logical strategy for an assailant if, but, only if, the parties are due to meet in court. Then the question of guilt is decided on the credibility of the parties involved. But here there is a difference, and that is that Katrine is dead. If the motive for the killing of Katrine Bratterud was to conceal a rape, with the intention of silencing the victim, why would he admit intercourse afterwards? That's the same as putting your head on the block, isn't it!'

'So you don't think Kramer killed her?'

'I didn't say that. But if he did kill her, he must have had other motives than wanting to conceal a rape.'

Frølich sighed.

Gunnarstranda continued. 'It would be totally illogical of him to admit to sex with Katrine if he had killed her to cover up a rape.'

'So we don't arrest him,' Frølich said.

'What do we know so far?' Gunnarstranda asked with a show of impatience.

'We know she was alive at three o'clock in the morning.'

'If Kramer is telling the truth.'

Frølich nodded. 'If he's telling the truth, she was alive at three in the morning. We have to assume she was killed soon thereafter because she was found five to six hundred metres from where she was last seen by Kramer.'

'But she wasn't killed where she was found,' Gunnarstranda said. 'She was moved.'

'So it might have been a random encounter,' Frølich said. 'Any nutter might have bumped into her. In the tunnel, for example, which she had to walk through to reach her boyfriend's flat. Anyone could have picked her up, dragged her off somewhere and strangled her.'

'But there has to be a crime scene.'

'So we ought to look for the place where she was murdered?'

'Of course. We have to check all the places Kramer mentions in his statement, walk the route she is supposed to have taken to Holmlia and comb these areas for a crime scene. We also have to check Kramer's story and try to find witnesses to confirm what he has said. However, we also know that a group of guests left the party at more or less the same time as Katrine. We also know that a car followed Kramer and Katrine to Ingierstrand – is that not correct?'

'He didn't think anyone was following him.'

'But someone might have been. Let's say that someone was following him. The two of them in the car may not have seen the car until it drove into the car park in Ingierstrand.'

'Isn't that a bit far-fetched?'

'I don't care whether it is far-fetched or not; the point is that it is feasible,' snapped Gunnarstranda. 'Someone might have been following them. Or,' he continued, 'someone in this car in Ingierstrand can confirm what Kramer says. My personal opinion is that the attacker is a stranger. Someone who is turned on by this girl walking alone in the middle of the night.'

'We also have the guy who went for her at her workplace,' Frølich said in a low mumble. 'That is a specific violent incident. We have to find out what happened and hope that madam in there,' he nodded in the direction of the closed door, 'recognizes one of the faces.'

The police inspector nodded. 'If this man had a score to settle he might have followed Kramer and her in his car. He might have spied on her all day, all evening and all night and struck when she was alone.'

'But then you're presupposing that they were followed?'

'Let's find out. Put out a search for the car that drove into the car park in Ingierstrand. The best would be if it turned out that it was driven by lovers who didn't want to waste a summer night sleeping.'

'Three lines of enquiry,' Gunnarstranda concluded at last. 'It could have been a stranger who assaulted Katrine as she was walking on her own to Ole Eidesen's flat. It could have been someone who knew her: to whit, the man in the travel agency and others – for example at the party . . .'

'And the third?'

'Henning Kramer. He could have killed her.'

'I thought you just rejected that possibility.'

'Wrong. I said he can't have done it to cover up a rape. That's quite different. We have only his word for what happened between midnight and three o'clock in the morning.'

'What do we think about the murder victim's secret? Is that worth following up?' Frølich wondered.

'Not a lot to get our teeth into there, but I suppose there's nothing wrong with asking people.'

Gunnarstranda nodded. 'Make time in your programme to check out Kramer's statement – try Aker Brygge and Oslo Taxis. Dig up as much dirt as you can.'

12

The Green Exercise Book

Katrine Bratterud's flat was small but very appealing with bright wallpaper on the walls. The main furniture in the living room was a sofa bed, a TV and a desk. In front of the window there was a flower rack with three levels – a kind of pedestal on which some house plants had been arranged in a very refined way. There was a strawberry begonia, a large aloe vera and a very vigorous hoya that had coiled itself around the wooden frame and formed an impenetrable tangle. Gunnarstranda stuck a finger in the soil in the pot. It was dry, but it hadn't dried out.

He went over to the desk. There was a pencil case on top. Beside it a little wooden box. He raised the lid. Inside there were coins, badges, a few hairpins, a tampon in plastic packaging, a couple of lighters, buttons and other odds and ends. He replaced the lid.

Gunnarstranda opened the bedroom door. A broad double bed took up most of the floor space. It wasn't made. Two duvets lay entwined. The bed sheets were rumpled. A yellow bath towel lay strewn across the bed.

He opened the wardrobe. The clothes inside were hung in order. He closed the wardrobe and turned to the dresser under the window. There was a can of hairspray on the dresser. It stood on top of a small white cloth in which her name, Katrine, had been embroidered in red cross-stitch.

He breathed in before opening the top drawer. It was crammed full with lacy things for women – bras and panties. The next drawer was the same. On the left of the bed there was an old bedside table made of high-quality wood. The top was dusty. On it was a novel. *The God of Small Things* by Arundhati Roy. The novel lay on top of a magazine. *Tique.*

Gunnarstranda opened the bedside-table drawer. A pen rolled around inside. It was a shiny silver Parker. Under it an exercise book. Gunnarstranda took it out. It was an A4 format notebook. He opened it. There were pages of neat looped handwriting in blue ink. He read.

I drove down a straight road with green trees on both sides. Now and then I passed huge fields of yellow sunflowers nodding their heads to greet the sun. The road stretched on into eternity. But the car went slower and slower. It was running out of petrol. I didn't want the car to stop. I wanted to keep going, to be moving. However, in the end the car stopped all the same. I felt heavy, as always when things go wrong. I looked around. The car had stopped at a crossroads outside a wooden shed. It looked like some sort of garage; it was abandoned with smashed window panes and a crooked roof that someone had tried to repair with multi-coloured corrugated iron and faded green pieces of plastic. Beside the shed stood an abandoned car. It was an elegant red sports car, a Porsche. The contrast between the stylish red car and the derelict shed was beautiful, almost a pleasure to see. My gaze wandered to and fro between the shed and the car. It was as though I had to convince myself it was the contrast I wanted to see, not just the car. Yellow cornfields with the green marble effect of as yet unripe corn stretched along both sides of the road. Dark green spruce trees formed a threshold to the forest beyond and enclosed the field in the distance. Behind the field the mountains towered up towards the sky. On the road to the right a cloud of dust rose behind a car. The car created movement in a painting of a blue sky, white cauliflower clouds, looming mountains and the deli-

cate colours of the terrain. I turned up the volume of the radio and lit a cigarette, not because I felt like one but because the sight of a woman smoking in a car with the music pounding through the speakers made me part of the picture. It was confirmation that I existed.

Björn Skifs was singing 'Hooked on a Feeling'. The car coming closer was a rusty, beat-up Opel, an old model. The car didn't slow down for the crossing. It smashed into the side of the sports car, knocking the door into the passenger compartment and pushing the light Porsche across both carriageways and into the ditch. On the radio a male voice choir sang 'oggashakka oggashakka' and the driver of the Opel seemed to have his mind set on escape. The rear wheels were spinning, sending up a cloud of grit and road dust into the air. Then the car jumped backwards as it freed itself from the Porsche. Another cloud rose as it came to a halt. The red Opel shot forward and rammed the side of the Porsche for the second time, like an angry billy-goat. The sound of splintering glass was like a tiny rustle of paper against the roar of the music through the speakers. The Porsche rocked; it took the blow like a severely wounded stag. For a few seconds the music was all there was to hear, until the sound of a screaming starter motor rent the air. The Opel started up again. The same thing was repeated. Another crash. The Porsche was rocked again by the bang and slipped further into the ditch. At some expense to the Opel. It was stuck too. I switched off the radio. The silence was deafening. I crushed my cigarette in the ashtray and looked at the weird sculpture of two entangled cars as a transparent, sun-glittering cloud of dust fell to earth and cleared the air. The derelict shed was unchanged. The corn swayed in the light breeze and there was not a sign of life anywhere.

Suddenly the Opel moved. The window was rolled down on the driver's side. Something was thrown out and fell to the ground. It looked like two crutches. I opened the car door, put one foot on the ground and straightened my skirt. It was cooler outside than I had expected. The light wind was chilly. The gravel on the road cut into my bare feet. I stopped, unsure of myself. Then a foot appeared out of the Opel window. A black shoe, a leg. The leg with the shoe fell on to the ground with a thud. Another foot appeared in the car window. Another leg with a black shoe fell to the ground. The next thing to be seen in the window was a man's bald head. The man had a wreath of curly hair over his ears and wore glasses. After the head came his upper torso. Finally, the man tumbled to the ground head first. I closed my eyes because I didn't want to see him break his neck and die. On opening my eyes I saw him roll around and then lie still. But he was not dead. He soon crawled into a sitting position and wiped his face with both hands. The man had no feet and no legs. His legs had been amputated, and his thighs were two short stumps under loose trouser material. 'Can I help?' I asked, feeling stupid. The man didn't seem to hear me. He rolled up his trousers and attached the two prostheses lying on the ground. I went closer. I froze. 'Can I help you up?' I repeated and heard my voice crack.

The sight of my shadow made the man stop and look up. He was bleeding from the mouth and nose. 'I can't hear you,' he muttered and patted his ears. 'I think I've gone bloody deaf.'

I picked up the crutches and passed them to him. The look he gave me was one of surprise. He tried to stand up, but toppled over. I didn't know what to do, except to grab his arm. By supporting himself on the crutches as I lifted he managed to stand up. 'Thank you,' he mumbled and hobbled off. Soon he was gone. He looked like a clown swinging on a trapeze in a rat's cage. Click, clack, click clack.

I walked back to my car and got in. The hobbling figure was approaching the forest at the margins of the picture. I felt cold and lonely. The cripple hobbling away on his crutches became smaller and smaller. He didn't look back once.

Gunnarstranda lowered the notebook and looked up, deep in thought. He discovered that he was sitting on her bed. He hadn't noticed that he had sat down. On her bed. A long, blonde woman's hair lay looped on the sheet. He jerked around sensing that someone was looking over his shoulder. But no one was there. He sighed and flicked through the rest of the notebook. It was filled with writing. The same neat, light-blue handwriting, page after page. Just the last four or five sheets were blank. The policeman closed the notebook and put it back in the drawer. Then he stood up and slowly made his way back to the living room. He stopped at the front door and looked back at the attractive flat that had once belonged to Katrine Bratterud. Leaving the place felt different from entering it. It felt quite different. Closing the door and locking it, he wondered whether it had been a stupid idea to undertake this visit. I don't know, he said to himself. I don't know.

13

Mr Nice Guy

Frank Frølich saw the man sitting on the chair outside number 211 as soon as he turned into the corridor. It had to be Bjørn Gerhardsen. He was punctual but still appeared impatient, with his arms folded in front of his chest and one foot bouncing up and down in annoyance. Frølich looked ahead, passed him without a nod and continued on to the next door. Here he turned and glanced at Gerhardsen before entering.

The figure reminded him of one of the boys you find in the back row of the classroom, the type with ambitious parents and no spine. He seemed to be generating an image of himself from those times – rocking the chair, wearing designer clothing and puffing himself up with arrogance.

Frølich closed the door behind him and crept back to room 211 to write up his notes. Gerhardsen could wait a bit longer.

Ten minutes later there was a ring from reception.

'Hi, Frankie. There's a man standing here, name of Bjørn Gerhardsen. He was supposed to appear in front of room 211 at half past three.'

'Ask him to take a seat outside 211 and wait,' Frølich said without mincing his words and went on with the report.

The next time he looked up it was ten minutes to four. Gerhardsen was a patient man. Five minutes later there was a knock at the door.

Frølich swung round in his chair and watched the door. The handle went down slowly.

The policeman pretended to glance up from his papers as the door opened.

'Hello, I'm Bjørn Gerhardsen,' the man in the doorway said, unsure of himself.

Frølich looked up at the clock on the wall. Then, with raised eyebrows, he looked at Gerhardsen.

'I've been waiting since half past three,' the man said.

'I see,' said Frølich, getting up. 'I thought you would never come. Well, take a seat,' he said, pointing to an armchair beside his desk. 'Frank Frølich,' he went on, proffering his hand.

Gerhardsen sat down. He was business-like, but at the same time casually dressed in a dark suit jacket and lighter slacks, chinos, an expensive brand. Beneath the jacket he was wearing a garish yellow shirt and a tie that created a natural transition to the colour of the jacket.

'I'm sure you understand why we would like to talk to you.'

'Yes, indeed.' Gerhardsen cleared his throat. 'Do you mean . . . you've been waiting for me since half past three?'

Frølich glanced up from his papers, indifferent to his question. 'You are married to Annabeth Ås?'

'Yes.'

'And on the Saturday Katrine Bratterud disappeared you had both invited a great many guests to a party. Could you start by telling me your experience of this party?'

Gerhardsen fixed him with a glassy look indicating that he was not used to being insulted in this way. The look also said that he was not sure whether he would tolerate the insult. In the end he made a decision, closed his eyes and swallowed hard. Then he cleared his throat and said: 'There isn't much to tell. It was a successful party, easy-going, nice atmosphere. I think that was true for most people, at any rate.'

Frølich nodded. 'What sort of party was it? What was the occasion?'

'Just a private party. Annabeth and I invited good friends over for some food and wine.'

'But most of the guests had some kind of connection with the Vinterhagen centre, isn't that correct?'

'Yes, it is. In that sense I suppose it marked summer – it was a kind of summer party.'

'But not everyone was invited?'

'No, I guess it was the inner core. All that side of things was Annabeth's domain.'

'And Katrine Bratterud.'

'Yes, as you know, she had completed the programme at the rehab centre. She was due to be formally discharged, if that is the term they use. In fact, I don't know much about the details of these procedures.'

'You're the chairman there?'

'Yes, but not a therapist. I trained as an economist and economics is my professional field.'

'I see. You're the CEO of a financial institute?'

'Geo-Invest A/S.'

'Katrine was not a close friend?'

'Yes, she was, a good friend. That was one of the reasons she was invited. She had been a part of Annabeth's working day for years. And . . .' He opened his palms. 'What is there to say? She was attractive, she . . . had style, was talented . . . was intelligent . . . and had the best references from the travel agency where she worked.'

Frølich nodded to himself and scratched his beard. 'We can come back to that,' he mumbled and asked, 'Did you notice anything in particular about Katrine that evening?'

'She was ill.'

Frølich looked up.

'Yes, she felt sick and threw up, I believe . . . there was a bit of a hubbub around this incident. My guess is it happened at around eleven. At any rate, it was a while after we had left the table. We always stay at the dinner table for a long time . . . I didn't see what happened, but I understand that Annabeth spoke to her . . .'

Gerhardsen stopped as the door behind him opened. He turned in his chair. Police Inspector Gunnarstranda came in and stood in front of the mirror on the wall arranging his comb-over. 'Bjørn Gerhardsen,' Frølich said to Gunnarstranda and to the man: 'Police Inspector Gunnarstranda.'

The two of them shook hands. Gunnarstranda sat on the edge of the desk.

Gerhardsen asked: 'Should I continue?'

As the other two made no attempt to answer, he said: 'Annabeth had been talking to her when someone came from behind. Anyway one or two bottles of wine were smashed. As I said I didn't see anything but Annabeth was covered in . . .'

'You don't know who it was?'

'Pardon.'

'The person who collided with your wife, you don't know who it was?'

'No.'

Frølich motioned for him to go on.

'Well, there was a lot of mess, and then Katrine must have fainted, I suppose. Her boyfriend was there and helped her into the bathroom. Then I heard she had left after the incident because she didn't feel well.'

Gunnarstranda was fidgeting with a packet of chewing gum. The packet wouldn't open. With an irritated yank he broke the packet in two and put two pieces of gum in his mouth. He leaned over, rested his chin on one hand and listened with interest. His chin rotated like a sheep's lower jaw.

Frølich to Gerhardsen: 'But you didn't see this happen?'

'No.'

'Where were you?'

'I was round about, somewhere or other. I was the host after all.'

'Did you notice Katrine leave? When did that happen? How did it happen?'

'No. That is – I did register that she was quarrelling with her boyfriend.'

'Quarrelling?'

'Yes, that was after the wine incident, or the fainting or whatever I should call it. I passed them in the hallway. Needed . . . well, I needed . . . a pee. They were having a row.'

'A row?'

'Yes, or so it seemed, but they went quiet as I passed them, and then I heard them start up again as I closed the door. But I have no idea what they were rowing about.'

'Did you talk to Katrine at any point during this party?'

'A little. We sat together at table, or opposite each other, so we talked or to be more precise, we made conversation.'

'How long did the party last?'

'Until about four o'clock in the morning. That was when the last guests left.'

'Can you remember who the last ones were?'

'There were quite a few in fact. Some were being picked up. There was a lot of fuss with taxis and so on. Some had to wait for taxis. But there were some who went before, earlier in the evening, though I certainly didn't notice who went when.'

Frølich conferred with his notes. 'How can you know that when you weren't there?' he asked breezily.

Gerhardsen gave him a hard look. 'I was there in fact,' he answered.

'We have heard that you left the party soon after coffee was served, with a certain Georg Beck and a number of others.'

'Yes, indeed, that is correct. But I was back before four.'

'By taxi?'

'No, I drove one of the company cars.'

The two policemen exchanged glances. Gerhardsen noticed and

coughed. 'We have two cars belonging to Geo-Invest, a van and a smaller saloon – a Daihatsu. Since I'm the CEO I can use the cars on the odd occasion. That night I took one to drive home – so that I didn't have to queue for a taxi.'

He coughed and continued as the two detectives still made no move to interrupt. 'We have offices in Munkedamsveien. These two cars are in the garage and I couldn't bear the thought of waiting for several hours in the taxi queue, so I unlocked the garage and drove the saloon car home.'

Frølich cleared his throat. 'Were you intoxicated?'

Gerhardsen shrugged. 'I presumed I was not over the limit.'

'But you had been drinking alcohol and continued drinking all night.'

Gerhardsen returned a flinty stare. 'I presumed I was not over the limit.'

'Who left the party earlier in the evening?' Gunnarstranda interrupted. 'Who else apart from you?'

'There was Goggen, Georg that is. Then there was his boyfriend – a man whose name I don't recall, but Annabeth knows him through some connection or other. Then there was another woman who was a temporary teacher at the centre during the winter at some point. Her name's Merethe Fossum. And then there was Katrine's boyfriend – Ole. Can't remember his surname.'

'When did you leave?'

'At midnight, more or less.'

'Where did you go?'

'We went to Smuget.'

Gunnarstranda sent an inquiring look to Frølich, who explained: 'Restaurant at the bottom of Rosenkrantz gate.'

'That's just by Aker Brygge, isn't it,' Gunnarstranda said.

'Walking distance,' acceded Gerhardsen. 'Right across from the City Hall square.'

'What happened then?'

'Well, we went to Smuget. And split up.'

'Split up? What do you mean?'

'Mm, there are several rooms there. In one of them there was a blues band, in another disco music. There were all kinds of music and it was packed. We went our own ways.'

'And what did you do?'

'I circulated a bit, had a few beers and a few mineral waters, talked the usual rubbish to whoever was at the bars.'

'Why did you leave the party you yourself had organized and hosted?'

'I usually do.' Gerhardsen sat up straight in the chair. 'I know this may sound strange to some people,' he began, 'but Annabeth and I have no children. We've been married for sixteen years. We know each other so well and accept that we're different and we like to amuse ourselves in different ways. Annabeth is the kind of woman who likes objects, by which I mean she collects Royal Copenhagen porcelain – the seagull series. She likes antiques and is very keen to have a home that is modern and reflects good taste. I'm not like that. I'm a simple man with a stressful work pattern, a tough job. When she invites people back they tend to be from her circle of friends and if I see that there are other things I can do . . . Well, we all know that some guests come out of loneliness, some because they feel they have to come, some to be with good friends whose company they enjoy. People's needs vary and that applies to me and Annabeth, too. That is where we are today. At least Annabeth and I have come to terms with it and we are pretty happy living in this way . . .' He grimaced and weighed his words before continuing. 'In practice this means that a party like the one we held on Saturday often ends with Annabeth sitting and chatting with other women about interiors and . . .' He extended his arms to show the range of topics in his spouse's conversation. '. . . about . . . about the job, the centre and wallpaper patterns too, for all I know. But I . . .' He tapped his chest with his first finger. 'I prefer to hit the town and have fun.'

Frølich nodded to himself. 'What's your impression of Ole Eidesen?' he asked.

Gerhardsen shrugged. 'Common sort of young man.'

'Common?'

'Yes, usual.'

'But you used the word *common*.'

'Yes.'

'Did you mean anything derogatory by that?'

'Not at all. He seems like a decent sort. We were on the same wavelength, anyway.'

Frølich made a note. 'And afterwards? Did you see him again in Smuget?'

'The odd glimpse. We were spread out, the music was too loud and the room was too cramped to enjoy any conversation. I guess he was dancing and enjoying himself.'

'When did you leave the place?'

'At around three.'

'And what did you do then?'

'There were no taxis around, just long queues, so I strolled up to the garage in Munkedamsveien and fetched the car and drove home.'

'And afterwards?'

'Afterwards? You mean after I arrived home? Well, I helped to empty ashtrays and dispose of the bottles and then I went to bed.'

'With your wife?'

Gerhardsen nodded.

'What time would that have been?'

'About four maybe. Can't say when.'

'And then you slept?'

'I slept sweet, dreamless sleep until late in the morning.'

'Can anyone vouch for that, do you think?'

'That would have to be Annabeth, but I assume she was asleep, too.'

'So you don't have a witness?'

Gerhardsen, annoyed now: 'Ask Annabeth. I haven't asked her if she lay awake watching over me that night. But let's stop beating about the bush. Why don't you ask me if I killed her and get it over and done with?'

'Did you kill her?'

'Of course not.'

Frølich fell silent and looked across at his colleague, who after fiddling with his comb-over took the chewing gum out of his mouth and glowered at it.

'Was it your idea or your wife's to invite her?' asked Gunnarstranda, continuing to chew.

'It was Annabeth's idea.'

'Can you remember the first time you met Katrine?'

Bjørn Gerhardsen groaned with irritation and looked up at them. They said nothing. Gerhardsen deliberated. In the end he made a decision.

'I met her first a few years ago in a brothel close to Filipstad, on the corner of Parkveien and Munkedamsveien. I paid her fifteen hundred kroner for intercourse. I had not seen her before. I didn't know who she was until she came in to massage me. She was a screw, if I can put it like that. I am sure I would have forgotten her had it not been for . . .'

He closed his eyes as though searching for the right words. And pulled a face. The two policemen watched him in silence. Gunnarstranda blew a bubble which burst. Gerhardsen took it as a signal to go on.

'When she was offered treatment at Vinterhagen, Annabeth brought her home. I didn't recognize her, but I think it is highly probable that she recognized me. She absconded from the centre soon after meeting me that afternoon, you see. When Annabeth brought her home and I greeted her, she was a skinny little drug addict, a fragile wreck who had been helping Annabeth with the shopping. That same evening she ran away from the block she was in. They didn't find her . . .'

'And you interpreted this disappearance as a reaction to her recognizing you?'

'Yes.'

'When did you come to this conclusion?'

'Later, but I'll come to that.'

'Go on.'

'I was the one who found her. I was in town for a meeting and went down to Bankplass to find a prostitute. That was about three weeks later. I didn't know it was her until she got into the car. We had agreed a price through the window . . .'

'So you picked her up?'

'Yes . . . She sat next to me in the car without saying a word and I had no idea who she was. I drove across Bispekaia to find somewhere to park where we wouldn't be disturbed. At some point I glanced across and recognized her. She laughed out loud and enjoyed the shock I had. She also reminded me of our encounter at the massage parlour. There were a number of other things she said – I don't remember what – but the essence was that I was a bad person. I countered that I had never claimed to be any better than anyone else. I also said that I wouldn't be buying any sexual services off her after all. And I asked her if I should run her up to the rehab centre. Then she asked me if I had thought about what I would say as an explanation of how I came to find her. I said it would not be a problem; I would say I had bumped into her in town. She asked me if I was wondering what her version would be . . . to Annabeth. I stopped there and then, and said I had no more to say. She could leave and keep all the money she had been given. I also gave her a bit more. Then she sat in the car staring at me without saying anything.'

Gerhardsen paused again, as if he had reached a difficult point, then went on:

'I asked if I should drive her back to the city centre, but she said no and added that she didn't want to owe me anything. She repeated that twice. Used exactly the same words: *I don't want to owe you anything at all*! Then she performed oral sex and got out of the car.'

The silence hung between the walls.

Bjørn Gerhardsen cleared his throat after a long pause. He said, 'I ought to add that she turned up at the rehab centre a few days later and from that moment followed the full course until she was declared clean, had caught up on her schooling and was rehabilitated. From my knowledge of her over recent years she was resourceful and excellent in all ways.'

'Have you had sexual intercourse with her since?'

'Never.'

'How . . .'

Gunnarstranda interrupted Frølich by bursting another bubble and said: 'There's one thing I was wondering regarding the car ride.'

Gerhardsen raised his head.

'I visualize a number of shifts of mood here,' Gunnarstranda said. 'You drive round in the red light area, you pick up a prostitute who takes your fancy and then you have a shock when you recognize her. Following that there's a kind of discussion between you . . . a discussion that has overtones of . . . shall we say . . . morality. At that moment you become a representative of what we might call Norwegian respectability. At least you play the role of a representative of *normality*, the model that your wife also represents when she meets her patients . . .' Gunnarstranda formed inverted commas with his fingers. '. . . *The normal world* . . . whether you like it or not. So you and your wife become the *model* that patients have to imitate!'

'Of course,' Gerhardsen interrupted. 'But you don't need to moralize to me in this way!'

'I'm not moralizing,' Gunnarstranda stated. 'I was merely wondering what shifts of mood there were in the car. I'm trying to imagine the signals that you sent each other during the conversation you had. In other words, you were lustful, you wanted a quickie and you went about this by driving up to someone you regard as an anonymous whore in Bankplass. You agree a price through the open car window, she gets into your car, but you have a shock when you recognize her. You then have a sort of morally indignant discussion with her which ends up with you buying yourself a pardon by letting her keep the money without rendering any services. But in the end you experience the sexual climax you were in fact after as she, to your surprise, supplies a sexual service. Have I understood you correctly?'

'They're your words. It's not my version,' Gerhardsen answered in an aloof tone.

'But you agree that it can be described in that way?'

'I cannot refute it.'

'And two days afterwards she goes to your wife of her own accord and submits to long-term treatment of a social and medical nature?'

'Yes.'

'What was your experience of the relationship between you two in the car, from a psychological point of view?'

'What do you mean now?'

'Well, what roles did you play? Were you the dominant male buying a quick blow-job off a down-and-out junkie in need of money for a fix?'

'I've never thought about it like that.'

Gunnarstranda: 'Are you sure? Which of you had the upper hand, in a psychological sense, during the car ride?'

Gerhardsen: 'I've never thought about it like that, but I would guess that she did. I, for my part, was keen to get away.'

As the two policemen were silent, he continued. 'Or . . . maybe at the beginning . . . when I didn't know her, she was expecting me to recognize her. She must have recognized me when I stopped the car and rolled down the window. I assume she felt she had . . .' He coughed. It was his turn to use his fingers to express inverted commas: '. . . *the upper hand psychologically,* as you call it . . . because she had recognized me, I suppose. I can tell you with absolute assurance that I felt pretty small when I realized who she was . . .'

'But afterwards?'

'I don't understand what you mean.'

'You must do. She humiliates you by revealing that she knows who you are and thereby exposes your misery. What has the psychological balance between you been like since then?'

Gerhardsen closed his mouth and kept it closed.

Gunnarstranda beamed a white teeth smile. 'It's not dangerous to tell the truth, Gerhardsen. You've been very good so far. It's very understandable, very normal to want to take revenge for the little humiliation in the car.'

Gerhardsen, stiff: 'I have never taken revenge for anything.'

'Fine, but you did take your revenge,' the policeman smiled. 'You have made approaches, haven't you? We know that you even tried it on during the party.'

'I didn't try anything on during the party.'

'Our witnesses tell us something different!' Gunnarstranda snapped. 'Don't start lying to me. I know you made advances and suggestions to Katrine Bratterud during the party!'

'And so what if I did?'

'So what?' Gunnarstranda's smile was white again. 'If it happened that night, it could have happened before, couldn't it?'

'But it didn't happen before.'

'How can we know that? How can we know that she didn't feel she was being sexually harassed by you the whole time?'

'Talk to her therapists.'

'Your wife?'

'Yes, do that. I don't keep any secrets from her.'

'Do you mean to say your wife knew you had bought sexual favours from one of her patients?'

'Yes.'

'Excuse me,' said Gunnarstranda, exasperated, 'but you're the chairman of the Vinterhagen Rehabilitation Centre, aren't you?' He didn't wait for an answer, but ploughed on. 'Have you never had the concept of ethics on the agenda?'

Bjørn Gerhardsen, eyes closed: 'I have a vague feeling this conversation should not be about Vinterhagen's ethical foundations.'

'No, let's return to the night in question,' Gunnarstranda said in a calmer frame of mind. 'Quite a number of professionals would, however, frown on key drug-rehab staff inviting addicts to royal piss-ups.' He raised his voice as Gerhardsen tried to interrupt. 'But we can leave that for the time being. My problem is that I have to imagine what happened the night the girl was murdered. I have to find out exactly what happened that night.'

'Of course,' Gerhardsen said with indulgence. 'That's why I am sacrificing my valuable office time and trying to tell you what happened.'

'Did you meet Katrine Bratterud in Oslo city centre after getting out of the taxi?'

'Katrine? In the city centre?'

'Answer the question.'

'No, I didn't meet her.'

'Did you see her?'

'No.'

'Let us imagine what you have said now is not true,' Gunnarstranda said gently. 'Let's say you met her in Aker Brygge that night . . .'

'I certainly did not!'

'Let me finish,' snapped Gunnarstranda. 'We know that you tried it on with her at the party. We know you took a taxi to the City Hall square. We know you regarded her as another screw. That's your word. Let's imagine you followed her, repeated your advances, she resisted and you found some string to tie round her neck to make her more compliant . . .'

The policeman's eyes flashed white at Gerhardsen who was cowering in his chair.

'You're barking up the wrong tree,' he said at last.

'So tell me what happened!'

136

'I had a party at home. I was host to lots of nice people. I went to the centre to dance and have a good time . . .'

'Not to look for another screw?'

'No.'

'Can you prove what time you took the company's Daihatsu that night?'

Gerhardsen lowered his head to think. 'No, I don't believe I can. It's a normal garage in a basement you open with a key, and I have no idea if anyone saw me . . .'

'Can you prove what time you left Smuget?'

'I don't know. Someone must have seen me.'

'There was no one in your group who spoke to you before you left?'

'No.'

'But that's very strange, isn't it?'

'You might think that, but . . .'

'But what?'

'I don't think so.'

'Do you know if any of the guests at the party that night had a score to settle with Katrine?'

'I cannot imagine that.'

'What about your wife?'

'Annabeth? What would she have against Katrine?'

'She might be jealous.'

Gerhardsen angled his head. 'Yes . . . well . . . but not jealous in that way.'

'In which way was she jealous?'

Gerhardsen heaved a weary sigh. 'Listen,' he began, raising his palms as if in an attempt to calm troubled minds. 'Listen,' he repeated. 'I was forced to tell Annabeth about my relationship with Katrine. There was no alternative. When Katrine started treatment it was only a question of time before she said something about me to someone at the centre. I had to pre-empt her – not with everyone, of course – but with Annabeth. I couldn't walk in dread day in day out that . . .'

'When did you confess to your wife?'

'I don't remember.'

'A long time afterwards?'

'Well . . . a while. I told her when it was clear that Katrine was going to stay at Vinterhagen and had stopped doing bunks.'

'So it's a number of years since you told her?'

'Yes.'

'So your wife has treated Katrine for several years knowing that you paid for her services as a prostitute?'

'Yes.' Gerhardsen seemed tired.

The two policemen exchanged glances. Frølich cleared his throat and raised his eyebrows as a signal to his boss, who nodded in return. 'Do you think this affected the relationship between the two of them?' Frølich asked cautiously.

'Annabeth is very professional,' Gerhardsen answered. 'With patients she was professional, but this matter triggered a crisis in our marriage of course.'

'What sort of relationship did the two of them have? Was it warm?'

'No, but I don't think that had anything to do with me. A lot of water has passed under the bridge since I told her, you might say. The reason the relationship between Annabeth and Katrine was not warm was more to do with chemistry.'

'But you just said your confession triggered a marital crisis.'

'Yes, but that was between Annabeth and me.'

'Nevertheless it was Katrine who caused the crisis. It would be surprising if your wife did not take out her emotional response on her, wouldn't it?'

'It may sound strange but I don't think she bore a grudge against Katrine.'

'Are you on first-name terms with all the patients at Vinterhagen?' Frølich interjected.

'Heaven forfend, no.'

'Why Katrine?'

'She'd been there for quite a few years. She was a success. She was rehabilitated. That's quite an event of course.'

'But that doesn't make it natural for you to be on first-name terms with her.'

Gerhardsen sighed. 'She was a special patient for me.'

'So you made advances during the years she was there.'

'No,' Gerhardsen said in desperation. 'But this girl had a position of trust. I read reports, I interviewed her . . .'

Gunnarstranda broke in: '. . . without your pasts as punter and prostitute colouring the situation?'

'Yes. How much more are you going to hassle me about this?'

'Until we find out something important we can use,' Gunnarstranda said, taking out his chewing gum, grimacing at it and flicking it into the wastepaper basket beside Gerhardsen's right leg. 'Could your wife have left the party that night?'

Gerhardsen stared at him in silence.

'Come on, answer the question.'

'For how long?'

'For an hour.'

'I doubt that very much.'

'Why do you doubt it?'

'Because she would have been missed by the guests at the party. Annabeth loves having this kind of get-together. She loves being at the centre of things and she was the one who sent out the invitations. Her leaving the house while there were still guests would have been inconceivable.'

'Were there any others who went missing for shorter periods?'

Gerhardsen deliberated. 'It's possible,' he said at length. 'But who . . . ?' He shook his head. 'You'll have to ask Annabeth. As I said I wasn't there for a few hours.'

'Did anyone else at the party have a grudge against Katrine?'

'I don't know anyone who did.'

'But now you're contradicting yourself,' Gunnarstranda said with a smile.

'I certainly am not.'

'You claimed just now that Katrine had been arguing with her boyfriend.'

'But I don't suppose he would have killed her. My goodness, I can assure you, such a decent man . . .'

'What were they arguing about?'

'No idea.'

'So you didn't see an argument?'

'No, but . . . it was more that they weren't speaking. I could sense an atmosphere.'

'You said they were having a huge row.'

'I retracted that.'

'Has it occurred to you they may have been arguing because of you?' Gunnarstranda asked.

'Me?'

'You had just tried it on with her. Perhaps he was jealous?'

'He wouldn't have been able to hide that from me when we took the taxi to town. The atmosphere in the car was terrific.'

'He may have taken his anger out on Katrine,' Frølich said. 'Have you thought about that?'

Gerhardsen puffed out his cheeks and closed his eyes. His brow was sweaty. 'No,' he said, his eyes still closed. 'I didn't think about that. Is there going to be any more of this?'

Frølich sent an enquiring look to his boss who waved his hand in a deprecatory manner. 'Not for the time being,' Frølich said. 'But we will contact you to clear up some of the points in your statement.'

'Surprise, surprise,' Gerhardsen said, getting up.

* * *

The two policemen sat staring at the walls after Gerhardsen had gone. Gunnarstranda produced a box of matches and tried to make a toothpick from a match.

'Bl-oo-dy hell.'

'Yes, so much crap you need a spade,' Gunnarstranda replied, fiddling with his match-cum-toothpick. 'Geo-Invest, what's that?'

'Offshore,' Frølich said. 'Some oil guff to do with arbitration – it's the kind of job you need to have trained for to understand what it involves.'

'Have we got any interviews this evening?'

'Eidesen – the boyfriend.' Frølich flicked through the blank sheets of paper on his desk. 'What do you think?' he asked. 'Could it have been Gerhardsen – or his missus?'

Gunnarstranda shrugged. 'There's no doubt he must have been in real torment when she turned up at the centre for the second time.'

'Do you think he's lying?'

'Why should he lie? The whole prostitute business is very delicate, isn't it? He must have known or assumed our girl would have confided in someone and that in some way or other we would find out about his blunder. That's why he takes the plunge and admits everything here. It suggests he has nothing to hide as far as the murder is concerned.'

'But his wife?'

Gunnarstranda's face distorted – he seemed to be in great pain. 'Mmm,' he mumbled. 'But why wait for so many years?'

'Might have been the last straw that night. Kramer said Gerhardsen had been molesting Katrine B that night at the party. His wife might have noticed . . .'

'Yes, and then?'

'She sees it and loses her temper and . . . well . . . and so on.'

'Yes.' Gunnarstranda nodded. 'But Kramer claims he looked after Katrine until three in the morning. We'll have to check the arrangements with this car Gerhardsen took home. But it's an incredible coincidence that Henning and Katrine drive down to the same part of town where the gang of party-goers leaves the taxi. It seems quite extraordinary that none of them saw any of the others!'

'Henning and Katrine went to McDonald's in Aker Brygge. The others are on the other side of the City Hall square outside Smuget. They wouldn't necessarily have seen each other.'

'But if they did . . .' Gunnarstranda said with a meaningful look. 'Gerhardsen and/or Ole Eidesen see Katrine in a clinch with Henning Kramer . . .'

'Gerhardsen is the only one with access to a car,' Frølich added. 'Kramer claimed there had been a car following them on to Ingierstrand beach.'

14

Old Acquaintances

Gunnarstranda flicked the tiny cigarette end into the long-necked ashtray as he heard the knock at the door.

'Come in,' he shouted and picked up the photograph attached with a paper clip to the file on the table.

Frølich came in. 'You saw it?' He nodded towards the picture the inspector was holding between his fingers. 'The travel agency lady came up trumps. She named the thug.'

'Raymond Skau.' Gunnarstranda pulled a face as if the name had a sour taste. 'Sounds like a character from the Olsen gang films.'

'That's his name anyway,' Frølich said. 'The lady's a hundred per cent positive. This guy visited Katrine in the travel bureau the Saturday she was killed.'

Gunnarstranda studied the photograph again. 'Never seen him,' he mumbled and as he put it back he felt his fingers begin to tremble.

'Small-time crook,' Frølich said. 'Done time for receiving stolen property, and robbery. Known to hang around strip joints and that sort of area. May be a pimp, in other words. Been arrested a few times for selling hash to teenagers. But the most interesting bit is a case from a few years back – March 1995.'

'I see,' said the inspector, bending over the photograph. He interlaced his hands to keep them still. The man in the picture looked like hundreds of others in the same category. Prison mug shots. A man with a haggard face, a vacant expression beneath half-closed, almost sleepy eyelids, and dark or grey hair. A glimpse of a very uneven row of teeth was visible in the murky hole that constituted the open mouth. 'Has he broken a tooth?'

'Could have done,' Frølich said. 'But at that time – I mean in '95 – he was reported to the police by one Katrine Bratterud.'

Gunnarstranda whistled. Frølich's smile widened into a broad beam. 'The report came from the Centre for Battered Women. Bugger me if our friend there hadn't been living with our girl. And charges were brought against him for beating her up and trying to run her over with his car!'

'Run her over?'

'Yes,' Frølich said. 'Jealousy drama de luxe. And the case was not shelved, oh no. Frøken Bratterud presented herself in person at the police station and withdrew the charges.'

'And he was waiting outside?'

'We don't know, but it's possible.'

'How was she? After the car incident?'

'She escaped with a fright. I can't remember the pathologist mentioning any lasting injuries anyway.'

'Jealous,' Gunnarstranda mumbled as he sat flicking the photograph. 'We like that word.' He stood up and strolled over to the window.

'There was no one at home,' Frølich said.

'Where was that?'

'Grønland, council flat, one of the old blocks in Grønlandsleiret.' Frølich nodded and studied the photograph as well. 'Raymond Skau,' he said. 'What a name.'

'He doesn't have to be ashamed of his name,' Gunnarstranda said. 'He can't do anything about it anyway.' He sat staring into the distance. Frølich stood by the door.

'Mm,' Gunnarstranda said, rapt in thought.

'The boyfriend,' Frølich said, pointing to the door. 'We agreed we would see Ole Eidesen together.'

15

A Man with Cuts

A woman jogged up the stairs in front of them. Frank Frølich kept a close eye on her. Her face and hair were masked by a veil. However, what nourished Frølich's imagination were the nicely shaped hips and breasts whose contours he could make out beneath her ample and airy clothes as she rounded the bend in the stairs.

'There,' Gunnarstranda said, pointing to a door with OLE EIDE-SEN printed in white on a red plastic strip beneath a bell.

The Muslim woman lived on the same floor. She stood fumbling for her keys, let herself in and took off the veil before closing the door. Frølich couldn't believe his eyes. 'Did you see that?' he asked.

'What?' Gunnarstranda rang Eidesen's bell.

'The woman. Her hair was blonde.'

'So what?'

'But she was wearing a veil!'

'You're allowed to be a Muslim even if you are Norwegian.'

'But . . .' Frølich swallowed and cleared his throat. At that moment the door to Eidesen's flat was opened. Ole Eidesen appeared to be around thirty years old. He was slim and of medium height. There was a conspicuous ring in his left eyebrow. He had tried to disguise a growing bald spot on his crown by shaving off all his hair. A dark shadow across his skull revealed the growth pattern of his hair. But the most noticeable thing about him was a series of scratches and red marks down his face.

'Eidesen?' Gunnarstranda asked.

'Yes,' the man said, looking serious. His eyes wandered from one policeman to the other.

Gunnarstranda kept both hands in his jacket pocket as he introduced himself.

'Come in.'

'This is Frank Frølich.'

Eidesen had long, slim fingers. His handshake was light but firm.

The sitting room they entered was light and smelt of perfume. There were several windows, the hessian wallpaper was painted white and the room was spartanly furnished. A stereo system stood on the floor against the wall. A white leather sofa and two manila chairs encircled a glass table. One chair creaked as Frølich took a seat.

Eidesen sat down on the white sofa; under his shorts his legs were tanned and muscular. He looked nervously at Gunnarstranda who stood thinking and biting his lower lip.

Frølich sorted out his notepad on his lap before focusing on the man on the sofa. 'This is about Katrine Bratterud,' Frølich said.

Eidesen nodded.

'You've had an accident?' the policeman asked.

Eidesen shook his head. 'I fell flat on my face.'

'Fell on your face?'

Eidesen fidgeted. 'I can't keep still. I think about her all the time. It's worst at night, so I run.' He stretched his face into a tired, apologetic smile. 'I ran last night and . . .' The smile broadened into a nervous, sardonic smile. 'I tripped over some scrub and fell flat on my face with a bang.'

Frølich nodded slowly. 'Has the priest contacted you?'

Eidesen became serious and shook his head. 'I heard yesterday.'

'What did you hear?'

'That it was Katrine they were writing about in the newspapers.'

'Who did you hear it from?'

'Someone called Sigrid who works at the rehab centre.'

Frølich consulted his notes. 'Sigrid Haugom?'

Eidesen nodded. 'I rang them.'

'What did Sigrid Haugom say?'

'I rang and she said Katrine had been killed. That it was Katrine they had found dead by Hvervenbukta.'

'Did she say how Katrine was killed?'

Eidesen coughed and, unsure of himself, shook his head.

The art is to be patient, thought Frølich. Always be patient, he thought, oblivious of why the boss was letting him run this show, but there would be some plan behind it. That he did know. 'How long did you know her?'

'Hm?'

Frølich repeated the question.

'A few months. I knew who she was long before that. We met on a course. Spanish.'

'You can speak Spanish?'

'Yes.' He added, 'My mother is Spanish. I teach Spanish in the evening. Adult education at the folk university.'

'And Katrine was a student there?'

'Yes.'

Frølich waited. Eidesen cleared his throat. 'I asked her out,' he began and cleared his throat again. 'On the third evening we ate at the Spanish restaurant in Pilestredet. I just don't remember . . .'

'Do you remember what clothes she was wearing at the party on Saturday?' Frølich asked. 'Try to give me an exact description.'

'A black top with buttons and sort of . . . sort of . . . transparent sleeves,' Eidesen said, thinking carefully. 'Over a sort of grey skirt, dark grey, light and summery, not one of the shortest, it reached down well over her knees and the shoes I'm not sure . . . They were black, I think, or grey, bit of a heel on them.'

'Lingerie?' Frølich asked.

Eidesen rolled his shoulders. 'I have no idea. She got dressed in the bathroom after taking a shower. We were at her place – then we took a taxi to the party.'

147

'But what lingerie did she wear as a general rule?'

Eidesen shrugged again. 'The usual stuff – both bits, if I can put it like that.'

'Colours?'

'As I said, I don't know. I would guess it was something dark because she was wearing a black top. She was precise about things like that . . . I mean nothing vulgar.'

'Anything else?'

The question came from Gunnarstranda. The man's sensitive lips were trembling. He always had this expectant expression in his eyes. An expression that did not invite a head-on confrontation, but still presaged something undetonated.

'A bag, a little shoulder bag . . .' Eidesen fixed his gaze on Gunnarstranda, who took off his coat, walked a few paces over to the free manila chair, placed it opposite Eidesen and sat down. He then rested his head on his hands and said in a low voice, 'I always lay my cards on the table and I never lie.'

'Is that right?'

'But I'm a real bastard, Eidesen, a real bastard. Did you know that?'

Eidesen, puzzled, shook his head

'But that's how the game's played,' Gunnarstranda said. 'Now and then there are certain advantages to being a bastard. From what I understand you were, or had been at some point, Katrine's boyfriend. Right now I cannot make allowances for that. The most important thing is to find out who killed her and, for all I know, that could have been you. I don't know. No one knows except the killer.'

Eidesen nodded again. He was ill at ease.

'Did you kill Katrine Bratterud?'

Eidesen winced. 'No.'

'She died what pathologists here call a gruesome death,' Gunnarstranda said.

Eidesen looked up.

'We don't know why the killer did what he did. The conclusion, however, is that she took a very long time to die. A very long time.'

Eidesen was breathing with his mouth open. There was silence in the flat; only Eidesen's heavy breathing was audible.

In the end Gunnarstranda broke the silence again. 'The fact that it took a long time means that the killer had time and the opportunity to stop and let her live. So what, one might ask? Does it matter when she's dead anyway? Well, the time it takes to kill her suggests two very important pieces of information. It means we're talking about malice aforethought.' He stared at Eidesen in the ensuing silence.

'And?' Eidesen asked with face raised.

'If someone is hellbent on eliminating a threat someone poses, there can be two causes for what happens. Two causes that seem feasible. The killer may be trying to protect his own life. But I don't believe that to be the case here. Even strangulation must have taken several minutes, which means she put up some resistance. She must have been lashing out with her arms and legs. So we have a situation in which the assailant is waiting for her to die. This killer wasn't defending himself, which may mean that he was blinded by fury – or quite unemotional at the time of the crime.'

From the kitchen they heard the refrigerator switch itself on. Frølich also heard a hollow ticking sound in the silence. It was a small table clock on top of the television – a new black Philips.

Eidesen stroked the cuts on his face. 'I would imagine she resisted,' he mumbled.

The policeman nodded without saying anything. He looked into Eidesen's eyes and said: 'Were you and Katrine having some disagreements?'

Eidesen shook his head.

'Please articulate your answers.'

'Hm?'

'Answer my questions with words not body language. Frank Frølich, in the chair over there, will note down your answers.'

'No, we didn't argue very often.'

'On Saturday 7th June you both went to a party held by Anna-beth Ås. Is that corret?'

'Yes, it is.'

'Is fru Ås a friend of yours?'

'No, the invitation came via Katrine. Annabeth is the boss of the rehab centre where Katrine was a patient, a part-time patient.'

'How long did you stay at the party?'

'I left at about midnight.'

'Did you leave alone or with someone else?'

'Alone . . . that is there were several of us splitting the taxi fare.'

'And Katrine?'

'She was ill and went home.'

'Before you?'

'I think so.'

'Why do you think she left the party before you?'

'She was in a bad way, throwing up.'

Gunnarstranda furrowed his brow; his interest was caught. 'Did she have a habit of throwing up?'

Eidesen: 'A habit? She was ill.'

'But did she suffer from an eating disorder? Did she often throw up?'

'Not at all.' Eidesen continued in a dry voice, 'After we had eaten, a good while later, she went to the bathroom and threw up. She said she didn't feel well.' He fell silent.

'So you interpreted this behaviour of hers as a case of illness, gastric flu or something like that?'

'Yes, that is, at first I thought she might have been drinking.'

'But she hadn't been?'

'No. She said she hadn't touched a drop all evening.'

'But did she seem drunk?'

'No.'

'What did you do? Ring for a taxi?'

'No.'

Gunnarstranda waited. Eidesen cleared his throat again. 'I think she did that. She said she wanted to go, and a little later she was nowhere to be seen.'

'But you didn't see her go?'

'No. I didn't see her anywhere, so I presumed she must have left.'

'Did you have a row?'

'No.'

'Why didn't you say goodbye or make sure she found her way home OK?'

'There was a bit of tension between us.'

'So you did have a row?'

Eidesen shrugged.

'She was ill, wanted to go home. You wanted to stay. You couldn't agree. You had a row?'

'We didn't have a row.'

'If I were to say a guest at the party saw you involved in a loud altercation before she left, what would you say?'

'OK, that's true. But I don't remember it being loud. It was more the atmosphere that was unpleasant. She didn't want me to stay.'

Gunnarstranda was quiet. The sunshine broke through the large south-facing windows and specks of dust danced in the air. 'Ole,' he said. 'May I call you Ole?'

Eidesen nodded.

'In cases like these, out of self-respect, you must stick to the truth from the very first moment. Otherwise you'll get into a lot of trouble. Do you understand?' Without waiting for a response he went on: 'Well, Ole, did you have a row or not? If you did, what did you row about?'

'She wanted to leave the party because she was ill, but I didn't want to go. It was fun there so then she got, well, she got . . . annoyed with me. That was what it was. She was annoyed that I wouldn't accompany her home.'

'Did she say that? That you should accompany her?'

'No, but I interpreted her annoyance in that way.'

'Tell me about her illness.'

'Well, she just fainted, sideways. We were standing and chatting to some women from the centre, including the one whose house it was, Annabeth Ås. All of a sudden Katrine collapsed, towards me, with her eyes rolling. Out cold. There was a bit of a palaver and I went to the bathroom with her. She had just fainted for a second or two, then she threw up in the toilet bowl.'

'Did she give any explanation for this attack?'

'No.'

'Had this happened before?'

Eidesen jutted forward his lips and considered the question. 'Not like that. I don't think I'd ever seen her faint before, but she had been really dreading this party.'

'Why was that?'

'That's how she was. Couldn't quite manage social gatherings with people she didn't know. And she was dreading spending a whole evening with these particular people. She felt she was on display because she was a patient.'

'But did she express her terror that day?'

'Not in so many words. But . . .' Ole Eidesen pulled a face. 'She had been very bitchy earlier in the day. Argued with me a lot.'

'Argued with you?'

'Yes, we were at her place. I was watching football and then we started arguing. That is, she started.'

'What about?'

Eidesen shook his head. 'She wanted to use the phone and I wasn't allowed to watch TV. She turned down the sound and we had a row. It was the Saturday afternoon fixture for the pools coupon, wasn't it. She was in a real state!'

'And you interpreted this as a bout of nerves?'

'Yes.'

'And what was she nervous about?'

'Going to the party. She didn't want to go, but felt she had to.'

'Back to the party. What were you talking about when she fainted?'

'I don't remember. It was just chat. I think Annabeth was complimenting her on being so clever and all that. I don't remember her exact words.'

'Were you drunk?'

'I was in a good mood. There was wine with the meal and brandy afterwards, quite a lot of brandy.'

'Have you ever used any other intoxicating substances?'

'Eh?'

Gunnarstranda: 'You were in a relationship with a drug addict. You must understand what I mean. Did you consume other substances apart from spirits and wine that evening?'

Eidesen's face went rigid. 'She was not a drug addict. In a few months she would have been regarded as fully rehabilitated. And I do not use other intoxicating substances, as you put it!'

'So you didn't take any other substances apart from alcohol that night, is that what I am to understand?'

'Yes.'

'You each have your own flats. Had you thought about living together?'

'No, it was still early in the relationship. But we stayed over at each other's place now and then.'

'And you were considered a couple?'

'By some perhaps.'

'And you?' Gunnarstranda said sardonically. 'Did you consider this a relationship?'

'Of course.'

'Did you leave the party alone?'

'No, I took a taxi with some of the others after Katrine left.'

'Who was that?'

'The guy who lived there, Bjørn, and a gay man called Goggen with his partner – a guy whose name I don't remember – and a woman called Merethe Fossum.'

'When was this?'

'Around midnight.'

153

'But you had just told your girlfriend that you didn't want to leave the party?'

'Yes, but there was this group of people in party mood. Goggen, he's such a funny man, and Bjørn was all right.'

'The lady?'

'Yes, she was all right, too.'

'Did you already know Merethe Fossum?'

'No.'

'You met her there for the first time? At the party?'

'That's correct.'

'Where did you go?'

'To the city centre, to Smuget, a restaurant.'

'The taxi dropped you off outside the restaurant?'

'Yes.'

'Then?'

'We paid and went in.'

'Everyone?'

Eidesen thought about this. 'I think so. I mean three of us did. The two gay men wanted to go to another place. We three went into Smuget.'

'You and the lady and Gerhardsen?'

'There was a bit of a queue outside. I stayed with Merethe. Gerhardsen went off on his own, but I would guess he paid and went in.'

Gunnarstranda glanced at Frølich. 'Do you often go to restaurants where you have to pay to go in?'

Frølich: 'Smuget is not a restaurant in its normal sense; it's more a club with dance floors and stages for live music . . .'

Gunnarstranda turned back to Eidesen.

'Did you see any of the others as you went in?'

'I saw Merethe mostly.'

'What did you do?'

'We danced a little, listened to music, had a few beers . . . and . . .'

'And Gerhardsen?'

154

'I have no idea.'

'You didn't see him in there?'

'We were together in the queue, but after that . . .' Eidesen shook his head.

'What time did you return home?'

'I didn't look at my watch, but it was late. It was light and I was worried. Katrine was not here and we usually spent the weekend together – the nights. So I had somehow expected to find her here.'

'Did you see any signs that suggested she had been here?'

'She may have been, but I don't think so.'

'Why not?'

Eidesen rolled his shoulders. 'How could she have been here? I mean no one had made any food, no one had touched anything. If she had been here I would have noticed.'

'So you came back, but she wasn't here. What did you do then?'

'I rang her place.'

'In the middle of the night?'

'Of course. It was crazy that she wasn't here, with her being unwell and all that.'

Gunnarstranda got up and walked to the window. 'But suppose you had been ill,' he said. 'Suppose you had felt nauseous and had thrown up and hadn't felt like being with other people, wouldn't it have been natural to go back to your own place, go to bed and hope you woke up fit and well the next day?'

'Yes, it would, but I would have left a message on the answer machine of the person waiting for me.'

'And there weren't any messages on the machine?' Gunnarstranda lifted up a black object beside the white telephone on the window sill. 'On this?'

'There wasn't a message, no.'

'And she usually left you messages?'

'Yes.'

Gunnarstranda nodded. 'Did she pick up the phone when you called?'

155

'No.'

'What did you do?'

'I went to sleep.'

'Yes, and then?'

'Well, I slept.'

'I thought you ran into the forest and got scratched by thorns. Wasn't that what you said?'

'No, that was last night. I couldn't sleep after I heard what had happened.'

'But that night you slept?'

'Yes, like a log.'

'Even though she had vanished without a trace?'

'She hadn't.'

'Hadn't?'

'I mean I wasn't aware she had vanished. I thought she was asleep.'

'But she didn't answer the phone.'

'No, but she had been ill and had gone home. I assumed she was sleeping.'

Gunnarstranda nodded slowly. 'Can anyone confirm that you did not have the cuts on your face on Sunday?'

Eidesen shrugged. Silent. 'Maybe.'

'Name?'

'If you like I'll write down the names of the people I met on Sunday.'

'Fine. You slept. How long did you sleep?'

'Until nine, more or less.'

'Did you try to get in contact with her?'

'Yes, several times. On the phone.'

'What were you thinking?'

'How do you mean?'

Gunnarstranda, irritated: 'Well, you were anxious. What were you thinking? What hypotheses had you formed in your mind after your girlfriend had stayed away all night and was ill?'

'None.'

'None?' the policeman gasped.

Eidesen stood up and walked around the table. He was two heads taller than the short, lean policeman with the comb-over and the anthropoid jaw. 'I don't know how you are supposed to behave in cases like this,' he said in a tremulous voice.

Frølich didn't move as his boss still seemed to be in control.

Eidesen: 'I'm no expert at reactions and feelings, but I have just lost a person of whom I was fond and if you had any respect left in . . .'

'Are you thinking these thoughts now or did you fear these things on that morning, too?' the small policeman barked, moving two steps closer to the athlete who involuntarily retreated. The policeman repeated, 'Did it occur to you on that morning that something might have happened to Katrine? That she might have been hurt?'

'No.'

'And why not?'

'Because . . .' Eidesen was quiet, thinking, it appeared.

'Why?' Gunnarstranda barked.

Eidesen sat down on the sofa with a deep sigh.

Gunnarstranda sat down too, took out his packet of roll-ups and found a cigarette for nervous fingers to fidget with.

Eidesen seemed drained, but said nothing.

'Did you think she was with someone else?'

Eidesen stared out of the window.

'Come on,' Gunnarstranda said. 'Your girl stayed out all night. She may have been sick or unwell and you do nothing, not even check out the people you must have known were closest to her. You don't report her missing. Even when the news on Sunday is full of stories about a dead young woman found in Mastemyr, it doesn't ring a bell with you. It's so obvious why you didn't do anything. You must have thought she was with someone else, unless you killed her.'

'What did you say?' Eidesen's reaction was perhaps divided between shock at the question and annoyance at Gunnarstranda's aggression.

'I'm not saying anything,' the policeman explained, unruffled. 'I'm weighing the options. Either you were at ease that morning because you knew how things stood – that she was dead – or you were unconcerned because you had a good reason to assume nothing had happened. In which case, if you assumed everything was fine with Katrine, you must have assumed she was elsewhere. Both options are possible. You look as if you have been fighting with someone with claws . . .'

'An accident,' Eidesen interrupted.

'Indeed. And, off the top of your head, you cannot tell me the names of anyone who could confirm your assertions. But let us suppose you had nothing to do with the murder. Well, you say you were not concerned about Katrine that morning. So my question is: Where was she? Or to be more precise: Where did you think she was?'

Eidesen stood there with his head hanging. He was considering the situation. That much was obvious. When he finally straightened up he did so with a worn, somewhat resigned expression on his face. 'Henning Kramer,' he mumbled.

Frølich coughed and took notes.

Gunnarstranda: 'Why did you think she was with the conscientious objector?'

'She spent a lot of time with him.'

'A boyfriend?'

'According to Katrine they were . . .' Eidesen curled both index fingers, '. . . just good friends.'

'But you didn't believe that?'

'Are you starting again?' Eidesen looked tired.

Gunnarstranda shook his head. 'I would like to know your opinion. What kind of relationship did the two of them have? It makes me especially curious when you assume she has spent the night with the man. What kind of person is Henning?'

'What kind of person?' Eidesen shrugged. 'A skinny guy, long hair, bit of fluff on the end of his chin, grins a lot, obsessed by philosophy.'

'Philosophy?'

'Yes, philosophical questions, sitting and thinking, writing poems, likes cooking, obsessed with Buddhist tosh – every woman's dream guy.'

'Can I take it that you neither like cooking, writing poems nor debating philosophical questions?'

'You can take whatever you like. But I do not like and have never liked Henning Kramer. That's no secret.'

'But you believe he and Katrine were having a relationship.'

Eidesen took his time. 'Relationship,' he mumbled. 'I would guess they were very good friends, as they say. In any case Katrine claimed Henning was a friend and not a lover. Nevertheless, now and then I did wonder. They seemed to know each other so well.'

'Explain.'

'They were very intimate with each other, the way married people can be. They did have something private going between them.'

'And you thought she was with Henning that night?'

'Yes.'

'You must have thought there was something going on between them.'

'She claimed Henning was like a girlfriend.'

'A girlfriend? Is he gay?'

'Don't think so, but they were friends.'

'She didn't have any girlfriends?'

'No.'

'None at all?'

'None that I know of.'

'Isn't that strange?'

'Maybe, I didn't think about it. She may have had female friends, but I don't know of anyone close anyway.'

Gunnarstranda looked down. 'All right,' he mumbled, then homed in on the young man's eyes again. 'Were you jealous of Henning?'

'I have been.'

'Were you that night?'

'No.'

'Why not?'

'No idea.'

'But you come home at night expecting to find your girlfriend there. She isn't and you conclude as a matter of course that she is with another man. Yet you are not jealous?'

'I wasn't jealous.'

'And I find that a little hard to believe!'

'Fine,' snapped Eidesen. 'You want me to be jealous so what the hell does it matter? If you want, I can say I was. If that makes you feel better. Yes, I can say I was jealous. Are you happy now?'

'No!'

'And why *not*?' Eidesen stood up and screamed the word into the face of the policeman, who calmly said, 'Sit down.'

Eidesen sat down and Gunnarstranda cleared his throat in a formal-sounding manner. 'I want to know what happened,' he said in a quiet voice. 'As I mentioned before, I don't bluff and I don't tell lies. I am a civil servant, that is all, and have nothing to gain by either bluffing or lying. I only want to do my job, which is to discover the truth. You have confronted me with two possible hypotheses. Either you were jealous or you were not jealous. Let's imagine you were jealous that night. She was found murdered two to three kilometres from here. Let's say she was on her way here that night. What are the consequences of this hypothesis? Suppose we say you met outside or that maybe you went out – restless because she was not here waiting for you. It was beginning to get light and you met her on the way here. Perhaps you asked where she had been. Perhaps

160

she admitted what you suspected, that she had been with Kramer. Perhaps that started a row with a fatal conclusion. That fits the facts of the case very well – the killer must have been furious with the victim. If the victim had cheated on or deceived the killer you can understand the fury. Do you understand? Was that how it happened?'

'No,' Eidesen said in a resigned tone.

'She could have come here,' the policeman continued. 'For all I know, you may have killed her here, in this chair.'

Gunnarstranda sat watching Eidesen running two fingers down the sides of his nose. The silence persisted.

Frølich could feel that he was hungry. As if on cue his stomach rumbled. Both Eidesen and Gunnarstranda glared at him. Frølich cleared his throat and changed sitting position.

'Why did you let her leave the party so early on her own?' Gunnarstranda asked at length.

'The party? She felt unwell and I was enjoying myself.'

'But you were a stranger there, weren't you?'

'No more of a stranger than Katrine was.'

'A bit more of a stranger than Katrine was. She knew the hosts. You knew no one in the house.'

'I was a guest like everyone else and it was a good party.'

'Good in what way?'

'There were some good stories told. They were good people.'

'You left with, amongst others, this woman, Merethe Fossum. She's about your age, isn't she?'

'A bit younger.' Eidesen's eyes were now those of someone who was concentrating on not looking away.

'You had a good time. I mean it was just you two, wasn't it?'

'It was packed with people, but we danced a little, chatted a little.'

'We? So you were a couple?'

'We were not a couple. I was with Katrine!'

'But you and this Merethe got on well, had good chemistry even before Katrine left the party, didn't you?'

'No.'

'That wasn't why Katrine left, was it? Because you were coming on to other women?'

'I did not come on to anyone.'

'But you danced with her. And you admitted you had a row with Katrine.'

'We didn't argue about things like that.'

'Where does she live?'

'Who?'

'Merethe Fossum.'

'In Gagleberg, on the bend at the start of the road up to Ryenberget, Vålerenga.'

'How do you know?'

'We split the fare home. She got out there.'

Gunnarstranda motioned to Frølich, who stood up and went to the door. But then he remembered something. 'One last thing,' Frølich said as his colleague unbuttoned his jacket and rolled himself a cigarette.

Eidesen raised a weary head. 'Yes?'

'We know the clothes she was wearing, but this was a party. What jewellery was she wearing?'

'Jewellery . . .' Eidesen mused. 'A thin gold chain around her neck. Maybe a couple of bracelets. She had an incredible eye for bracelets. Always wore some round here.' He illustrated by holding his wrist. 'They jangled. She thought it was cool if they jangled.'

'Any more?'

'Nothing stands out.'

'No rings?'

'Yes, of course, she always wore a lot of gold.'

'And in her ears?'

'Yes. I bought them myself. A present. Two cannabis leaves – in gold, one for each ear.'

'I thought she was clean.'

'She was.'

'But cannabis leaves . . . ?'

'Yes, what about it?'

Frølich waved him away. 'Nothing,' he mumbled, waiting for Gunnarstranda, who shouldered his way past the much taller and stronger Ole Eidesen. 'You are instructed to attend the Institute of Forensics within the next twenty-four hours,' said Inspector Gunnarstranda, putting a cigarette in his mouth. 'There you need to give a DNA sample. You have twenty-four hours. Good evening.'

16

Discussions in the Rain

The rain was attempting to wash away a small, narrow biro mark on Frølich's left thumb. A raindrop struck the line about every third second. He hardly felt it; he was about as wet as it was possible to be. The material of his rain jacket was as stiff as cardboard, and the water trickled down his sleeves and dripped off both hands. The blue line contrasted with the summer-brown skin of his hand.

He went into a crouch and checked around the area of the trodden-down raspberry bushes. He examined the ground and tried to trample as little vegetation as possible. Whether the flattened edge of the ditch had been a crime scene or not was of less importance now as the pouring rain was washing away any clues there might have been. His green jacket hung down to his hips. On his legs he was wearing dark jeans and high green waders. He had tried to fold the stiff rain jacket at the bottom so that not too much rain would trickle down on to his thighs. But it was no use. Both his trouser legs were dark blue with the rain, and every time he moved he had the unpleasant sensation of his trousers sticking to his skin. His hood fell forwards like a helmet and obstructed his vision on both sides. Every time he turned his head, he had to pull back the hood with his right arm in order to be able to see anything apart from the inside material. Frølich stood up and headed for the other crime scene investigators.

'I don't know,' he said.

He didn't need to say any more. The others understood what he meant. Someone may have committed a murder in this place, but it could equally well have been deer moving around and trampling scrub and thicket.

'No clothes anyway,' said Yttergjerde, the oldest policeman in the group, a bow-legged man with a powerful, almost barrel-shaped upper torso, long upper arms and a stooping posture.

'Have you been on leave yet, Frankie?'

Frank shook his head inside the hood.

'You haven't been out to catch the great pike?'

Frank, who knew of Yttergjerde's passion for pike fishing, said, as was the truth, 'I tend to concentrate on trout.'

'Pike have never turned you on?'

'No,' said Frølich, staring into the rain. 'Fly fishing is an art form all its own – finding out what's in the area, making up the right fly and holding on when you have a bite.'

'Pikes are toughies,' said Yttergjerde. 'On Sunday I caught one weighing four kilos.'

'I'm never allowed to go away at the weekends,' Frølich responded. 'My partner isn't at all interested in fishing.'

'Four kilos,' Yttergjerde repeated. 'I had to kill it with a hammer axe, bang away at the head until it cracked, and afterwards I put the pike in a black bin bag at the bottom of the boat while I tried for a couple of hours to catch a few more. When I arrived home the missus wasn't in, so I put the pike in the utility sink and wrote a message to Mum to scrape it and make fishcakes for supper! That evening the missus came home and went looking for a knife. The pike flapped its tail and jumped into the air. Yup, it had been lying there, drying out and breathing air for half a day, but down on the floor it wriggled over towards my missus snapping its jaws like a hungry croc!'

Frølich gave a weak smile. 'Must have been one of the ones that eats kiddies swimming in the river,' he said drily.

'You think I'm bull-shitting, don't you,' Yttergjerde said. 'But it's almost impossible to kill them. They're jungle creatures. Bury themselves in the mud when it's dry season. As the pools dry out in July you can see them burying themselves with their eyes poking out. The good old boys take time off to go and kill pikes day in, day out, but the buggers are hard to kill! Then the rains come and they smack their tails on the surface of the water like small whales and swim off.' He was not smiling. There were deep furrows in the man's face. He had long, narrow teeth he hid by pressing his lips together, which gave him a surly expression – and which gave even the tallest of fisherman's tales an appearance of credibility.

Frølich nodded. 'Long time yet to a dry summer,' he said looking up at the sky. 'What have we found so far?'

'A crushed, empty can of Coke,' Julius read from a list he had made. 'A used condom – washed out and rotten, several bits of paper that were once packets of cigarettes . . . a load of rusty beer-bottle caps . . . and an electric motor, a water pump at a guess.'

'Who would throw away a water pump?' Frølich asked.

'Anyone, if it was knackered,' Yttergjerde said. He nodded towards the water's edge further down. 'Just wait until you deploy the divers. We'll be wallowing in stolen cars and caravans.'

'We're only looking for fresh clues,' Frølich said in a tired voice, rubbing the blue biro mark on the back of his hand. 'Clothes, a woman's party frock, I suppose nylons with lace, that sort of thing . . . underwear . . . and jewellery.'

Yttergjerde shook his head in despair. At that moment a young constable came round the bend with an object in his hands. Both Frølich and Yttergjerde turned to face him. Rain was dripping from the shadows on the young constable's police cap; there was one drop hanging from the underside of his nose. The policeman held out what he had found. It was a woman's high-heeled shoe soiled with mud and dirt. 'That must have spent at least three winters in the woods,' Yttergjerde said gloomily. He focused on Frølich and heaved a wordless sigh, which expressed what they all felt, all of those who were searching the area in the torrential rain. 'Shall I put the shoe on the list?'

The policeman who had made the find was standing in the same military posture as Frølich, at ease, so as not to feel the soaked clothes on his skin. 'There were a couple of empty plastic bags, too,' he commented.

'She was last seen on her way up to Holmlia,' Frølich said. 'And she was found less than five hundred metres from here.'

He pointed past the white bathing hut and across to the other side of the inlet. 'There,' he said, 'where the road bends and there is just the safety barrier leading down to the beach. Someone tipped her over the barrier. She was strangled somewhere close by.' He looked at his watch. 'Hope you can stand a bit more,' he mumbled. 'I have . . .' He cleared his throat as he searched for the right word. 'I'm afraid I have . . . an interview with a witness.'

He left them and strolled over to the car. They could think what they liked. There were more useful things he could do elsewhere.

* * *

He found an old plastic bag in the boot of his car and put it on the seat before getting in. He needed dry clothes and so drove home first. As he was unlocking the door he heard the telephone ringing in the sitting room. At once he remembered he had promised to phone Eva-Britt. He took the call on the cordless and continued to search for dry clothes while talking. Eva-Britt reminded him of the arrangement they had on Friday night. That was just what Frank had been dreading. 'I may be able to make it on Saturday instead,' he answered airily, taking a pair of dry jeans out of the wardrobe. The silence on the phone did not bode well. 'I know you don't like that,' he mumbled, wondering whether he had an ironed shirt. Doubtful. 'But I can't say no to Gunnarstranda, not on that day. When the man asks me to his mountain cabin, it's not a cabin, it's the Holy Grail.'

He found socks in the drawer and a pair without holes in the heel while Eva-Britt was gasping for air, wherever she was. Holy Grail or not, that was not the point. The point was that he was a past master in putting her in second place. It was humiliating and it made her doubt his feelings – it was the usual story. He put the cordless down on the window sill, lay on the bed and peeled the saturated trousers off his thighs as her voice cut through the room: 'Are you listening to what I am saying?'

Frank grabbed the phone. 'Oh shit,' he said.

'What?'

'I dropped the phone. Can you repeat the last thing you said?'

He wrenched off his trousers as her voice crackled like a radio. Eyed himself in the mirror. Too fat, too white. He picked up the phone again and raised it to his ear. 'I see that,' he said as she paused for breath. 'And I am really sorry. But can you do Saturday or not?'

She was stuttering with anger. This was the phase before she began to lay into him. He had to interrupt: 'Then I'll buy a bottle of red wine for you and some beer for me. I'll invite you to salted cod, bacon and mushroom ragout, which you can make – and I won't start work on Sunday until ten, I promise.'

He held the phone away from his ear before she progressed into mid-rant.

'Well,' he repeated. 'I'm afraid appeals won't help. I have to work on Sunday.' He put down the phone again, pulled on his dry trousers and buttoned up the fly. Then he lifted his trousers from the waistband and studied his stomach side on.

The telephone! He put it to his ear. It was dead. He hunted through the wardrobe, found a drip-dry shirt and inspected it – bit of a wrinkle on the breast pocket but it would have to do. He rang her and pulled faces at himself in the mirror as the phone rang. He let it ring forever. 'We must have been cut off,' Frank said before she could get a word in.

'At times you don't seem at all interested,' she bawled.

'Don't start all that again,' he parried. 'I promise to be here all Saturday evening. I promise not to be late. I promise to switch off the phone. I promise not to watch TV. I won't put on any 70s music. I will be fascinated by all the problems you're having at work. I won't hire a film. I promise to drink red wine with the meal. I will think up at least five compliments and I promise to light candles on the table. All right?'

'My goodness, you're such a romantic, aren't you,' her voice groaned.

'I can be if I want to,' Frank grinned, pulling faces at himself in the mirror. He was dry, and ought to be presentable enough for the force now.

17

Out of Shape

Georg Beck worked at the Nydalen Skills Centre, a kind of institution where most of the patients seemed to be psychologically handicapped. Frølich entered, but couldn't catch anyone's eye in reception. The young man sitting there was chewing gum and disappeared without bothering about the approaching policeman. Frølich ventured further into the low-ceilinged building and stopped a man in his forties coming out of a door. Frank assumed he worked there since he was carrying a file under his arm. A man with a short brown beard, a crooked mouth and a crooked fringe. An eloquent smile played on his lips at the mention of Georg Beck's name. Then he showed him the way through the corridors to a red door inscribed with ACTIVITY ROOM II in white letters.

Frølich knocked and went in. There were two people inside. A thin elderly woman was sitting in a wheelchair by a table. Georg Beck was leaning over her. The two of them were trying to glue together two pieces of cardboard. Beck was plump, medium height, with brown hair and a fine middle parting and kiss curls over his forehead. 'That's it, Stella,' he said in an amicable tone and with a wink to Frølich. Beck camouflaged the flab well with loose clothing: a blue V-neck jumper, baggy white cotton pants and sandals. He guided the elderly woman's hands towards one of the bits of the egg box on the table. 'Hold this, Stella,' he said with infinite patience. 'You've had your fingers in lots of things over the years, Stella. Grip this, that's it, yes. And now the tube of glue.'

The ageing woman in the wheelchair sat with her mouth half-open and concentrated. The egg box in one hand and the glue in the other. A drop of saliva gathered on her lower lip, stretched into a long, viscous thread of slime and slowly reached her lap before she had taken the decision to cast off.

'No, no, dear Stella!' the man said in an affected voice, wiping her mouth with paper and gently closing her mouth. 'We don't sit like that, do we?' Georg Beck winked at Frølich again. 'Not when we have strange men here!'

The old woman shrieked with laughter and a smile revealed bluish-grey false teeth. Her arms were so thin that the skin hung off her forearms. Her lined fingers were splayed out and she was staring at a point in the far distance.

'Now, now,' Beck reproved in a gentle tone. 'That's how to squeeze the tube. You can do it, Stella. Squeeze the tube! Not so hard, Stella! Not so hard. You've squeezed tubes before, Stella!'

He winked again at Frølich, straightened up and stood for a few seconds looking at the woman in the wheelchair. Her hands with the egg box and the tube of glue sank into her lap and stayed there, immobile. She sat unconcerned, with her mouth half-open staring ahead of her.

Beck shook his head in despair and turned to Frølich. 'Right, handsome, fire away!' he said producing a grin that exposed a large gap between his front teeth.

'It's about the party at Annabeth Ås's house.'

'Oh, my God, what a dramatic end!' Beck put on an affected expression. 'Come with me,' he exclaimed and wiggled his way to some free seats beneath the window. 'Don't bother about Stella. She can't hear anyway. I was there and, with my sense of timing, I left before it happened. That's what I call being off-form, not smelling a scandal when the word is written in capital letters and flashing neon lights.'

Beck gave the policeman a cool once-over and held out a chair for him. 'Whatever you do, Chief Inspector, don't rattle the handcuffs here or we'll all swoon!'

'What's your connection with Gerhardsen and Ås?' Frølich enquired.

'Oh, I just cast a bit of glamour over the gathering,' Beck said with a giggle. 'But Annabeth is so *lovely*. She's the one who arranges for me to go there. When she asks it's *simply not on* to say no. I only work freelance . . . for Vinterhagen; I don't have the *energy* for any more. But I do enough to be invited to parties. Then he brings out the best cognac, Bjørn does – the good-time Charlie.'

'The good-time Charlie?' Frølich asked.

'Whoops,' Beck exclaimed, putting a hand to his mouth. 'Have I said too much already? There you see – me and good-looking men, not a good combination.'

Frølich stared.

'I mean Bjørn's feelers were out for the poor girl, or his hands might be a more apt expression,' he said with a meaningful glance. 'My goodness, where that man has had his hands. It doesn't bear thinking about.'

'You mean he . . .'

'Yes, he was playing footsie under the table. What do you say to that? During the meal. With that poor girl, not that I am a complete innocent, and she wasn't either, I'm led to believe . . .' Beck laughed out loud and winked. '. . . Not that we need to go any deeper into that side of the case, eh? Anyway, Bjørn was sitting at the same table as Annabeth, wasn't he. Not that that made any difference. On the terrace he had one hand up her skirt.'

'Katrine Bratterud's?'

'Yes, I suppose that was her name.'

'You saw that?'

'Not only me. Annabeth did, too. She was grinding her teeth so hard we were beginning to think there were mice behind the walls.' He laughed again. 'And perhaps that turn of phrase says it all.'

'How did the girl react?'

'My God, I have no idea. I retreated – at once because Annabeth was clenching both fists and on her way to the terrace. I hadn't come to the party to ring for an ambulance. Anyway I sat down and started chatting to some other people.'

'But how . . . ?' Frølich searched for words. 'Were they being intimate? On the terrace? I mean Katrine and Gerhardsen – or did she seem to be rejecting him?'

'I have no idea. Maybe, maybe not. They didn't meet much resistance anyway – his hands I'm talking about.'

'But did you see how it finished up?'

'Look, handsome . . .'

Frølich cleared his throat. 'I mean, did you see what happened when fru Ås joined them?'

'No, and thank God I didn't. I would guess Annabeth made Bjørn control himself.'

'But if something had happened on the terrace, something *scandalous* . . . I presume you would have known?'

'Of course.'

'But you think the advances Gerhardsen made to the murder victim led to an emotional response from Annabeth Ås?'

'Lordie, the way you speak. *The murder victim.* I'm all on edge.' He gesticulated and put on a serious face. 'But yes, she was affected by the situation, there is no question.'

'Were you aware that the girl became ill during the party?'

'I heard about it and that is what I cannot forgive myself for. The scandal was already in full flow. I left straight afterwards.'

'You left the party alone?'

'No, there were five of us. It was so boring there. We went to Enka.' Beck winked. 'That is, we dropped three of them off at Smuget. Lasse and I went on. Lasse, he's my man of the moment.' He smiled.

'Who was in the car?'

'There was Bjørn, well oiled as always . . .'

'Annabeth's husband?'

'Yes, and there was the boyfriend of the girl we're talking about . . . a cutie with particularly attractive legs, and a woman who was clinging to him.'

'You dropped these three off at Smuget?'

'Yes, Bjørn and the woman and the athlete . . . Ole. Nice name, isn't it? I always go very solemn when I hear that name. I think of the violinist, Ole Bull, you know, the piece of music *The Herb Girl's Sunday*.'

'*The Herd Girl's Sunday*.'

Georg Beck gasped and patted his forehead. 'There you see. This is putting me all on edge.'

'Why didn't you and Lasse go to Smuget?'

'We wanted to go to Enka, but the others, above all Bjørn, wanted to go to a place with more of a hetero feel. So we dropped them off. Lasse and I went to Enka where we met another couple and we went back to my place at half past three, all four of us. I suppose, that's what you call an alibi, isn't it?' Beck put on a roguish smile and leaned forward. 'Would you like me to go into detail?'

Frølich sighed and tore a sheet from his notebook and passed it to Beck. 'Could you jot down the names here, please,' he said, and stood up.

18

Directions

The two policemen sat comparing the various witnesses' statements. Frølich fed all the material about the murder victim's movements into the computer. Gunnarstranda had been sitting and looking at the prison photo of Raymond Skau for a long time. 'This man is central,' he concluded.

'He's never at home, anyway,' Frølich remarked over his shoulder.

Gunnarstranda stood up. 'We'll have to try his door several times and if that does not produce results we'll ask someone to batter it down,' he continued, and went quiet when the telephone rang. A few seconds later he put down the receiver with a grunt and got to his feet again. 'That was Yttergjerde,' he mumbled in his excitement.

'What happened?' Frølich asked.

Gunnarstranda fumbled with his coat. He couldn't get it on fast enough.

'The clothes. They've found her clothes,' the police inspector said. With that he about-faced and went off in a flap. His coat fluttering behind him. His arms outstretched. Nose bent over like a beak. He resembled a hungry seagull floating on an up-draught behind a ferry, cheerfully pensive and excited at the same time.

* * *

Frølich turned off the road, drove into the gravel car park and came to a halt. The two detectives walked the last part, the older one a good two metres ahead. Yttergjerde and his men had blocked off the area beneath the road.

'This is not far from where she was found,' Frølich mumbled.

Yttergjerde met them. 'Floated along in a plastic bag,' he said. 'That is, it was bobbing up and down in the water between the rocks over there.' He pointed.

The two of them followed. The items of clothing lay on the ground packed in transparent plastic on which big puddles had collected in the drizzle. Frølich could make out a black bra, black panties, a grey shirt, a blouse, but only one shoe.

'The other shoe?' Gunnarstranda asked.

'This is all there was,' Yttergjerde said. 'And the bag, of course.' He pointed to a white plastic bag advertising the supermarket chain Joker in green writing. The colour was faded.

'And the bag was found there?' Gunnarstranda pointed to some large rocks at the water's edge. They jutted out into the water beneath the trunks of two enormous pine trees.

'Yes, and it was knotted, so I suppose it will go to the lab?'

'Did the bag float there or was it thrown?'

'Hard to say, if it wasn't thrown from up there . . .' Yttergjerde nodded towards the road where an ageing blue Volvo full of inquisitive youths was slowly trundling past. '. . . It can't have happened very far from here.'

'No jewellery, handbag or personal effects?'

Yttergjerde shook his head.

'We'd better have a look around,' Gunnarstranda said, walking up to the motorway. 'How far away are we from the place where the body was found?'

'Two or three kilometres.' Frølich, turning, nodded towards the west. 'And about the same distance to the area where Henning and Katrine were parked.'

'The killer threw the clothes first, then the body?'

'That's possible,' Frølich mused. 'Depends which way the car was going.' He looked up and down the road. 'The plastic bag on the right hand side of the road, the body on the left . . .'

'If the car was going west from here towards Oslo city centre,' Gunnarstranda added. 'Henning Kramer said the girl walked up towards Holmlia, and if she was picked up there, the car must have been on its way out of Oslo. In that case he got rid of the body first and then the clothes?'

They got into the car. Frølich started the engine. 'Did you notice the clothes?' he asked.

Gunnarstranda: 'What do you mean?'

'Is it significant? I think it looked as though she had undressed herself.'

'Disagree,' said Gunnarstranda. 'The clothes didn't seem to have been ripped to shreds, which is quite another matter. We'll have to see what the lab people say.'

Frølich nodded, drove out of the car park and headed back towards Oslo city centre. As they approached Hvervenbukta Frølich slowed down and pulled into the side. On the left they could make out the white bathing hut on the jetty, the green lawns leading up to the car parks and the pine-clad ridge of Ljanskollen.

'No problem at all,' Frølich said. 'If the killer drove as we have just done and pulled in where we are now, he must have carried her across the road and then thrown her over the safety barrier.'

'That suggests then the car was going in the opposite direction,' Gunnarstranda said. 'So the killer drags Katrine into the car, rapes and strangles her, strips her, drives seven or eight hundred metres down the road, stops, lifts her over the barrier, gets back in, drives on and . . .'

'In that case the driver would have had to stop in the middle of the bend,' Frølich interrupted. 'There is nowhere to pull in,' he pointed. 'Would you have stopped in the middle of the carriageway to get rid of a body?'

'Maybe in the middle of the night,' Gunnarstranda said, but was sceptical, and added: 'There's something not right with this.'

'It's much more likely that he parked here,' Frølich opined. 'On this side of the road.' He glanced at his boss. 'Kramer came this way,' he stated with emphasis.

Gunnarstranda returned a cryptic smile. 'Whichever way the killer was going, this is the place to stop,' he concluded. 'If he was driving towards us, towards Oslo, if he swung over on to this side of the road and pulled up, why did he carry her over to the other side of the road?' Gunnarstranda wondered aloud. 'He could have dumped her here in the ditch. No,' he decided. 'The killer must have been coming from the other direction, from Oslo – and stopped in the bend.'

They got out of the car. They crossed the road and looked over the barrier and down on to the crag where Katrine Bratterud's body had been found a few days before.

Gunnarstranda: 'If the car came from Oslo, that may fit with Kramer's statement. On the other hand, the killer may have disposed of the body and the clothes in this way so as to confuse us.'

Frølich shrugged. A car passed them and he had to shout to be heard over the noise. 'It all depends on when and where she was murdered. If she was picked up while she was walking up towards Holmlia and was murdered somewhere between there and this place, I assume she would have been killed in the car park up there.' He nodded towards the other side of the inlet where two cars were parked. 'Then the same car kept going and the driver threw the body out here first and got rid of the clothes later where Yttergjerde found them.'

Gunnarstranda leaned over the barrier and peered down. 'But no attempt was made to hide the body.' He thought aloud: 'The body was found without any jewellery, but there was no jewellery in the bag, either. So . . .'

'The killer seems very cold-blooded,' Frølich concluded. 'Cold-blooded with a singleness of purpose. Clothes separate, jewellery separate and the body separate.'

He cast a last glance over the fjord and followed Gunnarstranda, who was already on his way to the car.

'There are a couple of things I don't like about this theory,' the police inspector said as they drove on.

Frølich: 'Which theory?'

'That the killer was coming from Oslo. The problem is that we seem to be groping in the dark. If the car came east from Oslo the killer might be in Sweden now and we would be none the wiser.'

19

Foreground – Background

She was sitting and waiting at their usual table at the back of the restaurant. She must have been sitting there for a while because there was a half-empty bottle of Farris mineral water beside her. The sunlight from outside made her thick, dark hair shine. She was reading, and had already seen him because she was packing away her papers. He gave the cloakroom attendant his denim jacket, having put his wallet in his back pocket first.

They gazed at each other. She was wearing a light summer dress. It was different. She tended to dress more formally on weekdays. He stood for a couple of seconds and studied her; her shoulders were tanned, summer-brown, golden.

'The usual?' she asked.

He nodded and sat down.

'Good,' she said. 'I've already ordered.'

'What do you think of tattoos?' he asked.

She raised her eyebrows in query. 'You're not telling me you have . . . ?'

'No, I mean for you. Have you ever thought about it? Having a tattoo?'

She shook her head. 'Me with my job?' She pushed out one shoulder and peered down at it as though there were a design there. 'Me with my image . . .'

'The murdered girl had a tattoo, a big tattoo on her stomach.' His hand circled his stomach.

Eva-Britt looked at him sideways. 'Do you think it's sexy, Frankie?'

'Maybe. But not on a dead body. But what do you think? Could it be tasteful?'

'If you're a stripper, maybe.' She made room for the waiter to place the food on the table. 'But I'm not,' she added and began to sprinkle parmesan cheese over the spaghetti.

'Lena has a tattoo, I gather,' Frank reminded her. Lena was Eva-Britt's girlfriend from way back.

Eva-Britt reconsidered the idea. 'It might be tasteful,' she decided.

'Because Lena's got one?'

'No, Lena has quite a tasteful motif. It's a comic figure. The little yellow bird with the big head . . .'

Frank had no idea who she meant.

'In those old Daffy Duck comics,' Eva-Britt said. 'The bird that always fought with the cat.'

'Tweety and Sylvester,' Frank said.

'Mm,' Eva-Britt nodded. 'Tweety.' She pointed to her bare shoulder. Lena has a tattoo of Tweety here. It's quite tasteful because it's a bit downmarket. And then it's quite funny. Roses and birds and that sort of thing are worse because they are supposed to be sexy. It means you have to think about what clothes you wear. In my job you can't walk around with a cartoon on your shoulder. As a woman . . .'

'What's so special about your job?'

'Are you being sarky?'

'No,' Frank assured her. 'I'm curious. I'm thinking about this girl with the large flower on her stomach.'

'Well, she could always cover that one up,' Eva-Britt nodded. 'But being the manager of a medium-sized company with many male colleagues . . .' She threw him a lopsided smile and shook her head. 'I can't provoke men into fantasizing about my body, Frankie. A tattoo is downright unthinkable.'

'So you have considered having one?'

She glanced up, but ignored the question. 'And that's without even mentioning the fact that tattoos are hard to remove. I just consider them ugly. I once saw a young woman in Felix. She had a snake tattooed over her leg, a python wrapped around her thigh going down under her knee. Every single man she meets will be fantasizing about where the rest of the snake is. Do you understand? I'm sure it's fun for her when she is young and crazy and attractive. But she won't ever be able to last a day in a serious job that demands respect and professional distance.'

'Now I don't understand what you mean,' Frank said. 'I thought you were for women's rights and against sexual harassment.'

'But I am!'

'But should it count against her that she's got a snake tattoo that excites men's fantasies?'

'Listen to what I'm saying. It should not count against her, but she sidelines herself because every man will focus on her sexuality more than her other qualities when he meets her.'

'Hm,' Frank said.

'Have you learned something new?'

'Don't know,' Frank said. 'You have a point.'

'Just imagine,' Eva-Britt went on. 'I can also feel sexy, feel like being sexy . . .'

'Bring it on,' Frank said contentedly.

She ignored him. 'But why should I paste it all over my body and never be able to free myself from it again?'

Frank grew serious. 'What I'm wondering is whether the tattoo says anything about her.'

Eva-Britt smiled. 'And what do you think?'

He deliberated. 'I think she was trying to create a new life for herself. Everyone says that. She was trying to find freedom.'

'But then a symbol of that kind can be interpreted in a great many ways,' Eva-Britt said. 'If the tattoo is old, she may have regretted ever having it done. But it could also be a useful reminder.'

'Useful?'

'A kind of stigma, the symbol of something that should never be repeated.'

He absorbed her comments. 'You're on the ball today,' Frank said. He started to eat as well, but was soon lost in thought again.

Eva-Britt: 'What are you thinking about?'

'Ragnar Travås says you can become addicted to tattoos, like cigarettes.'

'Cigarettes?'

'Yes, he says one tattoo is fine, two is OK too, but three – then you're hooked. It's just a question of time before the whole of your body is decorated.'

'That is definitely grim. People like that look as though they have been made in a factory.'

He nodded.

'Talk about something else, Frankie,' Eva-Britt said with raised fork. 'Just don't talk about going to the cabin with that mad boss of yours.'

Frank gulped. 'What do you feel like doing afterwards?' he asked at length.

'Cinema,' she said.

'To see what?'

Eva-Britt put on a mischievous smile. 'It doesn't matter so long as it's sexy.'

20

Dust Thou Art, and to Dust Shalt Thou Return

The previous day might have been wet, but this day was drier than white wine. Police Inspector Gunnarstranda rolled down the car window and watched the sturdy figure of Frank Frølich approaching. The car park was empty apart from the odd car frying in the sun. Through the opening in the cypress hedge that divided the car park from the cemetery came a female gardener. She was pulling off a pair of filthy gardening gloves and plodding around in shorts and heavy boots covered in soil and clay. Clumps of earth fell off, leaving a trail behind her. She wiped the sweat off her brow and lit a cigarette which she stood smoking while staring pensively at the ground. A minibus trundled into the car park, passed the gardener, and Frølich too, before parking. A logo with the name of the rehab centre was painted in large, hazy, colourful letters on the side of the bus: VINTERHAGEN. A crowd of well-dressed young people piled out. They seemed fragile in their fine clothes, almost as though they had been rolled in starch to ensure that they remained erect. Frølich gave them a nod. The youths looked around with their hands buried deep in their trouser pockets before ambling off to the chapel where a gentleman in dark clothes from the funeral parlour was waiting for them. Ole Eidesen was there too. He stood with his nose in a booklet for the funeral ceremony. He was dressed in black.

Frølich got into Gunnarstranda's car bringing with him a strong smell of deodorant and sweat. 'Those are the VIPs,' he mumbled, nodding towards the youths in front of the chapel. 'Shall we go in?'

Gunnarstranda shook his head. 'Let them have half an hour to themselves.'

Frølich rolled down his window. 'Christ, it's hot,' he groaned. 'And now I have done most of this area, but there's still no sign of Raymond Skau.'

The youths from the minibus stood hanging around the entrance to the chapel.

'Loads of bloody great gravestones here,' Frølich said at length.

'You don't say!'

'Yes, obelixes and stuff.'

'Obelisks.'

'It was wordplay. A comic series.'

'Really?'

'A Gaul, a fat guy who carries around obelisks on his back – called Obelix.'

'Well, I never.'

'Yes, indeed.'

'Well, well.'

'Have you seen anyone?' Frølich asked.

'Henning Kramer, Annabeth Ås and the crew you saw from the centre. Ole Eidesen is around . . .' Gunnarstranda motioned towards the entrance where Eidesen had gone in.

'Talked to anyone?'

'No.'

'Perhaps we ought to give Kramer another grilling?'

'Not today. Besides, we'd better find holes in his statement first.'

'Seen anything of Gerhardsen?' Frølich asked.

Gunnarstranda checked his watch. 'He's still got a couple of minutes.'

'Do you think her mother's here?'

'I would assume so. After all, she is the next of kin.'

'Terrible business,' Frølich mumbled. 'Terrible business.'

'I suppose we should go through the park grounds again,' Gunnarstranda said.

'Should we go in and say hello to her mother?'

'I would like to, but this is not the time or place to do aggressive police work.'

'Right,' Frølich said, wiping the sweat with a tissue he produced from his jacket pocket. 'Right,' he repeated. 'I suppose that means I'll have to drive to her place.'

'For the time being the grounds seem quite appealing,' Gunnarstranda said.

'I don't think so.'

'Should I interpret that as a no to searching the grounds again?'

'Needle in a haystack.'

'Do you have any ambitions to be a public prosecutor at some point?'

'And that's why I should sweat in the grounds?'

'Not necessarily, but if there's any point in checking anything to do with this poor girl, there must be an underlying theory that the assailant is sneaking around in the bushes here or is sitting in the chapel listening to what a wonderful person he has destroyed. Look at Silver Fox . . .'

Gunnarstranda stopped talking and both policemen followed Sigrid Haugom with their eyes. She closed the door of a parked Mercedes. Frølich whistled. 'Jeez, what a body,' he mumbled.

'She's too old for you, Frølich. That's Sigrid Haugom. Katrine's confidante. The one who asked me if I liked my name.'

'Who do you think the old codger is?'

Gunnarstranda rolled his shoulders. 'Tax inspector from the outer isles – who knows. But the odds are it's her husband. In which case his name is Erik Haugom.'

Both men followed the couple with their eyes. She was graceful, with an hourglass figure, cultured and suitably dressed for the occasion; she even wore a black shawl over her shoulders. He seemed like a good-looking guy, straight back, firm backside with a sullen grin on his ruddy face.

'Guess what his job is,' Gunnarstranda said.

Frølich took his time to answer. Both policemen were following the couple with their eyes. As they passed the last parked car before the chapel, the man stopped, took a comb from his back pocket and combed his hair back in the reflection from the car window.

'No idea,' Frølich concluded.

'They live in Grefsen in an architect-designed house full of old junk they have accumulated from antiques auctions here and in London. The son studies at Yale and they each have a car of their own. He has a Mercedes; she has a BMW.'

'Suppose she must be trying to put something back,' Frølich mumbled. 'Since she rehabilitates drug addicts.'

'But how do you think he earns his living?'

'No idea.'

'Doctor, of course.'

'Doctor?' Frølich sneered. 'I know who the bugger is!'

'You do?' Gunnar said, uninterested.

'Yes, Erik Haugom? Doctor? He's a bloody celeb. The guy has his own column in several newspapers!'

Gunnarstranda stared at Frølich. His expression was reminiscent of someone who had just sampled tainted food. 'Did you say celeb? Do you use such words?'

Frølich was not listening. His face was one big, moist grin. 'I still read Haugom's columns. He calls himself a sexologist. The guy knows everything that is worth knowing about anal sex, group sex, urine sex . . . you name it.' He paused as though remembering something. 'They look quite respectable,' he mumbled. 'I mean . . . she's . . .'

Gunnarstranda – who was still observing the other policeman as if he were an object he would have to tolerate for the time being, but which he had high hopes would soon be off his hands – opened his mouth and said in a toneless but earnest voice, 'Don't come out with any more idiocies now.'

'No.' Frølich went quiet.

They sat watching the couple greet the man from the funeral

parlour. A gust of wind caught Sigrid Haugom's silver hair and she reacted with an elegant toss of the head. They went inside.

'Come on then,' Gunnarstranda said.

'Eh?'

'Say what you have to say.'

'You don't like me saying these things.'

'But say it anyway, for Christ's sake.'

Frølich cleared his throat. 'Well, she's a cracker, despite being fifty-something, isn't she? With that ass, I mean, she's a cracker.' He paused.

'Well?'

'Well, just imagine all that guy knows about sex . . .'

'Shut up!'

'I told you you didn't like the comments I make.'

'I'm going for a walk,' Gunnarstranda said, and got out. He crossed the car park and followed the female gardener who was strolling towards a grave. She knelt down and began to remove stubborn blades of wheat grass and goutweed from between the low-growing asters and sea lavender. Gunnarstranda threw his jacket over his shoulder and breathed in the perfume of freshly mown grass and sweet summer flowers mixed with the faint stench of decomposition. The silence surrounding the graves made him think of Edel. He strolled down to her grave. On the way he passed an open grave and a pile of earth covered with a tarpaulin. He went on to the area where Edel's urn was kept. The mauve carpet phlox he had planted the previous year had grown so big that it had spread across the little bed in front of the gravestone and on to the lawn. There were still a few small mauve flowers glistening between the seed pods against the green background. He crouched down and closed his eyes for a few seconds. He saw her in front of a window watering a potted plant. He opened his eyes and tried to remember when that had been and why he could visualize that particular image. But once it was gone, he couldn't picture it as clearly. He was unable to say how old she had been then or what clothes she had been wearing. Nor could he recall the type of plant she had been watering.

He turned away from the grave and strolled back towards the chapel, walked past it and by the south side where another funeral had just finished; grief-stricken mourners were observing each other, relaying their condolences and holding each other's hands. Gunnarstranda felt out of place and withdrew. A thin man in filthy jeans was sitting beside a mower on a lawn some distance away.

Gunnarstranda paused in the middle of one of the gravel paths that ran as straight as an arrow up to the huge cemetery. The path was broken by numerous other small paths crossing it and creating small squares all over the grounds, plots fenced off by tall, green cypress hedges. Some elderly women were walking down; a tractor crossed the path right in front of them, then re-crossed the path, closer this time. Gunnarstranda could see the hopelessness of the task of looking out for suspicious persons in the grounds. He walked around the chapel. In the east wall of the crematorium there were the urns of the first members of the Norwegian Crematorium Association. He stepped closer and tried to decipher the inscriptions on the urns. All of a sudden he recognized a name, an elderly neighbour from his boyhood days in Grünerløkka. He read the man's name once more and experienced a strange feeling of awe.

So this was where he had ended up. Gunnarstranda was reminded with a smile of the old crackpot in the window at the top of Markveien shouting propaganda for the crematorium. *I'm telling you, you young whippersnappers, the crematorium is the future!* he had screamed – and earned himself gales of laughter. Now he was here on the stand of honour – a handful of ashes in a clay pot.

Gunnarstranda kept walking and rounded the corner just in time to see Bjørn Gerhardsen sneaking in through the chapel door.

21

Mental Arithmetic

Frank Frølich found a gap for his car in Torggata between a kebab house and one of the greengrocers with a better selection of exotic vegetables. He remembered he should have gone shopping, but resisted the temptation, crossed the street and continued down the opposite pavement. A young man wearing colourful shorts and a helmet on his head was slalom-cycling between pedestrians. Frølich wormed his way through a group of Africans in expensive leather jackets embroiled in a heated discussion. A parked van was blocking the traffic. It was a clapped-out Toyota Hiace with large rusty holes in the sides. The rear door was open wide and the back of the van was crammed full with slaughtered animals. Arab-looking boys lifted the meat up on to their shoulders and ran a shuttle service between the van and one of the shops. Smuggled meat from Sweden, Frølich reckoned, and stood watching the unloading for a few seconds. In the end he tore himself away and walked up Bernt Ankers gate to the specialist publishing house where Merethe Fossum worked. He came to a general office with a central switchboard on the ground floor. The man in the office wore a uniform and belonged to a security service with a handcuff as a logo. He grabbed a telephone and asked Frølich if he was expected. Frølich took a risk. 'Yes,' he said. The man in the uniform rang through and passed the receiver to Frølich who put it to his ear and heard a phone ring twice. Merethe Fossum's voice was deep and a little husky. Sexy, thought Frølich, and asked if he could go up. She said it was time for lunch anyway and suggested he found himself a seat in the canteen.

He was shown to the basement by the guard. The company canteen was of the self-service variety with a long counter where you could help yourself to slices of bread and dry, dense rolls with traditional Norwegian *pålegg*: dark mutton sausage, liver paste and curved cuts of cheese garnished with red pepper. With your coffee you could have chocolate cookies in a plastic wrapper. A fat matronly type wearing a white apron asked for five kroner for a cup of coffee which looked as black and impenetrable as used oil from an old tractor. Frølich peeped into the milk jug beside the cash desk. It was empty. He coughed. Fatty knew what was required without turning. She took a red carton of milk from the bench behind the counter and placed it in front of him. He poured in a substantial quantity of milk but did not discern a hint of greyer tones in the black liquid.

It was clearly a kind of lunch break. A steady flow of people came down the stairs and the canteen began to fill up. Frølich found an unoccupied table by the entrance so that Merethe Fossum would not have any problems identifying him. As soon as she appeared he knew it was her. The woman cast tentative glances around the room until they found eye contact. She was delicate, slim and spry, not over one-sixty in height and dressed smartly in a black skirt with matching jacket. She put a pack of open sandwiches on the counter and poured herself a cup of coffee. He got up and cleared his throat. She spun round and her hair whirled around her head like in a commercial.

Her smile was inquisitive, almost quizzical. Then she sat down, slunk on to the chair and lazily arranged her elegant legs, revealing a generous strip of flesh above the knee. Her long fingers with red nails opened the sophisticated wrapping around the sandwich. She had fine, narrow hands with white, plump skin around the wrists. She studied the sandwiches beneath lowered eyelids, in secret. A lock of hair fell from over her ear and in front of her sensitive face.

Frank Frølich was in raptures. He couldn't take his eyes off her. Such pure and sensual features. Her face was oval, her eyes almond-shaped and ice-blue, her nose straight, her mouth broad and formed like Cupid's bow. The skin on her neck was more golden than white.

'You met Katrine Bratterud at a party in Annabeth Ås's house, I believe,' Frølich stammered, feeling like an overgrown gorilla beside this delicate, feminine apparition. He was sweating because she was sitting so close.

She glanced up and gave a quick nod. Hot energy poured out of her. The heat was absorbed by his jumper; that was what was making him sweat, he thought.

'And Ole,' she said with some reluctance.

'Ole Eidesen?'

'Yes, I didn't talk much to her; she left early on. But Ole is fantastic.'

In Frølich's mind her points tally sank from 99 to 89. He pretended to be studying his notes, but stole furtive glances as she raised her coffee cup and waved to a colleague.

'To what did you owe your invitation?' he asked, clearing his throat again. 'I mean why were you invited?'

'I had a few hours there, of teaching at the rehab centre. Most of them in the winter.'

'You're a teacher?'

'My major was in literary science. That's what I would really like to do.' She embraced the room with her glance. 'Began here in March, but I had a few hours of Norwegian, English and Social Studies at Vinterhagen in the winter.' She smiled.

'Did you teach Katrine?'

'No, she was working, of course, in the last phase. I had only seen her on the odd occasion before, from a distance. Don't think she knew me.'

The silence came between them.

'Nice canteen,' he said in panic, looking around.

'I don't like it,' she laughed. 'But I love the coffee.' Frølich took another ten points off for her remark about the coffee, but put her up fifteen points for beautiful teeth in an enigmatic smile. He loosened his tie, breathed in and braced himself to meet her sparkling blue eyes. She was holding a slice of bread between her slim fingers. For a few seconds she looked around for her colleagues who had gone to the back of the room. Then she turned back to the policeman and raised the sandwich to her mouth. Frølich looked up the second she opened her mouth and crushed the slice of bread into a lump of dough, and grey mutton sausage and green gherkin oozed to the side. She didn't take a bite, she stuffed the whole lot in and chewed it so that saliva and breadcrumbs seeped out between her lips. This was soon slurped back in, and the moment their eyes met she began to speak with her mouth full of food. She talked about Annabeth Ås and her house, about what wonderful people she and Gerhardsen were, and then she began to talk about the weather, the rain and how dreadful it was when your legs were sodden. Frølich's eyes hung on her broad mouth. His hands were trembling, but he couldn't quite tear his eyes away from the wet, open mouth. Her right cheek stretched like elastic. She had another open sandwich ready; she folded it like the previous one, stuffed it in and kept talking. Something about an umbrella, yes, it must have been something to do with an umbrella. Her slim fingers kneaded more bread; she shoved it in, to join the rest of the food creating a bulge in her cheek. She took a drink. Slurped the coffee. And then it was over. She folded up the greaseproof paper and licked her fingers clean. Frølich breathed out, through his nose. He didn't quite know what he had been through, he just knew that it was over – and he did not want to go through it a second time.

'You left the party early,' he said quickly.
'Who?'
'You and some others.'
'Yes, we went to the city centre.'
'Who?'

'Ole and I.'

'Any others?'

'Yes, there were five of us in the car. But the two gay men wanted to go to a gay place, and neither Bjørn nor Ole wanted to go there. I think that's fine, I do – gay bars and all that sort of thing. All the gay men I know are super.'

'So there were you, Ole, Bjørn Gerhardsen and two other men?'

'Yes, Goggen and Lasse. They're an item.'

'So what happened?'

'We went to Smuget. That is, Ole and I did.'

'Gerhardsen?'

'I have no idea.'

'Didn't he go into Smuget with you?'

'I'm sure he did. But I was with Ole and it was packed in there. I didn't see anyone I knew.'

'But you're not sure if Gerhardsen went in with you?'

'Why wouldn't he have done?'

'We-e-ell,' Frølich said. 'What happened then?'

'We left a bit later. Went back to my place.' She winked. 'Don't tell anyone. I promised I would keep my mouth shut.'

'You and Eidesen went back to your place, and he stayed with you?'

'Yes.'

Frølich stared and could feel his cheeks burning. Merethe Fossum picked her teeth with the nail of one of her slim fingers. She didn't manage to get hold of what she was looking for straightaway. So she opened her mouth and buried her finger in the recesses of her mouth, stretching her lips into a grotesque grimace.

'At what time?'

She shrugged and broke off from her excavations so that she could speak. 'It was light anyway. Maybe four o'clock.'

'Are you sure of the time?'

'No.' She sent him a vacant grin and, when she saw the policeman's face, added: 'I'm sorry. I don't know.'

'Do you know what time it was when you got to your flat?'

'A bit later. I'm so sorry, but I didn't look at my watch at all.'

'How long did he stay at yours?'

Merethe Fossum peered at a chunk of food on one of her red nails. She licked it off. 'Until eleven, or twelve, in the morning. Don't remember. Is it important?'

Frølich jotted down words, hardly knowing what to write, and made a private mental note of minus a hundred points.

He looked up. 'This is pretty important,' he said. 'Ole Eidesen was with you from midnight until eleven o'clock the next morning. Have I understood you correctly?'

She nodded.

'And he didn't leave the flat during that time?'

'I would have noticed.' She spoke with a faint, dreamy smile.

'He says you did not spend the night together.'

'Oh, God, poor boy.'

'I beg your pardon.'

She laughed. 'I suppose he's sticking to our agreement. We agreed we would keep it a secret. Well, now she can't find out anything anyway. She's dead, isn't she. The poor thing. It's a terrible business. But you have to think of those left behind. Ole has not had an easy time, either, has he? When the person you're with ends up like that.'

'That's true.'

'Indeed it is!'

'Have you kept in touch since?'

'Dear God,' Merethe sighed.

'Sorry?'

She was grinning, but caught herself. '. . . I mean, do I look like a one-night stand?'

Frølich regarded her in silence.

'I have talked to him, once. Forgive me if it is wrong to do that, but this is not so easy . . .'

'Have you at any time, in any form or manner, discussed with

Ole what you should say to the police about your movements that night?'

Frølich made a note before she answered. 'No,' she said. 'Not at all.'

'Well, that's a bit strange.'

'Why is it strange?'

'His girlfriend has been murdered, the police are investigating, what on earth did you talk about if this case did not feature in your conversations?'

She stared at Frølich with big eyes. 'Is that wrong too? To invite a guy to the cinema?'

Strolling past the uniformed receptionist a little later Frølich checked his jacket pocket for his mobile. It wasn't there. He stopped. Could he have left it in the canteen? Either there or in the car. He turned and looked at the stairs. In the car, he thought. It could be in the car and, if it is, I won't have to go down there again. He winked at the guard and left.

22

The Conversation in
the Greenhouse

After the telephone call from Frølich, Gunnarstranda sat in the car looking out of the window. He was thinking about the funeral ceremony, the faces of those who had passed him on their way into the church. He thought about Gerhardsen and his energetic spouse. The clock on the wall above the door was reflected in the window. A few hours had passed now. It was time to visit Vinterhagen again.

On locking his car door half an hour later and gazing across the gravelled car park he wondered whether his idea would be a waste of time after all. A dense stillness hung over the large area. Everyone must have taken the day off because of the funeral. He stuffed his hands in his jacket pockets and walked along the same path he and Frølich had walked a few days earlier, but now he didn't meet a single person. He rounded the corner of the yellow accommodation hall and saw the dark, lifeless windows of the office building. He pulled up and decided to use the opportunity to have a look around. He searched for a cigarette end from his pocket, lit up and strolled around the vegetable patch by the greenhouse. The potatoes had been earthed up at some point. It had obviously been done with a small fork or a spade. Someone had been very thorough. Other rows had been earthed up so badly that the yield would be poor. The leeks and onions were pale, thin and straggly. They needed more nitrogen. The carrots were looking good. He walked on to the greenhouse and tried the door. It wasn't locked. He flicked the cigarette into a pile of sand and entered.

He stood avidly breathing in the warm, heavy, moist air of the greenhouse. Cucumbers and lettuces were being grown. Overhead, on the ridge, there were ventilation grilles which let in a fresh breath of cooler air that brushed his head. He walked down between two lines of potting tables and saw someone at the back, by the far wall. It was Annabeth Ås. She had changed out of her dark funeral clothes into a green overall, a flannel shirt and high green boots. She was watering plants, walking along the potting tables with a hose pipe to which a shower head had been attached. He coughed, but she didn't hear. He coughed again.

'Oh,' she gasped as she turned round. 'You gave me a start!'

'I didn't think the funeral was the right place to bother you,' Gunnarstranda said.

'I know why you've come,' Annabeth said, resigned, and continued her watering. 'My God, Bjørn and I have had this showdown so many times I had an inkling it would re-appear. Let me make it quite clear so that we can avoid all the pomposity and the embarrassing pauses. Bjørn, my husband, is a big boy. Yes, he did confess to me that he had used her in a moment of weakness. If I hadn't already been working at getting the poor girl on to an even keel, I would have dumped her in another institution. I'm telling you that straight. It is no secret.'

'But why didn't you do that?' Gunnarstranda asked, cleaning the dry leaves of some of the plants on the table.

'You might well ask. It's always easy to ask when it's all over. Don't you think I wanted to do that? Don't you think I considered the problem? But she liked it with us. She trusted us. She could function here, Gunnarstranda. Believe me, it wasn't easy.'

Annabeth lifted the hose pipe and dragged it along with her.

'I am quite sure it wasn't easy,' Gunnarstranda broke in again. 'But it can't have been right, either. The decision to keep Katrine as a patient when your husband was having a relationship with her could never have been right.'

'See!' Annabeth waved the hose pipe about angrily. 'There you go with your accusations. Why do you do that?' She sent the policeman a fierce look and continued in an aggressive tone. 'You say that because she was murdered. If this hadn't happened no one would have been any the wiser. She wasn't suffering any extra pressure. She was completely rehabilitated. The treatment was a success. So it hadn't been wrong to keep her.'

Gunnarstranda went quiet. She had a point. She glared at him from the other side of the potting table.

'Katrine had all the facilities she needed to succeed here. We had her confidence. She wanted to kick the habit. We could have sent her to other professionals – to a place where she had to live with other patients and work with new staff, but there would have been no guarantee that she would have managed any better. Well, what is done is done. No one can undo the dreadful mistake my husband committed in a moment of weakness.'

'A moment of weakness?' Gunnarstranda queried.

'Yes . . . going to a place like that – a massage parlour. But would his weakness at that time, so long ago, stand in the way of Katrine's chances of succeeding?' Annabeth tilted her head as though she were talking to a close friend. 'Would that have been right?' she asked in a gentle voice.

Gunnarstranda smiled with one side of his mouth. 'That's one way of looking at it,' he conceded. 'But it's not necessarily a right way of looking at it. You don't know how she would have fared with her treatment elsewhere. You don't know if she would have succeeded just as well.'

'But can't you hear what I'm saying?' Annabeth almost screamed. 'Katrine had every chance to succeed here. We were the ones who cured her. We were the ones who laid the world at her feet!'

'It was while she was here that she was murdered,' Gunnarstranda interrupted with annoyance.

Annabeth shut her mouth and threw the hosepipe down on the baked-earth floor. They eyeballed each other in the silence that followed.

There was no point discussing investigative theory with this woman, the policeman thought. He had a feeling he knew what she was after. It wasn't the desire to save Katrine Bratterud that had driven this woman to keep her as a patient. It had been the chance to succeed that had driven her. That and the council subsidy that must have come with the girl. And in her hunt for success Annabeth had swallowed camels, or, to be more precise, she had shut her eyes to her own professional ethics. 'No one knows for the moment what happened that night,' he said in a milder tone. 'No one knows why Katrine had to be buried today. So we had better not make any allegations. Let us just state that you had a patient who perhaps should not have been treated here. Were there others apart from you who knew about your husband's previous . . . experiences with Katrine?'

'No.'

'How can you be so sure?'

'Because such rumours cannot be kept secret in a place like this.'

'Did you ever take up this matter with Katrine?'

'Never.'

'You never mentioned a thing about it?'

'No.'

'Did she ever take the matter up with you?'

Annabeth, eyes closed, shook her head. 'No, never.'

Never, mused Gunnarstranda. Katrine must have known she knew. And conversely, the certainty that her husband had exploited her patient's social needs must have coloured the atmosphere every single time Annabeth met Katrine. And the patient, on her side, must have felt it. Anything else would be inconceivable.

The water from the hose reached his shoes and ran down both sides of the flagstone path he was standing on. 'Shall we turn off the water?' he said, trudging back to the tap attached to the hosepipe. He turned it off, straightened his back and observed her. She had not moved from the spot. 'I know you don't like talking about this,' Gunnarstranda said. 'But I'm obliged to probe for motives. If for a moment we assume that Katrine was an unscrupulous woman one could imagine that this relationship – I mean the fact that your husband as chairman had received sexual favours from Katrine . . .' He paused for a few seconds when she closed both eyes. Then went on: '. . . we might imagine that this fact gave Katrine a hold over your husband. Would she have blackmailed your husband or tried to exploit this hold she had?'

'Never.'

'You seem very sure.'

Annabeth took off her gloves and strolled over to him. 'My good man, Katrine wanted to be cured. That was why I kept her as a patient. Katrine was perhaps the most motivated client I have ever met. Just the very idea of blackmailing Bjørn – that would never have occurred to her.'

'But what you're saying now you could be saying to cover up the fact that pressure was applied.'

'Why would I cover anything up if she had gone as far as black-mailing Bjørn?'

'Because blackmail would give Bjørn a motive for murdering her.'

'Ha,' Annabeth laughed haughtily. 'Now you're chasing shadows. Bjørn! Would Bjørn have killed Katrine?' She laughed again. 'Excuse me, but the thought is too ridiculous. Believe me, Gunnarstranda. Bjørn Gerhardsen can crunch numbers and he might sneak into some dingy place to vent his male sexuality. But other than that . . . ? When we go fishing in Sørland in the summer it's me who has to kill the fish he catches. If there's a mouse in the trap in our mountain cabin, he can't even look at it. I have to clean up. The truth about Bjørn is that he's a good boy but as soft as marsh-mallow.'

Gunnarstranda didn't speak. He was thinking about what she had said while they were walking beside the potting tables and out into the fresh weather. Good boy, soft as marshmallow. She was demeaning her husband's masculinity.

They strolled by the vegetable plot towards the car park.

'Believe me, Gunnarstranda, your speculations are absurd. Katrine wanted to be rehabilitated. She chose us because we could help her.'

The policeman stopped and looked into her eyes. 'Did you at any point leave the party you organized on that Saturday?'

She still had a faint smile on her face as she shook her head. 'Not for a minute. Bjørn left with Georg Beck and a few others. He's already told you, I understand. But he returned, as soft and affectionate as the little kitten he is when he's been away from Mummy for more than two hours.'

Gunnarstranda studied her for a while before asking, 'Do you remember what time it was when he left?'

'Around midnight. He came back alone a bit before four and helped me clear up.'

'Did anyone else leave the party in the course of the evening?'

'No, as a matter of fact they didn't. There was a sort of mass departure at half past two, but it was some time before everyone had been packed off happily in taxis. It took an hour, maybe more.'

23

The Stripper

The waiting room was packed with people. Frølich tried to find his bearings. An elderly man in a green buttoned-up parka and trousers that looked like pyjamas gave a hollow, gurgling cough. The policeman looked away. His gaze fell on another old man, grey and pale with thick stubble and greasy, unkempt hair. A boy was sitting on his mother's lap. An elderly woman sat beside them knitting. Beside her was another elderly woman wearing a headscarf. She had thick brown stockings on her legs and worn slippers on her feet. Frølich was reminded of Erik Haugom's reputation as a sexologist and for a brief instant wondered what sexual problems these patients were grappling with.

A woman dressed in white looked up from what she was doing. 'Please wait outside,' she said.

'Excuse me,' said the policeman.

'I asked if you would wait outside.'

'I have a question,' Frølich said politely.

'Then wait until it is your turn.' She marched around the counter, a figure of authority in white trousers and a white blouse. She took the policeman's arm and tried to escort him out. When he pulled his arm away, she pointed to a red light outside. 'It's red. Can you see that?' she asked in an annoyed tone. 'That's the colour that signifies stop on our traffic lights. The red man. That colour means stop here as well. When it's green you can come in – if it's your turn, provided you have booked an appointment. If you haven't, you can ring between eight and nine o'clock in the morning. Have you understood? Comprendo?'

Frølich forced a smile. 'Darling!' he cried. The woman was taken aback as he gently pushed her back through the door and closed it. He placed his police badge on the counter.

'What's that?' The young woman seemed resigned rather than irritated now. She clumped back around the counter in her white clogs. She picked up the telephone and punched in a number with the receiver under her chin. 'If you do not go of your own accord, we will have to get someone to throw you out,' she said, staring into space.

'My name is Frank Frølich. I have come to speak to Erik Haugom, the doctor here,' the policeman said.

'Wait your turn,' the woman said into space.

'We have tried to ring, but for some reason or other no one answers the phone. I have a suggestion to make,' Frølich said with calm. 'I suggest you knock on Haugom's door and ask him to set aside ten minutes. The alternative is that I call him in for questioning at the police station. He has a legal obligation to appear, which would mean his losing four hours, at least. You can put down the phone and ask him which he prefers. It's his choice – not mine.'

The woman closed her eyes and put down the telephone. 'People are so bloody cheeky,' she said in a low mumble as she went into the room behind the counter.

Soon after she showed him the way through the same door. They walked through rooms smelling of medicine, rooms equipped with folding screens, recliners covered in paper towels and eye charts on the wall. A similar chart was hanging in Haugom's office.

Erik Haugom received him with an outstretched arm. A doctor with a ruddy complexion, the statutory white coat and a tuft of grey chest hair protruding at the top over the buttons. He ran his tongue round his teeth at the bottom of his mouth. His jaw resembled a filing cabinet drawer. 'You must excuse our ladies,' he said. 'You know this is a clinic and some of the oddest fruitcakes can make an occasional appearance. Two months ago – Inger Marie, you've just met her, was on duty at the time – a man appeared out of nowhere in reception. It was impossible to get through to this person. Decent type, properly dressed, you know, suit and tie and so on. And he just stood there without moving. Without saying a single word. Quite the shop window dummy. What do you do? They all tried talking to him while he stood there rooted to the floor. I don't think he even blinked for twenty minutes. In the end the man started undressing. Can you imagine that? Without a qualm, one garment after the other, nicely folded over his arm. And there he was, standing in all his horrid nakedness, then he walked right out in the buff, through the waiting room, down the stairs and into the street. Can you imagine that? The world has not been the same since for Inger Marie. Take a seat,' he said, holding a chair out for the policeman. 'Your name's Frølich, isn't it? The poor woman managed to remember that anyway.'

'Mm,' Frølich said, taking a seat. 'I won't detain you for long. This is about the party at Annabeth Ås's place.'

Haugom sat down behind the desk and nodded.

'Did you also know Katrine Bratterud?' the policeman asked.

'Not very well.' Haugom smiled. It was a strained smile – his tongue was playing with his lower teeth – a sort of nervous twitch that had become fixed and for that reason would not melt away.

'Sigrid, my wife, talked about her,' the doctor went on as Frølich was silent. 'She talks a lot about her work. The way women do. Isn't that right? A woman's thing – talking about your job come what may? I have a friend who teaches at the high school. That is, we play bridge together – Sigrid and I with this couple. And the man, Mogren's his name, Mogren tells us about these nightmare colleagues of his, women who talk ad nauseam about their problems instead of doing their job. You're a policeman. I'm a doctor. How would it be if I talked about every bloody patient and every genital wart or gonorrhoea-infected penis or hypochondriac I meet on a daily basis, eh?'

'I am aware of the problem.'

'I should think you are. But I don't suppose it was our marital difficulties you wanted us to talk about?'

'So you didn't know Katrine Bratterud?'

'No . . . Yes, by sight. Attractive girl, breasts, long legs, attractive girl, wasn't she?'

'My understanding is that you drove your wife to the party on the Saturday, and you picked her up later that night.'

'Indeed, that's correct. Wretched business this attractive girl getting murdered, isn't it!'

'When did you collect your wife?'

'Just after four o'clock in the morning.'

'That was very kind-hearted of you.'

'I'll tell you something, Frølich. I've done this job all through our marriage. I'm no modern man; I don't do anything in the kitchen and I don't darn my stockings. But I do what is expected of me as a husband. Which includes picking up Sigrid when she wants to come home.'

Frølich glanced up. What is expected of me as a husband, he thought. That was an ambitious objective. He looked down again.

'Did you sit up waiting for her to call?'

'Of course. I am her husband.'

The policeman took a deep breath. He could not quite come to terms with the transfixed grimace on Haugom's lips.

'How do you pass the time?' he asked.

'Here?'

'No, I mean while you're sitting up for your wife.'

'It's the sort of investment that pays dividends over time in a marriage,' the doctor said with a faint smile. 'In this field I can speak with a certain professional gravitas. There are many myths about the recipe for a successful relationship. The secret is the small investments that cost very little, for example patience and tolerance. Besides, I enjoy such moments. Night time is the best time, especially light summer nights. Just going for a walk, eh? The silence and the blue-grey light. Or sitting on the veranda and reading, smoking a good cigar. It takes over an hour; time slips away without your noticing. You should smoke cigars. I can see from your fingers you don't smoke much. Perhaps you belong to this hysterical generation that always has to do things right, stick needles in rather than take medicine, who think they can prevent cancer by eating wrinkled apples and unchewable black bread. Well, I don't know. Appearances can deceive. I'm sure you're a fine man, but you should smoke cigars. It gives your soul a more profound calm. Recommended by doctors, you might say. So that you don't have to suffer from an uneasy conscience.'

'When you arrived there,' Frølich asked, 'to pick up your wife, that is, were there many guests left?'

'None.'

'Just your wife?'

'Yes, she'd been helping to wash the ashtrays and clear away the bottles and so on.'

'Was Bjørn Gerhardsen there?'

'Yes, my understanding was that he had just returned from a little trip to town. Devil of a fellow. Goes to town and leaves his wife at home, eh? At another party, I wouldn't mind betting. He's a modern man, Gerhardsen is. But he knows how to enjoy the good things in life, even if he is modern.'

'Can you remember what the exact time was when you arrived?'

'Five minutes past four.'

'And did you have any idea of how long Gerhardsen had been there?'

'No, but it can't have been long.'

'Why do you say that?'

'I leaned on the bonnet of the car he had been driving, and the engine was still very hot.'

'Were they full of what had happened?'

'What had happened?'

'The business of Katrine's sickness during the evening.'

'I don't think so, no. It was the middle of the night after all. My goodness, they were as tired as hell, the three of them. It was already the day after.'

The policeman stood up. 'Thank you for taking the time to talk to me at such short notice,' he said. He went to the door, but turned as though he had remembered something.

'Yes?' Haugom said from his desk.

'Mm, I read your column now and then,' Frølich said after some hesitation.

'Which one?' Haugom asked, his chin in the air.

'Well, if only I knew,' Frølich said, lowering his eyes.

Haugom sent him an indulgent smile. 'You had a question perhaps?'

'It's gone from my head now,' Frølich said, grasping the door handle. 'I'll be in touch if I think of it.'

24

The Jewellery

Gunnarstranda was reading through Frølich's report and smacked the sheet in annoyance. 'Is she stupid or what?' he said, looking across at Frølich who was sitting in the low armchair beneath the window. Frølich was weighing a green dart in his hand. He took aim and let his forearm rock backwards and forwards as if on a spring until he threw the dart at the board he had positioned between two box files on the shelf above his desk.

'She can't be,' Frølich answered from a different world. 'She has a job and an education.' He took another dart off the coffee table beside him.

Gunnarstranda looked up from the report with a grim expression on his face. 'She can be stupid even if she's educated.'

Frølich took aim again. But the dart missed and disappeared behind the box files. He swore.

'You're educated,' Gunnarstranda said caustically.

'Eh?'

'But you don't seem that bright at this particular moment.' Gunnarstranda waved the papers in a fit of impatience.

Frølich got up from the armchair, drew a long breath and sighed. He crossed the room, sat at his own desk and pulled out the sliding keyboard on the shelf. He said, 'We know that either Merethe Fossum or Eidesen is lying. That much is obvious.'

Gunnarstranda nodded. He said, 'You and I put the squeeze on Eidesen that first night. He made up an unlikely banal story that left him without an alibi. If my memory is correct he claimed he went home expecting to find Katrine in his bed, but she wasn't there. Am I right?'

Frølich moved the mouse and found the file on the computer screen. He read, 'He said he came home between half past two and three.'

'And Katrine may still have been alive at that time,' Gunnarstranda said.

Frølich read: 'Eidesen said he rang Katrine but didn't get an answer.' Gunnarstranda nodded. 'And he went to bed. So he doesn't have an alibi . . .'

Frølich swung round on his chair. 'Whereas Merethe Fossum maintains she and Eidesen went back to her place and were in the same bed until late the next morning.'

'But why would Ole Eidesen lie his way out of a cast-iron alibi?'

'Well, to give a more appealing image of himself. After all, he was the dead girl's boyfriend, and it sounds a lot better if he was asleep in bed waiting for her while she was being killed. Better than saying he was in bed with another woman.'

'But if that's the case, he must have known we would see through a lie like that.'

'Of course,' Frølich persisted. 'But he was her boyfriend. He had no motive for bumping her off. And he has an alibi, but to avoid reproaches from others – remember Katrine was a popular girl – he waits before producing his alibi, Merethe Fossum. What will all her friends say to him letting Katrine go out into the night on her own, exposing her to all sorts of sexual offenders and predatory creatures, and bedding Merethe while Katrine was being murdered!'

Gunnarstranda: 'If Katrine's adventure with Henning Kramer made Eidesen jealous, he has a motive. Let's assume he was jealous. There are men who are suspicious of their girlfriends twenty-four hours a day. Let's assume he spied on her when she left the party and he saw her walking down the road, saw her getting into a rival's car . . . My goodness, there are many such murders committed every year in this country.'

'But why would Fossum lie?' Frølich asked. 'Everyone has confirmed that three people went to Smuget. Everyone has confirmed that those two stayed together. It's very unlikely that she would cover up for Eidesen by lying. She has nothing to gain. We have to suppose that Fossum is telling the truth and that Eidesen has an alibi. If Eidesen had found out Katrine got together with Kramer that night, all he did by way of retaliation was to sleep with Merethe. That is more likely than running off to kill Katrine.'

Gunnarstranda listened with a thoughtful groove in his brow.

Frølich continued: 'Gerhardsen is the only person without anyone to hide behind. Suppose Gerhardsen had been turned on by Katrine that night. According to Georg Beck, he was standing on the veranda, touching her up. So we have this fantastic coincidence that two cars leave the party at more or less the same time. They drive down to the city centre. The taxi stops outside Smuget. Kramer parks the Audi in Cort Adelers gate and the two of them walk down to Aker Brygge. Here they queue at a takeaway and buy food; she dances with a down-and-out. Time passes. For the sake of argument let's suppose that Gerhardsen never joined Ole and Merethe. After all, he was the gooseberry. Let's say he left them in Aker Brygge where there is no shortage of women. Then he saw Katrine and Kramer. His company car was in the garage close by. We know he took the car, but he might have done that a long time before. He could have taken the car and followed them, and struck when Kramer dropped off Katrine, before driving back home. He could have managed that in the time. Kramer said he dropped off Katrine between half past two and three o'clock. That gives Gerhardsen time to rape, strangle and dump her and still get home by four.'

They sat looking at each other. Frølich was excited by his speculation. Gunnarstranda was silent.

'What don't you like about this theory?' the younger policeman enquired.

Gunnarstranda got out of the chair and began to pace to and fro in the room. 'Nothing really,' he said, grabbing the last dart from the low coffee table. 'But I'm thinking about Henning Kramer. I like his statement less and less. We don't know, as far as self-control goes, whether he has a low threshold.' Gunnarstranda leaned towards the window, thinking, while his right hand fidgeted with the green dart. 'And if he's lying,' he mumbled, 'he's doing that to hide something, and what else could he have to hide other than . . . ?'

'. . . her murder?' Frølich concluded. They sat without speaking. Gunnarstranda fiddled with the dart. Frølich coughed. 'But can we afford not to examine Gerhardsen's company car?' he asked at length. 'If Katrine was in the car, we are bound to find substantiating evidence.'

Gunnarstranda nodded. 'We can't afford not to,' he mumbled.

The telephone rang. Gunnarstranda strode over to his desk and grabbed it. Frølich stood up and began to search for the dart that had disappeared behind the files on the shelf. He gave up and instead turned towards Gunnarstranda who was nodding and grunting on the telephone: 'Yes . . . yes . . . yes . . . right . . . well, well . . .'

He cradled the telephone.

They stared at each other. 'What jewellery did Katrine own again?' Gunnarstranda asked.

'Apart from the piercing?' Frølich frowned. 'There would have been quite a bit of gold. Rings, a gold bracelet and most likely a gold chain, a bracelet made of ivory . . . all we know for sure is that she was wearing some earrings that night, two gold cannabis leaves. A present from Eidesen – but we have just his word for that.' He grinned and looked up with a questioning expression.

Gunnarstranda was weighing the green dart in his hand. 'Duck,' he said and took aim.

Frølich kicked and rolled his chair back, out of the line of fire. Gunnarstranda threw. Bullseye. 'That was Yttergjerde,' he said with a smug grin. 'Yttergjerde and a couple of other policeman broke into Raymond Skau's flat. No one has seen hide nor hair of Skau, but in his flat they found some lady's jewellery among which was a pair of gold cannabis leaves designed as earrings.'

'Raymond Skau?'

Gunnarstranda nodded.

'He's got Katrine Bratterud's jewellery?'

'Time will tell,' Gunnarstranda said. 'Only Eidesen can give a satisfactory answer to the question of whether it is her jewellery.' He stood up. 'So now I have an excuse to get him back here. You continue the field work in the meantime – in particular, check out anything connected with Henning Kramer.'

25

The Epitaph

Ole Eidesen sauntered down the corridor with his hands buried deep in his trouser pockets. He was wearing a white tracksuit top with a colourful design on the front, some kind of aquarium with either sperm cells or tadpoles swimming around. The white tracksuit bottoms had a grass stain on one knee and seemed too big: they smothered his white trainers. Gunnarstranda's white porcelain teeth sparkled at the sight; he held the door wide open for the close-cropped, monk-like visitor who had to bend at the knees to shake hands – it was almost like a courteous bow. Eidesen stopped the second he was inside. The cuts on his face were still red and angry, and his eyes were drawn to Gunnarstranda's desk. The paper had been tidied away, but the table space between the computer and the electric typewriter was littered with small objects.

'Take all the time you need and point out the things you think may have belonged to Katrine,' the police inspector said, guiding Ole Eidesen to the desk.

In the space there was a rusty old razor, a brass-coloured cylinder containing lipstick, a china hash pipe, a lump of black Afghani hash wrapped in transparent plastic, two gold earrings in the shape of cannabis leaves, a box of matches, a half-used sheet of contraceptive pills, two gold rings, one in the shape of a snake, the other with a green stone inset. A black disposable lighter with a figure 1 on the side stood next to a driving licence, a braided gold necklace, an ivory bracelet, a selection of thinner bracelets of unknown material and a small black shoulder bag.

Eidesen stared long and hard at the objects, then his eyes wandered over to the policeman.

'Take your time,' Gunnarstranda said, taking a seat. 'Take all the time you need.'

Eidesen cleared his throat and pointed to the bag. 'Could I see that, please?'

'The bag? Of course. Have a careful look.' Leaning back, the policeman pulled a drawer out of the desk and placed one foot in it. 'Take your time and take care.'

'This is hers,' Eidesen said, examining it.

'Sure?' the policeman asked.

'Yes.'

'How can you be so sure?'

'It was a present from me.' Eidesen pointed to the earrings. 'And these.'

'Are you sure?'

'Yes, I'm sure.'

'If I say I bought the cannabis leaves off someone in Markveien what would you say?'

Eidesen frowned. 'You may have done, but not the bag. I recognize it.' He opened it and turned out the white lining. 'See,' he said. 'She spilt nail varnish in it and I recognize the stain. This is her bag; I bought it in Spain. There are not very many bags of this type around. You might be able to trick me, but the earrings, the gold chain, the rings and the ivory bracelet, and the lipstick, Lancôme, that colour? They're Katrine's things.'

'Are you quite sure?'

'Yes.'

'Is there anything else you would have expected to see there?'

'I'm not sure.'

'And what does that answer mean?'

'I think she had another ring, one with two diamonds in it.'

'You mean she was wearing that ring on that night?'

Eidesen puffed out his cheeks. In the end he shook his head. 'It would be quite strange,' he mumbled, shaking his head gravely, 'if she had not been wearing it. She never took it off.'

Gunnarstranda nodded. 'Let's hold fire with the ring,' he said. 'Which of these things lying on the table belonged to her?'

Eidesen gathered the earrings, both rings, the bracelets, the gold chain and the bag into a little pile on the table. 'This, too,' he continued, adding the lipstick. He lifted the sheet of pills. 'Not sure about these.'

'Was she on the pill?'

'Yes.' He motioned towards the driving certificate. 'Could I see . . . ?'

'. . . the driving licence?' Gunnarstranda completed, and nodded. 'Here you are.'

Eidesen turned over the licence and saw Katrine Bratterud's face. He stood staring at it. 'Where did you find this?' he asked in a thick voice.

The policeman did not answer. Eidesen shook his head slowly. The photograph of his girlfriend's face had disconcerted him for a few moments.

'How come this girl had so much valuable jewellery?' the policeman asked.

'No idea.'

'Did you give her any – apart from the earrings?'

'No.'

'Are they stolen property?'

Eidesen glanced up and twisted his mouth into a scornful grimace.

Gunnarstranda sat watching him.

'There you have it,' Eidesen said, nodding towards the objects. 'Her epitaph – stolen goods.' His mouth had stiffened into a bitter scowl. He was in turmoil.

Gunnarstranda said nothing.

Eidesen cast around for something to sit on. Gunnarstranda pointed to the low armchair in the suite beneath the window. 'Please take a seat.'

'If you could change anything about that evening,' the policeman continued, 'what would you have done differently?'

Eidesen sighed, raised his head and stared at the wall, deep in thought. 'In fact, I have no idea,' he mumbled.

'Did you know Henning Kramer picked her up from the party?'

Eidesen's eyes widened.

The policeman nodded. 'She made a call from Annabeth Ås's house and asked Kramer to come and fetch her. He jumped into the car at once and she began to walk down towards the city centre – they met in Voksenkollveien. Did she tell you that Henning would pick her up?'

Eidesen shook his head in disbelief.

'She must have left either just before or just after the five of you took the taxi down to the city.'

'What?'

'She must have left after you because you didn't pass her. Well, I assume you would have known if your taxi had passed her.'

Eidesen said nothing.

'Why do you think she didn't tell you anything about Kramer picking her up?'

Eidesen waited for a few seconds before answering. 'I don't know what to say,' he said in a low voice. He cleared his throat. 'I don't know what to say,' he repeated. 'It's come as a complete surprise to me.'

'What was the relationship between Henning Kramer and Katrine?'

'Relationship?'

'Yes, were they friends or . . . ?'

'Lovers? I may have thought that . . .' He sat looking into space.

'. . . was she cheating on you?' suggested the policeman.

217

'I didn't say that.'

'Did you cheat on her?'

'Eh?'

'Did you go with other women?'

'No,' said Eidesen.

'Never?'

Eidesen shook his head.

'Not the night she was killed, either?'

Eidesen looked up at him without saying a word.

'Come on, Eidesen. I'm not asking you questions for fun. Were you with another woman when Katrine was killed?'

'You've spoken to Merethe,' Eidesen said, clearing his throat.

Gunnarstranda heaved a deep sigh.

'I wanted to wait until you had spoken to her. I had thought about telling you, but wanted to wait.'

'Eidesen,' Gunnarstranda said with a resigned intake of air. 'Imagine you had been charged as a result of this business and we were about to meet in court. The decision about whether you should be given a custodial sentence or not was hanging in the balance. You would have met your solicitor and do you know what he would have said? He would have whispered in your ear, *For God's sake, don't let them catch you lying. If you lie, you weaken your credibility.* In other words: If you lie once, who can be certain you haven't been lying the whole way through?'

They sat looking at each other in silence.

'I would like to change my statement,' Eidesen said at length.

'What would you like to change?'

'What I said about the taxi ride home after we were in Smuget.'

'What actually happened?'

'I went back to Merethe Fossum's place.'

'When did you get there?'

'Between three and four in the morning.'

'What did you do?'

'We opened a bottle of wine and went to bed.'

218

'Why should I believe this?'

'Because it's true.'

'Why did you say something different last time?'

'I don't know.'

'At least make this statement more credible.'

'What do you mean now?'

'Give me something, something that would help me to believe you,' the policeman shouted in despair.

'She's got a poster of Audrey Hepburn in her bedroom, a picture from a film . . . called . . . *Breakfast at Tiffany's* . . . you know, one of those fifties diva pictures.'

'You could have seen that before – or since.'

'I met her for the first time at the party.'

'But you could still have seen the poster in the days that followed the night.'

'She has a birthmark.'

The policeman sighed.

'On the inside of her thigh, high up,' Eidesen said.

'You could have discovered that since then.'

'Only if we had been together afterwards, which we haven't.'

'But why should I bother questioning her so many times?' Gunnarstranda stood up. 'You waste my time with nonsense and lies. You're obstructing my investigation.' He swept an arm towards Katrine's effects. 'Do you want us to arrest the person who created this epitaph for her or not?'

Eidesen didn't answer. He gently cleared his throat. Gunnarstranda strolled over to the window and placed his palms against the hollow of his back.

'There is one thing,' Eidesen said in a hoarse voice.

Gunnarstranda looked up at the blue sky. Over the ridge to the west a flying object was just discernible, a hang glider. He didn't answer, didn't turn around.

'Katrine did have a very colourful past,' Eidesen said. 'Imagine you were with someone who had done everything with everyone.'

Eidesen fell silent, and at long last Gunnarstranda came away from the window and rested his gaze on him. 'And what do you mean by that?' he asked airily.

'I don't know,' Eidesen sighed. 'That's what I have to say and either you understand it or you don't.'

'Do you know any of these men you have in mind?'

'I'm not interested in any of them.'

'Did Katrine mention a man called Raymond?'

'Don't think so.'

'Raymond Skau?'

'No.'

'Quite sure?'

'I've never heard the name before, neither from her nor anyone else.'

'What happened on the day of the party? When did you meet?'

'I was already at home when she arrived. She worked on that Saturday.'

'At home?'

'I stayed over at hers, from the Friday. We went to the cinema to see a film called *The Matrix*. Terrific film, I thought. But I don't think she enjoyed it very much. And it was crazy.'

'Why was that?'

'Because she liked that kind of film, action films, I mean, with tough-guy actors, CGI effects and so on, but she was very distant . . .'

'Distant?'

'Yes, distant, but afterwards we went back to her flat in Hovseter. It was late and we went to bed. I woke up as she was going to work . . . at about a quarter past eight, I think. They opened at nine, so she left in good time to be there for nine.'

Gunnarstranda moved away from the window. He crossed the floor and sat in the chair opposite Eidesen. 'And you?' he asked.

'I had a day off, so I stayed in bed. I slept a little, don't remember when I got up, but it was late morning. I went for some exercise, ran down to Bogstad and back, and afterwards I bought a couple of newspapers, read them and made some food for when she came back.'

'When was that?'

'Afternoon time – half past two – three maybe.'

'And then?'

'We ate. She took a shower and so on. I watched football on TV, Molde v Stabæk . . . finished in a draw, 0–0.'

'What did she do?'

Eidesen shrugged. 'Don't remember. She just did her own thing, trying on clothes and so on.'

'Clothes?'

'Yes, she was a bit stressed about what to wear in the evening.'

'And otherwise?'

'She was on the phone . . .'

'Who did she ring?'

'No idea. I was watching the football. It finished at about six.'

'Did she still seem distant?'

'A bit. But nervy too. Distant and nervy.'

Gunnarstranda waited.

'It was my impression she was in a flap because of the party.'

'Are you sure?'

'How do you mean?'

'Well, she might have talked about other things. Something might have happened at work.'

Eidesen shook his head.

'So she didn't say anything about her job?'

'No.'

'How many calls did she make?'

'Several. I wasn't following.'

'But did you hear what she was talking about?'

'No. She closed the door. The telephone's in the hallway, and I think the football was making quite a bit of noise, so she closed the door.'

'But how do you know she called several people?'

221

'Because she hung up, paced up and down, sat on the sofa for a bit and then called again.'

'How many calls did she make?'

'No idea.'

'More than two?'

'It must have been.'

'Three? Four? Five?'

'Three or four, I guess.'

'Do you know if she spoke to Sigrid Haugom?'

'It's possible, but she didn't tell me who she spoke to.'

'And you weren't curious as to why she made four calls?'

Eidesen pulled a face and shook his head.

'That's rather odd,' the policeman said. 'I mean, most people would have wondered what he'd got the girl into, wouldn't they?'

'I assumed she was chatting, the way that girls do chatter to each other.'

'Are you sure she wasn't trying to talk to you about something special that day and you may not have realized?'

'I don't understand what you mean.'

'Well, let's suppose something had happened at work and she wanted to talk to you about it, but you were so busy watching TV that you didn't twig that she wanted to talk about something important, so ...'

'No,' Eidesen said categorically. 'I would have sensed that.'

'But was she upset?'

'She was in a flap. But it was because of the bloody party. She was as nervous as shit about the party.'

'How did her nervousness manifest itself?'

'She tried on a pile of clothes and she was ... well ... bitchy.'

'Bitchy?'

'Yes, almost pre-menstrual, nagging me about every sodding thing.'

'About what for example?'

'Well, she was angry that I was watching football, that I hadn't

222

folded up the newspaper and that my jogging gear was strewn all over the bathroom, that sort of thing.'

'So she was grumpy?'

'Grumpy is too mild. Bitchy is better.'

'But was that because of you?'

'What do you mean now?'

'I was wondering whether these outbursts were unusual or whether she considered you lazy as regards tidying up.'

'No, no,' Eidesen reassured him. 'This was unusual.'

'According to another witness Katrine was wound up on this particular day because she had a secret she didn't want to tell.'

'A secret?'

'You didn't notice anything?'

'Nothing at all.'

'And the word *secret* doesn't ring any bells? You didn't share some deep secret no one else could be party to?'

'Not that I can think of off hand.'

The policeman nodded slowly. 'But there is one thing I don't understand,' he went on. 'Why do you interpret this mood as an attack of nerves before the party?'

'Because that was what she said.'

'Tell me what she said.'

'I asked her what was bothering her because she had thrown my tracksuit in my face, and she stood looking at me as though she was calming down and considering the question. Then she said she was nervous about the party.'

'What were her words?'

Eidesen furrowed his brow in thought. 'I said something like *What's up with you?* or *What is it now?* Something like that. And she said: *I'm just so on edge.*'

'And?' the policeman said.

'That's what she said.'

'*I'm just so on edge?*'

'That's what she said word for word.'

'Why did you interpret that as nervousness?'

'She was on edge . . . tense,' Eidesen added, on seeing the policeman's sceptical expression. 'That was what she meant when she used the phrase *on edge*. She meant tense, nervous.'

'But might she have meant something else? Could she have meant she was on edge about something that had happened or something that was going to happen?'

Eidesen gave the matter some thought. 'It would have to be the party. That was how I interpreted it, anyway.'

'Sigrid Haugom says she received a telephone call from Katrine that Saturday,' Gunnarstranda said. 'She says Katrine was anxious because something had happened that day – at the travel agency – and she wanted to discuss it with her.'

Eidesen shrugged his shoulders.

'We have reason to believe she felt threatened.'

'Threatened?'

'She didn't mention any of this to you?'

Eidesen shook his head. 'Not that I can remember.'

'I have to ask you to think back one more time to when she was explaining to you why she was irritable. What were the precise words that she used?'

'She said: *I'm just so on edge.*'

'Are you still sure it was the party that was making her nervous?'

'Not now, not after what you said about threats. What sort of threats were they?'

'How much did you know about Katrine's past?' Gunnarstranda asked in a compassionate tone.

'Depends what you mean by knowing. I didn't want to know that much.'

'Just now you talked about being with someone who had done everything with everyone.'

'That side of her past was no secret.'

'But why did you get together?'

'I liked her.'

'What did you know?'

'That she had been on drugs and had done a lot of crazy things.'

'And you knew about her life on the streets?'

'There's one thing you have to understand about Katrine and me,' Eidesen said in a low voice. He cleared his throat and paused as if to search for words. 'I wasn't interested in her past.'

Gunnarstranda waited. At that moment Ole Eidesen seemed very centred.

'What happened happened. The Katrine who walked the streets was a different person from the Katrine I knew. I was not interested in the person who walked the streets and took heroin. I was interested in Katrine.'

'My understanding was that Katrine never took heroin,' the policeman said. 'She was on amphetamines, cocaine, Ecstasy . . .'

'Don't you think she tried heroin? She was on the streets because she was a drug addict.'

'I don't think anything,' Gunnarstranda answered. 'But I've read reports about her. Didn't you talk about her past?'

'Never.'

'Why not?'

'As I said, I wasn't interested.'

'Were you jealous of her past?'

'Of course not.'

'Seems like that to me.'

'Then you're the one with the problem.'

'What happened at those times when she wanted to talk about the past?'

'I told her to shut up.'

'Were you violent?'

'I've never hit another person.'

'Not Katrine, either?'

'I wouldn't dream of it.'

'Did you ever hit her?'

'Never. The fact that you ask me shows just how little you know about me. Just asking shows you didn't know her.'

'But you asked me to try to understand your torments. You asked me to try to understand how you suffered being with a woman who had done everything with everyone.'

'That wasn't what I asked.'

'But I perceived it as such. Your saying you didn't want to discuss her past seems to me as though you were jealous of her past.'

'I wasn't jealous. I've never been jealous. Why are you so obsessed with this?'

'Because I sense a motive.'

'You're barking up the wrong tree. I would never have hurt Katrine. And, as you said yourself, Merethe Fossum is my alibi for that night.'

'Indeed, but let us imagine that Katrine insisted on talking about her past that Saturday. Let's say you refused to listen. It does not seem improbable that this may have caused a row in the light of your emotional attitude to her past.'

'But I told you I did not have any emotional attitude to her past.'

'We know Katrine was out of kilter that Saturday. She was out of kilter – because of something that had happened at the travel agency. Perhaps it had something to do with her drug-taking years. It does not seem too improbable that she took this feeling of despair home with her. In fact, we know she did. She rang Sigrid Haugom and told her about the incident while you were sitting in another room. You and Katrine were lovers. You were on intimate terms. You were in and out of each other's flats. Why would she keep such an important incident from you?'

'Because I wasn't interested in her bloody past.'

'Now you seem to be suppressing some aggression towards this past of hers.'

'I am not.'

'Yes, you are.' The policeman smiled. 'You're very angry now. I can see that you are sitting there and fuming.'

'And what's it got to do with you?'

'You're angry with her and the fact that she was a prostitute.'

'I told you I didn't give a shit about what she had done.'

'And I don't believe you.'

'I don't give a stuff what you believe!' Ole Eidesen yelled.

Gunnarstranda leaned back in his chair. It was a waste of time provoking this young man. After all, Eidesen had an alibi. In fact, he was probably wasting his time questioning him.

He pulled out a desk drawer and took hold of the prison photograph of Raymond Skau. He passed it to Eidesen. 'Do you know him?'

Eidesen put down the photograph on the desk and examined it carefully. He coughed. 'No,' he said.

'Have you seen him before?'

Eidesen shook his head. 'Don't think so.'

'Never?'

'No.'

'Think about it.'

'I'm thinking as hard as I can.'

'You're absolutely sure you've never seen this person?'

'Yes. Who is it?'

'It's someone from Katrine's past.'

'Who?'

Gunnarstranda smiled. 'Interested?'

Eidesen gave a groan of despair. 'Don't give a shit,' he sighed.

'I don't give a shit or you don't?'

'All right, I don't give a shit. I don't give a fuck who it is.'

'I've got your point now,' the policeman said, thinking. 'Now there's just one thing I don't understand.'

'And that is?'

'You haven't asked me yet what happened on the Saturday – in the travel agency.'

26

The Lie

The police inspector was sitting with a plate of chips in front of him on the desk when Frølich rang. With the receiver under his chin he tried to squeeze the ketchup out of a little foil packet and over the freshly washed Cinzano ashtray. He swore as a spot landed on his tie.

'Breakthrough,' Frølich said.

'What are you talking about?'

Frølich: 'We can make an arrest.'

'Arrest whom?'

'Henning Kramer.'

Gunnarstranda was eating. 'Why?' he chewed.

'I've been talking to two taxi drivers who have confirmed Kramer's version of events through to Aker Brygge. Both remember the girl. No question it was Katrine B – a real knockout in a skirt and black lace bra. The two of them had given the impression of being a couple, and she in particular was in a good mood – seemed quite high. A waiter at Lekteren – one of the restaurant boats – also remembers the girl well. She had been waltzing with some of the men on the wharf. A girl working at McDonald's recognized both of them. They bought cheeseburgers and Cokes and left. The guy at Lekteren also remembers Kramer, but he couldn't understand how such a stupid-looking guy could have a woman like her.'

'Everyone agreed they had had a nice time,' Gunnarstranda interrupted, dipping a handful of thin chip-stalks into the ashtray filled with ketchup. 'Get to the point!' The chips splayed out as he was about to stuff them into his mouth.

'Listen to this,' Frølich said, excited. 'One taxi driver's name is Kardo Bukhtal. He was driving a late-night party-goer home that morning. He remembers the trip because it was a long one, out to Ski. And on the way back he took old Mossevei and drove past the car park where Kramer thought they had parked. And he's willing to swear he saw the car there.'

'Kramer's car?'

'Yes, Kramer's car, an Audi open-top sports car, green with a grey hood. Well, this guy thinks cars like this are pretty stylish and he slowed down as he passed. The car was there at half past six that same morning, when Kramer says he was sleeping sweetly in his own bed after dropping off Katrine by the roundabout leading up to Holmlia.'

'In other words, Kramer is lying.'

'Like a presidential candidate.'

Gunnarstranda's fingers were covered in ketchup. 'Where are you?'

'In Holmen.'

Gunnarstranda stood up. He put the receiver under his chin, wiped his fingers clean on a serviette and patted his pockets for cigarettes. 'In Holmen. What the hell are you doing there? I want Henning Kramer here, now! With handcuffs on!'

'I'm sitting in my car outside his mother's house,' Frølich answered drily. 'The guy isn't at home. But I was given his brother's address. That must be where Henning stays when his brother is away.'

'The address?'

'Behind Deichmannsgate. Fredensborgveien 33.'

'See you there.' The inspector was already on his way to the door. He drank the rest of the Coke running down the stairs. His coat-tails fluttering behind him.

If Frølich had spoken to this idiot's mother she could have

warned him on the phone and put the boy on his guard. Gunnarstranda took the next flight in three strides and caught a glimpse of
Yttergjerde's stooped figure down in reception. Yttergjerde glanced
up. They exchanged looks. Gunnarstranda pointed his index finger
ahead and circled it above his head. That was enough. Yttergjerde
broke into a run.

* * *

The needle on the speedometer touched 110 kph. Shop windows
and pedestrians were just grey shadows. Cars in front of them
swerved to the side and in their panic drove on to the pavements
with a jolt. Yttergjerde drove in the middle of the carriageway, between lines of cars with casual nonchalance, crossing the lights on
red, pushing into the wrong lane and back again, his mouth going
like a taxi driver's all the while. 'Went to the Glomma last weekend,' he said. 'Flooding its banks, it was. In June, just imagine. Went
on to Mingevannet with my brother-in-law, down the lake, by Sarp.
We were sitting in a boat, casting lines towards the shore. Do that
in early summer, we do, when the pike's in the reeds. Only caught
a few littl'uns though, tiny buggers no longer than an index finger.
You wouldn't think they'd bite the spinning bait that was twice as
long as they were, would you? And so aggressive! It was ...'

'Watch out!' Gunnarstranda shouted, grabbing the glove compartment with both hands to brace himself for a collision.

However, Yttergjerde swung the wheel round and slung the car
to the left, into the lane of the oncoming traffic. He maintained
speed, driving towards a parked lorry unloading goods. Behind
the lorry was a queue of cars; their line of sight blocked, they had
not seen the police car. The first car came out and overtook the
lorry on its way towards them. Yttergjerde coughed and accelerated as he aimed for a gap between the two vehicles and one of the
cars that had swerved to the side. 'Could use them as bait, you
know. Save taking them off the hook. Pike are cannibals, too. My

brother-in-law caught one weighing three kilos and do you know where the hook was? In the pike's skull. My brother-in-law had bloody hooked a pike in the skull and hauled it in. What about that! Three kilos!'

'Bloody hell!' Gunnarstranda grabbed the strap over the door to his right as a cyclist was forced to throw himself and the bike on to the pavement.

Yttergjerde shrugged. They were already in Fredensborgveien. The howl of a siren echoed between the blocks of flats. Yttergjerde jumped on the brakes and screeched to a halt in front of another patrol car. Gunnarstranda was out of the car and already on his way to the front door. What was a second patrol car doing here? Frølich could never have made it here so fast.

He raced up the stairs with long strides. Behind him, Yttergjerde was more composed. Gunnarstranda didn't stop until he reached the second floor and was standing in front of an open door. A uniformed policeman stood in the doorway. Gunnarstranda walked past him and entered the flat.

* * *

The dead man was hanging from a hook intended for an electric light. It might have seemed solid enough for a chandelier, but now it seemed fragile. Someone had taken the cable off the hook and laid out the dead man.

'I took down the body and laid it on the floor,' said the uniformed constable by the door. 'Hope that's not a problem.'

Gunnarstranda scowled at him, but said nothing. The constable shrugged and leaned against the door frame. Apart from the constable, Gunnarstranda and Yttergjerde there was another stranger in the room. Without uttering a word, Gunnarstranda watched the stranger trying to give Henning Kramer heart massage. It didn't seem to be helping. The man sat over the dead body, the back of his white shirt wet with sweat. Every time he thumped the dead man's chest the corpse shook. Every time the man tried to pump the heart into life the lifeless legs thudded against the wooden floor. As did Henning Kramer's head. The man astride the dead body took a small break, gasping for air, and went back to pressing Kramer's chest. Two lifeless feet and one head banged against the wooden planks.

Gunnarstranda motioned to Yttergjerde who was leaning over the two on the floor. With a pair of nippers he cut off the rest of the cable, still coiled around the dead man's neck. The man attempting heart massage glanced up, mumbled something and went on pumping.

Gunnarstranda cleared his throat and asked the constable, 'Was he cold?'

'As ice,' the constable answered.

Gunnarstranda pointed to the man giving the heart massage. 'Who is this?'

The constable in the doorway gave a shrug.

At that moment Frank Frølich walked in through the door. He took one look at the dead body and heaved a heavy sigh. He and Gunnarstranda exchanged glances.

'He found the body,' the constable said, pointing to the man they had spoken about. 'But he has just started doing this.'

Frølich shouted to the man on the floor: 'Hello, are you a doctor?'

The man turned round. 'Vet.'

'He's dead,' Gunnarstranda said to the vet.

'We have to open his chest,' the man said. 'We have to try to squeeze his heart into life by hand.'

'What?' Gunnarstranda said.

'Squeeze his heart into life by hand.'

'Are you out of your mind?' Gunnarstranda's lips trembled with irritation. 'The man's dead. Can't you see that? He's almost transparent. He hanged himself from the ceiling several hours ago.'

'Rubbish,' said the vet who stood up and dashed into the kitchen.

Soon he reappeared in the doorway with a large meat cleaver. The expression on his face was concentrated and he was sweating. He brandished the cleaver. 'We have to open him up!'

'I make the decisions here,' Gunnarstranda said roughly. His voice shook with suppressed rage. 'He's dead.' His voice cracked on the word *dead*.

'But it works with the rats at the institute. This is something I do every day. We just open the chest and squeeze the heart into life.'

Gunnarstranda stared dumbstruck at the vet with the cleaver. Yttergjerde was crouched down examining the corpse as though it concealed profound secrets about his life. It was impossible to find eye contact with anyone in the room. No one was at ease. *They don't like my tone of voice*, thought Gunnarstranda. *They're afraid of what I might do. They think I'm going to crush this poor man. He's in shock. Take it easy*, Gunnarstranda told himself. *The man's in shock.*

There was a clunk as the man in the kitchen doorway dropped the cleaver. His hands were shaking; his jaw was quivering. He was obviously on the verge of a breakdown. The policeman, who was relieved that the man had dropped the cleaver, turned to the window and pointed to the weary, grey cactus leaning against the glass. 'Can you see the cactus?' he asked.

'I don't understand what you mean,' the man in the doorway said, stroking his forehead, exhausted.

'It's growing.'

'So what?'

'The window sill isn't growing.'

'Hm?'

'You can't make wood grow again however much you water it.'

The veterinary doctor stared at the cactus in bewilderment. He spun round to face the body on the floor.

'But he's my brother,' he cried.

Gunnarstranda took his arm. He's about to snap, he thought, and looked into the man's eyes. 'May I offer my condolences?'

'Don't you understand that I don't want to lose my brother?'

'Stand still,' Gunnarstranda ordered as the man bent down for the cleaver. In a gentler tone he continued: 'I'm sure you're a good vet and a good researcher, and you've had lots of success with the rats you work with, but you must not forget that this body was a man once. Even if his heart did beat again after you opened his chest, you have to remember that blood has not circulated through his brain for a long time. He would have to lie in a respirator with brain damage until someone was kind enough to switch it off.'

'You're right,' the man said quietly. 'I hadn't thought about that.'

Gunnarstranda pointed to the cleaver on the floor. 'Where did you find it?'

'What,' the man said, in a distant world.

'Where did you find the cleaver?'

'In the kitchen.'

'So it belongs to the flat?'

'Of course.'

'And you're the brother?'

'Yes.'

The others in the room breathed out and began to move again. Gunnarstranda could feel their eyes on him. There was a body on the floor and he was standing with the dead man's brother in his arms. He could not question him here.

Gunnarstranda looked around the flat. It was full of book-shelves up and down the walls. The room was attractive, decorated with taste. A few African masks and art posters hung from places where there was no shelving.

'So this is your flat?' Gunnarstranda had another look around. His gaze fell on a small wood-carving of a horseman balancing precariously on the bookshelf. Just inside the door was a suitcase with a British Airways label still hanging from the handle and a bag of duty-free goods beside it. 'Been travelling?'

The vet followed the policeman's gaze and nodded.

'For long?'

'Ten days or so.'

'Quite a welcome home,' Frølich interjected.

The vet slumped into a chair and stared into the distance with a blank expression on his face. 'I'm worn out,' he said, shaking his head dejectedly. 'I haven't slept for over a day. My body is riddled with jet lag. And I come here and find Henning hanging from the lighting fixture. It's too much. I can't cope.'

'What did . . . ?' Gunnarstranda started to say, but Frølich stopped him and hunkered down in front of the vet whose eyes were still glazed. 'You have our full sympathy,' Frølich said in a gentle tone. 'We understand that this must be a terrible strain, but we are nevertheless obliged to clear up a few matters, even though this is your flat. If you wouldn't mind coming with me, I'll book you a hotel room until tomorrow.'

'This is my flat,' the man in the chair stated from faraway.

'Of course it's your flat.'

'So why don't you leave? Why can't I be alone?'

'We have to take your dead brother with us,' Frølich said. 'And we have to let a few forensic technicians go through the flat to ascertain how this happened.'

'But it's obvious how it happened.'

'Herr Kramer,' Frølich insisted, taking the suitcase into the hall. 'Could you come with me, please?'

Gunnarstranda watched through the window until they appeared in the street. Frølich, large and broad with a rolling gait; the other man grey, almost a smudge, with hair whirled up by the wind revealing a bald patch as they strolled towards the police car. With a little twitch of the mouth, Gunnarstranda involuntarily raised a hand and patted his comb-over.

At that moment two ambulance men came in through the door. They were carrying a stretcher and a body bag. Gunnarstranda looked down at the deceased Henning Kramer.

'We need some technical assistance here,' he said tersely. 'After that I'm off for the weekend.'

27

The Palace

It was Friday afternoon and the summer traffic in Drammensveien was desperately slow. But as soon as Frølich turned off to take the old Lier hills route, the traffic eased. In Hurumlandet there were almost no other cars to be seen, especially after leaving the main road and taking the winding track linking the farms. Here and there the road went through a farmyard where an idle elkhound or a St Bernard lay with its head between its front paws, opening an indolent bloodshot eye to follow the car. Then he passed through an area with fields and meadows on either side. He slowed down as the road narrowed for a bridge over an old dyke and passed some mountain crags where some hardy fellow passing himself off as a farmer had released a few cows that either grazed between mounds of rock or waited with listless, hanging heads by a shelter made with round poles.

Frank Frølich was never very sure of the way after the tarmac came to an end and the road entered the forest. The tyres rumbled and the stony track was dry – it hadn't rained for a few hours – as the dust was swirled upwards causing Frank to close all valves and vents. The sunshine cut through the foliage at the side of the road and still he was passing lines of green postboxes for outlying properties, or crossroads where the track split and a tractor's tyre marks or cattle trails led into the wild. Frank never remembered where he should stop; he wouldn't remember until he saw Gunnarstranda's red Bölanz ride-on mower. If he could locate the mower he would have his bearings again. It was always like this, and every time he thought the way seemed longer than on the previous journey. He passed a small farmyard where graceful horses with shiny coats were strutting around a well-trodden paddock. He passed another farmyard where more graceful horses jerked nervously as the car went by. He drove past cabins with barred windows, past cabins with colourful postboxes, but he didn't slow down until he spotted a green rubbish skip for cabin owners. Five hundred metres up the mountainside he saw Gunnarstranda's mower parked higgledy-piggledy under some pine trees. He parked beside the mower, opened the boot and took out a sleeping bag, a parcel of meat for the barbecue, a six-pack and a bottle of Ballantine's whisky. He locked the car and ambled down the narrow path between the trees leading to Gunnarstranda's holy of holies: the cabin he called the Palace.

He found his boss on the veranda. In a track suit. He looked like he had been rolled in dough, but the baking operation had been abandoned. On a chair sat something white with a head protruding from the top, two arms at the side and two clumpy, almost unused trainers resting on the balustrade. The man's fingers were rolling a supply of cigarettes.

Frølich started by delivering his report on Henning Kramer's brother. 'The brother's the one who owns the car – the Audi. Henning was allowed to make use of the car when his brother wasn't there. His brother had been away for ten days; he says Henning was living with his mother, but he kept an eye on the brother's flat, too. He may have slept there – on the odd occasion. They had no special agreement this time, except that Henning was to pop by and water a few plants. That cactus, among others.'

Gunnarstranda lowered his feet, stood up and threw more charcoal on the brick grill in the corner where the fire was blazing with dry, cracking noises.

'Get some glasses,' he said and started unpacking the marinated meat from the carrier bags.

Frølich went in through the broad glass doors straight to a shelving system that separated the sitting room from the kitchen. Here he found two large beer tankards which he took outside.

'I've made some salad,' Gunnarstranda mumbled and gave a nod of acknowledgement as Frølich poured beer into the glasses.

'The brother says Henning often used his flat. He also says he spoke to Henning on the phone. Henning rang him on Thursday.'

'What time of day was that?' Gunnarstranda asked.

'Eight o'clock in the evening, Norwegian time, and as it was Henning who called, the brother sees that as evidence that he was making sure he wouldn't be disturbed while he hung himself.'

'How so?'

'First of all, because it was three in the morning – in the Philippines. Henning respected his brother and would never have rung him unless it was for something special – his brother thinks. The conversation boiled down to a question about when the brother was coming home. Henning had never called his brother when he was abroad before.'

'Thursday evening. Wonder what I was doing then,' the police inspector mumbled to himself.

'I was in the cinema anyway,' Frølich said.

'You waste your time going to the cinema, do you?'

'I wasn't alone. I had a lady with me. Besides it was one of the most violent films I've ever seen. It was the film that Katrine Bratterud saw the evening before she was bumped off, *The Matrix*. By the way, one of the characters had the same beard as Kramer. In fact, he looked very much like him.'

'You don't say. Was he a hero or a villain?'

'Villain,' Frølich said with a grin.

'What did they talk about?'

'Who?'

'Henning and his brother.'

'Life, the meaning of life, whether things were predetermined or you had control over your own life . . . destiny.'

'That doesn't have to be depressing,' Gunnarstranda said. 'You can do that with a sense of wonder.'

'In that case he could have waited until his brother came home.'

'He may have had other motives for ringing. He may have been trying to articulate something – after all, the man did have a philosophical bent.'

'But if he takes his own life afterwards . . .'

'We don't know that he took his own life,' Gunnarstranda interrupted. 'Have you never wondered who you are and where you come from?'

'It's pretty obvious . . .'

'I mean, seeing yourself as a mortal and wondering what the meaning of life is, whether there is a purpose.'

Frølich smirked into his beard, but stopped the moment he felt he was being observed. He shrugged. 'Not that often.'

The older policeman regarded Frølich with irritation. 'Sooner or later you will. Everyone does. Perhaps Kramer was just quick off the mark. Did his brother have any idea where Henning might have concealed a letter?'

'No.'

Frølich peered down into his tankard. The remaining froth formed a spider pattern on his glass. White bubbles rose in the brown liquid. Frank raised his glass to his mouth and drank with great gusto.

Gunnarstranda walked through the wide veranda doors into the kitchen where he rummaged around. Frank turned and gazed across the forest that ended in fields, which in their turn led to the mouth of the blue Drammen fjord. In the distance there was a cluster of yachts bunched together, presumably sailing in a regatta around the marker buoy.

Gunnarstranda came out with plates and salad on a white wooden tray. He set the table and put the meat on the grill, which soon began to smoke and spit.

'Would you have hanged yourself in your brother's flat?'

239

Gunnarstranda asked, raising the whisky bottle, twisting off the cap and smelling.

'I don't have a brother.'

After receiving a stern look from Gunnarstranda, and taking a seat, Frølich amended his flippant remark: 'I wouldn't have hanged myself – not in a relative's house, nor anywhere else.'

'That's the point,' Gunnarstranda said, pouring whisky into the cap, sampling it and, with closed eyes, contorting his face. He went on: 'The typical suicide victim tries several times, isolates himself socially, feels sorry for himself and drops hints to everyone and everything about how awful life is, but Henning Kramer didn't do that.'

'Yes, the brother was in total shock, but you saw that, didn't you. I dropped the man off at his mother's. He's going to stay there a few days. There's just the two of them now that Henning's dead. The father died some years ago. Car accident.'

'Henning Kramer was not a typical suicide victim,' the police inspector asserted with conviction. 'The process of suicide is like an upturned funnel. It starts with small signals that can go in several directions, but as the psychosis develops suicide becomes a kind of obsession.'

'We know nothing about him of that nature. Although he may have been going for regular psychiatric treatment.'

'Very unlikely. Anyone employed at the rehab centre has to go through a thorough examination. A psychiatric patient would never have passed the test.'

'The tests can't be that bloody good,' Frølich grinned. 'Kramer smoked home-grown marijuana. His window sill at his mother's house was like a greenhouse.'

Gunnarstranda gave a sigh of desperation.

'But he may have been pretty depressed,' Frølich went on. 'If he killed her – Katrine.'

'That's the point!' The two of them stood staring into a void, rapt in thought.

'He may have done it,' Frølich repeated, meekly folding his hands. 'He may have killed her.'

Gunnarstranda: 'How did her jewellery get into Skau's hands?'

'No idea.'

'Raymond Skau will have to come up with something very good to explain away the jewellery.'

The younger policeman was not finished with Henning Kramer. 'From the evidence of this taxi driver I spoke to, Kramer was lying through his teeth about what happened that night.'

'But why would he kill himself?'

'He couldn't stand it any longer.'

They both grinned at the empty rhetoric.

The older policeman went to the grill and turned over the meat. Frølich drank more beer and enjoyed the view.

At last Frølich spoke. 'We have some hard facts: the girl was killed and Henning Kramer lied about what he was doing that night. So far we only know for certain that Henning had a specific opportunity to take her jewellery. For all I know he could have sold it to Skau.' He pointed to clouds gathering in the south. 'Look,' he said. 'Storm clouds brewing again.'

Gunnarstranda peered at the sky for a few seconds, then produced a cigarette, lit up and held it covered in his hand. 'It's the same clouds you always see over Nesodden when we're in Oslo. It won't rain here; it follows the water – the fjord.'

He lifted a piece of meat to examine it before putting it back on the grill. 'The question comes down to why Kramer would remove her jewellery,' he said at length. 'Why would he remove her clothes and jewellery after killing her?'

'To remove clues,' Frølich said, but on seeing his colleague's critical glare continued on the defensive: 'I have no idea what he was thinking, not an inkling, but the fact of the matter is that he . . . I mean the person who killed her . . . must have removed the jewellery. And why? Maybe he wanted a souvenir, or perhaps he thought it would come in handy.'

'Or perhaps the person in question simply robbed her,' Gunnarstranda said in a quiet voice. A coughing fit was on its way up his creased neck.

While Gunnarstranda wrestled with the paroxysm, Frank began to pick at the salad. 'Would Kramer rob Katrine?' he wondered.

'Not Henning. If robbery was the motive it must have been Skau.' Frølich didn't think that was likely. He wrinkled his nose.

Gunnarstranda had his breath back and was thinking aloud. 'Raymond Skau is the perfect perpetrator,' he decided. 'He's the brutal assailant we've been searching for, the man who bumps into a semi-clad babe in the middle of the night, a girl with whom he once had an intense relationship and whom he beat up in a bout of jealousy. The fact that he is in possession of the jewellery makes perfect sense. But then – our basic premises are no longer solid. The picture crumbles because Kramer lied. Hell!' Gunnarstranda banged his fist on the table.

'At any rate, we have to find Skau,' Frølich said, composed. 'And now I assume Gerhardsen is beyond suspicion.'

'No one is beyond suspicion,' Gunnarstranda barked with irritation.

Frølich sighed. 'All we know for certain is that Henning drove to this car park by the lake. Observations of the car tally with what he told us.'

'So?'

'Suppose Henning killed her,' Frølich reasoned calmly. 'Henning knew Katrine. He may have known about Raymond Skau. He may have known about her problems with the guy, and he may have known that Skau visited her at work earlier in the day. After all, Katrine made a lot of phone calls and one of them may have been to Henning. Imagine the two of them in the car. Her, a tasty looker, semi-naked, happy. Him, aroused, turned on by her. Suppose they were not on the same wavelength. He was lusting for sex; she was thinking about quality of life. He put his arms around her.

242

She tried to brush him off with a joke, but he wouldn't relent. He lost control, raped Katrine and strangled her. According to criminal logic, the natural thing for him to do would be to remove all her clothes and jewellery, to hide any clues, but at the same time he knew the police would find semen in the body. He's read about DNA testing. Henning must have known that the semen would lead the trail back to him. So he devised a plan. He sold us a line about the two of them having consensual sex in the car and he kept her jewellery. Perhaps he sold it on afterwards.'

'That's a bit thin,' Gunnarstranda said.

'OK, you suggest something better.'

'I suggest we eat,' Gunnarstranda said, grabbing a plate and marching towards the barbecue.

They ate in silence for a while. Salad, marinated steaks and fresh white bread. They drank cold beer. Frank had in fact never believed that an afternoon with this misery guts could turn out to be so promising.

It was Gunnarstranda who broke the silence. 'In the first place, Henning admitted picking up Katrine outside Annabeth Ås's house. Raymond Skau might have been there, standing outside the house waiting for Katrine. He turned up at her work earlier in the day, didn't he. He might have followed her and Eidesen to the party – we have no way of knowing. Suppose he stood waiting outside the house. He saw Katrine jump into Henning's car, so he followed them. We know Henning and Katrine drove down to Aker Brygge and bought food at McDonald's. They drove off. According to Henning, a car followed them into the car park by Ingierstrand.'

Gunnarstranda fell silent and ruminated on what he had said.

Frølich filled both their glasses.

A white wagtail landed on the veranda balustrade and wagged its tail. 'We have an audience,' Frølich said. 'A spy.'

'If we focus and think logically,' Gunnarstranda resumed, 'it's clear we are dealing with a casual assailant. Once we have Skau, we'll get the forensics team to run a DNA test on him. That takes

243

two weeks and then we'll know if the skin under Katrine's nails belongs to Skau. Then it's just a question of time before we find her hair on his clothing. By which point this damned business will be an open-and-shut case.'

'But where is Skau?'

'In Sweden, I suppose,' growled Gunnarstranda, buttering a slice of bread. 'That's typical too. I've caught two killers before who thought they could slip into Denmark or Sweden to take the heat off themselves. In a couple of weeks Skau will be back, and then he's ours.'

The two policemen sat gazing into the air. Gunnarstranda was chewing and thinking. Frølich crossed his legs and turned his face to the sun – relaxed.

'I don't remember seeing any scratch marks on Kramer,' Gunnarstranda said at length.

Frølich beamed. His boss still had not dropped the idea of Kramer as the killer. 'We don't know where she scratched him,' he said. 'The pathologist will be able to say whether there are any scars resulting from scratches.'

Gunnarstranda pulled a face, as though suddenly remembering his role as host and Frølich's as his guest. 'Nice to see you,' he grinned.

'Thank you. And thank you for the spread.'

'Thank *you*. Do you play chess?'

Frølich's heart sank. Chess. Just as he was feeling at home. Chess – the game with one piece called a bishop, another a knight. One of them can jump over other pieces in an L shape. He gained time by taking a good swig of beer. Chess, he thought. The game where either the king or the queen has to stand on a square marked D1.

'I knew it,' Gunnarstranda said, contented. 'A good policeman loves chess.'

Frank thought of how sometimes he hated chess. Always having to make strategic decisions, always thinking three steps ahead before you made a move. 'It's a rare occasion for me to play,' he said with care.

'Come on,' Gunnarstranda said, leading him into the cabin to a low table with a black surface. 'Friday evening, out in the wilds, whisky, beer and chess,' he continued with a smile. 'You've landed in paradise.'

28

The Pin-up Girl

The next morning Frølich left Gunnarstranda's mountain cabin for Drammen, but instead of branching off to Oslo, he bore left for Kongsberg. He left the motorway, continued for a good half an hour and didn't stop until he reached the turn-off for the road through Nedre Eiker. He sat in the car looking across the small valley. The housing estate must have been built at some time in the seventies. The houses stood in neat lines. An attempt had been made to blend them naturally into the terrain, but it had failed as the area consisted of two large surfaces sloping downwards into a V-shaped hollow where a stream must have flowed at one time. Along these surfaces ran rows of two-storey terraced houses seasoned with the occasional low, single-storey, prefabricated house. Everywhere shingle-covered flat roofs and unsympathetic, square double-glazed windows prevailed. Here and there more ambitious buildings popped up, some with huge verandas and walls with 'prosperity pustules' – bulges in the walls with a small-paned window in the centre; others had more kitschy accessories: imitation Greek pillars at the entrance or multi-coloured leaded windows. In most of the gardens, however, bushes and fruit trees had succeeded in reaching maturity.

Frølich got out of the car and walked into the estate. Somewhere a lawnmower motor droned; a small girl was sitting alone and forlorn on a seesaw. She stuck a finger in her mouth and stared at the passing policeman with big eyes. On a veranda further away a boy sat astride a plastic tractor making *brum-brum* noises. Frank discovered the Bratterud house long before he saw the number on the wall. A sense of hardship emanated from the fragile construction, from the black holes in the roof, the stains on the flaking paintwork, the crooked postbox, the overturned dustbin, the grass that had grown so long that wispy flower stems dotted the lawn and the delicate front steps that threatened imminent collapse.

The woman who answered the door was plump around the waist and had unusually big bags under her eyes and reddish, curly hair. Frølich remembered her from the funeral. She was the woman with a handbag permanently hanging from her arm, who had shaken Annabeth Ås's hand after the service.

Frølich introduced himself. There was a burning in the woman's eyes, a muted yellow glow, a spirit flame nourished by the bags under both eyes.

'Long way from home here,' she said. 'This is Buskerud.'

Frølich responded with a smile worthy of a TV preacher. 'My main reason for coming is to talk about Katrine on . . . an informal basis,' he said, patiently placing his hands on his hips.

'Why's that?'

'To get to know her background . . . upbringing . . . just to know a little more.'

A big lock of curly, red hair fell across her brow. The woman stroked the hair away with a club of a hand. Her fingers were short and stubby, and inflamed with eczema.

'I would have liked to ask you in, but it's a mess here.'

'We can go for a walk,' Frølich said blithely.

'Stroll round the estate with the police? You've got to be joking!'

She turned her head and looked daggers at his profile. Hers were the eyes of a deranged bird the second before it flies at someone. Frølich looked away and noticed that the grey, damp-damaged wood was coming through the paintwork on the front door. A leak, he thought, and noticed why the steps were crooked. The base was beginning to rot.

The silence lasted for what seemed an eternity. An insect – a bug of some description – with six legs and a three-sided shell lumbered cautiously along the hand rail of the steps. Its two feelers looked like aerials and the creature flourished its antennae in the same way that the blind tap with a stick to detect dangers ahead. Wonder if it knows where it's going, thought Frølich. He looked up again to meet the woman's fierce gaze.

'Well, you'd better come in then,' said the woman at last, turning with difficulty.

'Sit wherever you like, but not in the cat's chair,' she panted, brushing the lock of hair off her brow again. It fell back at once. She pushed forward her lower lip and blew it away. 'That's the cat's chair. If you sit there you'll have to go home and wash your trousers right away!'

Frølich looked around and found the kitchen, where the sun was coming in through the window and making the stains on the floor shine with a dry, matt lustre. He took a wooden chair from the little table under the window and carried it into the sitting room.

'She hadn't been home for a long time . . . to visit you . . . before she died, I mean . . . had she?' he asked, sitting down.

'She never came home.'

Frølich said nothing in the silence that followed this outburst.

'Well, now she's dead, and it's sad, but things were bound to go wrong for her. She was a pathological liar who knocked about with boys and men from the time she was so big.' One club-shaped hand indicated a height of a metre off the floor.

'What do you mean by a pathological liar?'

'That's what she was. She lied about everything and everyone, and nothing was good enough. I wasn't good enough. When she dropped by a couple of years back I cooked for her. I remembered the food she had always loved as a child. But it wasn't good enough. No, you should have seen the woman with her, the fine lady who wouldn't accept any of my things, walking round the sitting room with her arms crossed as though frightened she would be infected by some disease. These people drove expensive cars and ate more elegant food. I wasn't good enough. No, Katrine had a high opinion of herself. She thought she came from better stock, her, the daughter of someone who couldn't take care of her own children.'

'You adopted her, didn't you?'

'Yes, we did.'

Frølich waited for more. It didn't seem to be forthcoming. In the ensuing silence Frølich considered how to formulate his next question. But to his surprise she spoke up first: 'Katrine was fond of her father. My husband. They were inseparable. And for as long as he was alive she was all right. But then he died, of cancer. When she was eleven, I think. And she was a difficult teenager. We never really got along.'

Frølich cleared his throat.

She interrupted, 'Now they'll be together, at last. I'll put her urn on his grave.'

Frølich tried to read what lay hidden behind the cheerless eyes, but gave up. When the silence had lasted long enough he asked in a light tone: 'Why adoption?'

'I couldn't have any children.'

'I mean . . . why Katrine?'

'Her real mother was dead. That was all we knew. And then Fredrik died a few years later. Yes, and then it wasn't many more years before I had the task of chasing the men away. That was Katrine's problem. She never got over losing her father.'

'What did she die of, Katrine's biological mother?'

'No one knows. But that fed the girl's imagination of course. She fantasized about everything from here to Monaco.'

Frølich nodded and lowered his eyes. He didn't like to think about children with unattainable dreams.

'You know, she thought about plane crashes and car accidents, reckoned her real origins were the Soria Maria palace.'

Frølich recalled a job he had been on years ago, with two others as muscle for the child welfare authorities – a case of gross neglect as a result of which the child had been placed with the social services. The girl had been around seven. How old was she now? Eighteen? Nineteen?

'But the woman could have been a drug addict or could have died of cancer like my husband for all I knew. We were told nothing and didn't want to ask. We didn't want to know.'

'Does the name Raymond Skau mean anything to you?' Frølich asked.

She pulled a bitter grimace.

'So you do know the name?'

She nodded. 'He was the one who got her into the mess. Much older than her. He was one of the worst good-for-nothings round here. Moved to Oslo as well. He's off the scene now, but they were a couple. She moved in with him as soon as she was old enough.'

'How old was she then?'

'Fifteen maybe . . . or sixteen? I went there, I did, and dragged her back. He even tried to go for me. *Be careful*, he shouted. *I'm warning you. I've got a black belt in karate!* Well, I mean to say. But I gave him a mouthful. *Go home and get it then and I'll whip your back with it!* I said.'

Frølich proffered a courteous smile.

Beate Bratterud smiled, too. 'Yes, it's easy to laugh now, after the event. But it went wrong of course. For Katrine, I mean. It's a terrible thought. Even though it was good that she managed to get out of the mess. But it was a pity she couldn't do it without bitterness. She needn't have been ashamed of me, or her home. We gave her what she needed and we fought for her. We did. But you have to say that she didn't have it easy.'

Frølich stood up. 'Excuse me for a couple of minutes,' he said, taking his mobile phone from his jacket pocket. He tapped in Gunnarstranda's number and sent a cheery smile to the cheerless face on the other side of the table.

It rang three times.

'Please be brief.'

'It's me,' Frank said.

'Spit it out.'

'Thanks for everything last night,' Frølich said in a crabbed tone. Then he went on: 'I'm at Katrine Bratterud's house, as we arranged. She says Raymond Skau comes from here. She knows Skau, who it seems was Katrine's boyfriend during her teens. I suppose he got her on to the streets.'

'Well, well,' Gunnarstranda said eagerly. 'Go on.'

'That was all for the moment.'

'We'll have to see what significance that has,' the voice on the telephone said. 'Some activity in Skau's flat has been reported. If you jump into your car now you may be able to catch them interviewing him.'

Frølich rang off and sat staring at the mobile in his hand. After a while he put it in his pocket. 'You say Katrine fantasized about her origins,' he said, looking up at Beate Bratterud. 'What do you mean by that?'

'What I said.'

Frølich waited.

'Sometimes her origins were all she had in her head. But she never did find out anything.'

'In practical terms, what did she do?'

'Well, now you're asking. Salvation Army maybe. Social services couldn't help. I could have told her that. These women at social services can endure the job for about two years and then they're burnt out. Those that aren't just stand there going on about client confidentiality. The only people who could tell her anything about welfare cases twenty years ago are the welfare cases themselves. I told her, but I don't think she was listening. I don't think she had much luck tracing her parents.' Beate Bratterud sat up straight in her chair. 'In the years after my husband died all this stuff took over full-time. They were very close. Katrine and Fredrik. But she never liked me. I was never good enough.' The woman with the curly hair rose to her feet with difficulty, lumbered over to a work-table in the corner and pulled out a drawer. She returned with a small box. In the box there were photographs. 'Here,' she said taking out the photos, looking at some, discarding them or passing them to the policeman, who studied them with polite interest. They were younger versions of Beate with long, curly hair. She was slimmer and her face was less lined. In one photo she was smiling; her teeth were straight and pointed inwards, like fish teeth. Frølich examined the smile and wondered whether it would be true to say that she had been good-looking.

Beate passed him the whole box and clumped off to another chest of drawers. He flipped through the photos and found a folded, yellowing newspaper cutting. He gently unfolded it in his lap. It was a page from *Verdens Gang*. He read the date in the top corner: 11 July 1965. The page was dominated by a girl in a bikini posing on a diving block in a swimming pool. She had curls flowing down to her shoulders and was a bit podgy around the thighs and stomach. *Today's VG girl is Beate,* the caption ran. Frank subjected the newspaper cutting to closer scrutiny. Yes, that was a younger version of Beate Bratterud. He looked up and met her doleful eyes.

'The years pass,' she said in a sullen tone, turned and began to rummage through another drawer. Frølich had no idea what to say, but felt it would be wrong not to compliment her. He cleared his throat. 'Wow.'

She turned.

He lifted up the cutting.

'Yes, I heard you,' she said.

He could feel the blush warming his cheeks and concentrated on the photos again. They were pictures of strangers in the Constitution Day procession on 17 May – young people wearing flared pants, a young woman with a pram and a group photograph in the park. In a few pictures there was a dark, thin man with brushed back hair and elegant features. And there were a few of Katrine –

blonde and very good-looking with a sensual, slightly puffed-up lip. She didn't look much like her foster parents.

'There was a photo I thought I would show you,' Beate mumbled and finally found what she was looking for. 'Look here . . .'

The picture was of the thin man arm in arm with Katrine – in front of a wooden gate – a woodland track lined with spruce trees in the background. The father's arm was round the daughter's shoulder while she squeezed his waist. Two people who loved each other.

'We met in the way that people did in the old days,' she said dreamily from the other chair.

Frølich raised his eyebrows. 'You and your husband?'

'Yes, nowadays people advertise in the paper to get to know each other, or through the internet or goodness knows what else. I wouldn't be surprised if you can ring up for a partner, but in the old days . . . in the old days you went to dances . . .'

Frølich nodded, thinking about the bitterness the eleven-year-old girl must have felt for the world the day she was deprived of her father. 'Cruel,' he mumbled.

'At a village hall,' she went on. 'Where the girls stood around like wallflowers and the boys asked you on to the dance floor, after drinking Dutch courage on the steps outside first, of course. Real bands with real music. Where men fought for girls. I suppose you've heard of Alf Prøysen – his song about one step here and one step there and the girl who laughs when you miss a step – and about journeyman joiners. Well, Fredrik and I met at the village hall and he chose me and not the other girl. What I say is: If you've never experienced a proper dance at a village hall, you've never lived!'

'That's right,' said Frølich. He cleared his throat. 'Does the name Henning Kramer mean anything to you?'

'Nothing at all.'

'Ole Eidesen?'

'No.'

Frølich put the photographs back on the table. 'You said Katrine was a little ashamed of her family, or at least she didn't think it was good enough. Was that more or less what you said?'

'She was ashamed of me,' Beate said with bitterness in her voice. 'She was ashamed of this house, of my appearance. Katrine could never accept love from me. She became a snob. It's sad, but the truth is that as her treatment progressed she became even more of a snob.'

Frank gave a heavy nod.

'But this is not the first time, you know,' Beate said.

'The first time for what?'

'It's not the first time Katrine has died. The first time was ten years ago. The drugs almost killed her. And now she has probably been raped and strangled . . .'

The plump woman heaved a deep sigh.

Frølich nodded in sympathy.

'And all I can think is that she must have died many times in the course of those ten years . . .'

Frølich stood up and moved towards the door. Beate Bratterud had sunk into her own thoughts and he had no wish to drag her out again.

29

The Anniversary

The green door had a window with wired glass. A curtain had been pushed to the side and a head was peering out. Even though the wire distorted the facial features on the other side it was clear that the face did not belong to a man. Gunnarstranda signalled to the group on the stairs to retreat. Then he moved his hand towards the door bell and rang again. The person inside fiddled around with the lock and a very young woman opened up. She could have been fifteen, sixteen, seventeen or eighteen years old. Gunnarstranda wondered whether she wasn't fourteen. But he concluded that it was unlikely. She had to be over fifteen. However, she was wearing a lot of make-up; her skin was so stiff it was like cardboard. She had painted her lips dark red and was scantily clad. It was the minimal clothing that gave away how old she was: thin thighs with no flesh – she hadn't finished developing.

'Is Raymond at home?' the policeman asked with a beaming smile.

'No,' she said with a return smile.

'Who are you?'

'I'm his girl.'

Gunnarstranda nodded. 'Good morning, good morning,' he said.

'Hi,' she said.

Gunnarstranda turned to look up at the armed policeman who had positioned himself higher up the staircase, out of the young woman's field of vision. The man withdrew without a sound and left. Gunnarstranda turned back to the young woman and asked in hushed tones: 'Will he be long?'

'He should be here any minute. I thought you were him now.'

'I'll wait indoors then,' Gunnarstranda said, stepping inside. The hall had been painted in dark colours; it was long and narrow as halls often are in old blocks of flats. He stopped in front of the bathroom door and opened it wide. He peered in. The bathroom seemed unusually modern and very clean. He also opened the next door wide.

'Bedroom,' the girl behind him said.

Gunnarstranda glanced at the dresser drawers scattered across the floor. On the broad, unmade bed were thrown socks, underpants and other things that must have come from the drawers. Gunnarstranda closed the door again and continued through the flat with the young woman at his heels. It was clear that she wasn't a hundred per cent sure of him. Gunnarstranda went into the sitting room, which was tidy. Raymond Skau collected old LP records. Three of the walls were covered from floor to ceiling with shelf after shelf of vinyl. There had to be thousands of records. Only two of the shelves were reserved for CDs. Several years of listening, thought Gunnarstranda, looking at the fourth wall, which had two high windows looking out on to the street. Beneath the windows and between them the wall was adorned with a huge hi-fi system. The speakers were two large, man-sized columns. He walked to the end of the room and glanced around the kitchen, which was just as messy as the bedroom. Several days' washing up, including encrusted plates, formed small edifices beside the sink alongside piles of cups lined with black coagulated coffee. The smell was testimony to the fact that it had been a long time since anyone had bothered to empty the waste bin.

The young woman stood in the middle of the floor wringing her hands. 'Who are you then?' she forced herself to ask.

Gunnarstranda walked back to the sitting room window, signalled to the officers below, shook his head and took out his mobile phone.

'I'm a friend of Raymond's,' he confided, wasting no words.

'My name's Linda,' the girl said, smiling the way that well-brought up girls do when they are uncertain of themselves, but are willing to take a chance that everything will turn out fine.

Gunnarstranda's mobile phone rang. 'Yes,' he said, walking to the window. 'No, Skau isn't here, but he's expected, so I'll wait here until he shows up.' He switched off the phone and pointed to the sofa with an air of authority. 'Sit down,' he said to the young woman.

She sat down. Gunnarstranda seated himself on a chair opposite her. 'Have you known Raymond long?' he asked.

'We've been together for two months.'

Gunnarstranda nodded.

'Tomorrow,' she said, 'is our anniversary.'

'Two months is an awfully long time,' Gunnarstranda said with a hint of irony.

'I can hardly believe it,' she said in her naivety, and smiled as though she couldn't believe it.

'Did you meet Katrine?' Gunnarstranda asked.

'No, I don't think so.'

'Blonde hair, quite good-looking, but a bit older than you.'

The girl called Linda shook her head.

'Works at a travel agency,' Gunnarstranda said.

The young girl rolled her shoulders.

'But I suppose you go to school?'

'Project week.' She giggled.

'So you don't need to go to school?'

'We do but . . .' She giggled again.

'How old are you?' the policeman enquired.

'Fourteen.'

Gunnarstranda's lips extended into a satisfied smile.

'What are you laughing at?' The young girl blushed, as if she thought the policeman was laughing at her.

'I'm laughing at Raymond.'

'Raymond's cool, isn't he.'

'Cool,' Gunnarstranda nodded. 'Dead cool,' he mumbled, revealing that hip yoof talk was not something he practised on a daily basis. 'Where is he in fact?'

'With the oinkers,' she answered.

'Oinkers,' Gunnarstranda repeated, mystified.

'With the cops,' she said. 'He rang me from the cop shop. He should have been back ages ago.'

'Do you live here?' Gunnarstranda asked in a friendly voice. 'Do you live with Raymond?'

'Are you crazy?' the girl said. 'I would never have been allowed to do that.'

'But you have keys?'

'Yes. I collect the post and that sort of thing.'

'That sort of thing?'

'Yes, cook and . . .'

'And?'

She came to a halt with a grin. 'Housewifely things.'

Gunnarstranda nodded in an eloquent way. 'Housewifely things,' he repeated and winked at her.

The girl blushed again. At that moment the policeman's mobile phone rang. He put it to his ear, listened to the message and smiled at the girl on the opposite side of the table. 'Great,' he said. 'Go to it.'

Soon afterwards there was a ring at the door and the young woman jumped up. 'That's Raymond,' she said, excited.

'Of course,' Gunnarstranda said without moving from his chair.

Then there was the sound of running feet followed by a thud and someone cursing in a gruff voice.

The girl called Linda glanced up in fear at Gunnarstranda, who staggered to his feet and went to the door. 'Pack your things together,' he said to the young girl. 'I'll arrange for someone to drive you home.' He opened the door and watched the scuffle on the floor of the staircase. A silent man was wriggling and twisting under the weight of two uniformed policemen. The man's arms were forced up behind his back and handcuffed together. As he swung round to see what was going on, his greasy hair hung like a thick curtain in front of his face.

Gunnarstranda smiled to the girl. 'But before going home you'll have to talk to some nice people about your boyfriend.'

30

The Toilet Lid

Frølich spotted Gunnarstranda's lean back as he rounded the corner of Prinsens gate. His boss was passing the shop Steen og Strøm. Frank walked faster. 'Congratulations on finding Skau,' Frank said as he caught up with his colleague. Gunnarstranda gave a brief smile and both strode on without another word about the case.

They crossed Egertorget between the bookshop and the dense group of people standing around the street musicians playing by the stairs leading down to the Metro. 'Have we anything to celebrate?' Frølich asked at length. He had to shout to be heard above the pan pipes and the singing.

'No,' Gunnarstranda said, forcing a path through the crowd.

'Not even Skau?'

Gunnarstranda shook his head. They continued down the slope on the right of Karl Johans gate. Frølich glanced over the picket fence of Dasslokket, the street café called the toilet lid because it was situated above the public conveniences. Even though it was some time since it had stopped raining, the plastic chairs outside were still wet. The tables and chairs covered by a canopy appeared to be dry, but there wasn't a single customer under it. The open door of the serving wagon was the sole evidence that the place was not closed. A warmer day would have been nice, he thought. With sun and designer sunglasses. 'Let's have a cup of coffee,' he said, patting his boss on the shoulder. Gunnarstranda followed him through the gate.

'Do you know why we couldn't find Raymond Skau?' Gunnarstranda asked, finding himself a relatively dry chair by the fence facing Lille Grensen street.

Frølich shook his head.

'Because he was in custody.'

'Say that again,' Frølich exclaimed.

'No,' said Gunnarstranda.

Frølich called to the young waitress slouching towards them. 'Two coffees, please.'

They sat looking at each other.

'So he was in custody,' Frølich said in a thinly disguised ironic tone.

Gunnarstranda nodded. 'Skau was arrested on the evening of 13 June. A call-out to Sagene Video, a small shop by Sagene church. A young girl on the cash desk reported a robbery – Skau was arrested behind Sagene church, in the area leading to the Akerselva the evening after Katrine was murdered. He was held under suspicion of robbing Sagene Video for a few kroner and some films in CD format.'

'DVD format,' Frølich corrected.

'The worst thing is that the shop's right by where I live and the man's been in custody until now,' Gunnarstranda said.

'And the warrant for his arrest was issued several days ago.'

Gunnarstranda scowled. 'Don't tell any journalists.'

'But he still could have killed Katrine on the Saturday night.'

'Possible, but it doesn't seem very likely any longer.'

'But he had her jewellery.' Frølich extended his arm outside the canopy. 'See,' he said. 'Now it's raining again.'

Gunnarstranda glanced up at the sky and took out a cigarette; he lit it and cupped his hand to shelter it from the rain.

'When I went to Skau's place I was let in by a girl of fourteen. Her name's Linda Ros and she says she's Skau's girlfriend.'

'Fourteen years old! The man's almost forty!'

The police inspector had one of his famous coughing fits. While

Gunnarstranda was struggling, the rain hammered down on the canopy making them feel as if they were sitting in a tent.

As the cough subsided Frølich burst out: 'What's happened to the coffee? There are only two of us here. It can't take that bloody long to brew two cups of coffee!'

'Yes, but the problem is this girl maintains she was the one who took the jewellery into the flat. Our people found Katrine's jewellery in the handbag lying on the sitting room table. The girl says it had come by post and she put the bag on the table.'

'Post?'

'That's what she says. The bag came by post on Wednesday or Thursday.'

'Is she telling the truth?' Frølich asked.

'It's very probable. The girl's head over heels in love.'

'But Skau can still have killed Katrine on the Saturday night.'

Gunnarstranda wrinkled his nose. 'The girl is stupid, but not stupid enough to make up this story. And why would Skau send Katrine's jewellery to himself?'

'Why did Skau turn up at her work – at the travel agency?' Frølich asked in turn.

'He claims Katrine owed him money.'

'How much?'

'He wouldn't say. Nor would he say why she owed him money.'
Frølich nodded.

'Keeping his mouth shut won't help him. Skau's the usual sort, an old acquaintance, as the saying goes, and he thinks he has something to gain by withholding information. Anyway, two narks, quite independently of each other, tipped off Yttergjerde that Skau owes money everywhere. That explains why he was so desperate and went for Katrine at her workplace.' Gunnarstranda paused and reflected on what he had just said.

He took another cigarette from his pocket and lit it from the stump of the last.

'Skau is supposed to have been doing amphetamine deals with

some Vietnamese. That explains why he was desperate. They're tough on debtors.'

'Well, here comes the coffee at last,' Frølich said with glee. He took the cups and found the money to pay. 'Got a lot on today, have you?' he asked the girl, who was sullenly gazing into space. Her pout deepened after the sarcastic remark.

31

The Name

'I refuse to make a statement,' Raymond Skau said as he was pushed through the door.

'That is your legal right,' the detective inspector said from his chair with a yawn. He pointed a weary finger at the red plastic chair. 'Please take a seat.'

Skau, unshaven and red-eyed, dressed in a loose-fitting, grey track suit, stood looking at the chair and repeated: 'I refuse to make a statement. Something wrong with your hearing?'

'Does that also mean you refuse to sit down?' Gunnarstranda asked drily.

Skau looked from the policeman to the chair and back again.

'Of course you may remain standing if you wish.'

'Drive me back to my cell.'

The policeman checked his watch. Ten minutes past midnight. He pulled a glum face and informed the man: 'The first transport to leave here will be at seven tomorrow morning.'

'You have no fucking right to do this.'

'What have we no right to do?'

'To refuse me transport to my cell.'

'But I'm not refusing you transport to your cell, am I?'

'Well, then you can drive me back.'

'There is no transport for six hours and fifty minutes. Would you like to stand for the duration?'

'I'll report you.'

'Be my guest.'

'I'll report you to the police complaints authority, SEFO. My solicitor will report you.'

'Please do. It's your legal right. In the meantime perhaps you wouldn't mind sitting down. As I said, you have over six hours to kill.'

Gunnarstranda stood up and walked over to the window. 'Your girlfriend claims she received a parcel in the post, a parcel containing Katrine's jewellery,' he said with his back to the detainee.

'We've talked about this before – I refuse to tell you anything more,' the man behind interrupted. 'There's no point starting this bollocks again. I refuse and it is my legal right.'

Gunnarstranda turned. Skau had sat down and was resting both forearms on the table. He glowered up at the policeman from beneath two narrow, finely arched eyebrows. Gunnarstranda went closer. The white parting in the man's hair ran as straight as an arrow from the forehead to the back, not a strand out of place. Gunnarstranda stuck his face right up close to his. The man's eyebrows had been touched up with a pencil. 'Do you wear make-up?' the policeman asked, unable to believe his eyes.

'So what if I do?' Skau snapped. 'Besides, I don't like your breath.'

Gunnarstranda straightened up. He stood looking down at Skau with a smile playing around his mouth. 'It's fine by me if you don't want to make a statement,' he said. 'I don't think it's very clever of you, but you're within your rights to refuse to make a statement. Nevertheless, I would like you to listen to what I have to say since you are here, anyway. Have you any strong objections to listening to what I believe?'

'I object to being bloody tricked into saying things that can be used against me later.'

'But do you have any reason to fear saying something that can be used against you?'

Raymond Skau did not answer.

'Your girlfriend,' Gunnarstranda began. 'Linda. Of course she may be lying. The jewellery story may be something she made up to protect you. For some reason she's in love with you. Of course she is entitled to be. But that kind of love is ephemeral. I speak from experience. I say that because you are going to be charged with corruption of a minor and sexual exploitation. She is only fourteen years old.'

'I didn't fucking know that!'

'Of course not. But that's not the point. She has admitted the actual state of affairs, so you will be convicted whether you like it or not. The consequence, irrespective of how much in love with you she is now, will be that her love will pass. If she is lying about the jewellery it is therefore just a question of time before she tells the truth. And then you're in a bit of a spot. On the other hand, she may be telling the truth. She may indeed have got the parcel through the post. The question is then who would have sent you the jewellery. Let's ask the question: Who could have done this?'

Skau stared into the distance with a darkened brow.

The policeman coughed and said, 'You may have done it yourself. You might have put the jewellery in the postbox.'

'Why would I do that?' Skau interposed.

Gunnarstranda pretended not to hear. 'I have no idea why you did it, but I have been thinking about finding out. I intend to find that out and why you attacked Katrine at work the day before she was killed.' Skau tried to interrupt, but the policeman held up his palm in the air. 'You claim that Katrine owed you money, but you won't say why she owed you money, or how much. Well, suppose that's true. I assume it is true because two informers – independently of each other – said you have been desperate for money these last two weeks. Rumours are going round that you owe a Vietnamese a lot of kroner for amphetamines you sold on and didn't pay for.'

Skau frowned and said darkly: 'Am I going to be charged for that as well now?'

'I don't give a shit what you do with drugs,' the policeman answered drily. 'I have other things on my mind, but let's assume for the sake of argument that what the two informers have whispered in our ears is true. What I do know is that you went to Katrine's workplace and demanded the money she owed you. We know you were so angry that you resorted to physical violence with Katrine even though someone else was present. It's this fury of yours which is interesting. The very same fury, and behaviour, when you met her alone – in the middle of the night – with no witnesses present – that's interesting too.'

Skau said nothing.

Gunnarstranda observed him for a few seconds in silence before continuing. 'That's why it's important for me to find out what happened after you left the travel agency. It was one o'clock in the afternoon when you left Katrine's workplace. It closed at two because it was a Saturday. Let me hypothesize what might have happened.'

'Save your breath,' Skau hissed.

'You hid,' Gunnarstranda ventured. 'You knew the shop closed early because it was a Saturday. That was why you waited for her. You sat on a bench not too far away and waited until you saw her come out. Then you followed her home to the block in Hovseterveien. You waited there until she reappeared. But she came out with her boyfriend, so you hesitated, then followed them anyway.'

'Why don't you give it a rest,' Skau said, tired. 'You're talking shite and you know you are.'

Gunnarstranda checked his watch. 'We've got plenty of time,' he mumbled. 'This is just a hypothesis, but let's say it happened. You followed the couple. You followed the taxi that picked them up. The taxi went to Voksenåsen and dropped the pair of them outside a house in Voksenkollveien. Now it was just a question of waiting for the party to finish. Let's assume you did that. Or let's assume that night you had a little recce around where the two of them lived, in Holmlia or the area around Hovseter so that you could waylay her. That would be quite logical. You're under a lot of pressure. Katrine owes you money. Why wouldn't you wait for her that night? You're desperate. Between three and four o'clock she walked up the road to Holmlia on her own. An hour later she was dead. Her body must have been lifted into a car. The killer drove a little way, stopped and threw her body over the barrier, where it remained. The car went on, stopping only to get rid of a bag containing her clothes. And three days later our people found her jewellery in your flat. Goodness me, Raymond. Can't you see that you're in a bit of a tight spot?'

'I'm always in a tight spot in this place.'

'Everything points to you. You owe money to everyone and his brother. You had x thousand kroner owed to you by Katrine. We know you threatened her that Saturday. The jewellery in your flat is conclusive evidence that you had been in touch with her that night . . .'

'I have no idea where the jewellery came from!'

Gunnarstranda ignored him. 'You didn't get the money that night either, so you took her jewellery. Whether it covered your debts or not, I don't know, but your desperation was real enough. You were so frantic for cash that you robbed Sagene Video for the till takings. We know what your temperament's like and can just imagine what happened as she walked towards you without any money that night.'

'I didn't see her that night.'

'You shut up and listen now,' Gunnarstranda barked. 'If you didn't do this you'll have to understand one thing and that is that we, or rather I . . .' Gunnarstranda pointed to his chest with a bony, nicotine-stained finger. 'I am the one person who can do the legwork to establish that you didn't do it. And if you want me to take the heat off you, off the petty crime you're sitting up to your neck in, then you have to give me something, even if it's all you have, at least give me something, a straw, anything – just something that suggests it wasn't you who killed Katrine.' He took a pile of papers from his bag on the floor, banged it on the table and said, 'Here! This is your first statement. You are unable to account for your movements all Saturday night and Sunday.'

'I was asleep.'

'Where?'

'At home.'

'And again you're giving me circumstantial evidence that you put the parcel of jewellery in your own postbox.'

'How do you work that out?'

'If you say you were sleeping on Saturday night you're admitting you were at home. You had strangled Katrine and taken her jewellery. You were at home, but you couldn't keep the jewellery in your house. You were seen attacking Katrine at the travel agency and you knew we could come visiting at any time at all.'

'Are you hard of hearing or something? It wasn't me!'

'Shut up, will you!' The policeman's spittle was white. 'You killed her and robbed her. You had to know we would be knocking at your door and with the jewellery in the house your position would not look good. At the same time, however, you needed something of value in case a debt collector came round. That's why you put the jewellery in your postbox, because you thought we wouldn't think to look there. You could easily have done that in the time between killing her and being arrested on Sunday night.'

'Use your head. Why would I put jewellery in my own postbox, so near to my own flat?'

'You needed quick access if one of your creditors came to the door. You were planning a robbery. In fact you were arrested for a robbery that same afternoon.'

'What the fuck do you want me to say?'

'Tell me why you visited Katrine on Saturday.'

'She owed me money.'

'What for?'

'Old debts.'

'But what for?'

269

'For a name.'

Gunnarstranda sat down with a deep frown imbedded in his forehead. 'A name?'

Raymond Skau nodded.

The inspector waved his fingers at him in irritation, to move him on.

'Tormod Stamnes.'

Gunnarstranda was waving his fingers like a man obsessed.

'Tormod Stamnes was working for child welfare in the Nedre Eiker district when Katrine was assigned new parents. He was responsible for her case.'

'And Katrine was interested in this?'

'She wasn't interested in anything else. That was all she had in her head. Finding out about her past.'

'And what did this man say?'

'No idea.'

Gunnarstranda was sceptical. 'You have no idea?'

'I never asked him about things like that. I found out quite by chance . . .' Skau glared across the table. 'What will you give me?'

'I don't understand what you mean.'

'You just said you would do me for sex with a minor. What will you give me in exchange for what I can tell you?'

Gunnarstranda stared at him.

'What about dropping the charge against me?'

Gunnarstranda's eyes darkened. 'Don't play games with me, boy. I'm giving you your only chance. Tell me what you know!'

Skau looked up through his fine eyebrows. He was thinking. Thinking and swallowing. At last he took a decision. 'I used to drink with an old dipso who's been on the social for ever.'

'Who?'

'His name's Arne and he's in a wheelchair. He told me who was working at the office when Katrine was placed with Beate and Fredrik Bratterud at the age of two.'

'Where does this Arne come from?'

'Krokstadelva.'

'But how do you know it was this Stamnes who dealt with the case?'

'Arne told me that child welfare and social security were under the same roof in those days. And in those days Tormod Stamnes did everything, but he's pretty old now. He stopped work several years ago. What happened was that, out of the blue, my pal Arne remembered his name. And, eventually, I found out where he lived. He said he remembered the case when I spoke to him about it.'

'And how much did Katrine pay you for the name?'

'She owed me ten thousand.'

'Ten thousand?'

'Ten thousand spondulicks isn't much to find out the truth about yourself, is it?'

Gunnarstranda rose and walked towards the door.

'You can't leave me sitting here until the morning,' Skau yelled.

The policeman closed the door behind him without another word.

32

The Traffic Menace

Frølich went on foot because it turned out that Tormod Stamnes lived close by in Uranienborgveien, a four-storey brick-built block with fine balconies and a secure front door. He rang down below but without attracting a reaction of any kind, no buzz and no one on the stairs. In the reflection of the glass door he glimpsed a thin, young woman in her mid-twenties walking across the road. She was accompanied by two thin hounds. All three had the same bouncing gait. Frølich moved to the side. The woman unlocked the door and threw him an appraising glance before letting in her two dogs, which skipped in through the narrow opening without a sound. The woman followed and made sure the door was locked properly.

Frølich took a decision, turned round and ambled down Uranienborgveien. An electric wheelchair was moving down the middle of the road driven at a crawl by a man wearing a hat. Cars were queuing behind the vehicle, which had yellow blinkers and indicated left at the crossing with Parkveien. It was strange to see the erect back of the man in the chair turning left. He seemed to be leaning backwards against a whole procession of cars and holding them up.

Frølich turned left, too. It was drizzling and there was a chill in the wind. The streets were empty, hemmed in by shiny, hostile, impenetrable windows. An occasional black-clad silhouette drifted out of sight between the tree trunks in the park behind the palace.

It was morning in Oslo. Frølich wandered aimlessly up Parkveien passing an opulent art gallery and finding himself outside the old Lorry restaurant. Frølich sniffed. His nose for beer had led him to the source. He cast around, went up the staircase to the front door in two strides and grabbed the door handle. It was open.

33

The Ashtray

Henning Kramer's mother lived in a semi-detached house in Stas-jonsveien. There were beautiful shrubs in the garden, with a trim sibiraea hedge growing alongside the fence and preventing passing motorists from prying. The nameplate on the door was made of copper and had turned green. Kramer was engraved in the same Gothic type as the logo of the *Aftenposten* newspaper. Police Inspector Gunnarstranda rang the bell beside the sign. From deep inside he heard a hollow ring. A shadow behind the kitchen curtain window told him he was being watched. He stood with his back to the door and observed the traffic.

There was a rattling of chains on the inside and he slowly turned around.

'Your son,' Inspector Gunnarstranda started when both were standing in the small but very tidy kitchen with the window facing the road. As he eyed up the woman opposite him, he considered what he would say. She was around sixty years old with a face that was worn and now marked with grief. Her eyes were red-tinged and her cheeks bloated. She pulled a tiny grimace. Her quivering lips and a twitch revealed that she was fighting to control her feelings. She returned his gaze with vacant eyes, neither friendly nor unfriendly, nor curious, eyes that kept going despite the pain and the stoical suffering. He cleared his throat. 'Your son didn't leave a letter.'

She continued to gaze with the same empty eyes, full of apathy. 'What letter?' she asked after a while, bewildered.

'Most suicide victims leave a letter,' the detective explained in a neutral tone, his eyes fixed on hers. He sensed a storm brewing inside her and was on his guard.

She grabbed the oven handle of the ceramic stove. Apart from that one movement, she didn't react.

'Letter,' Gunnarstranda repeated with a slight nod.

There was no storm. Even though she wound herself up to speak, her intonation was flat and languid. 'I can see that you might make mistakes,' she said. 'It's easy to make mistakes when you judge someone you don't know. If you had known Henning, you wouldn't think as you do.'

She was breathing through an open mouth, as though it had cost her a great effort to say these words.

'What do you think?' Gunnarstranda asked at length.

'About what? What do you want me to think about?' Her temper seemed to flare up. 'I don't feel as if I'm here. I know he's dead, but I still expect to see him coming through the door. I thought it was Henning when you rang just now.'

The policeman stood on the same spot with his jacket open and his hands buried deep in his trouser pockets, keeping his eyes fixed on her. She was taller than he was. She had tears in her eyes, and was leaning against the stove now, which made them the same height.

He said: 'What do you think about the way he died?'

'I don't think he killed himself, if that's what you're asking.'

'You mean that this was a . . . murder?' He dragged the question out so that the last word fell after a longish pause.

She straightened up in reaction to his choice of words and the way he said them. She sensed the unspoken, quivering in the air now. She turned and looked out of the window through which they both glimpsed the odd car passing the opening where the wrought-iron gate had been left open.

'You'll have to find out, won't you,' she declared.

Gunnarstranda nodded. 'That's one of the reasons I'm standing here asking about a letter. From what I understand Henning was not very communicative . . . about depression or other troubles that may have afflicted him in recent months.'

'No, he wasn't.'

'Nor his feelings about Katrine Bratterud's death?'

'He grieved of course, but he didn't confide in me.'

'Did he talk about his relationship with her at all?'

'Not very much.' She faced him again, assessing her words, their meaning and regarding him with renewed interest. Gunnarstranda, for his part, could see his outline in the kitchen window, a thin figure with a round, almost bald head and protruding eyes that appeared double in the reflection.

'I knew she meant an awful lot to Henning. He was in love with her.' She coughed and repeated with a sigh: 'Love – Henning struggled with that sort of concept. He always had to scrutinize everything from all sides. He made fun of words like love; after all, love is based on spontaneous emotion and I suppose he was frightened of that – talking about feelings. Henning was the intellectual type.'

Gunnarstranda nodded.

'But she was on his mind a lot of the time. He thought she was important for him and he for her. I was never introduced, though.'

'So in the last few days he wasn't down or different from normal?'

Her eyes filled with water. Her mouth trembled. 'He was grieving, but he would never let the grief stop him. That was just the way he was, the way he thought. If he was in love, I mean . . . if he experienced pain or pleasure because of a feeling like that – jealousy, too, for that matter – he would regard it as a deception, something that would pass. Goodness, it's impossible to explain. As I said, taking his own life for love – you're talking about someone else.'

'But how do you see the case?' she asked tentatively as Gunnarstranda was still silent.

'It depends on the particular circumstances,' he answered in a toneless voice.

Disconcerted, she raised her eyebrows.

'I would have liked to find a letter that told us why he chose to take his own life,' the policeman started to explain and at last moved away from the spot where he had been standing. 'If I can put it like that,' he mumbled and headed for the small kitchen table under the window, drew out a chair and sat down. With great care he crossed one skinny leg over the other and fidgeted with a cigarette. 'What would you think if it was proved beyond any doubt that Henning died by his own hand?'

The woman's shoulders slumped and she let go of the oven handle. She sat down, too. The detective put a cigarette behind his ear while studying her at the same time. She didn't give the appearance of crying. All the same, tears were running in two fine lines down her cheeks. The dour expression on her face was chiselled into her features, as though the trickle of tears was part of her facial repertoire that had always been there. Her breathing was normal; her expression and the stream of tears were all that revealed her internal state. Gunnarstranda realized this was the first time in this case that he had met undisguised, unforced grieving. And he realized that his last question had been put too soon.

'Let me put it in another way,' Gunnarstranda said in a low voice, leaning across the table. 'Whether Henning was responsible for his own death or not – there are two working hypotheses I have to have validated or invalidated. The reason I am working on this at all is because your son had a close relationship with the woman who was murdered.'

'So there is a link between Katrine's death and Henning's death?'

'I consider that highly probable irrespective of whether he killed himself or not.' Gunnarstranda didn't say any more. She was no longer crying. Her complexion seemed paler, but the significance of what he had said had sunk in and was now being internalized.

'You agree with me,' she whispered. 'Henning was murdered.'

'Stop right there.' Gunnarstranda stood up and walked to the window. 'I didn't say that.'

He looked outside without finding anything of interest on

which to settle his gaze but, still contemplating the street, he asked, 'What was your impression of Katrine Bratterud?'

'I didn't have one . . .' she said.

'Because,' the policeman added, 'you only know her through what your son said about her. You've already said that. But, like it or not, he was having a relationship with her, and he did mention her to you, so you must have formed some kind of impression, some concept of the kind of woman she was, at least for your son.'

'Yes, I did,' she nodded. 'Henning was twenty-five years old, he lived at home and didn't seem to have it in him to do much more than immerse himself in his own interests. He was doing his military service at the drug rehab place. He thrived on that and liked her. She was a patient there, I understand, trying to get off drugs. She was one of the ones who were successful, I understand . . .'

'What was Henning interested in?'

'As I said, Henning had to get to the bottom of everything, like with love. *What is it? What is it, in fact?* That's what he was like from when he was a little boy.' She gave an embarrassed smile.

'And his interests?'

'Travelling, literature . . . my God, you should see all the books . . .' She tossed her head in the direction of another room. '. . . they're as fat as bibles, and he read and read . . .'

'Travelling?'

'Yes, he spent all his money on travelling.'

Gunnarstranda nodded. 'Did you meet her?'

'The girl from the rehab centre? Never.'

'Did you know your son occasionally took drugs?'

She sat up erect and the expression that had brightened up for a few moments when she was talking about her son's literary feats, darkened again. 'Does that make him a bad person?'

'Of course not. Did you know?'

'Yes.'

'Let me be honest with you, fru Kramer. There is a strong likelihood your son died by his own hand.'

The woman on the sofa was taken aback and was on the cusp of objecting again, but Gunnarstranda held up a hand. 'The reason I cannot exclude such an eventuality is threefold: first, the way he died – so far it looks like an undeniable case of suicide. Second, the fact that he was a drug addict . . .'

'He was not,' the woman interrupted with vehemence.

Gunnarstranda raised his hand in defence. 'Let's not squabble about that. The fact of the matter is that many occasional drug-users often suffer from depression, long and short-term. A psychiatrist would be able to say something more intelligent than you and I could about whether Henning's death was due to an acute depression, drugs or no drugs. The third fact that suggests your son hanged himself is his relationship with Katrine Bratterud.'

'But why would the death of this poor girl suggest Henning would take his own life?'

Gunnarstranda turned to the window again. In the street a middle-aged lady wearing pink shorts and a white blouse walked past. She was pushing a pram. 'Give it some thought,' he said.

'What do you think I'm doing? I've been doing nothing else for the last day or so, but it doesn't make sense to me.'

'What if Henning killed Katrine?' Gunnarstranda said.

'Are you crazy? He loved her!'

'I can understand your reaction,' the policeman said. 'But since I've been employed to clear up this case, it would be unforgivable of me not to keep the option open that he might have killed her. If Henning did do it, you could understand this resulting in a depression, which in turn may have led to suicide, especially if he loved her as you say he did.'

'But why would he have killed her?'

'Good question,' Gunnarstranda said. 'Until the answer to that becomes apparent, we have to work on finding out what actually happened the night Katrine died.'

'Nothing happened that night. Henning was at home and asleep when she was killed.'

'Was he?'

'What do you mean?' The woman at the table was fidgeting with her handkerchief.

'I mean,' Gunnarstranda said, 'that Henning's statement doesn't ring true. There's something that's just not right. He claimed he left a car park by Lake Gjer at three o'clock in the morning – and arrived here at half past three at the latest. But he didn't. A taxi driver is willing to swear in court that he saw Henning's car parked in the same place at seven in the morning – the very morning that Katrine was killed. And he swears that Henning's car was in the exact same place that Henning claimed he had left over four hours earlier. Now I'm asking you, and I know it's difficult, but your answer will and must be used in court: When did Henning come home that night?'

'At the latest at half past three in the morning.'

'So my witness is lying?'

'I didn't say that.'

'But you're saying the car was here at half past three. How could it have been parked by the lake at seven?'

The woman bit her lip.

'Answer me,' the policeman whispered.

'He went back.'

'Have you just made this up or is it really true?'

'It's true. He went back.'

'Why?'

'Because . . .'

Gunnarstranda couldn't stand the tension. He knocked the cigarette down from behind his ear. He lit it with his stained Zippo without giving her a glance and inhaled. He opened the window and politely blew the smoke through the crack. 'Come on,' he prompted. 'Why did Henning go back?'

'Because he was worried about her.'

She stood up and fetched an ashtray from one of the kitchen cupboards. It was made of solid glass.

'He was worried about her?' Gunnarstranda asked, unconvinced.

'Yes. I told him to go back.'

Gunnarstranda flicked the ash off his cigarette.

'Have you one for me as well?' she asked.

Gunnarstranda passed her the tobacco pouch. She began to roll a cigarette, but had to give up when the paper split. The detective put his roll-up in the ashtray, made one for her and flicked the Zippo.

Henning Kramer's mother took a deep breath. She blew a cloud of smoke towards the ceiling and watched it. Then she told Gunnarstranda how she had sat up waiting for Henning and how he had told her why he was worried about Katrine.

'He had gone to sleep with her in the car earlier that night. When he woke up she had disappeared!'

'She wasn't there?'

'No, vanished. He got out and went looking for her but she was nowhere to be seen.' Kramer's mother put the roll-up in the ashtray and stood up as the policeman was about to interrupt. She stopped in the doorway to the living room and turned to him. 'He drove here and woke me up. I know it was half past three because I couldn't understand why he was in my bedroom and waking me up, so I glanced at the alarm clock. Henning was nervous, unsure what to do. He said he had no idea where she could have gone and when I saw how nervous he was, I advised him to go back and search the area.'

She went into the hall and Gunnarstranda shouted. 'What was the time then?'

'He left before six,' she shouted back. And in a louder voice: 'I made him something to eat and we talked for quite a long time.'

She appeared in the doorway.

'When did he leave?'

'I only know it was before six o'clock.'

'When did he come back?'

'At eight.'

'And he hadn't found her?'

'No.'

'Why did your son keep this quiet?' Gunnarstranda asked.

The woman in the doorway just shook her head. She sat down and, with an apologetic expression, produced a packet of Marlboro Light. 'Yours are a bit strong,' she said, putting one of her own in her mouth and allowing the policeman to light it.

'And why did Henning lie to us about what happened?' Gunnarstranda pocketed the lighter.

'He was afraid you would suspect him.'

'But, as you said yourself, why would we believe he had killed her?'

'I have no idea, but he was all over the place. He didn't know what had happened to her and he had a bad conscience about not carrying out a more thorough search when he woke up to find her gone. He was convinced she had to be close by. She could have lost her way or someone could have prevented her from shouting for help. And he was even more convinced that was what had happened when he came back the second time.'

'But he didn't find anything?'

'I'm not sure.'

'What do you mean by that?'

'That I'm not sure. I asked him if he had found her. He said no and gave me a very funny look. I wanted to ask more questions, but he told me to be quiet, not to say any more.'

Gunnarstranda watched the woman take a lungful of cigarette smoke and exhale with her eyes closed. 'I think something must have happened when he went back,' she said.

'Like what for example?'

'I don't know, but I have my own ideas.'

'What ideas?' Gunnarstranda asked.

'He found the corpse. Her dead body.'

Gunnarstranda crushed his cigarette in the ashtray. 'Did he say anything else about her?'

'No.'

'Did he talk about his police interview?'

She nodded.

'What did he say?'

'He said he had lied. He hadn't told you about going back to search for her the second time. I said that was stupid of him. I said you would see through the lie.' She paused.

'How did he answer?' Gunnarstranda asked in a quiet voice.

'He said: "We'll cross that bridge when we come to it,"' she replied.

'How do you interpret that?' the policeman asked.

'Don't know.'

Gunnarstranda mumbled, 'We'll cross that bridge when we come to it . . .'

They exchanged glances.

'I don't know,' she said. 'But I do know he didn't kill her.'

Gunnarstranda waited. In the end, she glanced up and said with a joyless smile: 'Mothers know that kind of thing.'

The policeman nodded to himself. 'Your son's death is tragic and I appreciate you don't like to think about the events, but what you have told me now may have had an effect on Henning. He may have felt guilty about what happened and gone into a depression . . .'

The detective's face was tired and lines of resignation began to appear around his mouth and eyes.

'I know he didn't do it,' she whispered.

'From what you've told me, I cannot exclude the possibility that he killed her.'

'But I think he was serious about this girl.'

'What do you mean by *serious*?'

'That there was something more between her and Henning than with anyone else.'

'You mean their relationship was special. But there is very little to suggest that is the case, fru Kramer. Katrine Bratterud had a boyfriend.'

'But she still felt something special for Henning. She was also precious to him.'

'Of course, the special relationship between them, if he did kill her, must have meant that the final act would have brought on a very bad depression.'

'Would you kill the person with whom you were going to share your life?'

'Share your life?' Gunnarstranda opened his eyes wide. 'You just said he was sceptical about concepts like love.'

'Being sceptical about such concepts does not mean he stopped loving her. What bothered Henning was that words like love camouflaged other things. He wanted to go deeper, to the core, beneath her skin.'

She sat looking into space, and added: 'And that is in fact the essence of love, isn't it?'

In silence, the policeman stared into the middle distance. He was thinking about his conversations with Edel, his own loss and his longing for isolation. 'I'm sure Henning was a very intelligent young man and a wonderful human being,' he said by way of a conclusion and sprang to his feet. 'But we in the police have to work with hard evidence and facts, so we would be interested in anything you might turn up . . . or remember.' He grasped her hand and took his leave.

34

The Archives

Gunnarstranda had just put a pan of potatoes on the stove when the telephone rang.

'I know what you're going to say,' Frølich said before Gunnarstranda could answer with his usual arrogance. Frølich went on: 'I'm ringing from the archives.'

Gunnarstranda watched Kalfatrus swimming restlessly around his glass bowl. The water was beginning to get dirty. Algae and sediment. 'Why's that?' he asked looking down at himself. In his hand he was holding a knife with a blob of butter on the tip and a fork.

'Because of Tormod Stamnes – the social worker who administered Katrine Bratterud's adoption. The guy's over seventy years old and in reduced circumstances,' Frølich said.

'Reduced in what sense?'

'He goes to Lorry during the day. He's one of the boys who hangs his head over his beer glass for ten minutes, then drains it in one go.'

'I see.'

'How much would you be willing to pay for a good motive?' Frølich asked with a grin.

'That's how you want to top up your pay, is it? I've got a frying pan on the go in the kitchen,' Gunnarstranda growled.

'Stamnes was involved in the relocation of Katrine in 1977. But that's not the most interesting bit. The crazy thing is that this guy spoke to Katrine the day before she was killed.'

Gunnarstranda put the kitchen utensils down beside Kalfatrus's bowl. His eyes glowed with the fiery intensity of old as he bit his lip and inhaled.

'This guy seems a bit dodgy,' Frølich said. 'For a long time he pretended he didn't understand what I was talking about. But then when I mentioned her name and said she was dead it gave him a shock. There was a real reaction and it all came out. She'd been there and he'd given her the name of her real mother. Katrine had got everything he knew out of him. The day before she was killed!'

'What was her real name?'

'Lockert,' Frølich said. 'Katrine's real mother's name was Helene Lockert.'

'There's something about that name,' Gunnarstranda muttered, thinking hard.

'I thought you would say something like that,' Frølich whinnied down the line. 'Does it ring a bell?'

'Not at this moment.'

'Helene Lockert died when Katrine was two years old. But that's not the most interesting thing. The most interesting thing is the cause of death.'

'And that was?'

'The Lockert case. In Lillehammer in 1977. Helene Lockert was strangled and left for dead in her house. Killer unknown.'

35

The Clean-Up

After the policeman had gone she plucked up her courage and began to tidy Henning's things. The thought of being in contact with his clothes still repelled her. Seeing his things lying around, where they'd been left, knowing he would never use them again, every little detail reminded her of him, reminded her that he was dead. Outliving your children is a terrible fate, she thought. It is the worst thing that can happen to anyone. When she had finally brought herself to enter his room, she stood studying the room as though it were the first time she had seen it.

The policeman had asked about a letter. But she dreaded going through his drawers, touching his things, confronting her grief, her loss, her emotion. She was exhausted from thinking thoughts about what he would never achieve, what he would never learn, what he would never do or the joys he would never bring her. You should never have dreams, she thought. It's dangerous to dream because dreams make you vulnerable. Dreams that plummet to earth create the greatest pain. She should never have nurtured dreams for Henning. Everyone has enough to deal with inside themselves. She stood in a daze, contemplating sweaters, trousers, shoes that would never be filled with his body, his spirit or his personality.

I have to think about something practical, she said to herself. She didn't want to lift the clothing. It was impregnated with his scent and she knew that would be too much for her. I have to reconcile myself to the fact that Henning is dead, she thought, that he will never come back – not here, not to this life. Her gaze fell on a red book on the bed. The author was Carl Gustav Jung, one of Henning's favourite gurus. Henning had said Jung was the internalized Hindu; Jung had a theory that time was an illusion. Those were the words he had used. *The soul isn't reborn, Mum. We live different lives all the time. While you are living this life as my mother you're living another life, in another time, maybe as a French citizen in a Paris commune, maybe as a Stone Age woman, maybe as a camel!*

'Camel!' she had screamed in consternation, rejecting his suggestion. The incident still made her smile. She sat down on the bed. Of course he was right. There had to be something after death. Something roaming other places, beyond the mortal frame, whether it was called a soul or a spirit or energy. But Henning had not done away with himself, she was certain of that. The mere idea of doing away with yourself would have been totally alien to him; it wasn't a way of thinking he would have been able to accept. She should have said that to the policeman. In those precise words. Henning did not understand what suicide was.

If Henning was living on some other transient spiritual plane, there was still hope. Hope of a spiritual plane, some form of mental substance – a god. But how would Henning meet God? After all, he had criticized the Bible as no more than a collection of myths and good stories, and called himself a religious agnostic.

Her eyes fell on the white marble box he had brought back with him from India last summer. She stood up and wondered whether she dared to hold it. A small marble box decorated with onyx and mother of pearl. She studied the box, fought against her feelings, overcame her desire to turn away and lifted the box up. At once she flinched. There was something inside. A low, dry sound indicated that something slid around every time she moved her hand. There was something in the little box. A flood of new emotions streamed through her. It had to be precious. And therefore something secret. Henning had a secret. Would it be right to pry? Or to be more accurate: did she have the strength to pry? Would another un-achievable dream issue forth only to dash all her hopes yet again, with all the injustice of fate?

She fought an internal struggle. With tears in her eyes she re-moved the lid from the little marble box. And found herself look-ing at a ring.

A ring. She put the box down on his desk and lifted the ring. A heavy ring, a broad ring with two stones inset. She examined it. The ceiling lamp was reflected in all the facets of the two jewels. The light seemed to be sucked into the stones and to explode out again. This was no cheap bauble. She scrutinized the ring. There seemed to be something engraved on the inside. *Katrine*, she read and burst into tears. The box had contained a vain dream, a dream that might have been better remaining a secret.

36

The Detective

Gunnarstranda used his legs and strolled down Maridalsveien to Beyer Bridge. He needed to think and he hated changing buses, so he decided to take a tram instead, a tram to the other side of town. He crossed the Akerselva on foot. By the bridge there was a kind of art installation with balloons. He continued down Thorvald Meyers gate towards Birkelunden. He tried to imagine Katrine Bratterud at the moment she found out the truth about her biological mother. Katrine at the end of her quest. A social worker who would open the door for her, the door out of a life lived in dreams. Would she have been disappointed? He supposed not. The discovery that the mother had been a murder victim of an unknown killer simply threw up yet more secrets.

Gunnarstranda's attitude to the new development in the case was split. On the one hand, it was not good to extend the confines of the investigation too far since it is important to concentrate your energies on the most fertile, and the most logical, ground. In this sense, a murder committed many years ago in a different location could be a dead end. On the other hand, the information about Katrine's biological mother was so sensational that it would be a dereliction of duty to ignore it.

Gunnarstranda sat down on a bench at the tram stop to wait. An elderly woman was inspecting the litter bins in the park and found two empty bottles which she stuffed into a large bag. A young couple who were walking hand in hand stopped to admire the foliage at the top of a birch tree. Gunnarstranda was on the point of lighting a cigarette when the pale blue tram rounded the bend in Schleppegrells gate.

* * *

The building in Drammensveien was the kind that Johan Borgen's Little Lord might have grown up in: a three-storey stone building – the plaster was an attempt to approximate the colour of sandstone – with two balconies adorning a façade of which even the King and Queen would have been proud. The feudal character was emphasized by the Doric pillars at the front entrance. On the wall beside the heavy door was a sign saying Horgen AS, squeezed between a consulate's sign and a sign for an embassy representing one of the states that had recently broken away from the old Soviet Union. Axel Horgen himself opened the door and his bulldog-like face split into a wet grin as he recognized Gunnarstranda on the doorstep.

If the façade was impressive, the hall inside was more confused because of repeated unsuccessful renovation work. The staircase curving down from the first floor was one of the original features. The sculpture filling one of the niches in the wall probably was, too. But the floor had been laid with linoleum and the walls were covered with inelegant hessian. The stucco work in the ceiling had begun to disintegrate; in one place it sagged. Axel Horgen drew him into this low cave, past a fierce woman who ruled the centre of a ballroom furnished as an antechamber. She was sitting on a wooden chair in the middle of the room and, with a clear view of the window, desk and fax, she kept an eye on passers-by like a spider lying in ambush in its web. The corridor did another couple of twists before the two men pushed open a door into Axel Horgen's spartan office. Even though the desk was huge, it seemed very lonely in the corner of the room. There were two armchairs in another corner. But the height of the ceiling created acoustic reverberations that made their heels sound like echoes in the Alps.

Gunnarstranda studied Axel Horgen's certificates and diplomas hanging on the wall. 'Impressive,' he mumbled. The other man seated himself at the desk and rested his legs on an open drawer. 'No flattery, Gunnarstranda. Cut the crap. You didn't come here to examine my wall decorations.'

'Oh, I was thinking more of how impressive it is that you take such good care of all these papers . . . *Russian course*,' Gunnarstranda read aloud while looking at one of the framed documents. 'Do you attract clients because you can speak Russian?'

'We attract clients with anything that smacks of serious political work. Have you thought of changing to pastures new?'

Gunnarstranda shook his head.

'We need old foxes,' Horgen said and seemed to mean it.

With eyebrows raised in query, Gunnarstranda took out a cigarette from his coat pocket.

'Be my guest,' Horgen said. 'So long as we close the door and open the window, we still hold sway in our own offices.'

Gunnarstranda lit his cigarette and took a seat in one of the deep armchairs. It was like lowering your backside into a large wad of cotton wool. On his way down his feet lost contact with the floor and ended up pointing towards the facing wall. 'I'll never get out of this chair again,' Gunnarstranda said, stretching his legs.

'If you had been a potential client, I would have dragged you out when you were ready to sign the contract.'

'Are you making ends meet?'

'There's enough to butter your bread and a bit left over.'

'Expensive rooms?'

'Cheaper than in Aker Brygge.'

'I can believe you,' Gunnarstranda said, and added, 'I'm working on the case of the corpse they found by Hvervenbukta.'

Horgen nodded. 'I've heard.'

'Twenty years ago when you still had a sense of decency and worked for Kripos,' Gunnarstranda said, 'a woman was killed in Lillehammer. Name of Lockert.'

Horgen nodded. He had the expression of a listener, but was experienced enough not to show whether he was listening with interest or not.

Gunnarstranda inhaled.

'True enough,' Horgen said. 'True enough.'

They watched each other in silence.

'You were on that case,' Gunnarstranda stated.

Horgen pulled a face. 'Gunnarstranda,' he said with a grave air. 'I had been working there for six months. I was still wet behind the ears. The only thing I did was write reports as long as novels on that case. Have you read them?'

'I will do.'

'Read first, Gunnarstranda, and ask afterwards.'

Gunnarstranda shook his head. 'I need a briefing.'

'Why's that?'

'I have to know what I'm looking for.' Gunnarstranda played for time, flicking the ash into his open hand. He leaned forwards, breathed in and braced himself. At the second attempt he managed, with some effort, to release himself from the chair. He walked over to the high window, opened it a crack and threw out the ash. He stood observing the traffic. A blue tram rattled down Drammensveien. The sound boomed inside the room. He watched the tram disappear. Slowly other sounds returned: a door slamming on the other side of the street, a car horn honking in the distance, the scraping sound of a woman's stiletto heels on the tarmac and behind the green hedge the voices of two children playing. He turned to Axel Horgen. 'The girl who was killed was the daughter of Helene Lockert.'

Horgen whistled.

They looked at each other for a long time. Horgen lifted a corner of his mouth into a wry smile. 'That case has tormented more policemen than me over the years.' He lowered his feet on to the floor and straightened up in the chair.

'But you're the one I know,' Gunnarstranda said.

'So what if your corpse was Lockert's daughter?' Horgen said at length. 'We all die.'

'The girl was strangled.'

'I've heard rumours that she was raped.'

'That's not definite.'

'Not definite?'

'One witness maintains he had consensual sex with her.'

'And why hasn't he already confessed?'

'He's dead. Hanged himself.'

'Why haven't I heard anything about a moving suicide note detailing his confession?'

'There's no letter, not yet anyway,' Gunnarstranda said in a fatigued voice.

'Helene Lockert was strangled, but there was no sex involved at all.'

Gunnarstranda: 'I hope the Lockert case is not connected. I can't put a man on a case that is twenty years old. And definitely not a case that was never solved.'

'Well, what is there to say?' Horgen shrugged. 'Helene Lockert was left to look after her daughter. Single mum. The father was a seaman. If anyone in the world had a watertight alibi it was him. He was working as a second officer on a Fred Olsen boat when Helene Lockert was killed. I don't think there was ever anything serious between Helene Lockert and this seaman. If there had been, he would have looked after the daughter. She was small, anyway, not more than a couple of years old and unable to say anything. Helene was killed in her own home while the daughter was strapped into the pram or a play pen. And that's all there was. A struggle in the middle of the day in a peaceful little town in mid-Norway. A struggle that ended with Helene's death. Unknown killer. Still unknown.'

'Arrests?'

'None. But . . .'

'Yes?'

'We wondered for a long time about charging a man who was engaged to Helene. He had a sort of an alibi, though. And there was no motive. The guy was about to marry the victim. They were just a couple of days away from the wedding. Another hypothesis was jealousy. Lockert and this man – what the hell was his name again? . . . Buggerud, Buggestad, Bueng . . . yes, that was it, Bueng – he was getting on even in those days, by the way. He was at least twenty years older than her, if not more . . .'

'The second hypothesis?' Gunnarstranda asked when Horgen went quiet, as if a thought had struck him.

'Oh that? Well, Bueng was a ladies' man, a Casanova, had a number of women on the go. We had a theory about jealousy and brought in a stack of women for questioning, but that trail petered out, too. Hell, I hate cases that are never cleared up!'

Horgen rose to his feet. 'They never give you any peace,' he added to himself.

Gunnarstranda threw the cigarette out of the window and folded his hands in front of his chest. 'Gut instinct? Was it Bueng, off the record?'

'No . . . or I don't know. I think he was given a pretty thorough going-over.'

'But what do you think deep down?'

Horgen gave a laconic smile. 'Forget the Lockert case. It's nine to one that the suicide victim raped and killed Helene Lockert's daughter. Are you a betting man?'

Gunnarstranda shook his head. 'This Lockert trail may be a shot in the dark, but I had an idea,' Gunnarstranda said. 'If you've given the case a lot of thought, and I am sure you have, then you've kept tabs – haven't you? – checked a few things out, and my idea was . . .'

'Your idea was . . . ?'

'. . . that you might know where I could find old Bueng.'

37

The Golden Section

No one answered his knock. He opened the door and walked in. 'Hello,' he shouted, still without any response. There was a solitary armchair situated under a window. He went in further and stopped where the wall ended and the room turned a corner. An elderly man lay sleeping on a bed in the alcove to the right. The old man was fully dressed. The policeman hesitated, in two minds. He looked round at the bare walls. A room devoid of any personal touch. For one brief moment he saw himself living his last days in this way. It was a possibility after all. He was alone. Or he might become ill. Seeing himself on the bed for that brief instant made him see the room with new eyes. The man living here had done nothing to personalize the room. A creeping sense of shame overcame Gunnarstranda for bursting in, for standing there as if the room were his own, an intruder in another man's home, a man who didn't know he was there.

The man on the bed was sleeping soundlessly. Only the heaving chest covered with the grey woollen sweater bore witness to the fact that he was breathing. Gunnarstranda's eyes flitted across the dressing table with the closed drawers and the shelves of the bed-side table. An old portable radio, a Radionette, stood on the dresser. The aerial was broken and its shiny stump pointed into the air at an angle.

Gunnarstranda ran his eyes over the sleeping man once more. Bueng was thin, long and grey-haired with a sharp profile: his skin was wrinkled, but the nose was straight; his chin long and pointed; his lips sensitive but severe.

The policeman exited and closed the door behind him. In the corridor he stood looking around, perplexed. Perhaps you weren't allowed to personalize your room, he wondered. Perhaps there were house rules, barracks regulations, like in the army. The walls of Bueng's room were bare. No pictures, no books.

A woman in a long skirt with a shawl over her shoulders came tramping down the corridor. She looked fifty-ish and seemed to be an employee of the institution. There was something quite natural about the way she held herself; she entered the corridor with self-assurance as though she had paraded down it countless times. A woman with auburn hair, kind eyes and a charming slanted smile. 'May I be of help?'

'Bueng,' Gunnarstranda said.

'Right behind you.'

'He's asleep,' Gunnarstranda said.

'Aha,' the woman said with another charming slanted smile. 'I see.'

Gunnarstranda nodded and experienced a rare moment of gentle tenderness for a stranger.

'Wait here,' she said, patting him on the shoulder, and continued down the corridor from which she disappeared into an office. Soon afterwards Gunnarstranda heard a bell ring in the room behind him. It rang for a long time. Eventually the sound was cut short and a gruff voice said something inside. The office door at the end of the corridor was opened and the woman with the shawl peered out. 'Knock on the door,' she mouthed and mimed knocking motions with her fist.

Gunnarstranda followed instructions.

Bueng opened the door a crack. 'Yes,' he said in a friendly, inquisitive voice.

Gunnarstranda introduced himself. 'I'm a policeman,' he added.

'Oh yes?' Bueng said. 'Policeman, yes. Policeman.'

The man suffered from Parkinson's disease. The shaking of his arms caused him to keep hitting the door frame with his hand – as if he were tapping a melody.

Gunnarstranda glanced towards the office door whence the woman with the shawl sent him her broadest beam yet.

Gunnarstranda took a deep breath. 'Would you like to come for a walk with me?' he asked and heard the woman with the shawl approaching from the right.

'Bueng's legs are not very strong,' she explained. 'But we have some wonderful benches in the garden.'

* * *

Bueng managed to walk unaided although his progress was slow. His hands and arms shook without cease. Gunnarstranda held the front door open for him. They exchanged glances. Bueng raised one shaking arm. 'Bloody shakes,' he mumbled and shuffled slowly into the sun. It was a beautiful garden with high cypress hedges, gravel paths and fine, wax-like begonias growing in lines along the edging stones by the path. But those who tended the flowers didn't have a clue about roses, the policeman noted. In the middle of the lawn was an ailing shrub rosebush with no flowers. A strong, thorny, light-green sucker had shot up between the sparse leaves, like a spear. In front of this monstrosity of a rose was a green bench around which a dozen or so small sparrows were hopping and pecking at biscuit crumbs on the ground. The two men took a seat on the bench. The conversation flowed without a hitch as long as they talked about nurses and medication. However, Bueng clammed up when Gunnarstranda asked about Helene Lockert. 'This is about her daughter,' the policeman explained. 'Katrine. She has been killed.'

'The daughter,' Bueng mused.

'Yes,' said the policeman.

'Births can't be undone,' Bueng mumbled, then added, 'It's the only dream you wake up from and you can never go back to sleep.'

'Mm . . . ,' Gunnarstranda said, wondering how to proceed.

'And now you say she's dead. The girl, too,' the old man declared. They sat looking into the distance. Gunnarstranda felt an ache in his fingertips to search his pockets for a cigarette.

'We were going to get married,' Bueng pronounced at length. 'Though nothing came of it.'

'No,' the policeman concurred.

Silence descended over both of them once again. Gunnarstranda stuffed his hands in his pockets to rummage around for cigarettes while trying to devise a strategy to proceed. On a bench further up two elderly ladies were sitting and eating muffins.

After a while they heard steps on the gravel and Bueng glanced up. 'Don't let him get his hands on anything,' he murmured. 'He ruins everything he touches. The other day he was fiddling around with the hedge clippers for hours and as soon as the handyman started them up they fell apart. Some help. And then afterwards he had to tamper with a brand-new lawnmower. It was kaput by the time he'd finished with it.'

'Who are you talking about?' Gunnarstranda asked in a whisper.

'Him over there. The one with the grey hat. Now he's off to do some repairs. I can see that by the way he's walking.'

The policeman followed his gaze and saw an elderly man wearing a grey beret on the gravel path, striding out with his legs splayed to the side. In his hand he was swinging a large wrench to and fro.

'Bueng, you had a lot of women apart from Helene Lockert in those days,' Gunnarstranda interrupted with a firmness of purpose. 'Now those days are gone. A lot of water has flowed under the bridge. No one is interested in past sins any longer. Who were you with at that time?'

'Ah, death, yes,' Bueng said philosophically. 'You only have to walk down Karl Johans gate to see how ineffective death is. No, you can see it here. Look at all of us!'

'OK,' Gunnarstranda said, impatient. 'I have a list here, from the police report made at the time. It says they questioned, among others, a woman by the name of Birgit Stenmoe, one called Grete Rønning, Oda Beate Saugstad, Connie Saksevold . . .' The policeman glanced up and sighed. 'Connie,' he grumbled. 'Imagine calling a poor Norwegian child Connie . . .'

'Connie was half-American,' Bueng said. 'She drank coffee with milk and sugar, and then she had psoriasis. Terrible complexes she had because of psoriasis . . . although it was mainly in her scalp. Who cares whether a woman has dandruff in her hair? You should have seen Connie's legs. They were as smooth as polished aluminium.'

'I have been led to believe these women considered themselves to be in love with you while you were engaged to Helene Lockert?'

'It's not easy to say no all the time,' Bueng said in reflective mood. 'It's not easy to disappoint others.'

'No, it's not easy,' Gunnarstranda said.

'But things have a tendency to go wrong if you lie too much.'

'That's right,' Gunnarstranda said.

'Two lovers at once, that's fine,' Bueng said. 'Three at once is too much. It's difficult to remember what you said to one and not to the other, and then there's the problem of time. Most women want at least two nights a week and with three the week is too full . . . it's difficult to make things fit. You drive yourself mad with the lies.'

'You had five,' Gunnarstranda said.

'Yes, it had to come to a sorry end.'

'Right.'

'But two lovers – that's fine. You don't get locked into specific patterns. Of course you know that women's tastes vary. Their kissing does, too.'

'Indeed,' said Gunnarstranda.

'You can tell a woman's nature from the way she kisses,' Bueng said.

'You must have been much older than her . . . than Helene I mean?'

'I was more than twenty years older, yes, but age is not important in love.'

'Did she have a daughter?'

'Yes. She's dead now, you said.'

'Helene Lockert's daughter, did you see much of her?'

'I don't remember her very well. It was the mother I was interested in.'

'And she was killed, of course.'

'Yes, that was a sad story. We didn't get married. And I never got married later, either. I had never imagined I would grow old alone.'

'Have you ever received a visit from Helene Lockert's daughter?'

Bueng twisted his upper body round. His head shook as he regarded the policeman. 'What do you mean by a question like that?'

'We have reason to believe that she knew the identity of her biological mother . . .'

'But my dear man, who doesn't know the identity of their mother?'

'This case is complicated, Bueng. Please answer the question. Have you ever received a visit from Helene Lockert's daughter?'

'Never.' Bueng stared into the distance again. A puff of wind brushed a lock of white hair across his forehead. 'Never,' he repeated to himself.

'It will be my destiny to die alone . . .' Bueng continued in a louder voice. 'And I would never have imagined . . .'

'So you gave up the idea of marriage after Helene?' the policeman asked.

'Helene knew it wasn't always easy.'

'She knew about her rivals?'

'They were not rivals in fact. There was only Helene.'

'However, one of the police's theories was that one of her rivals . . .'

'I didn't agree with the police.'

'Did you have any suspicions as to who might have killed her?'

301

'I think it must have been one of Helene's ex-lovers who killed her.'

'But witnesses – many witnesses – said they had seen a woman walking down the street where she lived, a woman behaving in a strange manner, at roughly the time Helene was killed.'

'Yes indeed, but the only man they checked was the girl's father and he had an alibi. But Helene was a good-looking woman . . .'

'But the witnesses . . .'

'. . . so he must have dressed up, I reckon. Men wearing women's clothing is nothing new.'

'The years have drifted by now,' Gunnarstranda said with a sigh. 'You've thought about this case for many years now. Are you sure that . . . ?'

'You mentioned Connie,' Bueng interrupted. 'And you mentioned Oda Beate . . .'

'Grete Rønning,' the policeman read from his list, 'Birgit Stenmoe . . .'

'Yes?' Bueng said, waiting.

Gunnarstranda said nothing.

'Yes?'

The policeman cleared his throat. 'There are no more names.'

Bueng turned his head and they exchanged glances.

'I have to go now,' Bueng said and staggered to his feet. 'I'm tired.'

* * *

Gunnarstranda watched him go. The figure tottered down the gravel into the building. There was no doubt that he did not look like a murderer. But appearances can deceive. He had discovered that before.

The policeman took a cigarette from his jacket pocket, lit up and inhaled deep. He crossed his legs and wondered whether he ought to be annoyed. He had no idea. A moment later something made him turn his head. The woman with the long skirt and the shawl was standing by the entrance. She made an embarrassed movement with her arms when she realized she had been seen. Stuffing some papers under her arm, she advanced at a measured pace. She stopped by the bench. Gunnarstranda stood up and gave an involuntary smile upon realizing they were the same height.

'Do you know Bueng well?' she asked after they had sat down.

He sighed and shook his head. 'I'm a policeman.'

She was quiet and waited for him to go on.

'It's about an old case.'

'He almost never has visitors,' she said.

Gunnarstranda managed a faint smile. 'He didn't want a visit from me, either.' He glanced over at her. Read her name on the badge fixed to her shawl: Tove Granaas. She assumed a serious face until it softened with her captivating, slanting smile. 'He usually loves talking to people.'

'But then I suppose he doesn't talk about himself,' Gunnarstranda said.

'That's true,' she grinned and fell silent.

Gunnarstranda wanted to extend the conversation. 'Lovely garden,' he said. 'Lovely begonia semperflorens.'

'Yes,' she said, pointing to the ugly rose in the lawn in front of them. 'But we can't do much for that one.'

'Roses are pruned from the rootstock,' Gunnarstranda said with a nod towards the protruding, pale green, thorny spear. 'When that happens, it means the root has decided to grow on its own.'

'You don't say?' She seemed impressed. 'Fancy me meeting someone who knew what the problem was. A policeman who knows about flowers.'

'It's just an interest, a hobby.'

'So you must have a beautiful garden, I suppose.'

'No.' He added, 'I have a mountain cabin,' when he saw her tilt her head to show interest. 'What does he like talking about?'

'Hm?'

'Bueng, what does he like talking about?'

'Would you like to try again?' Tove asked.

'No, I'm not sure it's worth the effort.' He put the cigarette in the matchbox and closed it with care. 'He's a witness from an old case, over twenty years ago. I don't even know if he can remember that far back.'

'We call him Elvis,' she said.

'Why's that?'

'He sings like Elvis. Perhaps he looks a bit like Elvis.' She chuckled. 'Although he doesn't quite have the leg work.'

Gunnarstranda nodded. 'Parkinson's, isn't it?'

'Yes.'

They sat staring ahead. She seemed to be thinking. 'You don't have any kind of ID, I suppose?' she asked all of a sudden. Gunnarstranda was charmed by the look accompanying the question. The purpose. He took out his wallet with the police badge and showed her. 'Nice name,' she said.

'There are not many of us,' Gunnarstranda replied.

'He's a bit of a charmer,' she said. 'Elvis . . . Bueng.'

'I can believe that.'

'And that means he never talks about himself.'

The policeman nodded. 'Has he had any recent visitors?'

'Oh, he seldom has any visitors,' she sighed. 'That was why it was nice that you visited him today. It was a bit of excitement.'

'When did he last have a visitor?'

'No idea, but it must have been a long time ago.'

'Are you absolutely sure he hasn't had a visitor in the last two weeks?'

'I doubt it.'

'But you're sure?'

'No, I don't work here every day – round the clock.'

'Could you find out . . . ?' Because then I could phone you, he had thought of adding, but paused not to appear ridiculous in her eyes.

She smiled. 'That should be possible.'

They stood up. 'Is there hope?' she asked.

He didn't understand what she meant.

'For the rose.' She motioned towards the strange growth in the lawn.

The policeman shrugged. 'Cut off the pale green shoot coming out of the ground. If it comes up again you can dig up the plant and chuck it away.'

* * *

'There was something there, Kalfatrus. I saw it,' Gunnarstranda mumbled as he cleaned the inside of the goldfish bowl with a wad of cotton wool. He looked down at the fish. It lay quite still in five centimetres of water. 'And I must buy some equipment so that this bloody bowl doesn't get so mucky,' he went on, pushing his glasses up his nose. He stood musing and muttering to the fish: 'Either the old goat noticed a name was missing off the list I read out or he was giving me a hint. Anyway, I don't think he's the killer. He seemed too frail and fragile for that. But suppose he gave me a hint. What would the purpose of that have been?'

He put the cotton wool on the shelf and went for more. He shouted to Kalfatrus, 'That would be too improbable, wouldn't it? Kripos work on that case for months and then twenty years later I go to a nursing home and the old Casanova suddenly remembers salient facts?'

He searched for something to put water in, thinking. 'It might have been something else, a detail. It doesn't have to be a person.'

He found a litre measuring jug, filled it with water and reached for a thermometer. 'In any case,' he muttered, 'if I stumbled over something of any significance to help solve the Lockert case, so what? It happened more than twenty years ago and there is no link between the two cases. Katrine Bratterud grew up somewhere else, several hundred kilometres from Lillehammer . . .'

He poured hot and cold water in the jug until the temperature was right. With great care he poured the tempered water over Kalfatrus, who reacted with wild flicks of the tail. Gunnarstranda observed the fish. 'You're happy now, aren't you,' he mumbled. 'You like to have water around you; you like the surroundings you know. Just imagine if you had landed on the floor, or in salt water. You would have ended up like poor Katrine. Asphyxiated and dead.'

He stood thinking. After a while he said to the fish: 'Perhaps that was what happened, eh? She wasn't in her natural habitat. But then what was her natural habitat? Or what was the wrong habitat?'

38

The Empty Chair

They were sitting in her kitchen, in the spacious dining alcove. They were alone. As Julie was with her father, the chair at the end of the table was empty. Eva-Britt was resting her head on her hands. She had finished eating a long time ago. She poured herself a little more red wine. Her mouth broadened into a smile and her eyes sparkled as he took another helping.

'You think you've won, don't you,' he said.

'Me?'

'I know I'm fat,' he said, taking more sauce.

She grinned. 'I didn't say that.'

He scraped the frying pan. 'But you were thinking about saying it,' he said, putting the pan down on the table and taking another potato. '*You're fat, Frankie*, you were thinking of saying, just like now you're thinking about saying: *Be careful. I put lots of cream in the sauce.*'

'Well, you're wrong there,' she said. 'I like it that you're well padded.' She gave another faint smile and pressed her hand against his shirt front. 'I like men who are well padded.'

'You like me,' Frank said. 'And you say you like men who are well padded because I'm fat. If you ask a psychologist . . .'

'I go to see a psychologist every week, and you don't ask psychologists anything; they ask you.'

'Well, when you're there next time you can discuss the quality of our relationship . . .'

'What do you think I talk about? I don't talk about anything else.'

'. . . You can ask him how it is you can stand me, someone who refuses to move in with anyone. He'll . . .'

'It's a she . . .'

'She'll say that your subconscious is tricking you into liking me because you have formed bonds with me – psychological bonds – just like a duckling follows a goat if there is a goat standing by the egg when it is hatched – you and I have been together for years and now you have formed a psychological bond with me. That's why your subconscious is trying to make you believe that I'm the right one for you.'

'You talk such rubbish Frankie,' Eva-Britt said, clearing away her plate.

'And in the end you say I'm a coward because it's the one hundred and fifty-five thousandth time we have slept together and I don't like you talking about living together . . .'

'I refuse to listen to your drivel!' She crossed her arms and stared at the reflection in the large windows to their right.

'Fine by me,' Frank said in a sour tone. 'We've been through this ritual a million times, too.'

'That's what I'm saying,' she grinned. 'We might just as well be married.'

'Well, I agree.'

'You agree?'

'Of course I agree!'

'But why do you protest every time we talk about these things?'

'That's where you're wrong,' Frank smiled. 'Had it been up to me we would have got married long ago . . .

'Yes, we would,' he continued as she made to interrupt. 'And you can take that one up with your psychologist because now I'm going to say the whole truth out loud. I'm going to state openly what we both know deep down, that you are the one who does not want to get married. You don't want to live with me. You always make out

308

that it is me who doesn't want to, but the main reason we live separately is that you don't want to and then you make out the entire thing is my fault. This is basic psychology, just like the fact that people in the society for the protection of animals are really perverts who fantasize about setting fire to kittens – and that all skinheads and neo-Nazis deep down are closet homos who dress up in women's panties and net stockings when they're alone in the bathroom.'

Eva-Britt shook her head.

'We can put it to the test,' Frank said. 'My thoughts and your thoughts. What am I thinking about?'

'I'm not interested.'

'But I definitely know what you're thinking.'

'Oh yes?' she said.

'You're thinking about Julie. For the first time we have been discussing cohabitation without bringing Julie into the discussion.'

'That's true.' She smiled. 'At least that's positive.'

Frølich stretched across the table and caressed her cheek with the back of his hand. They sat looking at each other.

'She's fond of you Frankie,' Eva-Britt said. 'You're as important to her as I am.'

He said nothing.

'You know that, don't you?'

He nodded and watched her from beneath lowered eyelids.

She took his hand. 'If we're going to live together, we have to learn to cope with silence.' She looked down. 'We mustn't compare hands,' she said in a distant voice, holding his forearm instead. 'My grandma always said it brought bad luck.'

He gave a silent nod. She looked up. 'What shall we do when we have no more to say to each other?'

'We do what they do in American films,' Frank said in a low voice.

She sent him a tender smile. They rose together. She put her arms around his neck and stood on tiptoe. The kiss lasted a long time. He ran his fingers down her spine, first once, then again. As she gently loosened her hold he enjoyed the sight of her supple body and her swaying hips move towards the window. They exchanged glances in the reflection. As she reached up for the string to close the blinds her muscles undulated beneath her dress.

* * *

Frølich awoke and gazed into the air. It sounded like a bad version of Mozart's 40th Symphony being played on a barrel organ. The telephone was ringing – his mobile on the floor. He bent down and pressed the right button. 'Hi,' he mumbled sleepily.

'Guess who this is,' Gunnarstranda said.

'Just a moment,' Frølich said with a glance over at Eva-Britt lying naked on her back in bed. She opened her eyes slowly and looked at him from deep inside a dream. With the mobile under his chin he lifted the duvet and covered her. Bit by bit her eyes closed again. He took the phone and tiptoed into the kitchen, with his trousers and jumper in hand. 'Now,' he said. 'Now I can speak louder.'

'You've got post,' Gunnarstranda said.

'Now, in the middle of the night?'

'It's half past twelve.'

'I'd just gone to sleep.'

'You go to bed too early and the letter's important.'

Frølich yawned. 'But why can't I read the letter tomorrow?'

'Because it was sent by Henning Kramer.'

'Oh, shit,' Frølich said.

The sound of paper being torn carried over the phone. 'As your superior officer I assume you entrust me with the task of breaking the seal?'

'Break away.'

'That's not so easy,' the police inspector mumbled. 'Have you tried opening a letter with two pairs of tweezers and a knife?'

'How come you only discovered the letter now?'

'Because it was in your pigeonhole. When did you last empty it?'

'Yesterday morning – I think, anyway.'

'Thought so,' mumbled Gunnarstranda. 'Are you ready?'

'As ready as I usually am after half an hour's sleep. Bet you ten kroner it's the suicide note.'

'The odds were low, but you won. So that's it,' the inspector muttered. 'We'll have to wait until tomorrow to have it confirmed, but it looks like the case is closed.'

Frank Frølich yawned.

'Our reasoning is written here in its entirety. He raped the girl, killed her, stole her jewellery and sent it in the post to Raymond Skau. Fair old confession.'

'Do you believe it?'

'I have my doubts.' Gunnarstranda whinnied.

'Why's that?' Frank asked.

'Listen to this last sentence: *I can't go on*. Hm?' Gunnarstranda seemed piqued. 'Would you have used such insipid language if you were going to kill yourself?'

'No idea.'

'Bloody hell, this man was deep, thoughtful. Surely he wouldn't express himself like that?'

'I have no idea. Let a psychologist have a look at it.'

'Irritating,' Gunnarstranda sighed from a distance.

'Does the note mean we're off the case?'

'Not for the time being. Kramer's autopsy report has come in. It says Kramer was doped up when he died.'

'That's not very surprising, is it?'

'I don't know. It wasn't speed. According to the pathologist he was full of sleeping tablets.'

'What shall we do?'

'Do you really want to go back to bed?'

'But what can we do?'

'Every single word in the letter has been typed. There's no signature.'

Frølich pondered.

'Do we believe in our heart of hearts that Henning Kramer wrote all this crap?' the voice on the phone asked.

'It's possible.'

'Is it likely?'

Frølich pondered once more. 'It's possible,' he concluded.

'Great help it was ringing you up, young man.'

'We have to do *something*!'

'I've arranged a briefing with the public prosecutor about the whole of this case for tomorrow. And unless this is going to end with a downgrading or a closing of the case, we have to find proof that Kramer did not take his own life.'

'Hang on,' Frølich said as his boss rang off. Too late. The engaged tone. He stood contemplating the phone. In the end it was his brain that reacted. He yawned. Oh well, he thought, scratching his stomach. He stood in the doorway to the bedroom and looked straight ahead. Inside, Eva-Britt had kicked off the duvet again. She was lying on her side with her face turned to his pillow, her body in the shape of an elegant Z. Fascinated, he observed how her feet beautifully rounded off and completed her body's imitation of a letter of the alphabet.

He had absolutely no wish to leave this woman. Not now at any rate. Not tonight. Now and then Gunnarstranda was prone to winding himself up into a stressed, hysterical condition. Of course the suicide letter would require the present stage of the investigation to be summarized and evaluated. But why did that have to be tonight? The man is obsessed, he thought. No, he's not obsessed. He doesn't have enough people around him. He doesn't have enough to think about. After working with the sourpuss for so long now, Frølich bore most of the man's whims with great composure. Of course I could go to work now, he thought. I could plunge into the darkness and sit and read reports. I could spend the rest of the night with a headache and the taste of lead in my mouth and reduce everything to a conclusion about how far it would have been possible for Kramer to hang himself or not. Or I could lie down next to the beauty in the bed, listen to her breathing, then think about Kramer, hope to sleep a bit and dream about Kramer – until I wake up with her. He grinned at the thought of how furious Gunnarstranda would be when he failed to turn up. He crept into the bedroom, lay down with as little noise as he could and stretched out in bed. Eva-Britt's regular breathing caressed his ear.

39

To and Fro

Fristad, the public prosecutor, sat with his legs crossed and both hands folded over his plump stomach. He was a man who cultivated his boyish image by letting his hair grow into a thick fringe down to two finely formed eyebrows. He signalled his intellectual side with a pair of thick horn-rimmed glasses, to which he had attached a black cord and which hung around his neck to ensure they didn't go missing. His glasses sat astride the tip of his large nose while the cord formed decorative loops on each of the clean-shaven cheeks. The public prosecutor tried to prevent his glasses from falling off by stretching his mouth sideways as far as he could. This grimace inflated both cheeks in such a way that they pushed the glasses back a millimetre, only to slide forward two millimetres. He continued like this until his glasses fell on to his chest, which caused him to sigh aloud, then retrieve and re-position them.

Frølich looked from him to Gunnarstranda, whose nocturnal exertions had left their mark. The detective inspector had dark coffee stains on his lips, his lean fingers trembled as he held the papers and the narrow rimless reading glasses – doubtless bought by mail order – were unable to camouflage the dark shadows under his eyes.

Gunnarstranda cleared his throat. 'The body was found on the Sunday morning in a ditch alongside Ljansbrukveien, just by the bathing area in Hvervenbukta. Presumably dumped from a car. There had been no attempt to hide the body, which was found by a pensioner out walking. His name is Jan Vegard Ellingsen and he has been eliminated from our enquiries. There is some reason to believe that the body was transported by car to where it was found. The victim had been stripped and had very few external injuries apart from strangulation marks and the odd graze or cut to the skin which, in the pathologist's view, were consistent with the approximately two-metre fall down the slope – before the body came to rest.'

He picked up the photographs of Katrine Bratterud's distorted and lifeless naked body with the staring eyes.

The public prosecutor lost his glasses and put them back. He peered at one of the photographs.

Fristad pointed to the picture. 'What's that around her navel?'

'A tattoo,' Frølich intervened. 'A kind of flower.'

The public prosecutor studied the photograph. 'Reminds me of Norwegian rose painting.'

Gunnarstranda coughed. 'Apart from the scratches, which must have been caused by the fall, you can see . . .' He placed another photograph on the table – a close-up of the head and shoulders. '. . . You can see the bruising to her neck which appeared after the strangling, a wound where the cord – I presume it was the curtain cord that was also found by the body – cut into the tissue during strangulation.'

'We've got that, have we?' Fristad asked. 'The cord?'

Gunnarstranda nodded. 'The victim had particles of skin under her nails, perhaps occurring during the fight with the assailant. The DNA analyses confirm that the semen found in the vagina of the victim belongs to Henning Kramer. Kramer himself admitted to having sex with the girl before she was murdered. In his first statement Kramer falsely stated what happened in the car after the victim left the party in Voksenkollveien.'

'Just a moment,' the public prosecutor interrupted: 'What about the particles of skin under the nails?'

Gunnarstranda: 'I'll come back to that.' He cleared his throat.

'The clothes?' the public prosecutor asked.

'A bag was found in the ditch down by Ljansbrukveien by Lake Gjer. It must have been thrown out of a car. It was found . . . well, I can start somewhere else first . . . we know for certain that the victim left the party at the house of Gerhardsen and Ås of her own free will. She was picked up by Henning Kramer close by, in all probability, at around midnight. The two of them were seen in Aker Brygge by several witnesses at some point between midnight and half past. They seemed to be having fun and, according to Kramer, they drove to Lake Gjer to talk about the stars and to . . . to . . .'

'. . . have a romantic interlude?' the public prosecutor rounded off with raised eyebrows.

'Yes . . . at a car park by Lake Gjer between Tyrigrava and the amusement park . . . what's it called?'

'Tusenfryd,' Frølich answered.

'That's it.' Gunnarstranda fumbled around with the paper. 'The woman's clothing, that is, most of her clothing – a shoe we haven't been able to trace is still missing – was found between the car park and the victim's body. This might suggest she was killed close to the car park where she and Kramer had sex and that the killer got rid of the clothes before the body. But I'll come back to that, too . . .' He searched through the pile of papers. Frølich and the public prosecutor said nothing while the police inspector flicked through his paperwork.

'There we are,' Gunnarstranda muttered. 'Lots of paper. And you've got to read through the whole bloody lot yourself . . .

'. . . Henning Kramer's version of events was that the two of them had a romantic interlude in the car park, they drove off and he dropped the victim at the roundabout over the E18 in Mastemyr at around three in the morning because she had expressed a wish to walk to her boyfriend's flat at Holmlia senter vei 13.'

'Boyfriend?' exclaimed the public prosecutor, grimacing.

The detective inspector looked at him in silence. The silence persisted and the public prosecutor pulled another grimace.

'Ole Eidesen,' Frølich interposed. 'Katrine Bratterud left her boyfriend Ole Eidesen at the party.'

Fristad's glasses fell on to his chest.

Gunnarstranda coughed. 'All right?' he asked.

Fristad nodded and put his glasses back.

Gunnarstranda: 'Later we had reason to doubt Kramer's statement. A reliable witness had seen the car Kramer was driving – it was a bit special, an Audi cabriolet – in the same car park by Lake Gjer more than three hours after Kramer claimed he had driven off. The sighting was made early in the morning at a time when Katrine was in all probability already dead. We never managed to confront Kramer with this witness's statement because Kramer died. However, in the course of our enquiries we interviewed Kramer's mother. Kramer lived with his mother, but spent occasional nights at his brother's flat when his brother was on his travels. Kramer's mother told us that Henning came home at half past three on the Sunday morning. He woke her up and was very perturbed. He told her he and Katrine had been for a ride in the car, they had fallen asleep and when he woke up – at about half past two – she had vanished without a trace.'

'He'd been very perturbed?' the public prosecutor queried. 'There could be many reasons for him to be perturbed. He may have been lying to his mother.'

'Of course. But according to his mother Kramer is supposed to have said he had been looking for Katrine, and afterwards he began to drive around to find her but without success. In the end he drove home and told his mother everything.'

'Has the time of death been established?'

'It's difficult to determine the exact time. All we have to go on is the contents of her stomach, a verified meal bought from

McDonald's in Aker Brygge at around midnight, the semen in her vagina and the state of rigor mortis. The pathologist believes death occurred at somewhere between two and five o'clock in the morning.'

'And this Kramer went back to the car park. Is that right?'

'According to the mother, he did, yes. She says he left home just before six that morning to resume his search for Katrine and he returned at eight.

'On the assumption that Kramer killed her he could have driven home to his mother first – with the corpse in the car – and then panicked. He could have told his mother some twaddle. She told him to go back and search and then he drove back. He could have stopped in Hvervenbukta and tipped the body over the crash barrier. Then he could have driven on a bit and thrown away her clothes.

'We therefore examined the car Kramer was driving and found some hair, some stains which could have been semen and a variety of textile fibres. But for the time being these things have only been recorded. The best evidence we have against Kramer is the semen. But, according to Kramer's mother, he was having a relationship with Katrine. So Kramer may well have been telling the truth when he said they had consensual sex in the car that night.'

'But it has not been proved that Kramer did not rape Katrine,' Fristad interjected in inquisitorial manner, without a grimace.

Gunnarstranda: 'There is, of course, a chance that Kramer did commit rape and then murder. That's what he claims in the suicide note.'

'But you don't believe the letter is genuine?'

'Not on the face of it.'

'What do the pathologists say about Kramer's body?' Fristad asked.

'They are holding both options open. But the strongest indication that he died by his own hand is that he was found strangled with the noose around his neck.' Gunnarstranda rummaged through the pile of photographs and found one of Kramer with the cord around his neck. 'In addition, we have the suicide note in which Kramer writes that he took Katrine's jewellery, posted it to Raymond Skau, thus laying a false trail to cast suspicion of Katrine's murder on to him.'

'But is that improbable?'

'Not at all. Kramer and Katrine were on very intimate terms. Kramer must have known a lot about Katrine's past and Raymond Skau constituted a large chunk of that past. Kramer could have had many motives for damaging Skau, about which we know nothing.'

'Ahhh . . . ,' Fristad said, lost in thought. He sat studying the photographs.

No one said anything. At length the public prosecutor raised his eyes. 'And?' he asked with a sideways grimace.

'The problem is the particles of skin under Katrine's nails. First of all, we didn't find any indication on Kramer's body that would confirm that he had been scratched. In addition, the DNA analysis shows that the skin did not belong to Kramer.'

Fristad was quiet. Everyone went quiet.

Gunnarstranda sorted his papers into piles.

'Does that mean she scratched someone else?' Fristad asked at last.

Gunnarstranda put down the papers. 'It's possible. But we don't know. It's feasible that she might have scratched someone else during the course of the evening. She might have bumped into someone at the party or someone in the queue at McDonald's in Aker Brygge. Nevertheless, if Kramer had lived, and he had been charged, this evidence would have given the defence very strong cards.'

'But the case seems pretty clear, doesn't it?' Fristad said in a loud voice. 'We have Kramer's confession. He says he killed her and he planted the jewellery on Skau because he knew she owed him money and all that other stuff about trying to shift the blame on to someone else. Then he committed suicide. Seems very tempting to drop the whole thing.'

'Except that the accused should be given the benefit of the doubt.'

'But the accused is bloody dead.'

'He should still be given the benefit of the doubt,' Gunnarstranda asserted with obduracy. 'If the particles of skin under Katrine Bratterud's nails belong to someone else, a person with a motive, then we have to ask ourselves why Kramer would make a false confession in a suicide note.'

'And?'

'If Katrine was killed by someone else, not Kramer, I don't understand why he would confess.'

Fristad pulled a wry face. 'Now you're making the case unnecessarily complicated, Gunnarstranda. We're talking about an ex-tart, aren't we? A bloody junkie. Why should a case like this be so damned complicated – and contain so many conspiratorial motives that involve premeditated murder and so on, and so on?'

'I'm not complicating the case,' Gunnarstranda yelled back angrily. 'I just expect it to be tied up in a correct manner! The only thing I want is for us to wait before we prioritize other work until all those involved have been checked out and we have completed the essential investigation.'

'What's so fishy about Kramer's death?' Fristad asked.

'Traces of sedatives were found in Kramer's body. If he killed himself he might have taken them to dull his senses. However, the problem with Kramer taking sedatives before dying is that we couldn't find a box of tablets or a prescription anywhere in the flat. The point is that, if he had taken sedatives, it doesn't make sense to me that we cannot find any traces of said sedatives in his flat.'

'But he was working at a drugs rehab clinic. He did a bit of hash and cocaine himself, I've read. Kramer must have had innumerable contacts, and getting hold of illegal drugs on the street is as easy as wink.'

Gunnarstranda glanced up at Fristad, who was nodding and grimacing. 'I'm just saying it's odd,' the policeman said. 'It's also strange that the suicide letter was not found where he died. There are no fingerprints on the paper or the envelope. It seems bizarre that it should turn up in a pigeonhole at the police station. And the letter was not signed. It was printed on a laser printer and written with a computer. But Kramer did not have his own computer. There was a computer in his brother's flat and there is no sign of this letter on his machine. He might have written the letter at work, at the Vinterhagen centre, but so far we haven't been able to trace the machine on which it was written.'

'The bit about the fingerprints sounds particularly odd,' the public prosecutor said as his glasses fell on to his chest.

'Agreed,' Gunnarstranda said. 'It is odd. But it's also odd that the suicide letter isn't signed and was not where he died. If he had to confess why not confess properly so that all doubts would be dispelled? Why a letter addressed to Frølich at Police HQ? Why not to his mother or to his brother? After all, he rang his brother to talk about the mysteries of life before he died. It's strange that he doesn't send his mother and his brother a final word.' Gunnarstranda waved the letter in the air. 'This is just a confession. It's not a suicide letter as I know them.'

'He might have sent it to Frølich to be sure it was found.'

'Of course,' Gunnarstranda conceded. 'But the oddest thing of all is that he actually admitted to having sex with the girl in his first statement. It seems crazy that he would kill to cover up a rape, and then he admits to having sex with her as soon as the police show up.'

'You've got a point,' Fristad said, losing his glasses again.

'It's also funny that he would go to a postbox, post a suicide letter, then go home, take sedatives and hang himself.'

The public prosecutor nodded, interlacing his fingers in front of him and banging his thumbs against each other. He thought aloud: 'The perpetrator rapes the girl, kills her, removes her clothes and other possessions to hide the evidence. But the motive must be the same whoever strangled her?'

'The jewellery,' Gunnarstranda said with emphasis. 'The jewellery turning up at Skau's place complicates the matter. We have established that Katrine was wearing jewellery that night and it turned up later in Skau's flat. Skau may, as we have said, have bumped into her that night. He may have killed her and taken her jewellery. The problem is that Skau's girlfriend, Linda Ros, maintains the jewellery came in the post. The posting of the jewellery tallies with what Kramer wrote in the letter.'

'What did the police officers who found the jewellery in Skau's flat say?'

'They said that everything was in a handbag on the table, which tallies with what the girl said. She said the handbag was in the postbox on Wednesday afternoon. But she didn't take in the post on the Tuesday or the Monday. We don't know when it was put in the box.'

'Could Skau have put it in the postbox himself?'

'He could have done it on the Sunday. From Sunday evening, the day after Katrine was murdered, he was in custody and he's in custody now.'

'But leaving the matter of the jewellery aside,' the public prosecutor said, 'I understood that Skau attacked Katrine at work. If he had met her in the night and attacked her again . . . then he could have killed her. Afterwards Skau could have forged the suicide letter – couldn't he?'

'That's a possibility,' Gunnarstranda admitted.

'Kramer's death could still be suicide even if the letter is forged,' Fristad said.

Frølich studied the police inspector. He thought he could discern the contours of a smile forming around the man's thin lips. The public prosecutor didn't notice. He was sitting with his eyes closed and a rigid expression on his face – proof that he was thinking. 'Let's imagine the following,' Fristad now declared. 'Katrine Bratterud left Henning in the car that night to get some fresh air. Her lover was asleep and she was awake. She went for a walk. She may have wanted to go to the toilet or smoke a cigarette or stretch her legs. She bumped into Raymond Skau. He killed her, stripped her and stole her jewellery. Are you with me?'

Frølich nodded. He had the impression the smile on Gunnarstranda's lips was even more pronounced. He had no idea what scheme Gunnarstranda had devised, but at that moment things were going his way, that much Frølich did know.

Fristad went on: 'The whole business with the jewellery stands or falls with the girl, Linda Ros, doesn't it? Right? You found the jewellery there, at Skau's place . . . then . . . a week later with Skau completely out of the picture . . . Kramer took his own life in a fit of depression. He felt guilty, perhaps because he had left the car park without finding her. The thought that she might have been lying on the ground being strangled while he drove away – that sort of thought could have pushed Henning Kramer over the edge. When Kramer killed himself, Skau saw a chance to save his own skin and forged the suicide note to lead suspicion away from him. He wrote an unsigned letter in Kramer's name confessing the murder.'

Fristad beamed in triumph. 'Is that how it could have happened? I'm asking! Could that have happened? Is it a possibility?'

His boyish face shone like in a TV commercial.

Gunnarstranda said nothing.

Frølich was about to say something, but the public prosecutor intercepted first. 'I like the theory about Skau,' the public prosecutor said with enthusiasm. 'Skau is stupid enough to write an unsigned suicide letter. He's unscrupulous enough. Isn't he? Eh?'

Frølich cleared his throat ready to speak.

Gunnarstranda's eyes were like an eagle's. 'Let the public prosecutor finish,' the inspector snapped.

'Yes,' repeated Fristad in a dream. 'I do like the Skau theory. It explains why this ridiculous suicide letter turns up in Frølich's pigeonhole. Skau was being held across the street, in custody. He just dropped off a letter in an envelope in the corridor when he was let into the yard for a walk. It was addressed to a policeman. He smuggled it out. What do you think? The theory is simple, plausible, could have happened. Remember, Gunnarstranda, this is not the first time . . .'

'Then we'll have to try to persuade Linda Ros to admit she was lying about the jewellery,' Gunnarstranda said in a soft voice. 'And then we just have to wait for the results of the DNA test, don't we?'

'Mm . . . exactly! We need the results of the DNA test,' the public prosecutor concluded automatically. 'If the particles of skin under the victim's nails belong to Skau . . .'

He stood up in his excitement. 'Then it's probable that Skau strangled her,' he repeated. 'We'll have to wait for the results of the DNA test,' the public prosecutor stated. 'Thank you, gentlemen.'

* * *

'It can't have been Skau,' Frølich said after the two policemen were on their own. 'How the hell would he have got access to a computer in custody?'

'Absolutely. Sounds unlikely.'

'But why didn't you say anything? Why should we leave here with that man's conclusions?' Frølich asked, tossing his head in the direction of the public prosecutor's door.

'I had my reasons,' the policeman said in a cutting tone. 'What I'm wondering about is what kept you last night.'

'I went back to sleep after you rang. Sorry.'

'Did you go back to bed after I had dragged you out of it?'

Frølich gave a sleepy smile. 'I had my reasons.'

'But if you leave me to do the dirty work on my own, don't stick your nose in my business, as you tried to do here,' Gunnarstranda chided, annoyed.

Gunnarstranda went down the stairs with Frølich in his wake. He already had a cigarette out. 'Fristad wants a simple, easy-to-follow case to plead. For that he needs evidence. He's relying on you and me to know what we are doing. And he wants more than half the glory. At the moment he thinks he's helped us on our way. So we have a free hand for a while yet.'

'A free hand to do what?'

'To find evidence, of course.'

'What evidence?'

'My dear colleague,' Gunnarstranda said in a patronizing voice. 'Hasn't it occurred to you that the DNA sample they found under Katrine's nails may not belong to either Kramer or Skau?'

'Have you been told that?' Frølich quizzed.

'I haven't been told anything, but I intend to find out.'

40

Uphill

Bente Kramer trudged up the hill the police station bestrode like a castle at the end of a footpath. A man wearing a cowboy hat was taking his dog for a walk on the green grass stretching across to Oslo prison. A group of homeless tramps were having a meeting on a bench under one of the trees. Bente Kramer stopped to collect her breath. A uniformed woman with a contented face and blonde hair in a pony-tail under a police cap came striding down the hill. Bente nodded to her. The policewoman nodded back, and puckered her brow in a questioning frown. Bente put on a tired expression and battled on. Having come this far, she would manage the last bit.

Inside the heavy doors, she stopped and watched the hectic activity around the reception desk.

'I would like to speak to Police Inspector Gunnarstranda,' she said to the kindest-looking of the men.

'Have you got an appointment?'

Bente Kramer shook her head.

The police officer picked up a telephone and called. A tired-looking man smelling of stale beer and garlic pushed to the front and shouted something across the desk. The man with the telephone ignored him and, with the receiver under his chin, asked: 'What's it about?'

Bente cleared her throat. 'It's about a ring,' she said. 'Tell him it's Bente Kramer with a ring that belonged to Katrine Bratterud.'

PART 3

THE LAST FIX

41

Hamlet

The scratch marks down his chest and side had faded; now they were mere pale, almost invisible red lines, not unlike the marks after a hot night with the woman you love. Beneath the nipple on his right hand side her nail had dug into him leaving a cut which was also healing now. With his eyes closed, he could still conjure up the sensation of her fingers scratching him, freezing, as death finally came to his rescue in the grass and took her into shadowland as violent jerks shook the young body for five seconds. Her final, but presumably her greatest climax ever. A gift – delivered after a few tender moments of doubt from his side. She had thought he was going to mount her. She had felt the pressure from his stiff member against her body and assumed he wanted to take her. She had relaxed in the hope she would be allowed to live. He had read that in her blue eyes. Eyes that now – at this very second – caused him to bend his head in pain and doze as the sweat broke out over his entire body – still – so long afterwards. *Just do it*, said the blue eyes. *Do what you want. Just let me live.* She had almost succeeded in bewitching him – forestalling her own destiny. But only almost. Even now he could still feel the same fury rising inside him. As the fury rose the memory of her eyes could cause him to pull up short at any moment, to immerse himself in profound thoughts, a memory that thus became the best way to maintain his aggression, to think about how she had just been asking for it – by spreading her legs and opening them wide to let him in. That was when he no longer had any choice. The hardness she felt was no precursor of sensual pleasure; it was a precursor of death.

There would never be such eyes again. He put on a white shirt and quickly tied his tie. Inspected himself in the mirror and threw his suit jacket across his shoulders. *Think of her. You're doing it for her. Think of her. Get it over with.*

* * *

'Hamlet,' Frølich said with a grin. 'Quite convincing, too. You should go on the stage.'

'At least I don't fall asleep,' Gunnarstranda answered, weighing the ring in his hand. Frølich was supporting his chin on his hand and said, 'What's the question?'

'The question is: If Henning Kramer posted Katrine's jewellery to Raymond Skau, why didn't he send this one?' Gunnarstranda held the ring between thumb and first finger while squinting through the hole at Frølich.

'Because he never posted anything.' Frølich mused on what he had said and at length asked, 'Do we know if she was wearing this ring on the night of the murder?'

'Eidesen noticed this ring was missing when we found her jewellery. We can prove it belonged to Katrine.'

'If Kramer had wanted to point the finger of blame at someone else I don't think he would have left a ring in his room that clearly belonged to her . . . so the logical explanation must be that Kramer never posted any jewellery anywhere.'

'You're getting warm, Frølich. Kramer didn't send any jewellery. All he had was this ring. Someone else must have posted the jewellery to Skau, and if there is a someone else, it must be a person who first killed Katrine Bratterud and then Henning Kramer. And then,' Gunnarstranda grunted, 'we're facing a problem I do not understand at all.'

'What's that?'

330

'I don't understand why Kramer had to die.'

'He must have known something.'

Gunnarstranda chewed on that. 'Possible,' he said. 'If you're right, Kramer must have invited the murderer over the night he was killed. That may also explain why he lied to you about what happened the night Katrine was killed. He may have suspected some people, or a particular person. And called him.'

'Why would he have called the killer?' a sceptical Frølich frowned.

'Because he was killed at home in his brother's flat, not in his room. Henning Kramer was quite unpredictable as regards where he spent the night . . .' Gunnarstranda mumbled with closed eyes. 'Well, that's how it must have been. Kramer asked to meet up and that resulted in his death. Afterwards the suicide letter was written. Since Kramer is dead, to all outward appearance by his own hand, it's easier to point suspicions in his direction than Skau's, who is alive and can still issue denials. For all the killer knows, Skau has an alibi. Looking at the facts, what do we know so far?'

'We know the killer was not a random assailant. He must have been in her circle of acquaintances.'

Gunnarstranda nodded.

'We know the killer must have known about the connection between Katrine and Skau.'

Gunnarstranda grinned. 'You're the one who's so keen on the theatre. What would Holberg's Erasmus Montanus have said?'

'A stone cannot fly. Mother Nille cannot fly. Ergo . . . is mother Nille a stone . . . ?' Frølich ventured.

Gunnarstranda shook his head. 'We know that Katrine rang friends and acquaintances before going to the party. We know Katrine made at least five calls and later that night she was murdered. Ergo,' he mumbled, 'it's possible the motive is to be found in the phone calls.'

'We've established that she had a strained relationship with Bjørn Gerhardsen,' Frølich said. 'We know that Annabeth Ås must have hated her, that Katrine couldn't choose between Ole Eidesen and Henning Kramer, and that she was hiding from her past while trying to clear up a period in her very earliest past – she owed ten thousand kroner to a violent pimp. We've established that on the day before the murder she visited the social worker who knew about her adoption.'

'The last one,' Gunnarstranda smiled. 'It means Katrine knew who she was. She didn't tell Ole Eidesen. Why not? Because she hasn't come to terms with the matter yet. She knows the name of her biological mother and she has had a shock. The circumstances around the adoption must have struck deep. Remember she had far-fetched fantasies about her biological parents dying in plane crashes and all that sort of thing. Now she has discovered the actual truth. What does she do then?'

'So you think the phone calls prove she was continuing to dig up her past?'

'Not necessarily. She may have simply revealed the news to some other person. Although she may also have rung someone who was in the know.'

'But how does that help us?'

'We know she made four or five calls, at least.'

'And we would never get a warrant to check the telephone line. Wait a minute,' Frølich said, excited. 'Gerhardsen,' he went on. 'Gerhardsen has money. He's loaded. Katrine might have called him to ask for a favour. She needed money to pay off Skau. Wow, this is a straight business deal for the two of them. Both Katrine and Gerhardsen have been in this situation before. She asked him for money. That explains why he treated her like a whore at the party afterwards. That explains why she was ill at the party. Suppose he had given her money and wanted repayment in kind – in the form of sexual favours?'

'You may be right. But why would he throttle her?'

Frølich considered the options. 'Because she didn't want to play along,' he concluded. 'And Gerhardsen doesn't have an alibi. He claims he went to Smuget, but no one has corroborated that, neither those who went with him nor the other two in the taxi. Neither Ole Eidesen nor Merethe Fossum remembers him entering. Neither of them can remember having seen the guy inside. But Katrine and Henning must have been five hundred metres away from his taxi outside Smuget. My God, his car in Munkedamsveien, everything fits. He has to cross the City Hall square to fetch the car. If he had gone for it right after the taxi dropped them off he would have seen Katrine and Henning. They were putting on their show on the wharf.'

Gunnarstranda regarded his younger colleague with a smile. 'You'd like to bang up Gerhardsen, wouldn't you.'

'Naturally.'

'Have you got something against him?'

'All the same, it's worth bringing him in for questioning again,' Frølich said.

They were interrupted by the telephone, and Gunnarstranda's face split into a huge smile after delivering his arrogant one-liner.

He coughed. 'Of course I remember you,' he said, standing up and fidgeting.

Frølich stood up as well.

'Just a moment,' Gunnarstranda said, holding his hand over the mouthpiece of the receiver. 'Yes, Frølich?'

The reserved expression caused his colleague to burst into a grin. 'A woman, is it?' He beamed.

Gunnarstranda, unmoved, coughed. 'What's the matter, Frølich?' he repeated in unapproachable mode.

Frølich was already by the door. 'Should Gerhardsen be arrested or just brought in for questioning?' he asked in a formal tone.

The inspector gave an impatient shrug and turned away. As soon as he concentrated on the telephone the features of his lean face softened. He sat down and listened with a big smile on his lips. 'And that,' he said with sympathy, 'that's usually a fertilizer problem . . .'

42

A Sucker

He drove in the vague direction of the city centre. He needed to find a multi-storey car park. It wasn't so important where he put the car. The main thing was that the place should be anonymous. A place where he would be given a receipt. It was at such moments, when there was no doubt about what had to be done, that all the tiny events put together acquired new meaning – that tiny events became a comprehensible whole. In a way he was back at square one; finally he was where he should have begun. Of course this was a weakness on his part – not starting at the beginning. However, perhaps it is humanity's greatest weakness: a tendency to walk around the target until there is no way back. It's always like that: it isn't until you stand by the quarry that you can see the shortest route – it's only then you know where you should have started.

He grinned. He knew where he should have started. After so much trouble he now knew. Because of the most common weakness in existence: not facing up to the real truth. You shrink from seeing small signs and signals of the illness until these same symptoms have grown so large that the illness keeping the symptoms alive can no longer be denied.

In all these years there had only been one real threat. He had accepted the threat. Not because he was stupid, not because he was weak, but because he had allowed himself to be duped by the symptoms when the malignant tumour began to stir.

But was it in vain?

Nothing is in vain. He turned the car radio up louder. It was the wrong question. That's why nothing is in vain. The car radio began to hiss as he drove down the hills in Fjellinjen. Cars whizzed by on both sides, young people racing by without knowing what it was they were racing after. Urban traffic is a study in impatience. He slowed down and turned off before he was through the tunnel and reappeared in daylight just before Filipstad. He turned right and drove slowly into the entrance of the multi-storey car park. The crackling in the speakers disturbed his thinking. He had to switch off the radio. The bends led him gently downwards. Nothing is in vain. It is the endeavour and the exertion that afford insight, that reveal the truth. The others did not die in vain. They had helped him to point out the real tumour. When the tumour can no longer be concealed there is only one solution: you get rid of it. He left the spiral ramp and drove into the parking area. Out of the darkness; into the darkness.

* * *

The sun was baking the policeman's back as he closed the wrought-iron gate behind him and slowly made his way up the garden path alongside a beautiful row of weigela plants whose bell-like flowers were coming to an end now. He stopped and took a spray of fragile, wax-like bells that were still in blossom. He could sense his dread. While he was standing there he heard the rustle of a newspaper from somewhere behind the hedge. So someone was at home. He moved away and walked the last few metres to the broad front door and rang the bell. Not a sound could be heard from inside. Either the bell didn't work or they didn't hear, he thought, and he raised his hand to ring again. At that moment the door opened a crack.

'Gunnarstranda?' Sigrid Haugom said in surprise. 'What brings you here this time?'

The inspector put both hands in his jacket pockets and tried to formulate an answer in his head. 'A sucker,' he said after a pause.

Sigrid Haugom opened the door wide and led the way. She was wearing a flowery dress. It looked as though she had just put it on. As if to underline the correctness of his assumption she stopped in front of a mirror and smoothed a few kinks over her bosom. 'Is that what you think?' she asked.

'About what?'

She glanced over her shoulder. 'That Katrine was a sucker?'

'I was thinking of a different kind of sucker,' the policeman said without further explanation, glancing to the left as he passed a veranda door. There was a sun lounger on the terrace, an open newspaper on the lounger, a pile of newspapers across the floor and a half-eaten apple on a plate beside the newspapers.

She sat down where she had done the previous time, by the oval table with her legs tucked underneath her on the sofa. Gunnarstranda walked over to the window and looked out at the sun bed. 'Have I disturbed you?' he asked, taking hold of the pot with the bonsai tree on the window sill.

'I'm off sick,' she said.

'Anything serious?'

'Just exhaustion.'

'Has it anything to do with the murder – Katrine?'

'It's a contributory factor.'

'You were good . . . I mean . . . you were close, weren't you?'

'That's putting it mildly, yes.'

The policeman was still holding the pot as he turned to her. 'This tree's dying,' he stated.

'If you've got green fingers,' Sigrid Haugom sighed, 'perhaps you can save it for me.'

'A bonsai tree,' Gunnarstranda said, lifting the pot. 'A Japanese work of art. It can't have been cheap.'

'It was a present,' the woman on the sofa said. 'I never ask what presents cost.'

'I would guess it's more than a hundred years old,' the policeman surmised. 'Trees like this one can grow to be five hundred years old, I've heard. I've seen a few and this one seems to be very, very old.'

'We all have to die some time,' Sigrid Haugom said in a soft voice, breathing in deep. 'I apologize, but I can't get Katrine out of my head. I try, but I can't do it.'

'Imagine if this tree was really old,' Gunnarstranda said, humbled. 'Imagine it was two hundred years old. If so, it would have been tended by six, seven, maybe eight generations of gardeners.'

'Fantastic,' Sigrid said, uninterested.

The policeman shrank back. 'Seven generations of gardening knowledge,' he said bitterly. 'Two hundred years of care, right from the French Revolution until today, a plant which as a result of careful nursing has managed to outlive Montesquieu, Napoleon, George Washington, Wedel Jarlsberg, Bjørnstjerne Bjørnson, Mussolini and Chairman Mao.' He put the plant back with a bang and said with emphasis: 'Until you were given it as a present and let it dry out on the window sill!'

Sigrid Haugom looked at him in silence with raised eyebrows.

'I saw the tree last time I was here,' the policeman said, crossing the floor and taking a seat opposite her on the sofa. 'It was the one thing in this house that didn't fit. The only unexpected artefact in this museum of lamps, signed by Louis Comfort Tiffany in person I have no doubt, of antiques, of Swiss bells, old tables and Italian designer sofas. The rug on the floor over there, from my knowledge of rugs, I would guess was woven by Kashmiri children. I noticed the cups you served the coffee in were made of Meissner china.' He pointed to the left. 'Even down to the charming hammer shaft you or your husband placed next to the stove as an adornment. But in this conglomerate mass of undefined taste and aspiring snobbery neither you nor your husband is capable of keeping an eye on what is happening on the window sill.'

'I suppose not,' Sigrid Haugom said gently, perplexed by the policeman's outburst. 'But then by a happy chance you have an eye for this kind of thing.'

'The sight of that poor tree in the dried-out pot told me all I needed to know about your character.'

'Oh yes?' Sigrid's voice had assumed a sharp edge of patrician arrogance.

'The sucker that has brought me here today grows in the garden of a nursing home. A sucker on an otherwise very attractive ornamental rose, a sucker that resembles a pale green spear planted in the ground in the middle of the lawn. Am I making myself clear?'

'Loud and clear,' Sigrid said with a dry voice, 'but I have no idea what you are talking about.'

Gunnarstranda smiled and stretched out his legs. He said, 'Isn't it the Chinese who have an expression for everything?'

'Bound to be.'

'The Chinese would, I assume, have said something like: Though your eyes may have rested on the rose sucker you were unable to see.'

'As I said, I have no idea what you're talking about.'

'I may not be that sure myself. The only thing I want is some answers to one question.'

'Then I think you should ask it,' Sigrid said with a sigh.

'On Friday, ten days or so ago, Katrine Bratterud called on a flat in Uranienborgveien,' Gunnarstranda said. 'The flat is owned by a pensioner called Stamnes. In his time this man worked for child welfare. Once he had been employed by Nedre Eiker council where he handled casework including, amongst other things, the relocation of children. The reason Katrine visited him was that Stamnes knew details about her own adoption case more than twenty years ago. Does that ring a bell, fru Haugom?'

'Hardly,' she said in a chilly tone.

'This Stamnes still felt constrained by professional vows of client confidentiality, but in the end yielded to Katrine's questioning. The likelihood that he would be able to help her was minimal. There were far too many relocations for that. However, he did remember her case. The reason he remembered hers in particular was that it was connected with the very tragic circumstances that necessitated adoption. The child's mother had been strangled by an unknown assailant and the child's father was an absent sailor who was neither married to the child's mother nor considered himself in a position to take care of the child. The little girl was therefore referred and given up for adoption. Stamnes told Katrine this. He couldn't remember the name of her father, just the name of her mother because it was all over the newspapers for ages at the time: Helene Lockert.'

The policeman paused. In the silence that followed all that could be heard in the room was the ticking of the antique clock.

'Katrine was in a very special situation that night,' the policeman said in a low voice. 'She was on the trail of her past, of where she belonged, where she came from. She was on the trail of understanding why she and the world were not in harmony. And what do you do in a situation like that? What is the logical thing to do or, perhaps better: What does it *feel* right to do? Would you try to trace your father or your mother's family? I have no idea what Katrine wanted to do first, but I know she was doing something.

'Later that evening Katrine and Ole Eidesen met outside Saga cinema to see an action film. This was to Ole's taste, but he told us Katrine was noticeably distant and unapproachable all evening. The day after, she went to work. Still she hadn't said anything to Ole about her big news. Why not? I wondered. I don't know the answer, but I think it was because Katrine had a lot to think about, a flood of thoughts swirling through her brain. One of the thoughts that bothered her was that she had bought information about Stamnes off an ex-boyfriend. This man, Raymond Skau, claims Katrine owed him ten thousand kroner in cash for the information. She didn't have the money. She still owed him ten thousand kroner and the money should have been paid the day before. I don't know what concerned her most: her biological mother's tragic fate or the sum of money she didn't have. What we do know for certain is that at one o'clock Raymond Skau entered her workplace to demand

339

payment. She said, quite truthfully, that she couldn't pay, which caused him to become violent and threaten her. He left the shop shortly afterwards. What we now know is that Katrine left at two o'clock and went back to her flat where Ole Eidesen was waiting for her. He has since told us she was still unapproachable and irritable. She wanted to be alone and spent hours in the bathroom. Until five or six in the afternoon. Then she rang around. She made several calls, here too.'

'That's no secret,' Sigrid said. 'I told you she rang, didn't I? She told me about this man who attacked her.'

'I remember,' Gunnarstranda said. 'But you didn't tell me about the whole conversation, did you? Helene Lockert had been about to get married,' he continued, 'but she never got that far. The man she was to marry is still alive. His name is Reidar Bueng and he lives in the nursing home with the garden where a rose-sucker has shot out of the ground. I met him there and we had a chat.'

Gunnarstranda coughed, once, and then again. He was hoping for a reaction to his long monologue, but was disappointed. Sigrid Haugom watched him with large eyes, but a gaze that was turned inwards.

'I've become acquainted with ...' Gunnarstranda paused, searched for words and coughed again. 'By chance I know the assistant matron at this place,' he continued. 'What she told me on the phone today is my small question to you, fru Haugom.'

Sigrid Haugom sat on the sofa, silent and distant.

Gunnarstranda looked straight into her eyes. 'I am wondering about the following: Why did you spend a total of one hour with Bueng at this home the day after Katrine Bratterud was murdered?'

43

The Messenger

He pursed his mouth and whistled as he bounced across Egertorget. He avoided two Japanese tourists; they were each holding a
map and looking into the air . . . *four little, three little, two little
Indians. One little Indian boy.*

It would be like visiting a sick patient. A quick, effective visit,
the way doctors did in the old days. *One little Indian boy.* The arm
with the attaché case swung to and fro. He followed the stream of
people down Karl Johans gate. A thin man with a harrowed face
and long, black hair hobbled towards him with a bent back. *An
angel in disguise,* he thought, with a cold smile. *To intercede.*

He laughed aloud at the beggar's pestering for coins. What an
angel! He ignored the remark the beggar shouted after him. He
didn't hear the words. If there was one thing in this world that was
of no consequence it was the junkie, he thought. The ones I loathe
most are the down-and-outs.

One small fix! The kind of fix that makes down-and-outs like
him spread their heavenly angel wings when he shoots up an overdose in his stupid, hedonistic desire for self-extinction.

He crossed Skippergata on red, and with his head held high
walked straight across Fred Olsens gate to the station square. He
ignored the hooting from the taxi that roared up behind him, then
veered left and raced into the taxi rank. One man among many.
Anonymous in the summer heat.

'You already know the answer, I assume,' Sigrid said. 'Otherwise you wouldn't have asked. In fact, I have thought about you a little, about the kind of person you are. You're the kind who tries to hide your real personality. You camouflage yourself and play the part of a fool with transparent vanity. The comb-over of yours that you arrange with such care, I suppose so that others, and particularly women, will feel sorry for you – nothing is as pitiful as transparent vanity. But I can see through your façade. You're an ordinary man, do you know that? No, you're not even that. You're an under-developed little pleb, a man riddled with complexes. You come here and you already know the answer to your question. Yet you drag yourself up here just for the pleasure of asking the question, to enjoy the sound of the question in your own ears. You are a con-ceited little worm. Do you know that?'

Inspector Gunnarstranda did not say a word in the subsequent long silence. He looked deep into the eyes of the woman on the other side of the table. There was a moist gleam in his eyes. However, Sigrid's cheeks burned red with anger.

She was the first to place her feet on the floor and break the silent battle between them. 'You remind me of a little boy with his chemistry set,' she said. 'You're so damned pleased with yourself. The only thing that means anything to you is to triumph, to show me that you know. But shall I tell you a secret? The secret is that you know nothing. You don't have a clue. You haven't the slightest concept of what is important, of what anything means.'

The policeman, who had been sitting there the whole time, un-moved, didn't stir now, either. His moist eyes remained focused on hers until she looked away. 'You don't need to look at me like that. It's pathetic. You know nothing, nothing of any significance. Nothing!'

'Did you say that to Helene Lockert, too?' Gunnarstranda asked in a brittle voice.

Sigrid Haugom gave a contemptuous chuckle. 'I was waiting for that,' she said, twisting her mouth into an ugly sneer and mimicking him: *Did you say that to* . . . no, fancy that, I didn't.'

'There were no suitable words, I suppose?'

'How the hell can words help at such a time?'

'So you strangled her instead?'

'Save your breath, Gunnarstranda.'

'You strangled her,' the policeman repeated stubbornly.

'Yes, I did,' Sigrid admitted in a testy voice. 'Do you feel better now? Do you feel a perverse potency when you hear such an admission?'

'Katrine,' Gunnarstranda said in a hoarse voice. 'Did she see her mother being strangled?'

Sigrid fell silent. Her face, the part around her mouth, froze in a distorted, pensive grimace. The silence in the room was numbing. All of a sudden she stood up. 'I can't take this silence,' she said quickly and went over to the window where she clung on to the sill with one hand. She held the other to her temple. 'I have a headache. You'd better go. This headache will be the death of me.'

Gunnarstranda turned in his chair and observed her. 'Did she see you doing it?' he repeated in a low voice.

'I don't know,' she said. 'I just do not know.'

'Why did you never ask her?'

'How could I?' Sigrid put her other hand to her face. 'I mean it. I get headaches. I can't have visitors here when I have a migraine,' she sighed.

'You mean Katrine was killed before you managed to ask her what she knew?'

'Gunnarstranda. Will you, please, go now.'

The policeman rose to his feet, breathed in and reluctantly crossed the parquet floor. He stood behind her. The sun was roasting outside. The June sun that baked the intermittent rain into the ground, creating fertile conditions for growth. Everything green would grow skywards in June, become strong enough to master flowering, seed setting and ripening through the summer and autumn. Beside the sun lounger, the newspapers and sunglasses on the terrace lay the remains of an old flower bed in which wheat grass and goutweed had taken over and colonized the whole area with fearsome energy and vitality. A few poor overwintering wild pansies hung their pale heads in the wilderness. The life-giving sun penetrated the living-room window and cast a bright yellow rectangle across the wooden floor and a small corner on the rug where she was standing. The same sunlight created a faint image on the window pane. It was an almost colourless image of the room they were in, the tables, the chairs, the clock on the wall and two figures. Gunnarstranda concentrated on the contours of the woman in front of him in the glass. She was standing with her eyes shut tight. Her skin was stretched taut across her forehead and the fingers holding her head were like the white veins of translucent leaves.

'Why were you never questioned by the police regarding the murder of Helene Lockert?' he asked.

Sigrid gave a start. 'Are you still here? Didn't I ask you to go?'

'Why is your name not in the interview reports?' the policeman repeated after clearing his throat.

Sigrid stood on the same spot without moving.

'That must have been a shock,' Gunnarstranda said, stepping closer to her back. 'Meeting her daughter again after all these years. Perhaps it was fate. Have you wondered about that? Sometimes things do have a meaning.'

'What are you talking about?'

Gunnarstranda drew in his breath and tried to see if there were any changes in the face whose flat contrasts he could just make out in the reflection of the glass. 'My wife died of cancer a number of years ago,' he said with a cough. 'All her life she had had one single dream. I mean a real, a genuine dream.' He paused.

'Yes?' Sigrid said at length, either impatient or genuinely interested.

Gunnarstranda had to clear his throat again. 'Before she died she was given the chance to experience the dream. But she was not the one to make it happen. She couldn't, she was too ill. She didn't know the dream was reality until it happened.'

'I didn't dream about meeting Helene's daughter again.'

'But it happened,' the policeman said. 'Perhaps it was meant to happen.'

'If it was . . .' Sigrid spun round. 'Why should she be killed? Can you tell me that? Was that meant to be as well?'

'I don't know,' the policeman said, looking into her eyes. 'I have no idea. But the important thing is that you met, that you had the chance to love her.'

Sigrid looked away. 'You may be right,' she said. 'But that will never be enough.' She paused. 'I thought that, too,' she continued at last. 'Katrine . . . when I first saw her in Vinterhagen after all these years . . . it was as though Helene was standing there. I knew she had to be Helene's daughter from the very first moment.' Sigrid raised a faint, dreamy smile. 'The same wonderful blonde hair,' she whispered. 'Helene's mouth, her body, her voice. I instantly knew who she was, and I did wonder in fact if she and I were meant . . . But why should she be killed?'

Sigrid's facial expression was genuinely questioning.

'Why were you never interviewed for the murder of Helene?' the policeman repeated without the slightest intention of capitulating.

'I don't know,' she said, drained. 'Maybe Reidar never said anything about me.'

'Reidar Bueng? He mentioned your name. There must have been some other reason Kripos crossed you off their list.'

'I was in Scotland. In Edinburgh.'

'In Scotland?'

'Officially.'

Gunnarstranda smiled with curiosity. 'Tell me more,' he said.

'At last something you didn't know. I'm a qualified engineer, a chemical engineer.'

'I thought you were a qualified social worker.'

'That, too. But I took chemistry at university in Edinburgh after my school-leaving exams. Engineering courses were the thing at that time. Unfortunately I didn't go into a job straight afterwards. When I was about to do so, after being a housewife for almost twenty years, my subject had changed and I hadn't kept up. So I tried a different job. One that was about giving, repairing. Will you promise to go if I tell you what happened?'

Gunnarstranda sent her an old-fashioned look.

'Always true to yourself, eh. Upright. Promise nothing. The apostle for the ordinary man.' Her smile was bitter. 'I went home on a stand-by ticket. It was supposed to be a surprise. In fact it is quite a banal story. I went straight to Reidar's place. I wanted to surprise him and thought there would be no one at home. But there was. In the bedroom. He was underneath her. My best friend. Do you think that's stimulating? Men can find that kind of thing stimulating. I thought it was loathsome. I could hear the noises and stood there like an intruder watching while she . . . do you understand? With my boyfriend. There's not much more to say.'

'Did you go into the room? To the two of them?'

'Are you mad? No. I went to her place. I waited for her. I knew she wouldn't be long. After all, she'd left her child in the playpen while she . . .'

'So you just waited for her?'

'Yes.'

'Why?'

'Because I wanted her dead, of course.'

'Couldn't that have been avoided? Her dying?'

'I don't know . . . maybe if I'd been different, with a different view on . . . on things.'

'Did you talk?'

'Of course.'

'But why did you kill her?'

'Because she was my best friend.'

'Yes . . . ?'

346

'My best friend. Don't you understand?' Sigrid gave a tired smile. 'Of course you don't understand. I don't have much of a defence. I know myself . . .'

'When did you leave the dead woman?'

'When she was quite still. She didn't make a sound. She had screamed out all the sound she possessed with him. And that made me furious that she had no sound left for me.'

'And then what did you do?'

'Went back to Scotland. The same day. On stand-by.'

'You never heard anything from the police?'

'Never.'

'So no one knew you were in the country?'

'No one.'

'Did Katrine know any of this?'

'No,' Sigrid said.

'But she rang you and told you she had found the name of her mother. That was what she actually told you in that call on the Saturday, wasn't it?'

Sigrid gave a heavy nod.

'Was it she who told you that Bueng was living at the nursing home?'

Sigrid shook her head. 'No, Katrine knew nothing about Reidar Bueng. She knew nothing about me. It was a shock. It was a terrible conversation. I thought I would have a heart attack when she told me what she had discovered. I knew where Reidar was. I've known where he is every single day since the day it happened.'

'What did you want from him? When you met him at the home the day after Katrine rang?'

'I wanted to be sure Reidar didn't tell her about me, I mean the relationship between Helene and me. I knew it was only a question of time before Katrine would find him. If she found her way to Reidar, sooner or later my name would crop up. It would be catastrophic for us both. I had to talk to Reidar first. I had to make sure he said nothing to Katrine about me.'

347

'Do you think Bueng knew you killed Helene?'

'Of course.'

'But he never gave you away?'

'Never.'

'He didn't say anything to me, either. Do you still love Reidar Bueng?'

She laughed the same chilling laugh and sneered again. '*Do you still love him*,' she mimicked with a biting tone. 'You ridiculous starched hypocrite.' She clenched her fists. 'What are you actually asking? What the hell do you mean by that question? Are you wondering whether I miss being with an old man who cannot walk unaided? Whether I miss physical contact with this man?'

'I'm wondering whether you love him,' the policemen repeated as unshakable as before.

They stood eyeing each other until she said: 'What does it matter? I've destroyed my life. I've lived half my life with a person who regards love as a muscular activity, like an exchange of body fluids.'

She gazed at the ceiling and gave a deep sigh. 'You know, I have no idea whether I loved Reidar or not. I haven't a clue. I have no illusions about love any longer. But I think I used to believe in it, at that time. It felt like being down for the count . . . did you, in your younger days, drink too much or were you so ill that you wished you were dead just to escape? That's how it was. But a hangover is soon over. Intoxication passes. In those days nothing just passed. I could go for long walks in the evening until I found a deserted place where I could stick pins or needles in myself and scream in an attempt to escape the plight that was mine . . . that was love. But now? I have no idea any more. I don't know what has any meaning. But if there is a worst part to all of this, it is not being able to remember that side of myself I used to regard as my most precious.' Sigrid clenched her teeth and hissed with spittle in both corners of her mouth. 'The only thing that never fades, the only truth left is that I hated Helene!'

'As much today as then?'

'There you go again,' she sighed, exhaling with her eyes closed. 'Sometimes, yes. As a rule, no.'

'It won't work,' Gunnarstranda said out of the blue.

'What won't work?'

'You won't be able to pass your resentment and bitterness on to dead Helene.'

'What do you mean?'

'I think your hatred and bitterness are reserved for another person.'

Sigrid shook her head slowly.

'You've told this story before, haven't you, Sigrid?'

Sigrid eyed him, on her guard. 'Why are we on such intimate terms all of a sudden? What do you want now?' she asked, but quickly closed her mouth again as if anxious not to say too much.

'I know who killed Katrine,' the policeman said in a quiet voice. 'And so do you.'

The sun shone on her silver-grey hair. 'I have no idea what you are talking about. Apart from that, my head hurts. You'd better go.'

'Katrine rang you that Saturday,' Gunnarstranda said, taking a step closer. 'She told you about Stamnes. She told you about her mother's true identity and about Raymond Skau, who had turned up at her workplace demanding money. I appreciate it must have been a shock, but you should never have told anyone else. When you told him you signed her death warrant. You knew that, didn't you.'

Sigrid had closed her eyes. 'I didn't know. I went to see Reidar on Sunday to prepare him for Katrine. It would never have occurred to me that she was dead.'

'But you must have known.'

'You're evil,' she said, and then repeated, 'You are evil.'

'You went to see Bueng even though you knew she was dead.'

Sigrid said nothing.

'He may have killed Katrine to protect you. I'm sure he thinks

349

he acted out of chivalry. Nevertheless, that's no bloody good. You know as well as I do he did it.'

'Suppose I did know,' she said with bitterness. 'So what? Can it be undone? Will regret make any difference? As for these ridiculous claims that he wanted to protect me . . . ha!' Her laugh was harsh and she bore down on the policeman with narrowed eyes. 'Hasn't it occurred to you that he wanted to protect himself?'

He stood looking at her for a few seconds. At last he took a deep breath and took two steps forward. She turned her head and looked at him as though she was actually surprised he had the effrontery to be in her house still. 'Imagine,' she said, twisting her mouth into a sneer of contempt. 'Imagine. The truth had not even dawned on you.'

'Sigrid Haugom,' said Police Inspector Gunnarstranda. 'I am arresting you for the murder of Helene Lockert. Would you please come with me of your own free will?'

44

Painful

The tram was jam-packed with people. There was not a seat to be had anywhere. People stood cheek by jowl in front of the doors and in the central aisle. He was squeezed up against a woman clinging to a strap hanging from the ceiling. She was wearing only a red singlet over her upper body. The hair under her arm was curly and moist with sweat. He looked at her. She had painted an unattractive yellow stripe under her eyes. Her hair was dyed blonde with darkened roots revealing the original colour. Every time the tram went around a bend he looked down between her neck and her blouse, into a gap revealing two small breasts with long engorged nipples. The sight made him think of the other girl and how the jerking of her body had become weaker and weaker, like a fish at the bottom of a boat. And then he was there again with one knee pressed into the damp grass and his other foot slightly stretched as her young body heaved its last.

A noise. He was startled by the look he received from the woman with dyed hair. The noise must have come from him. He cleared his throat and looked away to prevent anyone remembering him.

It was as hot outside as inside. In fact it was hotter, but not so clammy; the air wasn't as bad. Standing on the pavement as the tram passed he felt the woman's gaze through the window. It met his own. It was for these reasons you had to plan, by getting off the tram two stops too early, for example.

The problem with the sun was that people would be outside in the wonderful weather. But the heat made this less likely. Most old people go into the shade when the sun is too strong. The first time he passed by he tried to gain some perspective of what was going on in the lobby. It seemed quite still. He passed one crossroads, then another, felt his breathing accelerate. There was a kind of restless, tingling sensation in his arms. He stopped and raised his hand with his fingers outstretched. Not a tremble. Being tense is one thing. It's a good sign to be tense. Composure was in the offing, half an hour away. This was perhaps the simplest operation so far. But at the same time it was the most difficult. It was the first time that he had known inside himself for certain – the first time he had felt it in his body like a feeling of hunger – that the outcome would be death.

He took a left at the next crossroads and walked to the next street. Here he went left again, on his way back to the nursing home.

* * *

Sigrid Haugom walked with quick steps through the door to the left. Gunnarstranda followed her. They crossed a kind of dining room, in traditional Norwegian style, with a buffet along the wall and in the middle of the floor a dining table with a scoured surface surrounded by eight chairs. She stopped by the next door and turned as if to ensure that she had heard correctly. 'Are you following me?' Gunnarstranda nodded. 'I see,' she said, and continued down a shorter corridor and headed towards a staircase leading up to the first floor. Halfway up the stairs she stopped again. On the white wall above her head hung a modern painting with striking blue and yellow colours, a sky. 'He definitely did not do it for my sake,' she said, looking down at the policeman through the staircase railing. 'He is only interested in himself and his own needs.'

'Do you think he raped her?'

'Him?' She snorted. 'He would never do anything so banal. No.

352

His actions are imbued with one single purpose: to avoid the scandal a potential court case against me could produce.'

Gunnarstranda: 'Scandal? What scandal? Your husband wouldn't be involved in any case against you, would he?'

She assumed a patronizing smile. 'You misunderstand, Mr Smart Guy. He's not frightened of what I did to Helene. The only thing he's frightened of is the consequences of his own actions. He's afraid of what I would say about him and his abuse of me for half of my life.'

She tossed her head in despair at the policeman's expression. 'Has it finally got through to you? Erik is not the man people think he is. Erik is an animal.'

Gunnarstranda pulled a sceptical face at her choice of words. As she took a step down he took a step up. She grabbed the handrail. 'Scoff at me,' she whispered. 'Laugh at me. Don't try to think what it's like to lie naked on a bed, bound hand and foot, while your child is in the adjacent room, night after night. Don't try to imagine what it's like to serve a person night and day who finds his satisfaction in your pain – and to dress up afterwards to be your tormentor's companion at a dinner in some snobbish club, forced to choose clothes that conceal swellings and bruises, to smile and whisper sweet nothings in this same man's ear not to attract attention, but to maintain his noble façade. You can't, can you? Your imagination doesn't stretch that far. Imagine what it's like to have to grovel to a man like this just because once you were stupid enough to tell him about the greatest error in your life – that one act.'

'Why didn't you move out?'

'How can you ask!'

Gunnarstranda flung out his arms. 'Did he threaten to expose you? Did he threaten to go to the police with what he knew about the murder of Helene Lockert?'

'You're getting there, you clever little policeman.'

'Do you mean to say he killed that poor girl to . . .' Gunnarstranda searched for words. '. . . To keep the lid on the secret?'

353

'He killed Katrine so that no one would know who killed her mother. If everyone knew who killed Helene, he wouldn't have had a hold over me any longer. He could not have stopped me talking about what he has done to me.'

'Help me to catch him,' urged the police inspector.

She shook her head. 'You won't coax me into doing anything,' she said quietly. 'Let's be honest with each other now, Gunnarstranda. As far as evidence goes, you haven't got a leg to stand on.'

'That's true,' the policeman agreed. 'I have no evidence. Unless you help me.'

She laughed. 'Heavens above! Why would I help you?'

Gunnarstranda paused. Sigrid Haugom regarded him with a contemptuous glare.

'Because this cannot go on,' the detective replied at length.

She laughed again. A cold, harsh laugh. 'Can it not go on?' She mimicked him with a pursed mouth: '*Cannot go on!*' She took another step down the stairs. 'Have you considered,' she spat, 'that I've been living with blood on my hands for more than twenty years? Have you considered that what I have dreamt about for twenty years has been realized? Finally I know something and I have a hold over him! Finally, finally, finally, I am the one with the power!'

'But is that really what you want?'

'There's nothing in this world I want more!' Sigrid shouted.

The policeman observed her standing on the stairs, bent forwards, panting, her hair dishevelled, her face, in which hatred and fury had formed deep furrows, bare. A frothing drop of saliva bubbled on her lower lip. 'Then do it for someone else instead,' he pleaded. 'Do it for her sake. Look upon it as a chance to make amends. That was what you dreamt about, wasn't it? Making amends to Katrine?'

She took a deep breath as though to restrain another outburst. She stood there with her eyes closed until she made up her mind and signalled her decision with a shake of the head.

'OK, no,' he said. 'But you'll have to come with me all the same.'

When she did at last open her eyes they were shiny with tears. 'The case against me is time-sensitive,' she said, spinning round and continuing up the stairs with the policeman in tow.

'We'll see,' Gunnarstranda said to her back. 'Fortunately it is not my job to determine whether the case against Helene Lockert's murderer is covered by the statute of limitations or not.'

She came to a sudden halt.

Gunnarstranda continued speaking. 'I'm a policeman, not a judge. But I hope you won't resist arrest. It would just be embarrassing for us both.' He gave a wry smile.

'No, of course not,' she said, bewildered, running her hands down her dress as though wiping off something unpleasant. 'We are both adults.' She grabbed a door handle. 'I must change my clothes. What was it you wanted me to do?'

'Just ring him and tell him you were there, at the nursing home on Sunday.'

'Tell him I was with Reidar, that I visited him?'

'Yes.'

'Nothing else?'

The policeman coughed when he peered up at her now smiling face. 'What is it?'

'I've already done it,' she said. 'Funny.'

'You've told him? When?' Gunnarstranda's lean figure jerked. He ran over to her. His sensitive lips were trembling. 'No more bluffing. When did you tell him?'

'Early this morning.'

'You're lying.'

She shook her head. 'I've been lying to myself too much to do it any more.'

'But why today of all days?'

'Because today I . . .' She breathed in and closed her eyes again. '. . . Today . . . when I woke up . . .' She paused.

'What about today?' Gunnarstranda was staring at her. 'What do you mean?'

355

With a distant smile, she said: 'What makes you think you would understand me if I were to answer that question honestly?'

The policeman had his mobile out. He watched her with a concerned frown on his forehead, then turned away from her with the phone against his ear. 'Don't go anywhere,' he said in a low voice while impatiently waiting for an answer from Frølich. And added in an even lower voice, 'Surely you must understand what an insane thing to do it was to tell him you'd visited Bueng?'

'I don't understand anything any more.'

'I hope it's not too late,' Gunnarstranda said and swore. 'Where do you keep your toothbrush and toiletries? In the bathroom? Well, go and get them.'

He followed her down the corridor with the mobile to his ear. He trailed her every step. Something told him this woman should not be left alone for a single second.

45

The Telephone Call

A young man with an oversized head, big hair and a strangely frail body squeezed into a blue suit rounded the corner for the third time and looked at Frank Frølich, who jumped to his feet in his eagerness. 'Is Gerhardsen in or not?' Frølich asked, annoyed. He had been sitting and waiting for an audience for three quarters of an hour. The young man had protruding eyes and a swollen red pimple on his cheek.

'He's in a meeting,' came the answer. The young man didn't move.

'Did you tell him I was waiting?'

The young man nodded. He was wearing a dark blue shirt, which was the same colour as the wall-to-wall carpet on the floor. Around his neck he wore a brown silk tie. The knot was much too loose. *Young men with an irritating appearance should not be employed*, thought Frølich, and, impatient, shifted his weight from one foot to the other.

'The meeting's going to last a long time,' the young man said with a grin.

Frølich thought: *Men like you should be in the fields and woods.* He said: 'So your boss thinks he can psyche me out, does he?' He went back to the chair and sat down.

The young man stood there with his arms hanging down by his sides. What was it Eva-Britt always said? *I think men in dinner jackets can be quite sexy, but James Bond should understand once and for all that he should not run around in that kind of clothing.* Frølich leaned forwards and eyed the young man. *Young men in suits shouldn't stand so erect with their arms down by their sides,* he thought. *It makes them look like standard lamps.* 'Let there be light,' he said with a smile.

At that moment his mobile telephone rang.

46

Getting Warmer

The easy part was that the man was a patient. He looked down at his legs. Soft, light brown shoes and loose trousers. His legs were quite normal, his stride relaxed. The important thing is how it looks from the outside, not how it feels on the inside. The feeling of heaviness is sheer imagination.

He turned left again and at an accelerated pace headed for the nursing home. The lobby was deserted and quite still. A taxi was parked in front of the entrance. The taxi driver was waiting, so he was collecting, not delivering. He walked past the taxi and took the last few steps to the front entrance. As soon as he opened the door, the familiar smell hit him: the smell of old people, a pungent odour consisting of elements such as urine, dirt, dust, stale air and rotten organic material. It smelled like an open grave. The irony of this image made him smile. A young woman in a garish yellow sweater was sitting behind a low glass partition and speaking on the telephone. He went to the door and knocked politely against the door frame.

'Reidar Bueng?' he asked, leaning against the wall.

She put down the receiver with a startled expression. 'I'm on placement here, so I don't know my way around so well . . .'

'A student?' he smiled. 'Isn't there a list you can consult?'

'Yes, there is.' She put the receiver on the desk and searched through the paperwork. She was nervous she wouldn't find what she was looking for. Finally she looked up. 'Room 104.'

'Thank you,' he said and continued at a composed tempo down

the corridor. He passed room 104 without stopping, just a brief glance to see where he was in the corridor. Through the windows he could see white clover flowers in the lawn. An old man with a beret, white legs in enormous shorts and a spanner in his hand was standing over a dismantled lawnmower.

He went on and found a toilet further down the corridor. He entered, locked the door behind him and laid the briefcase on the toilet lid. At the bottom of the briefcase, each in their own compartment, were plastic gloves, a hypodermic needle and the serum. He put on the gloves and quickly assembled the syringe. Then he pressed down the plunger and sucked up one phial, then a second. He released two drops into the toilet. Ready for use. *Goodness me*, he thought. *Someone has been given the wrong medication today.* He hid the weapon in his jacket pocket. Then he inspected the pocket in the mirror. It looked as it should. He put his sunglasses back on and breathed in before opening the toilet door and walking slowly down the corridor.

Not a soul around, neither to the left nor the right. *Think about her. Feel her fury. Think how she would crush you!* He proceeded without hurrying to room 104. His breathing was regular: out, in, out, in; he knocked twice. Not a sound from inside. Time to complete the job, he thought, grasping the door handle.

* * *

'You're worried about me,' Sigrid Haugom confirmed after they had got into the car. 'You think I'm psychotic. Maybe you think I might harm myself?'

'I'm only doing my job,' Gunnarstranda said, donning his jacket, starting the engine and driving off.

'Is it part of your job to watch women sitting on the loo and having a pee?'

'I didn't watch you. It's my job to stay on the heels of arrestees. You are not the first in that regard.'

'You're a bad liar, Gunnarstranda.'

He looked across at her and said with a wry smile on his thin lips, 'You have to remember I've listened to lots of liars, all too many.'

'Strange,' she sighed.

'What's strange?'

'This moment.'

She went on: 'All the times I've tried to imagine what it would be like to be arrested. Thousands.' She glanced out of the car when he braked for a car coming from the right. 'Talk about an anti-climax.'

'I'm beginning to get used to it, too,' Gunnarstranda said drily.

They fell silent.

'I think . . . ,' he began after a while.

'Are you frightened I'll throw myself out of the car?' she interrupted.

'I think Henning Kramer discovered something,' Gunnarstranda persevered.

She sighed. 'God, now you're being tiresome.'

'I think he discovered something your husband had missed, something which made Kramer dangerous in his eyes. I want you to think. What could Kramer have discovered?'

She angled her head. 'I think that's pretty obvious, don't you?'

Gunnarstranda sent her an uneasy glance.

She was looking ahead with a scornful smile on her lips. 'It's staring you in the face. My God, if the rest of the police force is as stupid as you it's not surprising I got away that time in '77. Can't you see it? How could it never have occurred to you!'

Gunnarstranda kept his eyes on the road and stopped to let a car through from the right.

All of a sudden she became serious. 'It's my fault, too,' she said. 'I wanted to help Katrine that night at the party when she fell ill. So I rang Erik. I thought he could drive us home. I wanted to escape and I needed to talk to Katrine face to face. Erik didn't turn up. Henning came to collect Katrine, but Erik didn't turn up.'

Gunnarstranda nodded to himself. The picture was beginning to take shape.

'I waited for Erik at the party. When I saw Katrine leaving . . .'

'You saw her leaving?'

'Yes, I was on the veranda and saw her go out through the door, close it and walk to the garden gate. I saw her in the light from the street lamp outside the gate. I saw her walking down the road. I thought about shouting to her, but didn't. Instead I went inside and tried to ring Erik to tell him not to pick me up after all. He didn't answer the phone.'

'He was already on the way?'

Sigrid ignored the question. She said: 'That Monday you came to the rehab centre Henning was walking around in a trance. We talked about what had happened, all of us, about the party and about Katrine. Henning kept hassling us. We had to tell him again and again what had happened that night. All the time I could feel Henning's eyes on me. There is only one explanation for that. Henning saw Erik that night. He drove past Erik on his way up to Annabeth's at around midnight. He had Erik on his tail when he drove to collect Katrine. But everyone knew I wasn't picked up until four in the morning. It was repeated again and again at the meetings on Monday morning.'

She paused. The policeman said nothing.

She smiled at him. 'I'm beginning to like you, Gunnarstranda. You know how to be quiet in the right places.' She coughed. 'Henning called us the evening after the funeral. He demanded to speak to Erik.'

'What did they talk about?'

'I think Henning threatened to go to you with his suspicions and his sightings of Erik that night.'

'And your husband asked him not to,' Gunnarstranda completed.

She laughed a hollow laugh. 'It would never occur to him to ask anyone for anything.'

She looked out of the car window. 'No,' she said. 'Erik agreed to meet him so that they could talk it out, man to man.'

47

The Last Fix

Elvis Presley's low, metallic voice blared out from the radio's loud-speaker on the bedside table. But the room was empty.

He couldn't believe it. Couldn't believe it. Once more he went into the bathroom, into the kitchen and into the small alcove. Not a soul anywhere. He looked down at himself. A man wearing yellow gloves. They would have to come off. He peeled off the gloves and put them in his pocket. No, that wouldn't do. He took the gloves from his pocket and deposited them in the briefcase instead. Where to get rid of them? He sat in the armchair by the window and slowly ran his eyes across the room. He peered through the open door to the bathroom – at a dirty laundry basket. That was where. He slipped into the bathroom and dropped the briefcase into the half-full laundry basket.

'*Maybe I didn't treat you quite as good as I should have . . .*' Elvis sang.

He switched off the radio and stood listening. Not a sound to be heard. No mumbling, no rushing sounds in the pipes. For what must have been the hundredth time he checked the bulge in his jacket pocket. He was ready. More than ready and no one was at home.

It was very strange. He hastened back to the window and looked outside. The same lawnmower he had seen through a corridor window on the lawn, abandoned. Why had it been abandoned? Why was it so quiet?

He was getting hot and ran to the door. Stopped. He didn't want to go, not yet, not so close to the conclusion. *There's something wrong. Best to get out now!* He grabbed the door handle. Changed his mind yet again. Locked the door from the inside. Reached the window in two quick strides. He took the latch and pushed open the window. It had hinges on both sides, a window it should be possible to tilt open. A safety catch had been added. It wasn't possible to open the window wide. He tried again. The window wouldn't move. A meagre twenty centimetres of air was all the window was capable of supplying.

The blood froze in his veins as someone was pressing the door handle behind him. It could not be Bueng. It was someone else. Thank God the door was locked. He looked at the brown door – and turned back to the window. He thought: Smash the window. Now!

The person on the outside tried again. Jerked the handle downwards. Knocked.

How the hell were you supposed to open this window? He pushed at the frame. It gave way on the left-hand side. There. A little bolt you had to flick up. Two seconds later his left foot sank into a tangle of thorns. That didn't help. The rose bush snagged his leg. He was out. He closed the window behind him. Struggled out. The thorns tore at his clothes. He was sweating. But didn't stop to look around. He strode towards the gravel path dividing the lawn into two rectangles. The area was completely deserted. *You should have known. You should have known something was wrong when it was so quiet!*

Well, what had happened? A young woman in reception. That was all. And what had she seen? A man with sunglasses asking after a patient. That was all.

He stopped on the corner and cautiously looked around the house. A police patrol car was parked in the drive. It was empty.

Now! he thought. *Now! The car's empty. So there's only one or two of them. A couple of second-raters answering a call. They're investigating a call someone has made. No one is after you! Skedaddle!*

He set off towards the police car and walked past it and out. He turned left and kept walking, straight ahead. Every single muscle in his back was knotted. Every second he expected to hear a shout behind him. But nothing happened. He was twenty-five metres away now, forty. Five metres to the first crossroads. He forced himself not to walk fast. One metre to go. He turned left without looking behind him. He kept going, hidden now by a large block of flats. Five metres, ten metres. He breathed out. All was well. No one had seen anything.

The thought of the empty police car bothered him. Why had the car appeared? Had it been called because of him? That was very unlikely. If the police knew anything at all they would not have sent a single patrol car. It must have been called out for some other reason. But why had someone yanked at the door? He tried to consider the matter. He hadn't heard any shouting. That was a good sign. A policeman would have shouted if he was standing outside a locked door trying to contact someone inside. It couldn't have been a policeman trying to get in. So why had he panicked? Something must have gone wrong. But what? It was impossible to know. But if something had gone wrong what proof did they have against him? Nothing. The police were tapping in the dark. The question was: Had it been a blunder to go there, to the nursing home? *No! It hadn't been a blunder. Reidar Bueng was the only connection with Sigrid's case. The only person who knew anything at all. The only link of any significance.*

He stopped. He was crossing Bentse Bridge.

Just a feeling . . .

He turned round. No. No one stopped, no one following. He looked down into the river and pretended to go through his pockets, and turned round again. Nothing. Nevertheless, he was aware of a prickling sensation. On he walked, taking his time, up Bentse-bruagata to Vogts gate and the tram stop. He stopped here and turned round again. Nothing to be seen, just some youth shuffling along the pavement, a young woman locking her car and an elderly lady pulling a shopping trolley. The tram rounded the hill to the left by Sandaker. When it finally slid to a halt in front of him he went through one of the double doors in the middle. He was the only person to board. He smiled, began to work his way forward and approached the driver to pay. The tram came to a sudden standstill and he looked out, but there were no cars or pedestrians in the way. And then a door slammed behind him. His blood froze to ice. *Turn round. See who it is before the tram sets off!*

He slowly twisted his head to the right. Nothing. No uniforms, just people sitting, leaning against the steel poles, chewing gum, talking to each other in low voices. Nothing. Searching for coins in his pocket, he nodded absentmindedly to a bearded Sikh who had adorned his head with a dark red turban.

He found an unoccupied seat on the left. And went over the great fiasco in his mind. Either something had gone disastrously wrong or no damage had been done. But he had to find out which. A boy with long, black hair and a spotty face was talking about the relationship between language and understanding. 'If you're taking the piss, I want you to say you're taking the piss,' he said to his companion, a plump girl with a lot of sub-cutaneous fat on her thighs.

He craned his neck round and looked back. Nothing. Nevertheless a tingling sensation in his back. Between his shoulder blades he could feel an itch that was not of a physiological nature. Someone was there. There had to be. He was sweating. He rubbed his forehead with his fingers. Damp. He fought to stop himself turning round.

A mobile telephone rang. The man who answered spoke very good English. A Vietnamese-looking boy was playing some kind of game on his mobile telephone. It was hard to concentrate in these surroundings. The hardest thing of all, though, was not letting yourself turn around.

Well, what could have happened? Nothing. He glanced up. A woman was staring at him. What was she staring at? He couldn't

366

stand it any longer. He had to turn. He gave a start. For a few fleeting moments he thought it was *her*. But it was not. Even though the woman sitting in the seat right behind him was very similar. The blonde passenger lowered and averted her gaze.

He faced the front again. He must not behave like this. He had to be calm. Under control. Better go home, meditate and work out when to strike again. He alighted from the tram in Aker Brygge. Lots of passengers got off there. Lots of casually dressed people without a care, laughing. A few boys were doing BMX tricks on a ramp. A large crane had been positioned in front of the entrance to Aker Brygge. Three fit young men were offering bungee jumps.

He slowed down, trying to be the last in the group. He soon saw how hopeless that was. The whole of the City Hall square was teeming with people. He stopped by the large crane as an elderly lady was being strapped into position. She hung, dangled, over the tarmac like a cross between a slaughtered animal and Astrid Lindgren's Karlsson-on-the-Roof. She was really enjoying herself as she was hoisted upwards.

He tore himself away. A little boy shading his eyes as he squinted into the sky shouted: 'Grandma! Grandma!'

He proceeded along the wharf promenade with quickened steps. The itching in his back was still there. There was someone behind him. *Someone.*

He veered to the right towards the square, stopped and looked behind him. People. Throngs of people.

He walked close by the fountain and went into the multi-storey car park. He was alone in the lift. The doors closed. He leaned against the glass wall and registered a movement to his left.

* * *

Frank Frølich and Erik Haugom looked each other in the eye for what seemed like an eternity. Haugom had positioned himself at the back of the glass lift. They held eye contact as the lift moved downwards. Frank, on the staircase, was in no hurry. He ambled down with his legs akimbo. On the bends they exchanged glances. Every time Frank rounded the corner Haugom turned his head; it was lower at every bend. When Haugom's head was on a level with the policeman's knee, Frank brought his foot back and kicked the glass with all his might. Haugom's body jerked backwards. But his eyes gave nothing away. His face was closed, two vacant eyes above a tightly clenched mouth. Frank noticed that the doctor had birthmarks on his scalp. There were still a couple of bends left when he heard the metal door leading to the parked cars bang. Frank reached the door ten seconds later. Inside there was the sound of running feet. He stood still and smelt the heavy, exhaust-infested air. He tried to see the closed face from the glass lift, the expression on the man's face as he ran throwing hasty glances over his shoulder. But he could not. Still he stood without moving, trying to hear where the sound of running feet was coming from. But it seemed to be impossible. The parking area resounded with a slight echo from all parts at once – it came in waves across rows and rows of empty, darkened car interiors – an illuminated sign on the ceiling, yellow stripes over the concrete floor. Frølich lumbered along the central aisle, the broad driving lanes, with cars on both sides. On hearing the sound of an engine starting, he stopped. It sounded more like a scream than an engine starting. Haugom was becoming nervous. Frank gave a smile of satisfaction and wondered how stupid this man really was. Soon after there was a squeal of braking tyres. The man must be living on his nerves. The engine screamed again. Frank concentrated. He ran his eyes along the walls. Not a movement anywhere. Again the howl of an engine. The sound was coming closer. He just managed to throw himself to the side at the last moment. The coke-grey Mercedes raced past only one millimetre away from his foot. He caught a glimpse of an elderly man bent over the steering wheel. That was probably the most pathetic thing about this person, Frank thought, struggling on to his knees – the ill-placed single-mindedness and pugnacity this sad guy could mobilize. *When it comes down to it, all villains are just as bad as each other, but there's no doubt some villains look better on film,* as Eva-Britt always said.

Frank remained on his knees brushing down his trousers and watching Haugom's Mercedes brake into the bend and turn into the ramp leading upwards. The idiot had even managed to drive the wrong way.

He sighed and got to his feet, then strolled in the direction the car had just taken. This was a subterranean car park and it differed from all of the others in Oslo. This one you had to drive down to exit.

Frank jogged around the narrow bend Haugom had driven. On the floor above there was the shriek of brakes again. Screaming tyres. Now it was a case of getting to the top before the guy slalomed down at a hundred. He was beginning to pant. He was sprinting. His legs were leaden. The screech of brakes again above him. Frank could see the next level approaching. The opening was ten metres away. The tyres on the car above him were spinning. The engine was roaring. Inside his head, Frank imagined a coke-grey Mercedes hitting him at full speed. He saw his body – spine broken and hips crushed – landing on the car bonnet, rolling out of control towards the front windscreen and on to the roof from which it smacked down on to the floor with the dead weight of all his kilos, banging his skull and smashing it on the concrete.

Five metres to go. Frank had the taste of blood in his mouth. The sudden sound of a loud crash.

A collision.

As Frank reached the top a car door slammed. He stopped and his lungs gasped for air. His pounding heart sounded like thunder in his ears. He tried to regulate his breathing, but could not. The first thing he noticed was a woman standing by the lift. She was holding the hands of two small boys in short trousers. One of them was picking his nose. Sixty metres in front of him he saw Haugom's coke-grey Mercedes. The bonnet had almost carved a parked, small VW Golf into two. A man was staggering along the central aisle. It was Haugom. But there was something wrong. Haugom stood with his knees bent and a surprised expression on his face. He was holding his thigh.

Frølich set off. 'Stop,' he shouted to Haugom. 'Stand still!'

He was running. From the corner of his eye he could see the woman with the two children shooing them into the stair well. Haugom's knees gave way. Frank slowed down against his will.

Erik Haugom was rocking on his knees. 'Stop.' Frølich repeated, gentler this time, and continued walking towards the man who now had a distant, almost dreamy expression on his face. The bent figure fighting to remain upright resembled a spaced-out needle addict. Frølich ground to a halt as the man fell to his knees.

There were five metres between them as the man let go of his thigh. He was a strange sight. His jacket seemed to be glued to his right thigh.

'Help me,' whispered Erik Haugom, rolling gently down on to the concrete floor.

'What's up?' Frølich asked, bending over him. 'Have you been hurt?'

Haugom's breathing was a strained wheeze. He was fighting for air. His mouth moved. Frank stooped over him. 'In my jacket pocket,' Haugom whispered with a gurgle.

'What have you got in your jacket?'

'A hypodermic needle. Take it out.'

'You've got a syringe in your pocket?'

Haugom didn't answer. He fell on to his back and tried to straighten up. His face was scarlet; his breathing a barely audible rasp.

'Well, well, doctor,' Frølich mumbled to the figure on the floor. 'I think you need a medic.' He stood thinking, and alternated between looking at his mobile telephone and Haugom, who was now lying on his side, his fingers shuddering with spasms. 'Where are the medics when you need them?' Frølich asked himself in a low voice.

48

The Lost Girl

They were sitting in Café Justisen. They had taken seats at a table in the corner under a photograph of Oslo-born artist Hermansen. Gunnarstranda had just eaten a meatball and fried egg smorgasbord. Now he was washing it down with a cup of black coffee. Fristad and Frølich each had a draught beer.

'So now at last we can do what we should have done a long time ago,' Fristad said with a tiny smile followed by a broad grin. 'We shelve the case for lack of evidence. What did he have in the syringe by the way?'

Gunnarstranda glanced up from his coffee. 'A Norwegian killer nurse special. He had left his briefcase in a dirty laundry basket in Bueng's room. The original packaging was in it. Big dose.'

'Curacit?' Fristad gave a nod of acknowledgement. 'That's what I call suicide with style.'

'Bad luck I would call it.' Gunnarstranda turned to the other two. 'He didn't have a snowball's hope in hell. The dose of curacit would have paralysed his respiratory organs pretty quickly. The idea had been to kill Bueng. When you turned up at the home I suppose he had the syringe primed and ready in his pocket. It lay there then like an undetonated bomb until the collision in the multistorey car park. He must have got the whole syringe in his thigh when he smashed into the car. The pathologist had to cut the needle out it was stuck in so far.'

'Typical,' Frølich said. 'Bloody typical.'

'What was?'

'That he was out to paralyse Bueng's respiratory organs. Haugom must have been hooked on asphyxiation. Even the medication he used ended in asphyxiation.'

Fristad drank his beer and smacked his lips. 'I gather his wife has confessed to the murder of Helene Lockert. Why would the husband set out on this trail of murders?'

Police Inspector Gunnarstranda took his time. 'It seems he never believed she would confess,' he said at length. 'The truth about the Lockert woman's death had bound them together for good or ill for years. He had a hold over her. She claims he abused her, but she didn't dare to report him because he threatened he would tell all he knew about her killing of Helene Lockert. That Saturday . . . Sigrid Haugom had barely finished listening to what Katrine had told her before she told her husband about the phone conversation. Neither of them knew what to do. Not until Katrine fell ill at the party. Haugom's motive for killing Katrine was to prevent the Lockert case from being solved.'

Gunnarstranda chewed, swallowed and went on: 'As soon as Katrine knew who her biological mother was, it was just a question of time before she would start digging up the past. Sigrid's name would have popped up sooner or later. According to Sigrid, her husband feared her reprisals and was concerned about his own status. Sigrid's defence in a court case would have been to go for mitigating circumstances, in other words, to embroider on what a psychopathic animal of a husband she had tolerated. With her inside, he would have lost the hold he had over her. She would have reported him for abuse and nothing would have stopped her. In this way she would have had her revenge for all the humiliations to which he had subjected her over the years.

'Sigrid's role in Katrine's murder boils down to her call to her husband when Katrine fell ill at the party. He drove over and saw her walking in the middle of the road. He saw her jump into Henning Kramer's car. We will never know what his thoughts were at that time – whether he had already decided to throttle her, I mean. In any case, he followed them. He had claimed to his wife that he had followed them to talk to Katrine. Whether she believed that, I don't know.'

'But he must have been spying on them for several hours,' Fristad said. 'He can't have been intending to talk if he had stalked them for such a long, long time.'

'At any rate he can't have been intending to talk when he struck,' Frølich said. 'His upper body is covered in scratch marks. So he must have taken his clothes off before he attacked her. And so the murder must have been premeditated. He approached her naked so as not to leave clues on her body.'

'Did he go straight up and strangle her?'

'Yes, he did,' Frølich said.

'How come he didn't get any scratches on his face?'

'We found a mask in the car boot,' Frølich said. 'A kind of SM leather thing, with a zip in front of the mouth and so on. He must have looked a terrible sight – no clothes and a face like Hannibal the Cannibal.'

'Poor girl,' Fristad gasped.

'Girls,' Gunnarstranda amended. 'Poor girls. The mask was not unknown to his wife, either.' They sat staring into middle distance. Gunnarstranda unwrapped a sugar lump and put it in his mouth. He sipped coffee and sucked the sugar lump. 'Sigrid said she felt Henning Kramer was watching her,' he continued. 'But she didn't know why. She didn't know that Henning had seen Haugom in Voksenkollveien. Henning couldn't figure out why Sigrid had been picked up at four in the morning by her husband, but he had seen the man in his car when he went to collect Katrine.'

'She might be an accessory,' Fristad concluded. 'She ought to be charged.'

Gunnarstranda shrugged and drank more coffee. 'I don't think so. Sigrid maintains she didn't tell her husband any of this. She visited Bueng on Sunday, of course, before she knew that Katrine was dead. She visited Bueng because she feared Katrine would discover his existence and thereby find out the truth about the murder of her mother. Haugom, for his part, posted Katrine's jewellery to Skau in an attempt to pin the blame on him. What happened afterwards was that Henning phoned their house and asked to meet Haugom. On Wednesday. After the funeral, after Frølich had questioned Haugom in the office.'

'Haugom did meet Henning,' Frølich said laconically. 'The guy is the dutiful type.'

'We don't know if Haugom drugged Henning, but it's very likely, anyway. Then he hanged him from the ceiling.'

'Helluva guy,' Fristad said with a brief nod to two solicitors on their way out.

'Yes, it was clever. The so-called suicide almost made us decide to shelve the case.'

'Us?' Fristad laughed aloud. 'You, Gunnarstranda, you almost shelved the case. Unless I am much mistaken, I urged you to keep going.'

Gunnarstranda put another sugar lump on his tongue and sipped coffee in silence.

Fristad was still grinning and grimacing.

Gunnarstranda watched him from beneath heavy eyelids until the man's convulsions were over. Then he said: 'Sigrid had suspected her husband for a long time, but only understood the precise circumstances when Henning died. That led to some terrible fights between them. Which led to her taking sick leave and in the end telling her husband that she had visited Bueng at the nursing home.'

They sat looking into the air again. Frølich raised his arm and signalled the waitress with two fingers. She immediately brought two more beers on a tray.

'So Bueng was the final threat,' Fristad said in an earnest voice. 'The motive for killing the girl was to prevent the Lockert case from being solved. Henning was killed to cover up the first crime. The same motive triggered the attempt on Bueng's life.'

Gunnarstranda nodded. He turned to Frølich. 'At some point you could . . .' He bent down for a brown leather briefcase and put it on the table. He undid two zips and opened the briefcase to take out a green notebook. '. . . take this to Katrine Bratterud's mother,' he said, passing it to Frølich. 'I'm sure she would be happy to have it.'

'What is it?' Frølich asked, examining the notebook with interest.

'Her daughter,' Gunnarstranda said with a weary smile. 'The daughter she lost when her husband died.'